FUTURE WARS...

AND OTHER PUNCHLINES

★ ★ ★

10650557

Withdrawn from
Toronto Public Library

BAEN BOOKS EDITED BY HANK DAVIS

The Human Edge by Gordon R. Dickson

We the Underpeople by Cordwainer Smith
When the People Fell by Cordwainer Smith

The Technic Civilization Saga
The Van Rijn Method by Poul Anderson
David Falkayn: Star Trader by Poul Anderson
Rise of the Terran Empire by Poul Anderson
Young Flandry by Poul Anderson
Captain Flandry: Defender of the Terran Empire by Poul Anderson
Sir Dominic Flandry: The Last Knight of Terra by Poul Anderson
Flandry's Legacy by Poul Anderson

The Best of the Bolos: Their Finest Hour by Keith Laumer

A Cosmic Christmas
A Cosmic Christmas 2 You
In Space No One Can Hear You Scream
The Baen Big Book of Monsters
As Time Goes By
Future Wars . . . and Other Punchlines
Worst Contact (forthcoming)
Things from Outer Space (forthcoming)

To purchase these and all other Baen Book titles in e-book format, please go to www.baen.com.

FUTURE WARS...

AND OTHER PUNCHLINES

★ ★ ★

Edited by
HANK DAVIS

FUTURE WARS . . . AND OTHER PUNCHLINES

This is a work of fiction. All the characters and events portrayed in this book are fictional, and any resemblance to real people or incidents is purely coincidental.

A Baen Book

Baen Publishing Enterprises
P.O. Box 1403
Riverdale, NY 10471

ISBN 13: 978-1-4767-8080-1

Cover art by Alan Pollack

First Baen printing, September 2015

The quotation from *Charles Fort: Prophet of the Unexplained* by Damon Knight is reprinted by the kind permission of Richard Wilhelm for the author's estate. And the book is highly recommended if you can find a copy.

Distributed by Simon & Schuster
1230 Avenue of the Americas
New York, NY 10020

Library of Congress Cataloging-in-Publication Data

Future wars and other punchlines / edited by Hank Davis.
pages cm. -- (Baen ; 1)
ISBN 978-1-4767-8080-1 (paperback)
1. Science fiction, American. 2. Short stories, American. 3. Humorous stories, American. 4. War stories, American. I. Davis, Hank, 1944- editor.
PS648.S3F86 2015
813'.0876208--dc23

2015025458

Printed in the United States of America

10 9 8 7 6 5 4 3 2 1

CONTENTS

★ ★ ★

Copyrights of Stories

"A Funny Thing Happened on the Way to the Martian Front" by Hank Davis © 2015 by Hank Davis. Published by permission of the author.

"The Abominable Earthman" by Frederik Pohl originally appeared in *Galaxy*, October 1961. © 1961 by Galaxy Publishing Corporation. Reprinted by permission of the author.

"Honorable Opponent" by Clifford D. Simak original appeared in *Galaxy* August, 1956. © 1956 by Galaxy Publishing Corporation. Reprinted by permission of David Wixon for the author's estate.

"Sentry" by Fredric Brown originally appeared in *Galaxy*, February, 1954. © 1954 by Galaxy Publishing Corporation. Reprinted by permission of Barry Malzberg for the author's estate.

"And Then There Was Peace" by Gordon R. Dickson originally appeared in *If: Worlds of Science Fiction*, September 1962. © 1962 by Digest Productions Corporation. Reprinted by permission of David Wixon for the author's estate.

"Fool's Mate" by Robert Sheckley originally appeared in *Astounding Science-Fiction* March, 1953. © 1953 by Street and Smith Publications, Inc. Reprinted by permission of the Donald Maass Literary Agency for the author's estate.

"Airborne All the Way" by David Drake is © 1995 by Wizards of the Coast, Inc. All rights reserved. Magic: The Gathering® and Wizards of the Coast® are trademarks of Wizards of the Coast, Inc. Reprinted by permission of the author.

"Mr. Jester" by Fred Saberhagen originally appeared in *If: Worlds of Science Fiction*, January 1966. © 1966 by Galaxy Publishing Corporation. Reprinted by permission of Spectrum Literary Agency for the author's estate.

"Custer's Last Jump" by Steven Utley & Howard Waldrop originally appeared in *Universe 6*, © 1976 by Steven Utley and Howard Waldrop. Reprinted by permission of Howard Waldrop and Jessica Reisman for the estate of Steven Utley.

"Project Hush," copyright © 1954, 1982 by William Tenn, first appeared in *Galaxy*; reprinted by permission of the author's estate and the estate's agents, the Virginia Kidd Agency, Inc.

"The Day They Got Boston" by Herbert Gold originally appeared in *The Magazine of Fantasy & Science Fiction*, September 1961. © 1961 by Mercury Press, Inc. Reprinted by permission of the author.

"The Gentle Earth" by Christopher Anvil originally appeared in *Astounding Science-Fiction*, November 1957. © 1957 by Street and Smith Publications, Inc. Reprinted by permission of Joy Crosby for the author's estate.

"Who Goes Boing?" by Sarah A. Hoyt appears here for the first time. © 2015 by Sarah A. Hoyt. Published by permission of the author.

"Historical Note," copyright © 1951, 1979 by the Heirs of the Literary Estate of Will F. Jenkins; first appeared in *Astounding*, reprinted by permission of the author's estate and the estate's agents, the Virginia Kidd Agency, Inc.

"Into Each Life Some Periwinkles Must Fall" by Hank Davis appears here for the first time. © 2015 by Hank Davis. Published by permission of the author.

"Success Story" by Earl Goodale originally appeared in *Galaxy*, April, 1960, © 1960 by Galaxy Publishing Corporation. All attempts to locate the holder of rights to this story have been unsuccessful. If a holder will get in touch with Baen Books, payment will be made.

"The Spectre General" by Theodore R. Cogswell originally appeared in *Astounding Science-Fiction*, June, 1952. © 1952 by Street and Smith Publications. Reprinted by permission of Cathleen Cogswell.

DEDICATION

This one is for David Drake, a grand master of military science fiction (can you say, "Hammer's Slammers"?) and someone who really likes to laugh. And can probably be heard in the next county over when he does.

ACKNOWLEDGEMENTS

My thanks to all the contributors (and raise a glass to absent friends), and to those who helped with advice, permissions, contact information, and other kindnesses, including Katie Shea Boutillier, Cathleen Cogswell, Joy Crosby, Vaughne Hansen, Elizabeth Hull, Cameron McClure, Barry Malzberg, Jessica Reisman, Joan Saberhagen, Bud Webster, Richard Wilhelm, David Wixon, Eleanor Wood, and probably several other kindly carbon-based life forms which my decrepit memory has unforgivably overlooked. And, of course, thanks to the late Jim Baen (see the introduction for further details).

A FUNNY THING HAPPENED ON THE WAY TO THE MARTIAN FRONT

Introduction
by Hank Davis

"War is hell," as one general put it. "It is well that war is so terrible, otherwise we should grow too fond of it," another general observed. All very true, but listen to war stories of veterans sometime, and most of them will be about the ridiculous, absurd, incredible things that happened to them. The *funny* things. (I've got a few of those myself, but I'll spare you.)

War, like other grim parts of life, is often funny, though it might be "you had to be there" funny. It'd be too easy to trot out the old cliché about laughing to keep from crying, even though that's often the case, but a lot of things that go on in military life, including peacetime military life, are just plain hilarious. And often memorable.

I've often heard about veterans saying of their time in uniform that they wouldn't go through that again for a million dollars—but they wouldn't take a million dollars for it, either. If it happened that somebody (or some *thing*) could offer *this* veteran a million dollars for it and take it away, even paying inflated 2015 dollars, I'd probably say, "Sold!" (Hmmm, there might be an SF or fantasy story idea there—an alien or supernatural entity buying up the war experiences of veterans. For nefarious purposes, of course. But I digress . . .)

Humor in time of war has a long history. Jane Austen, in *Pride and Prejudice*, has bushels of humor, starting with the novel's first line, and has also lots of soldiers—officers, of course—on the scene ("officers enough . . . to disappoint all the young ladies in the country"). If she mentioned that England is in danger of being invaded by Napoleon, I don't recall it, but that is the larger situation. The only physical violence is a passing mention of a private being flogged. How politically incorrect of her to write of gala balls, romantic misunderstandings, and matrimony when there's a war on, with people dying (think of the children!).

Movies have been seeing the humorous side of war for a long time; for example, Buster Keaton's silent movie *The General*, and, with the advent of sound, the Marx Brothers' *Duck Soup*. Some people consider that demented side-splitter an "anti-war" movie, though I don't recall anyone arguing that *Horse Feathers* is an anti-football movie, or *A Night at the Opera* is an anti-opera movie. Later on, Bob Hope was *Caught in the Draft*, Henry Fonda, on stage and on film, played *Mr. Roberts* (which, unlike the book, did not reveal how to easily make a new song of "Jingle Bells"). *Stalag 17* was set in a German POW camp, but had comic episodes, and a teleplay called *No Time for Sergeants* became a hit on Broadway, then a movie, also making a star of Andy Griffith. A decade later, Paddy Chayefsky's *The Education of Emily* made sport of D-Day, and Blake Edwards' *What Did You Do in the War, Daddy?* went for pure farce. In between, *Dr. Strangelove* blew up the world for laughs. (Probably few remember now that many movie critics at the time were not amused.)

Getting back to books, Joseph Heller's *Catch-22* not only has been selling and selling for over half a century, it plunked a catchphrase indelibly into the language. (Incidentally, when a part of the novel was published earlier in a paperback original anthology that I once saw, the title had a different number than "22," though I don't now remember what it was.) And *M.A.S.H.* went from novel to movie to TV show, running far longer than the Korean War it supposedly was about.

As for science fiction, Harry Harrison wrote a *Catch-22*-like novel, titled "The Starsloggers" when a short version appeared in *Galaxy*, and later published in book form as *Bill, the Galactic Hero*. A bit later Kurt Vonnegut's *Slaughterhouse-Five, or the Children's Crusade* (which I read while in Vietnam, incidentally), which undeniably *is* science fiction, no matter how much Mr. Vonnegut denied being an SF writer. And then there's humorous military SF at shorter lengths . . .

Which brings me to Jim Baen and Baen Books. Jim had been making waves for some time by publishing military science fiction by David Drake, Jerry Pournelle, and others, first at Ace Books, then at Tor Books, and finally at his own company, Baen Books (you *did* notice the name on the spine of this book, surely). In the years after the Vietnam war/conflict/fiasco/whatever, anything to do with war was *infra dig* to all right-thinking decent people. Congress rewarded veterans, most of whom had been drafted, by doing away with the G.I. Bill (and later a Carter administration spokesman lied on network TV, claiming that it was still around, but that's a whole 'nother rant . . . and when present-day politicians claim that they "support the troops," don't believe 'em!). Anyone who suggested that war might continue into the future was obviously part of the problem and not part of the solution, and many book reviewers and book editors had an attack of the vapors like Victorian maidens at the thought of science fiction involving war and the military. They saw no distinction between militaristic SF, which glorifies war and bloodshed, and military SF which treats military themes seriously, examines the character of soldiers, both professionals and draftees, and realistically portrays combat. Only an idiot would think that David Drake's stories glorify war. Alas, unlike more essential resources, we have never been in danger of idiots being in short supply. For example, in the late 1980s (before I was working for Baen), at a meeting of a New York SF club I heard one sometime editor talking about Baen Books making "money from murder."

Unfortunately for all the fainting maidens and posturing twits, military science fiction sold well, no matter how many sneering self-righteous remarks about "the pornography of violence" were made, and it became a strong subgenre of science fiction. If it was upsetting the ranks of the perpetually offended in the process, Jim Baen didn't mind, since he enjoyed shaking people up.

Which might have been why in the late 1990s, Jim asked me to make up a list of military science fiction stories with gallows humor, sometimes called "black humor," for a possible anthology. He might have been thinking of shaking up a different bunch of people, but he's no longer with us and I can't ask him. Whatever he intended, I could only think of a few military SF stories with gallows humor, though I could think of plenty of SF stories which involved the military and were humorous, so I compiled a list of those. At the time, Jim was preparing to move Baen Books from New York to North Carolina, and the anthology didn't happen—until now.

Humor, like beauty, is in the eye of the beholder (and maybe also the ear of the behearer), so I won't be surprised if some readers think some of the stories herein aren't really funny, but you can't please everybody. Some might even argue that some of the stories aren't really *military* SF. In any case, and ignoring the one I wrote, I think all of the stories in this book are humorous, some gently and some laugh out loud uproarious. And yes, there's some gallows humor, but I'll leave the reader to decide which ones fit that description (see previous remark about the beholder). And many of the writers represented here wore a uniform at one time and knew whereof they wrote.

Mind, not all of the stories which might have been included are here. Arthur C. Clarke wrote a classic called "Superiority," but that one is available in another Baen anthology, *Citizens*, still available in paper and pixel versions. Then there's Ray Bradbury's "The Concrete Mixer" in *The Illustrated Man*, Howard Fast's "Cato the Martian," Harry Harrison's "Captain Honario Harpplayer, R.N.", many Eric Frank Russell stories, more stories by William Tenn and Christopher Anvil . . . stop me before I anthologize again.

In the meantime, I hope you'll enjoy this anthology. And I hope this is as close as the readers get to actual war, though I'll take no bets on that.

—Hank Davis
May 28, 2015

THE ABOMINABLE EARTHMAN
by Frederik Pohl

The alien invaders, behind their impenetrable force fields, had the war going all their way—and then the biggest goldbrick in Earth's forces surrendered to them.

★ ★ ★

While **Frederik Pohl** *(1919-2013) didn't found the world's first science fiction magazine (probably due to age discrimination, since he was only about six and a half when Hugo Gernsback launched* Amazing Stories*) he otherwise was everything and did everything in science fiction: writer, editor, agent, a talk show guest, an emissary bringing word of the wonders of science fiction to the heathen, er, masses, all of which makes most other SF stars look like dilletantes. Beginning with a poem published in a 1937* Amazing Stories, *his phenomenal writing career produced enough novels, story collections, nonfiction books and collaborative novels to fill a medium-sized library, and he was honored with four Hugo Awards, three Nebula Awards, two John W. Campbell Memorial Awards, a U.S. National Book Award, the SFWA Grand Master award for lifetime achievement, and many other awards. His celebrated novel* Gateway *won the Hugo, Nebula, Locus, and John W. Campbell Memorial Award for its year. While editor of* Galaxy *and* If *in the 1960s, he received three Hugo Awards for best magazine for* If. *As befits a legend, he also was inducted into the Science Fiction Hall of Fame. And throughout his career, he was an enthusiastic fan of science* *fiction. Wherever you are, sir, thank you for all of it. And for more fascinating Pohl polemics, go to http://www.thewaythefutureblogs.com/.*

One night when I was C.Q. at the 549th, the Officer of the Day came in, swearing, with a tall, dark-skinned private wandering sullenly along behind him.

We were up to our eyeballs in frantic work; Trenton had just been evacuated. "Get me the M.P. barracks," yelled the O.D. "What do you think? This rat's been selling rations to the civilians." That was Lt. Lauchheimer, who was a pale young man with enormous integrity. He looked at the prisoner as if he wanted to kick him. I could understand that.

The prisoner looked back at him calmly, without very much interest at all. He leaned back against the wall, put one elbow on the hammering teletype and sighed. Behind him was a poster of a great green bug being bayoneted by an American infantryman, captioned:

SIRIANS, GO HOME!

"Sit down," snapped Lt. Lauchheimer, "—you. Whatever the hell you said your name was."

"He's Private Postal, sir," I said reluctantly. "Pinkman W. Postal."

The prisoner looked at me for the first time. The orderly room was full and bustling, so it wasn't surprising he hadn't noticed me. "Oh. Hello, Harry."

I dialed the M.P. barracks without answering him, but it was already too late. When I handed the phone to Lt. Lauchheimer he glared at me. I said, "We took basic together, Lieutenant. We, uh—we weren't very close buddies."

"Sergeant, I didn't ask you."

I listened while he was talking on the phone, although I was supposed to be checking casualty reports resulting from the morning's assault on the Sirian bubble. It seemed that Pinky had been given a truckload of supplies for evacuees and told to deliver it to a relief center in Bound Brook. They'd picked him up in New Brunswick with the supplies gone and a pocketful of cash. It was about what I would have expected.

The M.P. jeep was there in less than five minutes, and Lt. Lauchheimer escorted Pinky out without another word to me. But he didn't forget. Two weeks later, when we were packing up for the move to Staten Island, he was in charge of my section and he put me on every rough detail he could think of. I guess I didn't blame him. I would have done the same. He didn't know me very well, but he knew I knew Pinky Postal.

Lauchheimer didn't get off my back until the Boston Retreat, when we were bombed-in together for twelve hours and had a chance to talk things over. After that we were pretty close. He asked me to come along when he volunteered for the Worcester booby-trapping mission that almost worked, which I did, so in a way you might say that Pinky Postal was responsible for my getting the Congressional Medal of Honor.

I'm glad I got it. There were fifteen awarded that day, including mine and Lauchheimer's. They lined us up alphabetically, and my name begins with "W". So, although my medal looks like all the others, it's pretty special. It was the last one issued. After that the Sirians englobed Washington.

When Pinky Postal got his bright notion of selling GI canned milk in New Brunswick he was twenty-three years old. He had been drafted at nineteen, out of Cincinnati.

He hated it—hated both. He hated being drafted; and he hated Cincinnati. He had never done a day's work. He liked to drive around down in Kentucky and try to pick up girls, but he was a poor man's son. The girls were not usually impressed by his wobbly old Ford. In basic training his unmade bed cost the whole platoon a weekend pass at Saturday inspection, so the platoon gave him a bit of a hazing. He wasn't hurt. But the next day he went AWOL.

He got as far as the railroad station. He spent the rest of the eight-week training cycle cleaning latrines after duty hours, and our platoon had the dirtiest latrines on the post.

By the time the Sirians landed three years later, Postal should have been out of the Army, except that he never stopped trying. He fought the Army with everything he had. A warrant officer called him a Dutch mudheel—well, something like that—and Pinky hit him. That was three months in the guardhouse with forfeiture of pay. A mess sergeant somehow got in the way of a toppling vat of boiling dried limas after a few words with Pinky, who had been on KP. The court-martial called it deliberate assault with intent to maim. While he was awaiting trial for that he got out of the stockade and went AWOL again, and . . . add it up yourself; he had enough bad time to keep him in as long as they wanted him; and he was still trying to make it up when the Sirians blew their bubble around Wilmington.

Pinky couldn't have cared less.

They weren't shooting at him, were they? So what difference did it make to Pinky? What was there to choose between a hopelessly inimical government of human beings, whose rules were beyond him, and a hopelessly alien government of green-chitoned bugs, whose rules were never explained?

The difference was too small for Pinky to bother with. Pinky was as much an alien as the Sirians, in his unattractive, angle-shooting way.

But the Army still thought of him as a soldier, after all. In the massive redeployment that tried to put an armed perimeter around the bubble, Pinky found himself put to work. He hated that most of all.

We were throwing everything we had at the Sirians. The troops in Delaware and Maryland lived in lead suits for a month because we tried to break in with hydrogen bombs. All we accomplished was to kill off every green thing and wild animal for forty miles south of Wilmington. The bubble didn't even bend, and the troops got plenty of chance to become pretty foul inside those suits. I remember it very well; I was one of them.

So was Pinky but, heavens knows how, he managed to get sent north. He was supposed to be driving a truck again in the evacuation of Philadelphia. The place he was evacuating was Bryn Mawr, and probably he mistook the girls' panic for another kind of excitement.

They screamed to the colonel. Pinky wound up in a punishment battalion once more, and there he met the missionary from inside the bubble, an exile from Eden.

"Give it to me straight, Rocco. What's it like in the bubble?"

"Go to hell."

"Come on, Rocco! Look, you don't like working in the boiler room, do you? Maybe I know how we can cut out of here."

"Shut up, Postal. The sergeant's looking at us."

Vindictively, Pinky turned the steam valve a moment before Rocco was ready for it. The high-temperature jet barely missed boiling his fingers.

"What the hell did you do that for? Get off my back, Postal!"

"Come on. What's it like?"

"Shut up, you two! Drag tail!"

Pinky sulked. The job of delousing refugee clothing took two men, one to lift the hundred-pound bundles in and out of the steam boiler, one to turn the valve. Pinky was twice the size of the little ex-prisoner of the Sirians, but it was Pinky who sat at ease with one gloved hand on the valve.

"Don't you want to get out of here?"

"Look, Postal. They won't take me back. Now leave me alone, will you?"

". . . Well, what's it like? Do they feed you?"

"Sure."

"Work you hard?"

The little man said dreamily, "There's a stud farm down in Delaware. Fifteen hundred women, they say. Only a couple dozen men. For breeding, see?"

"Breeding? You mean—"

"They're growing slaves, I guess. Well, I was working on a farm and they closed that up. I got friendly with the overseer and he put me in for the breeding farm. Plenty of food. Nothing else to do. I—"

"I'm warnin' you two! For the last time."

But then, after the last smelly, flea-ridden bale had come out of the sterilizer, Pinky had a chance for one more word with the missionary. Why couldn't he go back?

"Postal, I don't want to talk about it. They threw me out. I was all set, passed the overseers, right up to one of the bugs. He—he said I was too little. They don't want anybody under six feet tall."

Back in the barracks, Pinky slipped out of his dirty GI shoes and painstakingly marked his height off on the wall. The tape measure showed that nothing had changed. He was exactly six feet, one and a quarter inches tall.

II

Altogether, there were six Sirian ships that landed on the Earth—two in Russia, one in the United States, one in Canada, one in India and, the first one of all, one in New South Wales. The first we heard of them was when the Russian radio satellite began a frantic emergency message in clear, and then went dead before it finished. Then all the other space stations went dead.

Then the ship came down on Australia and, pop, up went the pale green bubble.

The bubbles were like a wall, except more flexible and beautifully controlled. The rule was: what the Sirians wanted to pass could pass; everything else could not.

Time passed; the other ships landed; there were more bubbles.

Then the bubbles grew bubbles. They clustered in groups, expanding. Sometimes the new bubbles were big, sometimes small. Sometimes a couple of months would go by without much expansion, sometimes half a dozen little buds would pop up in a week.

No metallic object could get through them at all after the first week. Evidently the Sirians had decided that was their simplest defense.

We tried non-metallic attacks, of course. We drifted poison gas and bacteria through them easily enough. But nothing happened as far as we could see . . . as far as we could see was, after all, only the outermost skin of the bubble.

A man could walk through—or most of the time he could—without feeling a thing, as long as he had taken off his wrist watch and laid down his gun. Not always. I was in Camden when the 5th Mountain Division sent in an attack with wooden spears and pottery grenades. Fifty men got through but the fifty-first bounced back, knocked unconscious, as though he'd hit a stone wall. I don't know what happened to the fifty men who got through. The only thing I'm pretty sure of is that they didn't much worry the bugs.

Some people did come back. The Sirians threw them out, like Pinky's missionary, Rocco. Probably the Sirians had chosen types who would have little of importance to tell, except how much they liked living under the Sirians. That's what they told, every one of them.

They were a problem to the Army. Most of them were soldiers, as it happened. The Army didn't much like the idea of sending them back to their units, whose morale was already hanging low, so they put the missionaries in special battalions, along with the goof-offs and low-grade criminals, like Pinky Postal.

Pinky heard the message of the missionaries loud and clear. He didn't like the punishment battalion at all. He got his chance when he was handing out tetanus shots for a line of children and a jeep skidded in the slush, side-swiping the medics' personnel carrier. The kids scattered like screaming geese. By the time the medic corporal got his detail rounded up again he had only five men instead of six.

Pinky was in the back of a truck, heading south along the old Turnpike. Snow was driving down on him, but he was very happy. He had outsmarted the Army. They would look for him, but they would look North. It is always easy to desert in the direction of the enemy in wartime; the traffic is all the other way.

He walked the last mile to the edge of the bubble, looming over him in the darkness like a green glass cliff. The snow was easing off and it was almost daylight as he stepped through.

The Sirians never intended to destroy the Earth, only to own it. Pinky's missionary was quite right. Almost at once they began breeding slaves.

It was exactly the sort of job that Pinky would seek. He was not a bookish man, but he was immensely erudite on prurience. He knew very well what a breeding farm was like. There were the dozens of helpless, tamable does; and there was the big stud stallion, himself. What would be closer to the heart of any red-blooded boy? He made his way there, finally, very much elated. There were fifteen others in the shipment, all tall, heavy, muscular men, all extremely cheerful. They rode in the back of an old Ford pickup truck, in warm sunshine. They didn't mind that it had a purplish tinge (green, Pinky would have thought, if he had thought about it at all; but the bubble reflected the green bands of the spectrum and what came through left the sun looking like a violet spotlight in the sky.) There were lavender clouds in a mauve sky, and all around them the bugs were busy with their reconstruction. Snow-white machines on wire-mesh treads were neatly paving over the rubble that had been a small Maryland town.

"Bring on the girls," bellowed Pinky, waving a bottle in one hand. It was only California sherry, but it was all he'd been able to find in the abandoned supermarket where they'd spent the night.

"Man!" cried one of the other eager breeders.

"Women!" Pinky dropped the bottle in his excitement, staring.

They were women, all right. They were flat on their backs on a grassy meadow, their legs in the air, pumping invisible bicycle pedals under the direction of a husky blonde girl. "*Vun,* two. *T'ree,* four! *Vun,* two. *T'ree,* four! All right, ladies. Now some bending and stretching, hurry up, *yoomp!*" As the breeding stock clambered to its legs, Pinky observed that they had in fact already been bred, some months before. It was only mildly disappointing. Where these were, there were bound to be others.

The truck slowed and stopped, and Pinky saw his first Sirian.

The creature was twelve feet high but flimsily constructed. It had a green carapace like a June bug's, jointed in the center. It was not paying any attention to the snorting volunteer stallions. It stood on four hind legs, holding in its front pair of legs an instrument like a theodolite. (It had two smaller pairs of legs clasped across its olive-colored belly plate.)

"Out! Everybody out!" bawled a man in a green brassard, circling respectfully around the Sirian toward the truck. "Nip along, you!"

Pinky was first off, and first to reach the man in the green brassard. He had at that time been in the bubble for less than thirty-six hours, but he knew who to butter up. Green brassards were overseers. They were the human straw-bosses for the Sirians. "Excuse me, sir. Say, I happened to get some good cigars last night, and I wondered if you . . . ?"

The Sirians were not hard masters, but they were firm. They knew what they wanted in the way of a slave population—strength, size, stupidity—and it was only a detail that they found it necessary to kill some of those who gave them trouble. The trouble did not have to arise from viciousness. As Pinky Postal was entrenching himself with the man in the green brassard, one of the other candidate breeders made the mistake of gawking too close to the Sirian, who moved, which startled the captive, who brushed against the horny edge of green chiton at the Sirian's tail. It was like green fire. The man did not even make a sound. Washed in a green blaze of light, he froze, straightened and fell dead.

At about that time the first dead Sirian fell into our hands—partly because of Lt. Lauchheimer and myself—and we had a chance to discover what the green fire was. Not that it helped us. It was a natural defense, like the shock of an electric eel; electromagnetic, at neural frequencies, it paralyzed life. Nothing else. It would not set off a match or stir a cobweb, but it would kill.

Pinky did not know this, but he knew what he had already known, that the Sirians were deadly. Shaken, he waited for the physical examination.

The overseer was not kind to Pinky because of the gift of cigars. He knew that kindness was not involved; it was a simple bribe. But as he shared Pinky's code, he repaid the bribe. He did not volunteer information, but he answered questions. Would all of them be kept for breeding stock? "God, no. Six jobs want to be filled, the rest of you go back." Was there any special trick to passing the examination? The overseer jerked his thumb at a door labeled: *Dr. Lessard.* "Up to the doc." And was it really what they said, inside, all girls and fun? The overseer laughed and walked away. There had only been two cigars.

The doctor had overheard part of the conversation. He was human, a dark little man with a dark little mustache. "I give you one piece of advice," he said grimly, "stay away from Billings."

"What?"

"Billings—him; the man you were talking to. He's been working for the bugs since they landed in Australia."

Pinky said, "But aren't you working for them?" The doctor did not answer, unless the extra, unnecessary twist of the blood-sampling needle was an answer. There were a lot like the doctor in the bubbles—policemen, doctors, a few elected officials of towns, who saw only one duty and that was to continue at their jobs. They worked for the bugs, but not as Billings did.

Twenty minutes later the doctor had completed his blood tests. "Do I pass? Pinky demanded eagerly. "You know, do I get to breed?"

The doctor looked at him thoughtfully. Abruptly, he laughed. He erased a little mark on the paper and substituted another. "I think you do," he said.

Pinky didn't understand the doctor's laughter for several hours.

Then the five of the lot who had been selected were led into a long, narrow, white room with a bank of refrigerators against one wall and a remarkable quantity of test tubes, flasks, glass tubing and other chemical-looking instruments on benches against the other. The five potent studs stared at each other, until a sour-faced human male, wearing a laboratory smock, came reluctantly in to start them on their duties.

There was a storm of questions; the man said, "Oh, shut up, all of you. I *hate* this job."

Meanwhile there was a war on, and we were losing it.

I don't know all the battles that were fought, I only know we didn't win them. I saw the atomic cannon on Cape Cod, I heard about the *George Washington*'s attempt to penetrate the Atlantic Coast bubble, which resulted in its flooding and sinking in a hundred fathoms of water. We heard that the Russians had managed to penetrate with a plywood missile, built with a ceramic skin and guided by a human kamikaze volunteer. There was a latrine rumor that the Canadians got through with a whole squadron of gliders. But whatever results were achieved were invisible from outside the bubbles.

The one small victory that went to the human race came through

Lt. Lauchheimer and myself. We buried ourselves in a little cave off a railroad tunnel, just outside Worcester, Massachusetts. We were there four weeks before the Sirians got around to expanding the bubble to include us. They finally did; and the gamble paid off.

We were inside the bubble with a live bomb.

According to Intelligence, its information derived from correlating the accounts of returned missionaries, our target was a Sirian scout vessel in the mathematical center of the sphere; blow that up, and the bubble would burst. We did. It did. We traveled at night and never saw a Sirian. At night the bubble was a wet-looking, faintly luminous lavender shroud. Lauchheimer had a portable electronic gizmo which triangulated the center for us. We found the center, located the ship, fused the bomb, had an hour to get away, did . . . and saw, in the first rays of the morning sun, a great mushrooming cloud that rose into a blue, bubble-free sky.

Paratroopers captured four live Sirians; eight others were found dead from the blast.

That was what gave Lauchheimer and me our Congressional Medals.

The hostages didn't stay with us very long. They were brought to Washington too, for study. Ten minutes after we got our medals—flicker, whine—there was a sudden surge of color and a distant sound; the sun outside the White House window went purple and we were all caught.

Some months after that I found myself sharing a kennel with Pinky Postal.

III

I had not expected to see him there, though I suppose I could have guessed it. I knew more than he, though. I knew that the Sirians' idea of breeding was by no means the joyous sport that had inspired troubadours and axe-killings for thousands of years. After all, we use artificial insemination on our domestic animals, why should the Sirians be less efficient?

I knew enough, in fact, to have tried to avoid the breeding farm, for more reasons than one. Destiny makes games of our intentions; I was selected out of a thousand casual laborers in the work camp near Bethesda, and trucked to the farm overnight.

Pinky was thin, pale, trembling. He recognized me at once. "Help me, Harry! I got to get out of this place."

I looked around the place. It had been the Bethesda Naval Hospital at one time, with changes made by the bugs. It was now one enormous lying-in home, with beds for eighteen hundred women, dormitories for thousands more in the grounds around, and a special small detention home for we fortunate donors.

"You got what you wanted, didn't you?" I said.

Pinky had lost forty pounds, and there was no more flesh on his arms than on a spider crab's, but he surprised me. Without a word he jumped at my throat.

I beat him off with difficulty. "All right! It was a joke."

He slumped in a heap, whining, "Oh, Harry! I been here fourteen months and one of the bug boys tells me I have a hundred and twenty-three kids already, and more on the way, and—And, I swear, the closest I've been to a woman is looking at them out the window. You know what? They've got some of my—they've got samples, you know, in the deep freeze. They could kill me tomorrow and I'd go right on having kids for maybe twenty years. Harry! I didn't know it would be like this at all."

I left him and looked out the window. There was an exercise yard, a mess hall, a community shower—and a wall. Donors were not allowed outside of it.

I said, "You ought to feel honored. There are only ten of these stud farms in the world."

"And they're all the same—all this artificial insemination?"

"All exactly the same, Pinky. I'm sorry." That was a lie, of course—about being sorry; why would anyone waste compassion on Pinky Postal? But I was committed to telling lies. I could not trust him with the truth.

"Maybe it will work out all right," I said vaguely, reassuring not him but myself.

It had to. *Something* had to. Of the twenty-five of us who were abruptly sworn in as intelligence officers when the bubble closed in over Washington—the last real hope of any organized effort against the bugs—I was pretty sure that I was the only survivor.

The only hope of accomplishing anything against the Sirians lay in the possibility of destroying their central high command which was not a Sirian, or at any rate not an organic Sirian, but a machine. A computer. It did not rule them, but it detailed their plans.

There was a chance, said the general who swore us in, that if we destroyed the computer they would be confused and weakened, then we might get at them with conventional arms.

I followed Pinky's example and made friends with the man in the green brassard, Billings. I had no cigars. "I want to help you," I told him.

"My oath." He sat down with contempt and lit a cigarette with loathing. "You chaps get queerer every day."

I wheedled, "You never know, Billings. They might put you on stud any day."

"Too true." But it had shaken him. "And what can you do to stop them?"

I built a dream castle for him. "I have something they want, Billings. I can tell you about something the bugs will want to know."

Scornfully: "Hell! There isn't anything they want to know. They've a shootin' big machine that tells them everything they need."

"But the machine only knows what it's told. There's something the bugs have never known to tell it."

He looked impressed for a moment. "Dinkum? But—"

Then he shook his head. Casually he flicked ashes on my shoe. "I know what you're up to. You fellows are always coming to me with crook stories about how this is going to help me and that's going to save my life. It's no good. You can't fool me, cobber. And if you could, I can't fool *them*."

I said persuasively, "Let me try, won't you? It's a matter of human nature."

"What is?"

"What information they've given the computer. You were caught in the first landing, weren't you? Don't you remember what happened? They took a hundred men and women and subjected them to tests; the results made up a profile of human psychology for their computer." He nodded, watching me. "But they didn't have a Pinky Postal."

Billings said positively, "I don't know what the hell you're talking about."

But gradually I worked him over. I had to. Pinky was my ticket to the Sirian central headquarters. What I could accomplish there I did not know, but I knew that nothing at all could be accomplished on the stud farm. Besides, the argument was plausible—if not to Billings, then it would be to a Sirian. For what I had said was true. Their data was biased in favor of decent human beings, for their first captives were those who stood and fought. "Sure you know what you're talking about, pal?"

"I'm sure."

"You're not just sore because they wouldn't let you in with the sheilas?"

"I'm looking for a way out of here, Billings. That's all. Think it over. You'll see I'm right. They'll reward you."

He looked at me with contemptuous eyes. "You don't know much about them, do you? But probably they won't *hurt* me. Worth a try, no doubt. . . ." He said thoughtfully: "They'll be wild as cut snakes if this isn't right. And I'll be wild at you." But he finally gave in.

Pinky was pathetic in his gratitude. I was his only friend. He would never forget me; and, say, come to think of it, I was getting a break out of this too, wasn't I? How about giving him first pick of the food, for instance, or would I rather that he told the Sirians he couldn't react properly to their tests with me along?

He was reacting exactly properly, of course. But the trouble was the Sirians had their own ideas. Billings brought us down to the big barn where the only Sirian for miles around sometimes stopped by to check performance at the stud farm and, after waiting for some hours, the Sirian appeared. Billings, trembling, tried to explain what it was I had said. The Sirian grasped the idea very quickly; my promise was kept; the Sirian took the bait. He said something into a small spherical contraption he wore dangling from one middle leg and in a moment there was a Sirian plane, and Pinky and Billings were herded into it.

Just them. Not me.

For me it was back to the stud farm. Pinky had been my ticket to the headquarters and the ticket had just been punched.

The main Sirian headquarters on North America was in Maryland, on the site of what had once been the Bowie race track. Off to the south lay the horse barns. Where the grandstand and track itself had been, now tracelessly slagged over, stood the Sirian construction that they had flung up around their ship.

The building looked like a castle, worked like a palace. A palace is more than a home; it is workshop and office, an administrative center; so was this. But it did have a resemblance to a medieval castle, at least from a great enough distance in the air. There were things like towers and things like battlements. Closer up the resemblance was gone. The lobed wall that surrounded it was not for defense, as in a castle; it was the Sirian equivalent of a garage, where their ground and air vehicles were kept. The towers were viewless, except at the very top, where sweeping silvery needles performed a function like radar's.

Pinky and the Aussie came to it with suspicion and delight. Anything was better than the stud farm.

Or *almost* anything. But undeniably this was queer. They were sent to a hexagonal green-on-green room, small, bedless. Billings spat on the floor when he saw it. But even that satisfaction was denied him. The floor shimmered, the saliva collected in quick-silvery beads and trembled toward an almost invisible slit, where it vanished. Pinky said, "You don't like the accommodations?"

"It ain't Darling Point," said Billings. "You know what I wish? I wish that pal of yours was here. I've a notion of something I want to say to him."

But Billings had only been a straw-boss at the stud farm, Pinky had actually been one of the studs. "It's not so bad," he said with cheerful confidence, "and anyway we'll make out. Or I will." He hesitated and said: "You won't believe this, but I wish there were some women here."

The Sirians wasted no time. Considering the limitations placed on their researches by the lack of unimpeded communication (no human ever learned the Sirian speech, and they could manage human tongues only through a sort of vodor), they were thorough and complete. None of it made much sense to Pinky, of course. All he knew was that he and Billings were bored, annoyed and persecuted for twelve hours at a time with endless nibbling nuisances. Word associations, reflex tests, interpretive depth studies much like a Rorschach—the works. "There's not much in being a guinea pig," sighed Billings, exhausted and angry.

"Would you rather be a stud?" asked Pinky, very cheerfully. He was quite happy. He had discovered an angle to shoot.

IV

The heart of the Sirian headquarters was a room thirty feet tall, a hundred feet square, lighted with a sourceless green glow and inhabited at all times by several dozen of the bugs.

Pinky had seen the room from a gallery above it. The results of his tests and Billings' were fed into receptors in a little room just off the great one. It was there, banked like a horseshoe along three walls, that the central computer whispered and glowed.

The Sirians did not trouble with electricity in its grosser forms. The computers operated on what seemed to be neural impulses, projecting their data on soft green-ivory breast-shaped bosses in letters of light. There is very much about those computers which is mysterious, but some things are sure: For one, at least a hundred problems could be worked and answered simultaneously, so that the feat of juggling Pinky's personality quirks into the standard human profile could go on whenever convenient to the bugs, without interrupting the calculation of Hohmann trajectories for the remainder of their fleet (then approaching Orbit Pluto), the logistics of their Canadian enterprise, the setting of breeding quotas and the computation of field strengths for each bubble in their chain.

Not all of the answers were expressed numerically; some were translated directly into action in their factories; some were expressed visually. In the center of the room, for instance, was what (although Pinky could not have recognized it) was a situation map. The chart was of North America, but as the human convention of portraying bodies of water as featureless plains was not followed by the Sirians, Pinky could make of it nothing but a scramble of topography, as meaningless to him as the chart of the back side of the Moon.

If Pinky had had the wit to understand what he saw even he might have been shocked. The circles of Sirian bubbles were etched in fire. They had grown—*how* they had grown! All the Eastern seaboard was a string of fat Sirian beads now, and a beaded limb swung west as far as the featureless plain of Ohio. The last quick sproutings of bubbles had taken in and neutralized four Army Corps areas, eight SAC bases, the manufacturing centers of most of the eastern half of the continent and every center of population of importance north of Savannah and east of the Great Lakes. There was very little left.

Pinky Postal saw all that without comprehending. Or caring.

What he comprehended very clearly was that in the hours when he was not under scrutiny he was allowed to do as he liked.

The Sirians were not careless, they were merely confident. They had every reason to be. The few hundred humans at liberty within the headquarters had no weapons. All of them combined were no match for a single bug, who could effortlessly destroy them one after another at will. There was little prospect of effective sabotage in the areas available to the captives. Most rooms were featureless dormitories, halls, exercise areas, yards. The workshops and armories were closed to humans. The few chambers which had any strategic importance—principally the computer room—were never left untended.

Pinky restlessly prowled the headquarters and the abandoned human buildings surrounding it. He found treasures—in the old jockey's quarters, a wicker basket of champagne; in the Steward's office, a tin box full of money.

He waved the hundred-dollar bills in Billings' face, but the Aussie only snarled, "What's the use of *that*?"

"Oh, cheer up," said Pinky dispassionately. "What's the use of anything? But money's always good. You'll see."

"I'll see we'll spend the rest of our lives whingeing about here," groaned Billings. He had become very morose. He almost stopped eating and, as days passed, stopped speaking. In the tests he failed to cooperate.

Not Pinky. Pinky was a model of cooperation. He had learned that the way to get along with the bugs was to do what they wanted, and he was not surprised when one night as the tests were concluded Billings was detained. Pinky walked slowly toward their room, and did not even look back when from behind him he caught a flash of silent green light and heard a sharp, panicky sound from Billings, then silence. Too bad. But Pinky had his plans.

By then I was in the hills around Frederick, Maryland, with the freedom forces.

Well, we called ourselves that, for morale mostly; but actually my work lay mostly in nurse-maiding chitinous young Waldo, our ace of trumps.

I had not escaped from the breeding farm, I had been liberated. A fire and noise woke us donors one night; we saw human figures dancing around the flame of burning buildings, and in the confusion the raiders broke into our close-penned corral and led us away. It was none too soon for me, and I was not only grateful, I was astonished. For these were free men and women living under the bubbles!

It was inconceivable, but there they were.

Undoubtedly the Sirians could have hunted us down, but they didn't bother. Probably there were too many humans loose under their screens, like silverfish in an old house. They had ways of locating weapons as long as there was a metallic component like the barrel of a gun or shaft of a knife—magnetic or electronic detectors, no doubt—but while we kept free of metal they never troubled us.

So our weapon was the torch.

We killed bugs, too. We fried a dozen one night in firing a stand of yellow pine where they were—I don't know; perhaps camping. We clubbed a few, killed some from a distance with bow and arrow. Strike and run, we must have destroyed fifty of them in six months. That was not a small number. It was more than one per cent of all the Sirians on Earth.

It was relatively easy for us to move about because the expanding bubbles had swept so much of the human race ahead of them. The towns were deserted. The bug centers were easy to avoid. All of North America was now under the green umbrella; a mauve sun sailed over all of Europe and most of Asia. We learned, through such sparse communications facilities as were left to us, that Africa and South America were largely bug-free. Evidently the warmer parts of the Earth were not attractive to the Sirians. They were now a sort of game preserve, nearly all that survived of humanity packed into those two continents, almost two billion people crowded into the malarial Amazon basin and the hot savannahs of the Congo.

So we crept about under their feet and stung them when we could. We became ingenious in setting snares. With the high-octane gasoline from an abandoned storage tank we washed one of their landing strips one night, and set it ablaze just as one of their gull-winged flyers came in. The intention was to incinerate them all, and then for us to vanish tracelessly; but the Sirian pilot saw danger at the last moment and almost soared free. The flames caught him, and the ship pinwheeled into the side of a hill. And that was very fortunate for us, because that was how we captured Waldo.

Waldo was a small, dark-green creature the size of a puppy, newly hatched and not very dangerous.

He was our first living Sirian captive. We dared take time to poke about in the wreck of the plane, knowing that there would be investigation, and we found that only two of its crew were adult Sirians; the others were eggs or hatchlings. The crash had killed them handsomely. All but one. John Gaffney found the one; rummaging through the dark he suddenly screamed: "The little louse! He bit me!" But it wasn't a bite, it was a neural shock. It was Waldo. He was alive. As he was only a newborn, his shock was painful but not deadly.

We roped him and dragged him out onto the side of the hill. In the light of a quarter-million burning gallons of gasoline, pinned on his back with ten legs waving, he did not seem dangerous, only comic. "Kill him," said Gaffney, rubbing his leg.

"No." I had a better idea. "They'll never miss him. Why don't we keep him? He can be—We can use him for—"

"What?" demanded Gaffney. "No, kill him!" But I had my way finally. We had no plan for a captive Sirian, because it had never occurred to us we might catch one. But surely something would turn up!

So we swung him in a hammock and lashed him tight, and we got out of there minutes before the Sirian rescue parties were circling the sea of flame.

It was months before we had any idea of what to do with him. As I had insisted on kidnapping him, he was given me to raise. This was not pleasant. He was a painful pet, and difficult to handle.

I mention only the difficulty of feeding him. Infant Sirians were nurtured on a sort of nectar, probably once secreted by Sirian adults but now, in their dwellings, synthesized in quantity. We had none. We tried everything. Honey was good but hard to come by. Molasses made him drunk. Simple sugar solution he refused to touch. We finally settled on maple syrup with, after experimenting, a few drops of whiskey.

On this he thrived. I determined to try to teach him English.

I could not hope that he would ever speak it, but neither can a dog. He was much brighter than a dog. "Walk," "sit," "come"—he learned those before he was a month old. He showed that he could learn much more.

In the winter evenings he would cuddle in my lap and we would look at the pictures in magazines together, I pointing out "car" and "house" and "washing machine" and Waldo reaching out with a jointed, taloned leg to scratch at the picture on the page. He made a faint humming sound, and his hardening chiton was rather warm. I grew almost fond of him, he was so eager to learn. Yet I was kept from oversentimentality by the potent sting he carried with him always. He would fall asleep in my lap. Just as a human child will restlessly turn over a time or two before drifting off, so Waldo would emit one sleepy shock before the black, hard eyes unfocused and he went into the catalepsy that was their sleep.

As he grew larger (and he grew astonishing fast), those light love-pats in good night became more and more agonizing. Twice I was knocked unconscious.

We tried insulation. We wrapped him in rubber sheets, shrouded him in layer on layer of quilts. We tried keeping him off my lap, merely close by on a couch. Nothing worked. Always he drowsily reached out with one leg or an eyestalk or the corner of his backplate, just before he drifted off. And I leaped half out of my skin.

On Christmas day of the second year of the Sirian conquest, Gaffney brought us a new recruit.

I was not present when she arrived—I was out exercising Waldo, under the shelter of an overgrown old apple orchard—and I missed the questioning. By the time I got back to our camp she was asleep, worn out, but Gaffney was bubbling with news.

"She was actually in their headquarters! She drew us a plan of the whole thing, Harry—look!" It was crude, but if the girl was reliable it was all the information we had hoped for. We located the computer room, the Sirian sleeping quarters, the defensive installations, the shops, the laboratories. Slave quarters ringed one floor. Surveillance of half a continent was carried on in an observatory near the top. "And look here," said Gaffney in excitement, "see this line? The inner part of the headquarters is almost independent of the rest. Double walls, limited access, construction heavier, stronger inside. What does that suggest?" I opened my mouth. "A ship!" he cried, not giving me a chance. "The central part of the building is a ship!"

More than that, the girl had told him that that ship housed all the brains of the Sirian expedition. They had but one computer; it had landed with the first touchdown on Australia, but had been moved to the United States. If we could destroy that ship. . . .

"But that's the part that worries me," admitted Gaffney, downcast. "How do we get in? They let her wander about pretty much as she wanted, see—all the humans do. Fact, the humans are pretty much independent, long as they do what the bugs want. Even have their own, well, boss, a fellow who—Never mind. What I started out to say, the bugs can afford to let the humans roam around, because the corridors are booby-trapped. It's something like Waldo's shock. There are places where this girl couldn't go, because she would die, unless a Sirian was with her. It didn't bother Sirians."

We puzzled that over for a while. Waldo, beside me, rested one talon gently in my hand—he was very well-behaved and quite trustworthy except, as I said, just as he was drifting off to sleep. He loomed over us (being now more than nine feet tall), staring at the scribbled map with polite curiosity.

I turned and stared at him abruptly. "Waldo! *He* could help us!" Quickly I explained. If Sirians could pass the booby-traps, why, we had our own Sirian!

I said, "We'll have to ask the girl. Did they carry anything special? But she would have said so, and I think not. I think probably their own neural shock emanations screened off the radiations from the booby-traps, and if that's the case—"

"Don't guess," said Gaffney. "We've woke her up with all our noise. Here she comes now."

And there was the girl, coming drowsily into the room. She glanced toward me, stopped stark, her hand flew to her mouth, she screamed.

I threw a look at Waldo beside me.

"Oh, you saw him? Don't worry about him, young lady! He's perfectly tame. But no doubt he reminded you of the horrors you suffered while the captive of the Sirians.

She simmered down slowly, shaking her head. "No—no. I'm sorry to be such a fool. It isn't the *bug* I was worried about. It's just that seeing you standing there that way, so close to him—well. You scared me half to death. For a minute," she said with apologetic embarrassment, "for a minute I thought you were the boss. Mr. Postal."

V

Earth had now been conquered in all of its important parts. We knew that the great colonizing fleet that would follow the first wave had long been orbiting the sun, reducing its velocity, knocking off miles-per-second to match speed with the Earth and to land.

What we did not know was how tedious life had become for the conquerors.

Pinky Postal, however, had them right under his eye. He saw how little there was for them to do. These were soldiers, not intellectuals, not artists, not even home-builders; their work was to fight, and they were fought out. They had won.

Two days before Billings was killed, Pinky caught a glimpse of what might be. He found five quarts of champagne and got quite drunk. In his intoxication he blundered where he knew he should not go—into Sirian quarters—and it was only the providence of drunks that kept him from a booby-trap, but somehow he found himself in a small room where something heaved under a tarpaulin.

It was a queer sight, and he kicked it.

The tarpaulin flung free. There was a high-pitched Sirian chirp, and three great insect bodies bounded up from the floor, where they had been huddled. Gravely, drunkenly, Pinky realized that he was about to die. He had caught them at something, heaven knew what. And they would surely smite him low.

As he was drunk, he merely stood there, weaving slightly, breathing calm alcoholic defiance at the Sirian who bent dangerously toward him.

—But he did not die.

He did not die, and the next morning, through the pounding haze of his hangover, he wondered why. There were blanks in his recollection. But he remembered standing there, and he remembered that the killing bolt from the Sirian had never come.

He puzzled over it for a whole day.

Then, that evening, a Sirian came toward him and bent low.

Pinky was not drunk this time, and he was terrified. He tried to run, fell, squirmed and lay flat on his back while the great flat June-bug face swooped down at him.

Again the bolt did not strike.

The face hung there, for seconds and then for minutes. And by and by Pinky saw that the Sirian was twitching. It twitched and stirred. Then it definitely staggered. It stumbled, caught itself, almost fell athwart him, caught itself again. The faint cricket-chirp sounded, ragged and . . . and . . . *drunken.*

Drunken!

And Pinky, sleepless that night, staring at the black ceiling of his green-on-green cubicle, realized that he had found what he wanted.

He became a pusher. Of himself.

Of course the Sirians had their vices. What creature does not?

Carbon dioxide was their liquor. Their respiratory systems being what they were, it was only infrequently that their own waste gases reached their intake orifices; but the concentrated breath of a mammal could send them reeling; a few minutes inhaling a man's direct breath would stiffen them in a giggling paralysis.

But on their planet of Sirius, they had no mammals.

They did what they could with what they had to work with. Their most secret vice was bundling—two (or, rarely and most despicably, three or more) of the Sirians furtively huddled under an airtight sheet, exuding CO_2 and intoxicating one another. It was a fearful vice. It was also a dangerous one. It could not be practiced openly. And when done in secret there was always the risk that the drunks would pass out and ultimately die of hyperintoxication.

They were not merely drunks, they were alcoholics, a racial characteristic; for once they had tasted the happy gas exuded by gross mammalian chemistry they were addicts. Pinky collected his first addict by chance, but he was courageous enough and thoughtful enough to make more. It took courage. It took exposing himself to a chance bolt from a new contact, but once the first few moments were past, so was the danger. A new habit had been formed; the pusher had hooked a new customer. It was the sort of industrious empire-building to which Pinky was best fitted, for he was perceptive to all weaknesses of the flesh—even chitinous flesh hatched under alien, blue-white stars.

Pinky was supply enough for whole roomfuls of Sirians, such

clouds of intoxicant wafted from him. As days and weeks passed, more and more the work of the Sirian headquarters came to revolve around him. The business of occupying Earth tended itself well enough. The quasi-radars kept their vigil and marked their targets, the computers never stopped monitoring the approach of the fleet and correcting its course. They gave him a vodor, so that he could talk to them direct; he talked in commands. They obeyed his commands, for he was intelligent enough to bait them. He sent them on scrounging expeditions to find choice food—a good bargain for them for, as with Earthly topers, it was not the simple chemical paralysis that pleased them best but the subtle bouquet and tang of contaminants. What bliss in the reek of green onions on his breath! What tingling thrill in the stale scent of tobacco! They sent parties rummaging through the nearby abandoned towns, for canned cheese and garlic, for spearmint chewing gum and cinnamon drops.

Food and drink supplied, he next demanded control over the other humans in the Sirian headquarters. This too they gave him—why not? It was Pinky, after all, who knew how to brew those rare blends of flavor that made all the difference. If Pinky chose to exercise the human crew in ways of his own, he never failed to share their breath with his employers. For this reason the other humans grew to hate, fear and despise him, but they feared the Sirians even more. Pinky was perfectly happy for the first time in his life. He was not a king, he was more.

The Sirians ruled the world. And, in all but name, he ruled the Sirians.

It was into this earthly paradise of Pinky's that we snakes wriggled, bringing destruction.

The rest is history: how, emboldened by the increasing laxity of the Sirians, we attacked their headquarters; how Waldo, a happy child with no consciousness that he was betraying his race, led us through the trapped corridors into the Sirian fortress; how we were found out by that most Sirian of tyrants, Pinky Postal. For it was he who spotted us. He and his humans had ministered to the whole headquarters detachment, leaving them in a happy stupor, when the alarm bells rang, and though Pinky roused one of the bugs enough to locate us, the creature was far too tipsy to do anything about it.

It was the end of the world for Pinky Postal. His paradise was over.

He confronted us at the entrance passage, wild with fear and hate.

"Harry!" he brawled, screeching with rage. "You louse! You rat! You human!"

"Shut up," said I, and in truth I paid him little attention. I was wondering where the Sirians were. We didn't then know that they were all dead drunk, or almost all; we thought they might come ravening down among us with murderous shocks blazing left and right. Pinky danced before us, almost weeping; but when we deployed left and right, as we had rehearsed it so many times, he bolted away and, *crash,* a steel door slammed behind him.

We invested the outer shell of the Sirian structure with no trouble at all. It was all too easy, in fact. It turned out to be costly. Fifteen of us died in the Sirian takeoff.

Yes, the Sirian takeoff—which so many have wondered at—now the truth can be told. Two of Pinky Postal's retinue at the last, when they saw what was happening, fled with only seconds to spare back to the Earth Pinky was spurning. They told us how Pinky, raving, strove to arouse the bugs to destroy us; failing, tried to get them to lock us out; failing even in that, managed at the last only to sober one Sirian just enough to pull the master switches that blasted their ship loose from its shell, sending it screaming up, out and away, Sirians, computer, Pinky and all.

Fifteen of our raiding party died in its rocket-flames. It was a cheap price, of course.

But how are we to explain to history that the Sirian conquest of humanity was defeated not by our strength but by our vices?

And when it comes to that, what can I say to the President?

He is very sunburned and healthy looking from his summer on the Orinoco. He is a titan at the tasks of reconstruction. Life is almost normal again; and he assures me that, with what we have learned from the works the Sirians left behind, we shall have no trouble in fighting off their invasion if they dared to attempt it again. They left a hundred bubble generators, and now we know how to pierce any bubble. We have already mopped up their survivors. Young Waldo is busy every day, trying to learn to talk to his own kind and tell them that they have lost a war.

Naturally, the President wants to reward the man who made all this possible—at, says the President with sorrow and pride, the cost of his own dear life.

I wish I could stop it, but I don't know how. I don't mind, really, that mine should not be the last Congressional Medal of Honor after all.

But I resent it most keenly that the next should go in absentia to Pinky Postal!

HONORABLE OPPONENT

by Clifford D. Simak

The way the aliens fought a war made absolutely no sense—but that was because the humans hadn't been given an instruction manual yet.

★ ★ ★

***Clifford D. Simak** (1904-1988) published his first SF story, "The World of the Red Sun" in 1931, and went on to become one of the star writers during John W. Campbell's Golden Age of Science Fiction in the 1940s, notably in the series of stories which he eventually combined into his classic novel,* City. *Other standout novels include* Time and Again, Ring Around the Sun, Time is the Simplest Thing, *and the Hugo-winning* Way Station. *Altogether, Simak won three Hugo Awards, a Nebula Award, and was the third recipient of the Grand Master Award of the Science Fiction Writers of America for lifetime achievement. He also received the Bram Stoker Award for lifetime achievement from the Horror Writers Association. He was noted for stories written with a pastoral feeling, though he could also turn out a chilling horror story, such as "Good Night, Mr. James," which was made into an episode of the original* Outer Limits. *His day job was newspaperman, joining the staff of the* Minneapolis Star and Tribune *in 1939, becoming its news editor in 1949, and retiring in 1976. He once wrote that "My favorite recreation is fishing (the lazy way, lying in a boat and letting them come to me)."*

═ ★ ═

The Fivers were late.

Perhaps they had misunderstood.

Or this might be another of their tricks.

Or maybe they never had intended to stick to their agreement.

"Captain," asked General Lyman Flood, "what time have we got now?"

Captain Gist looked up from the chessboard. "Thirty-seven oh eight, galactic, sir."

Then he went back to the board again. Sergeant Conrad had pinned his knight and he didn't like it.

"Thirteen hours late!" the general fumed.

"They may not have got it straight, sir."

"We spelled it out to them. We took them by the hand and we went over it time and time again so they'd have it clear in mind. They couldn't possibly misunderstand."

But they very possibly could, he knew.

The Fivers misunderstood almost everything. They had been confused about the armistice—as if they'd never heard of an armistice before. They had been obtuse about the prisoner exchange. Even the matter of setting a simple time had involved excruciating explanation—as if they had never heard of the measurement of time and were completely innocent of basic mathematics.

"Or maybe they broke down," the captain offered.

The general snorted. "They don't break down. Those ships of theirs are marvels. They'd live through anything. They whipped us, didn't they?"

"Yes, sir," said the captain.

"How many of them, Captain, do you estimate we destroyed?"

"Not more than a dozen, sir."

"They're tough," the general said.

He went back across the tent and sat down in a chair.

The captain had been wrong. The right number was eleven. And of those, only one had been confirmed destroyed. The others had been no better than put out of action.

And the way it figured out, the margin had been more than ten to one in favor of the Fivers. Earth, the general admitted to himself, had never taken such a beating. Whole squadrons had been wiped out; others had come fleeing back to base with their numbers cut in half.

They came fleeing back to base and there were no cripples. They had returned without a scratch upon them. And the ships that had been lost had not been visibly destroyed—they had simply been wiped out, leaving not a molecule of wreckage.

How do you beat a thing like that? he asked himself. How do you fight a weapon that cancels out a ship in its entirety?

Back on Earth and on hundreds of other planets in the Galactic Confederacy, thousands of researchers were working day and night in a crash-priority program to find an answer to the weapon—or at least to find the weapon.

But the chance of success ran thin, the general knew, for there was not a single clue to the nature of it. Which was understandable, since every victim of the weapon had been lost irretrievably.

Perhaps some of the human prisoners would be able to provide a clue. If there had been no such hope, he knew, Earth never would have gone to all the trouble to make this prisoner exchange.

He watched the captain and the sergeant hunched above the chessboard, with the captive Fiver looking on.

He called the captive over.

The captive came, like a trundling roly-poly.

And once again, watching him, the general had that strange, disturbing sense of outrage.

For the Fiver was a droll grotesque that held no hint of the martial spirit. He was round and jolly in every feature, expression, and gesture, dressed in a ribald clash of colors, as though designed and clad deliberately to offend any military man.

"Your friends are late," the general told him.

"You wait," the Fiver said and his words were more like whistling than talk. One had to listen closely to make out what he said.

The general held himself in check.

No use in arguing.

No point blowing up.

He wondered if he—or the human race—would ever understand the Fivers.

Not that anyone really wanted to, of course. Just to get them combed out of Earth's hair would be enough.

"You wait," the Fiver whistled. "They come in middle time from now."

And when in hell, the general wondered, would be a middle time from now?

The Fiver glided back to watch the game.

The general walked outside.

The tiny planet looked colder and more desolate and forbidding than it ever had before. Each time he looked at it, the general thought, the scene was more depressing than he had remembered it.

Lifeless, worthless, of no strategic or economic value, it had qualified quite admirably as neutral territory to carry out the prisoner exchange. Neutral mostly because it wasn't worth the trouble for anyone to grab it.

The distant star that was its sun was a dim glow in the sky. The black and naked rock crept out to a near horizon. The icy air was like a knife inside the general's nostrils.

There were no hills or valleys. There was absolutely nothing—just the smooth flatness of the rock stretching *on all* sides, for all the world like a great spacefield.

It had been the Fivers, the general remembered, who had suggested this particular planet and that in itself was enough to make it suspect. But Earth, at that point in the negotiations, had been in no position to do much haggling.

He stood with his shoulders hunched and he felt the cold breath of apprehension blowing down his neck. With each passing hour, it seemed, the place felt more and more like some gigantic trap.

But he must be wrong, he argued. There was absolutely nothing in the Fivers' attitude to make him feel like that. They had, in fact, been almost magnanimous. They could have laid down their terms—almost any terms—and the Confederacy would have had no choice but to acquiesce. For Earth must buy time, no matter what the price. Earth had to be ready next time—five years or ten or whatever it might be.

But the Fivers had made no demands, which was unthinkable.

Except, the general told himself, one could never know what they might be thinking or what they might be planning.

The exchange camp huddled in the dimness—a few tents, a portable power plant, the poised and waiting ship and, beside it, the little scouter the captive Fiver had been piloting.

The scouter in itself was a good example of the gulf which separated the Fivers and the humans. It had taken three full days of bickering before the Fivers had been able to make clear their point that the scouter as well as its pilot must be returned to them.

No ship in all the Galaxy had ever gotten so thorough a study as that tiny craft. But the facts that it had yielded had been few indeed. And the captive Fiver, despite the best efforts of the experts in Psych, had furnished even fewer.

The area was quiet and almost deserted. Two sentries strode briskly up and down. Everyone else was under cover, killing time, waiting for the Fivers.

The general walked quickly across the area to the medic tent. He stooped and went inside.

Four men were sitting at a table, drearily playing cards. One of them put down his hand and rose.

"Any word, General?"

The general shook his head. "They should be coming soon, Doc. Everything all set?"

"We've been ready for some time," said the psychiatrist. "We'll bring the boys in here and check them over as soon as they arrive. We've got the stuff all set. It won't take us long."

"That's fine. I want to get off this rock as quickly as I can. I don't like the feel of it."

"There's just one thing . . ."

"What's that?"

"If we only knew how many they are handing back?"

The general shook his head. "We never could find out. They're not so hot on figures. And you'd think, wouldn't you, that math would be universal?"

"Well," said Doc resignedly, "we'll do the best we can."

"There can't be many," the general said. "We're only giving back one Fiver and one ship. How many humans do you figure a ship is worth to them?"

"I wouldn't know. You really think they'll come?"

"It's hard to be certain that they understood. When it comes to sheer stupidity—"

"Not so stupid," Doc replied, quietly. "We couldn't learn their language, so they learned ours."

"I know," the general said impatiently. "I realize all that. But that armistice business—it took days for them to get what we were driving at. And the time-reckoning system still more days. Good Lord, man, you could do better using sign language with a Stone Age savage!"

"You should," said Doc. "The savage would be human."

"But these Fivers are intelligent. Their technology, in many ways, has us beaten seven ways from Sunday. They fought us to a standstill."

"They licked us."

"All right, then, they licked us. And why not? They had this weapon that we didn't have. They were closer to their bases. They had no logistics problem to compare with ours. They licked us, but I ask you, did they have the sense to know it? Did they take advantage of it? They could have wiped us out. They could have laid down peace terms that would have crippled us for centuries. Instead, they let us go. Now how does that make sense?"

"You're dealing with an alien race," said Doc.

"We've dealt with other aliens. And we always understood them. Mostly, we got along with them."

"We dealt with them on a commercial basis," Doc reminded him. "Whatever trouble we might have had with them came after a basic minimum of understanding had been achieved. The Fivers are the first that ever came out shooting."

"I can't figure it," the general said. "We weren't even heading for them. We might have passed them by. They couldn't have known who we were. Point is, they didn't care. They just came piling out and opened up on us. And it's been the same with everyone else who came within their reach. They take on every comer. There's never a time when they aren't fighting someone—sometimes two or three at once."

"They have a defensive complex," said Doc. "Want to be left alone. All they aim to do is keep others off their planets. As you say, they could have wiped us out."

"Maybe they get hurt real easy. Don't forget we gave them a bloody nose or two—not as much as they busted us, but we hurt them some. I figure they'll come out again, soon as they can cut in."

He drew a deep breath. "Next time, we have to be ready for them. Next time, they may not stop. We have to dope them out."

It was tough work, he thought, to fight an enemy about which one knew next to nothing. And a weapon about which one knew absolutely nothing.

There were theories in plenty, but the best no more than educated guesses.

The weapon might operate in time—hurling its targets back into unimagined chaos. Or it might be dimensional. Or it might collapse the atoms in upon themselves, reducing a spaceship to the most deadly massive dust-mote the Universe had known.

One thing for certain—it was not disintegration, for there was no flash and there was no heat. The ship just disappeared and that was the end of it—the end and all of it.

"There's another thing that bothers me," said Doc. "Those other races that fought the Fivers before they jumped on us. When we tried to contact them, when we tried to get some help from them, they wouldn't bother with us. They wouldn't tell us anything."

"This is a new sector of space for us," the general said. "We are strangers here."

"It stands to reason," argued Doc, "they should jump at the chance to gang up on the Fivers."

"We can't depend on alliances. We stand alone. It is up to us."

He bent to leave the tent.

"We'll get right on it," said Doc, "soon as the men show up.

We'll have a preliminary report within an hour, if they're in any shape at all."

"That's fine," the general said and ducked out of the tent.

It was a bad situation, blind and terrifying if one didn't manage to keep a good grip on himself.

The captive humans might bring back some information, but even so, you couldn't buy it blind, for there might be a gimmick in it—as there was a gimmick in what the captive Fiver knew.

This time, he told himself, the Psych boys might have managed to outsmart themselves.

It had been a clever trick, all right—taking the captive Fiver on that trip and showing him so proudly all the barren, no-good planets, pretending they were the showplaces of the Confederacy.

Clever—if the Fiver had been human. For no human would have fought a skirmish, let alone a war, for the kind of planets he'd been shown.

But the Fiver wasn't human. And there was no way of knowing what kind of planet a Fiver might take a fancy to.

And there always was the chance that those crummy planets had given him the hunch that Earth would be easy prey.

The whole situation didn't track, the general thought. There was a basic wrongness to it. Even allowing for all the differences which might exist between the Fiver and the human cultures, the wrongness still persisted.

And there was something wrong right here.

He heard the sound and wheeled to stare into the sky.

The ship was close and coming in too fast.

But even as he held his breath, it slowed and steadied and came to ground in a perfect landing not more than a quarter of a mile from where the Earth ship stood.

The general broke into a run toward it, then remembered and slowed to a stiff military walk.

Men were tumbling out of tents and forming into lines. An order rang across the area and the lines moved with perfect drill precision.

The general allowed himself a smile. Those boys of his were good. You never caught them napping. If the Fivers had expected to sneak in and catch the camp confused and thus gain a bit of face, it was a horse on them.

The marching men swung briskly down the field. An ambulance moved out from beneath its tarp and followed. The drums began to roll and the bugles sounded clear and crisp in the harsh, cold air.

It was men like these, the general told himself with pride, who held the expanding Confederacy intact. It was men like these who kept the peace across many cubic light-years. It was men like these who someday, God willing, would roll back the Fiver threat.

There were few wars now. Space was too big for it. There were too many ways to skirt around the edge of war for it to come but seldom. But something like the Fiver threat could not be ignored. Someday, soon or late, either Earth or Fiver must go down to complete defeat. The Confederacy could never feel secure with the Fivers on its flank.

Feet pounded behind him and the general turned. It was Captain Gist, buttoning his tunic as he ran. He fell in beside the general.

"So they finally came, sir."

"Fourteen hours late," the general said. "Let us, for the moment, try to look our best. You missed a button, Captain."

"Sorry, sir," the captain said, fastening the button.

"Right, then. Get those shoulders back. Smartly, if you will. Right, left, hup, hup!"

Out of the corner of his eye, he saw that Sergeant Conrad had his squad moving out with precision, escorting the captive Fiver most correctly forward, with all the dignity and smartness that anyone might wish.

The men were drawn up now in two parallel lines, flanking the ship. The port was swinging open and the ramp was rumbling out and the general noted with some satisfaction that he and Captain Gist would arrive at the foot of the ramp about the time it touched the ground. The timing was dramatic and superb, almost as if he himself had planned it down to the last detail.

The ramp snapped into position and three Fivers came sedately waddling down it.

A seedy-looking trio, the general thought. Not a proper uniform nor a medal among the lot of them.

The general seized the diplomatic initiative as soon as they reached the ground.

"We welcome you," he told them, speaking loudly and slowly and as distinctly as he could so they would understand.

They lined up and stood looking at him and he felt a bit uncomfortable because there was that round jolly expression in their faces. Evidently they didn't have the kind of faces that could assume any other expression. But they kept on looking at him.

The general plunged ahead. "It is a matter of great gratification to Earth to carry out in good faith our obligations as agreed upon in the armistice proceedings. It marks what we sincerely hope will be the beginning of an era . . ."

"Most nice," one of the Fivers said. Whether he meant the general's little speech or the entire situation or was simply trying to be gracious was not at once apparent.

Undaunted, the general was ready to go on, but the spokesman Fiver raised a short round arm to halt him.

"Prisoners arrive briefly," he whistled.

"You mean you didn't bring them?"

"They come again," the Fiver said with a glorious disregard for preciseness of expression. He continued beaming at the general and he made a motion with the arm that might have been a shrug.

"Shenanigans," the captain said, close to the general's ear.

"We talk," the Fiver said.

"They're up to something," warned the captain. "It calls for Situation Red, sir."

"I agree," the general told the captain. "Set it up quietly." He said to the Fiver delegation: "If you gentlemen will come with me, I can offer you refreshments."

He had a feeling that they were smiling at him, mocking him, but one could never tell. Those jolly expressions were always the same. No matter what the situation.

"Most happy," said the Fiver spokesman. "These refresh—"

"Drink," the general said and made a motion to supplement the word.

"Drink is good," the Fiver answered. "Drink is friend?"

"That is right," the general said.

He started for the tent, walking slowly so the Fivers could keep up.

He noted with some satisfaction that the captain had carried on most rapidly, indeed. Corporal Conrad was marching his squad back across the area, with the captive Fiver shambling in the center. The tarps were coming off the guns and the last of the crew was clambering up the ladder of the ship.

The captain caught up with them just short of the tent.

"Everything all set, sir," Corporal Conrad reported in a whisper.

"Fine," the general said.

They reached the tent and went inside. The general opened a refrigerating unit and took out a gallon jug.

"This," he explained, "is a drink we made for your compatriot. He found it very tasty."

He set out glasses and sipping straws and uncorked the jug, wishing he could somehow hold his nose, for the drink smelled like something that had been dead too long. He didn't even like to guess what might have gone into it. The chemists back on Earth had whomped it up for the captive Fiver, who had consumed gallon after gallon of it with disconcerting gusto.

The general filled the glasses and the Fivers picked them up in their tentacles and stuck the straws into their drawstring mouths. They drank and rolled their eyes in appreciation.

The general took the glass of liquor the captain handed him and gulped half of it in haste. The tent was getting just a little thick. What things a man goes through, he thought, to serve his planets and his peoples.

He watched the Fivers drinking and wondered what they might have up their sleeves.

Talk, the spokesman had told him, and that might mean almost anything. It might mean a reopening of negotiations or it might be nothing but a stall.

And if it was a negotiation, Earth was across the barrel. For there was nothing he could do but negotiate. Earth's fleet was crippled and the Fivers had the weapon and a renewal of the war was unthinkable. Earth needed five years at the minimum and ten years would be still better.

And if it was an attack, if this planet was a trap, there was only one thing he could do—stand and fight as best he could, a thoroughly suicidal course.

Either way, Earth lost, the general realized.

The Fivers put down their glasses and he filled them up again.

"You do well," one of the Fivers said. "You got the paper and the marker?"

"Marker?" the general asked.

"He means a pencil," said the captain.

"Oh, yes. Right here." The general reached for a pad of paper and a pencil and laid them on the desk.

One of the Fivers set down his glass and, picking up the pencil, started to make a laborious drawing. He looked for all the world like a five-year-old printing his first alphabet. They waited while the Fiver drew. Finally he was finished. He laid the pencil down and pointed to the wiggly lines.

"Us," he said.

He pointed to the saw-toothed lines.

"You," he told the general.

The general bent above the paper, trying to make out what the Fiver had put down.

"Sir," the captain said, "it looks like a battle diagram."

"Is," said the Fiver proudly. He picked the pencil up. "Look," he said.

He drew directional lines and made a funny kind of symbol for the points of contact and made crosses for the sections where the battle lines were broken. When he was done, the Earth fleet had been shattered and sliced into three segments and was in headlong flight.

"That," the general said, with the husk of anger rising in his throat, "was the engagement in Sector 17. Half of our Fifth Squadron was wiped out that day."

"Small error," said the Fiver and made a deprecatory gesture. He ripped the sheet of paper off the pad and tossed it on the floor. He laboriously drew the diagram again.

"Attend," he said.

The Fiver drew the directional lines again, but this time he changed them slightly. Now the Earth line pivoted and broke and became two parallel lines that flanked the Fiver drive and turned and blunted it and scattered it in space. The Fiver laid the pencil down.

"Small matter," he informed the general and the captain. "You good. You make one thin mistake."

Holding himself sternly in hand, the general filled the glasses once again.

What are they getting at, he thought. Why don't they come flat out and say it?

"So best," one of the Fivers said, lifting his glass to let them know that he meant the drink.

"More?" asked the Fiver tactician, picking up the pencil.

"Please," said the general, seething.

He walked to the tent flap and looked outside. The men were at the guns. Thin wisps of vapor curled from the ship's launching tubes; in just a little while, it would be set to go, should the need arise. The camp was quiet and tense.

He went back to the desk and watched as the Fiver went on gaily with his lesson on how to win a battle. He filled page after page with diagrams and occasionally he was generous—he sometimes showed how the Fivers lost when they might have won with slightly different tactics.

"Interesting!" he piped enthusiastically.

"I find it so," the general said. "There is just one question."

"Ask," the Fiver invited.

"If we should go to war again, how can you be sure we won't use all of this against you?"

"But fine," the Fiver enthused warmly. "Exactly as we want."

"You fight fine," another Fiver said. "But just too slightly hard. Next time, you able to do much better."

"Hard!" the general raged.

"Too roughly, sir. No need to make the ship go poof."

Outside the tent, a gun cut loose and then another one and above the hammering of the guns came the full-throated, ground-shaking roar of many ship motors.

The general leaped for the entrance, went through it at a run, not bothering with the flap. His cap fell off and he staggered out, thrown slightly off his balance. He jerked up his head and saw them coming in, squadron after squadron, painting the darkness with the flare of tubes.

"Stop firing!" he shouted. "You crazy fools, stop firing!"

But there was no need of shouting, for the guns had fallen silent.

The ships came down toward the camp in perfect flight formation. They swept across it and the thunder of their motors seemed to lift it for a moment and give it a mighty shake. Then they were climbing, rank on serried rank, still with drill precision—climbing and jockeying into position for regulation landing.

The general stood like a frozen man, with the wind ruffling his iron-gray hair, with a lump, half pride, half thankfulness, rising in his throat. Something touched his elbow.

"Prisoners," said the Fiver. "I told you bye and bye."

The general tried to speak, but the lump was there to stop him. He swallowed it and tried once again.

"We didn't understand," he said.

"You did not have a taker," said the Fiver. "That why you fight so rough."

"We couldn't help it," the general told him. "We didn't know. We never fought this way before."

"We give you takers," said the Fiver. "Next time, we play it right. You do much better with the takers. It easier on us."

No wonder, the general thought, they didn't know about an armistice. No wonder they were confused about the negotiations and the prisoner exchange. Negotiations are not customarily needed to hand back the pieces one has won in a game. And no wonder those other races had viewed with scorn and loathing Earth's proposal to gang up on the Fivers.

"An unsporting thing to do," the general said aloud. "They could have told us. Or maybe they were so used to it."

And now he understood why the Fivers had picked this planet. There had to be a place where all the ships could land.

He stood and watched the landing ships mushing down upon the rock in clouds of pinkish flame. He tried to count them, but he became confused, although he knew every ship Earth had lost would be accounted for.

"We give you takers," said the Fiver. "We teach you how to use. They easy operate. They never hurt people or ships."

And there was more to it, the general told himself, than just a silly game though maybe not so silly, once one understood the history and the cultural background and the philosophic concepts that were tied into it. And this much one could say for it: it was better than fighting actual wars.

But with the takers, there would be an end of war. What little war was left would be ended once for all. No longer would an enemy need to be defeated; he could be simply taken. No longer would there be years of guerrilla fighting on newly settled planets; the aborigines could be picked up and deposited in cultural reservations and the dangerous fauna shunted into zoos.

"We fight again?" the Fiver asked with some anxiety. "Certainly," said the general. "Any time you say. Are we really as good as you claim?"

"You not so hot," the Fiver admitted with disarming candor. "But you the best we ever find. Play plenty, you get better."

The general grinned. Just like the sergeant and the captain and their eternal chess, he thought.

He turned and tapped the Fiver on the shoulder.

"Let's get back," he said. "There's still some drinking in that jug. We mustn't let it go to waste."

SENTRY
by Fredric Brown

Sentry duty is dirty, lonely, and usually boring—except when the enemy shows up.

★ ★ ★

***Fredric Brown** (1906-1972) was a writer with towering reputations in both the science fiction and mystery fields. After writing many short stories for the mystery pulps of the 1950s, he won the Edgar Award of the Mystery Writers of America for his first mystery novel,* The Fabulous Clipjoint *in 1947. He also wrote many stories for the SF magazines of the 1940s, and was a fixture of* Astounding Science-Fiction's *"Golden Age." He was a master craftsman in both fields, with a wide range of characterization, a lean hard-boiled style, and a sneaky touch of humor. In particular, he was the unchallenged master of the short-short story, a story so short it would take up only one or two pages, yet would have a tightly-controlled plot, and usually a surprise ending—often not a happy one. His sardonic sense of humor was displayed in such SF novels as* What Mad Universe *and* Martians, Go Home, *but he also wrote deadly serious novels such as* The Lights in the Sky Are Stars *and* The Mind Thing. *His short story, "Arena," was adapted into one of* Star Trek's *first season episodes (though there was an episode of* The Outer Limits *a couple of years earlier which had a suspicious resemblance to the same story). He inserted into a story of more usual length a story which has become known as the shortest horror story ever told: "The* *last man on Earth sat in a room. There was a knock on the door." While the story which follows is not* that *brief (though it's certainly more pithy than this introduction), it has its own sharp punch to the gut.*

He was wet and muddy and hungry and cold and he was fifty thousand light-years from home.

A strange blue sun gave light and the gravity, twice what he was used to, made every movement difficult.

But in tens of thousands of years this part of war hadn't changed. The flyboys were fine with their sleek spaceships and their fancy weapons. When the chips are down, though, it was still the foot soldier, the infantry, that had to take the ground and hold it, foot by bloody foot. Like this damned planet of a star he'd never heard of until they'd landed him there. And now it was sacred ground because the aliens were there too. *The* aliens, the only other intelligent race in the Galaxy . . . cruel, hideous and repulsive monsters.

Contact had been made with them near the center of the Galaxy, after the slow difficult colonization of a dozen thousand planets, and it had been war at sight; they'd shot without even trying to negotiate, or to make peace.

Now, planet by bitter planet, it was being fought out.

He was wet and muddy and hungry and cold, and the day was raw with a high wind that hurt his eyes. But the aliens were trying to infiltrate and every sentry post was vital.

He stayed alert, gun ready. Fifty thousand light-years from home, fighting on a strange world and wondering if he'd ever live to see home again.

And then he saw one of them crawling toward him. He drew a bead and fired. The alien made that strange horrible sound they all make, then lay still.

He shuddered at the sound and sight of the alien lying there. One ought to be able to get used to them after a while, but he'd never been able to. Such repulsive creatures they were, with only two arms and two legs, ghastly white skins and no scales.

AND THEN THERE WAS PEACE

by Gordon R. Dickson

After the war is over, there's always the problem of what to do with all the no longer needed equipment. Here's one solution.

★ ★ ★

***Gordon R. Dickson** (1923-2001) was born in Canada. After the death of his father, he and his mother moved to Minneapolis in 1937. After the U.S. Army and college, his first publication was a 1950 collaboration with Poul Anderson, followed a year later by four solo short stories. His major work was the massive Childe cycle, centered on the Dorsai future mercenaries, a series which unfortunately was left unfinished at his death. His fantasy series of novels which began with* The Dragon and The George *was also very popular. With Poul Anderson, he also wrote the hilarious series about the Hoka, aliens resembling large Teddy bears, who have no concept of fiction, and think, for example, the Sherlock Holmes stories or tales of the wild west are factual accounts, which they proceed to enact, driving all humans in their vicinity to the edge of sanity. In addition, he wrote over thirty stand-alone novels and more than a hundred short stories. He won three Hugo Awards, a Nebula Award, an August Derleth Award, the Skylark Award, and was inducted into the Science Fiction Hall of Fame in 2000. His stories often displayed protagonists who faced seemingly hopeless odds, but nonetheless prevailed against them; but he also turned out tales with a sharp sting at the end, as in this one.*

At nine hundred hours there were explosions off to the right at about seven hundred yards. At eleven hundred hours the slagger came by to pick up the casualties among the gadgets. Charlie saw the melting head at the end of its heavy beam going up and down like the front end of a hard-working chicken only about fifty yards west of his foxhole. Then it worked its way across the battlefield for about half an hour and, loaded down with melted forms of damaged robots, of all shapes and varieties, disappeared behind the low hill to the west, and left, of Charlie. It was a hot August day somewhere in or near Ohio, with a thunderstorm coming on. There was that yellow color in the air.

At twelve hundred hours the chow gadget came ticking over the redoubt behind the foxhole. It crawled into the foxhole, jumped up on the large table and opened itself out to reveal lunch. The menu this day was liver and onions, whole corn, whipped potato and raspberries.

"And no whipped cream," said Charlie.

"You haven't been doing your exercises," said the chow gadget in a fine soprano voice.

"I'm a frontline soldier," said Charlie. "I'm an infantryman in a foxhole overlooking ground zero. I'll be damned if I take exercises."

"In any case, there is no excuse for not shaving."

"I'll be damned if I shave."

"But why *not* shave? Wouldn't it be better than having that itchy, scratchy beard—"

"No," said Charlie. He went around back of the chow gadget and began to take its rear plate off.

"What are you doing to me?" said the chow gadget.

"You've got something stuck to you here," said Charlie. "Hold still." He surreptitiously took a second out to scratch at his four-day beard. "There's a war on, you know."

"I know that," said the chow gadget. "Of course."

"Infantrymen like me are dying daily."

"Alas," said the chow gadget, in pure, simple tones.

"To say nothing," said Charlie, setting the rear plate to one side, "of the expenditure of your technical devices. Not that there's any comparison between human lives and the wastage of machines."

"Of course not."

"So how can any of you, no matter how elaborate your computational systems, understand—" Charlie broke off to poke among the innards of the chow machine.

"Do not damage me," it said.

"Not if I can help it," said Charlie. "—understand what it feels like to a man sitting here day after day, pushing an occasional button, never knowing the results of his button pushing, and living in a sort of glass-case comfort except for the possibility that he may just suddenly be dead—suddenly, like that, before he knows it." He broke off to probe again. "It's no life for a man."

"Terrible, terrible," said the chow gadget. "But there is still hope for improvement."

"Don't hold your breath," said Charlie. "There's—ah!" He interrupted himself, pulling a small piece of paper out of the chow gadget.

"Is there something the matter?" said the chow gadget.

"No," said Charlie. He stepped over to the observation window and glanced out. The slagger was making its return. It was already within about fifty yards of the foxhole. "Not a thing," said Charlie. "As a matter of fact, the war's over."

"How interesting," said the chow gadget.

"That's right," said Charlie. "Just let me read you this little billet-doux I got from Foxhole thirty-four. *Meet you back at the bar, Charlie. It's all over. Your hunch that we could get a message across was the clear quill. Answer came today the same way, through the international weather reports. They want to quit as well as we do. Peace is agreed on, and the gadgets—*" Charlie broke off to look at the chow gadget. "That's you, along with the rest of them."

"Quite right. Of course," said the chow gadget.

"*—have already accepted the information. We'll be out of here by sundown.* And that takes care of the war."

"It does indeed," said the chow gadget. "Hurrah! And farewell."

"Farewell?" said Charlie.

"You will be returning to civilian life," said the chow gadget. "I will be scrapped."

"That's right," said Charlie. "I remember the preprogramming for the big units. This war's to be the last, they were programmed. Well—" said Charlie. For a moment he hesitated. "What d'you know? I may end up missing you a little bit, after all."

He glanced out the window. The slagger was almost to the dugout.

"Well, well," he said. "Now that the time's come . . . we did have quite a time together, three times a day. No more string beans, huh?"

"I bet not," said the chow gadget with a little laugh.

"No more caramel pudding."

"I guess so."

Just then the slagger halted outside, broke the thick concrete roof off the dugout and laid it carefully aside.

"Excuse me," it said, its cone-shaped melting head nodding politely some fifteen feet above Charlie. "The war's over."

"I know," said Charlie.

"Now there will be peace. There are orders that all instruments of war are to be slagged and stockpiled for later peaceful uses." It had a fine baritone voice. "Excuse me," it said, "but are you finished with that chow gadget there?"

"You haven't touched a bite," said the chow gadget. "Would you like just a small spoonful of raspberries?"

"I don't think so," said Charlie, slowly. "No, I don't think so."

"Then farewell," said the chow gadget. "I am now expendable."

The melting bead of the slagger dipped toward the chow gadget. Charlie opened his mouth suddenly, but before he could speak, there was a sort of invisible flare from the melting head and the chow gadget became a sort of puddle of metal which the melting head picked up magnetically and swung back to the hopper behind it.

"Blast it!" said Charlie with feeling. "I could just as well have put in a request to keep the darn thing for a souvenir."

The heavy melting head bobbed apologetically back.

"I'm afraid that wouldn't be possible," it said. "The order allows no exceptions. *All* military instruments are to be slagged and stockpiled."

"Well—" said Charlie. But it was just about then that he noticed the melting head was descending toward him.

FOOL'S MATE
by Robert Sheckley

The enemy had infallible computers and a foolproof battle plan—but whether or not a plan is foolproof depends on which fool is doing the planning.

★ ★ ★

***Robert Sheckley** (1928-2005) seemed to explode into print in the early 1950s with stories in nearly every science fiction magazine on the newsstands. Actually, the explosion was bigger than most realized, since he was simultaneously writing even more stories under a number of pseudonyms. His forte was humor, wild and unpredictable, often absurdist, much like the work of Douglas Adams three decades later. His work has been compared to the Marx Brothers by Harlan Ellison®, to Voltaire by both Brian W. Aldiss and J.G. Ballard, and Neil Gaiman has called Sheckley "Probably the best short-story writer during the 50s to the mid-1960s working in any field." This is one of his early stories, and his sardonic touch was present from the beginning.*

═ ★ ═

The players met, on the great, timeless board of space. The glittering dots that were the pieces swam in their separate patterns. In that configuration at the beginning, even before the first move was made, the outcome of the game was determined.

Both players saw, and knew which had won. But they played on. Because the game had to be played out.

"Nielson!"

Lieutenant Nielson sat in front of his gunfire board with an idyllic smile on his face. He didn't look up.

"Nielson!"

The lieutenant was looking at his fingers now, with the stare of a puzzled child.

"Nielson! Snap out of it!" General Branch loomed sternly over him. "Do you hear me, Lieutenant?"

Nielson shook his head dully. He started to look at his fingers again, then his gaze was caught by the glittering array of buttons on the gunfire panel.

"Pretty," he said.

General Branch stepped inside the cubicle, grabbed Nielson by the shoulders and shook him.

"Pretty things," Nielson said, gesturing at the panel. He smiled at Branch.

Margraves, second in command, stuck his head in the doorway. He still had sergeant's stripes on his sleeve, having been promoted to colonel only three days ago.

"Ed," he said, "the President's representative is here. Sneak visit."

"Wait a minute," Branch said, "I want to complete this inspection." He grinned sourly. It was one hell of an inspection when you went around finding how many sane men you had left.

"Do you hear me, Lieutenant?"

"Ten thousand ships," Nielson said. "Ten thousand ships—all gone!"

"I'm sorry," Branch said. He leaned forward and slapped him smartly across the face.

Lieutenant Nielson started to cry.

"Hey, Ed—what about that representative?"

At close range, Colonel Margraves' breath was a solid essence of whisky, but Branch didn't reprimand him. If you had a good officer left you didn't reprimand him, no matter what he did. Also, Branch approved of whisky. It was a good release, under the circumstances. Probably better than his own, he thought, glancing at his scarred knuckles.

"I'll be right with you. Nielson, can you understand me?"

"Yes, sir," the lieutenant said in a shaky voice. "I'm all right now, sir."

"Good," Branch said. "Can you stay on duty?"

"For a while," Nielson said. "But, sir—I'm not well. I can feel it."

"I know," Branch said. "You deserve a rest. But you're the only gun officer I've got left on this side of the ship. The rest are in the wards."

"I'll try, sir," Nielson said, looking at the gunfire panel again. "But I hear voices sometimes. I can't promise anything, sir."

"Ed," Margraves began again, "that representative—"

"Coming. Good boy, Nielson." The lieutenant didn't look up as Branch and Margraves left.

"I escorted him to the bridge," Margraves said, listing slightly to starboard as he walked. "Offered him a drink, but he didn't want one."

"All right," Branch said.

"He was bursting with questions," Margraves continued, chuckling to himself. "One of those earnest, tanned State Department men, out to win the war in five minutes flat. Very friendly boy. Wanted to know why I, personally, thought the fleet had been maneuvering in space for a year with no action."

"What did you tell him?"

"Said we were waiting for a consignment of zap guns," Margraves said. "I think he almost believed me. Then he started talking about logistics."

"Hm-m-m," Branch said. There was no telling what Margraves, half-drunk, had told the representative. Not that it mattered. An official inquiry into the prosecution of the war had been due for a long time.

"I'm going to leave you here," Margraves said. "I've got some unfinished business to attend to."

"Right," Branch said, since it was all he could say. He knew that Margraves' unfinished business concerned a bottle.

He walked alone to the bridge.

The President's representative was looking at the huge location screen. It covered one entire wall, glowing with a slowly shifting pattern of dots. The thousands of green dots on the left represented the Earth fleet, separated by a black void from the orange of the enemy. As he watched, the fluid, three-dimensional front slowly changed. The armies of dots clustered, shifted, retreated, advanced, moving with hypnotic slowness.

But the black void remained between them. General Branch had been watching that sight for almost a year. As far as he was concerned, the screen was a luxury. He couldn't determine from it what was really happening. Only the CPC calculators could, and they didn't need it.

"How do you do, General Branch?" the President's representative said, coming forward and offering his hand. "My name's Richard Ellsner."

Branch shook hands, noticing that Margraves' description had been pretty good. The representative was no more than thirty. His tan looked strange, after a year of pallid faces.

"My credentials," Ellsner said, handing Branch a sheaf of papers. The general skimmed through them, noting Ellsner's authorization as Presidential Voice in Space. A high honor for so young a man.

"How are things on Earth?" Branch asked, just to say something. He ushered Ellsner to a chair, and sat down himself.

"Tight," Ellsner said. "We've been stripping the planet bare of radioactives to keep your fleet operating. To say nothing of the tremendous cost of shipping food, oxygen, spare parts, and all the other equipment you need to keep a fleet this size in the field."

"I know," Branch murmured, his broad face expressionless.

"I'd like to start right in with the president's complaints," Ellsner said with an apologetic little laugh. "Just to get them off my chest."

"Go right ahead," Branch said.

"Now then," Ellsner began, consulting a pocket notebook, "you've had the fleet in space for eleven months and seven days. Is that right?"

"Yes."

"During that time there have been light engagements, but no actual hostilities. You—and the enemy commander—have been content, evidently, to sniff each other like discontented dogs."

"I wouldn't use that analogy," Branch said, conceiving an instant dislike for the young man. "But go on."

"I apologize. It was an unfortunate, though inevitable, comparison. Anyhow, there has been no battle, even though you have a numerical superiority. Is that correct?"

"Yes."

"And you know the maintenance of this fleet strains the resources of Earth. The President would like to know why battle has not been joined?"

"I'd like to hear the rest of the complaints first," Branch said. He tightened his battered fists, but, with remarkable self-control, kept them at his sides.

"Very well. The morale factor. We keep getting reports from you on the incidence of combat fatigue—crack-up, in plain language. The figures are absurd! Thirty percent of your men seem to be under restraint. That's way out of line, even for a tense situation."

Branch didn't answer.

"To cut this short," Ellsner said, "I would like the answer to those questions. Then, I would like your assistance in negotiating a truce. This war was absurd to begin with. It was none of Earth's choosing. It seems to the President that, in view of the static situation, the enemy commander will be amenable to the idea."

Colonel Margraves staggered in, his face flushed. He had completed his unfinished business; adding another fourth to his half-drunk.

"What's this I hear about a truce?" he shouted.

Ellsner stared at him for a moment, then turned back to Branch.

"I suppose you will take care of this yourself. If you will contact the enemy commander, I will try to come to terms with him."

"They aren't interested," Branch said.

"How do you know?"

"I've tried. I've been trying to negotiate a truce for six months now. They want complete capitulation."

"But that's absurd," Ellsner said, shaking his head. "They have no bargaining point. The fleets are of approximately the same size. There have been no major engagements yet. How can they—"

"Easily," Margraves roared, walking up to the representative and peering truculently in his face.

"General. This man is drunk." Ellsner got to his feet.

"Of course, you little idiot! Don't you understand yet? *The war is lost!* Completely, irrevocably."

Ellsner turned angrily to Branch. The general sighed and stood up.

"That's right, Ellsner. The war is lost and every man in the fleet knows it. That's what's wrong with the morale. We're just hanging here, waiting to be blasted out of existence."

The fleets shifted and weaved. Thousands of dots floated in space, in twisted, random patterns.

Seemingly random.

The patterns interlocked, opened and closed. Dynamically, delicately balanced, each configuration was a planned move on a hundred thousand mile front. The opposing dots shifted to meet the exigencies of the new pattern.

Where was the advantage? To the unskilled eye, a chess game is a meaningless array of pieces and positions. But to the players—the game may be already won or lost.

The mechanical players who moved the thousands of dots knew who had won—and who had lost.

"Now let's all relax," Branch said soothingly. "Margraves, mix us a couple of drinks. I'll explain everything." The colonel moved to a well-stocked cabinet in a corner of the room.

"I'm waiting," Ellsner said.

"First, a review. Do you remember when the war was declared, two years ago? Both sides subscribed to the Holmstead Pact, not to bomb home planets. A rendezvous was arranged in space, for the fleets to meet."

"That's ancient history," Ellsner said.

"It has a point. Earth's fleet blasted off, grouped and went to the rendezvous." Branch cleared his throat.

"Do you know the CPCs? The Configuration-Probability-Calculators? They're like chess players, enormously extended. They arrange the fleet in an optimum attack-defense pattern, based on the configuration of the opposing fleet. So the first pattern was set."

"I don't see the need—" Ellsner started, but Margraves, returning with the drinks, interrupted him.

"Wait, my boy. Soon there will be a blinding light."

"When the fleets met, the CPC's calculated the probabilities of attack. They found we'd lose approximately eighty-seven percent of our fleet, to sixty-five percent of the enemy's. If they attacked, they'd lose seventy-nine percent, to our sixty-four. That was the situation as it stood then. By extrapolation, their *optimum* attack pattern—at that time—would net them a forty-five-percent loss. Ours would have given us a seventy-two-percent loss."

"I don't know much about the CPCs," Ellsner confessed. "My field's psych." He sipped his drink, grimaced, and sipped again.

"Think of them as chess players," Branch said. "They can estimate the loss probabilities for an attack at any given point of time, in any pattern. They can extrapolate the probable moves of both sides.

"That's why battle wasn't joined when we first met. No commander is going to annihilate his entire fleet like that."

"Well then," Ellsner said, "why haven't you exploited your slight numerical superiority? Why haven't you gotten an advantage over them?"

"Ah!" Margraves cried, sipping his drink. "It comes, the light!"

"Let me put it in the form of an analogy," Branch said. "If you have two chess players of equally high skill, the game's end is determined when one of them gains an advantage. Once the advantage is there, there's nothing the other player can do, unless the first makes a mistake. If everything goes as it should, the game's end is predetermined. The turning point may come a few moves after the game starts, although the game itself could drag on for hours."

"And remember," Margraves broke in, "to the casual eye, there may be no apparent advantage. Not a piece may have been lost."

"That's what's happened here," Branch finished sadly. "The CPC units in both fleets are of maximum efficiency. But the enemy has an edge, which they are carefully exploiting. And there's nothing we can do about it."

"But how did this happen?" Ellsner asked. "Who slipped up?"

"The CPCs have inducted the cause of the failure," Branch said. "The end of the war was inherent *in our take-off formation.*"

"What do you mean?" Ellsner said, setting down his drink.

"Just that. The configuration the fleet was in, light-years away from battle, before we had even contacted their fleet. When the two met, they had an infinitesimal advantage of position. That was enough. Enough for the CPCs, anyhow."

"If it's any consolation," Margraves put in, "it was a fifty-fifty chance. It could have just as well been us with the edge."

"I'll have to find out more about this," Ellsner said. "I don't understand it all yet."

Branch snarled: "The war's lost. What more do you want to know?"

Ellsner shook his head.

"Wilt snare me with predestination 'round," Margraves quoted, "and then impute my fall to sin?"

Lieutenant Nielson sat in front of the gunfire panel, his fingers interlocked. This was necessary, because Nielson had an almost overpowering desire to push the buttons.

The pretty buttons.

Then he swore, and sat on his hands. He had promised General Branch that he would carry on, and that was important. It was three days since he had seen the general, but he was determined to carry on. Resolutely he fixed his gaze on the gunfire dials.

Delicate indicators wavered and trembled. Dials measured distance, and adjusted aperture to range. The slender indicators rose and fell as the ship maneuvered, lifting toward the red line, but never quite reaching it.

The red line marked emergency. That was when he would start firing, when the little black arrow crossed the little red line.

He had been waiting almost a year now, for that little arrow. Little arrow. Little narrow. Little arrow. Little narrow.

Stop it.

That was when he would start firing.

Lieutenant Nielson lifted his hands into view and inspected his nails. Fastidiously he cleaned a bit of dirt out of one. He interlocked his fingers again, and looked at the pretty buttons, the black arrow, the red line.

He smiled to himself. He had promised the general. Only three days ago.

So he pretended not to hear what the buttons were whispering to him.

"The thing I don't see," Ellsner said, "is why you can't do something about the pattern? Retreat and regroup, for example?"

"I'll explain that," Margraves said. "It'll give Ed a chance for a drink. Come over here." He led Ellsner to an instrument panel. They had been showing Ellsner around the ship for three days, more to relieve their own tension than for any other reason. The last day had turned into a fairly prolonged drinking bout.

"Do you see this dial?" Margraves pointed to one. The instrument panel covered an area four feet wide by twenty feet long. The buttons and switches on it controlled the movements of the entire fleet. Notice the shaded area. That marks the safety limit. If we use a forbidden configuration, the indicator goes over and all hell breaks loose."

"And what is a forbidden configuration?"

Margraves thought for a moment. "The forbidden configurations are those which would give the enemy an attack advantage. Or, to put it in another way, moves which change the attack-probability-loss picture sufficiently to warrant an attack."

"So you can move only within strict limits?" Ellsner asked, looking at the dial.

"That's right. Out of the infinite number of possible formations, we can use only a few, if we want to play safe. It's like chess. Say you'd like to put a sixth row pawn in your opponent's back row. But it would take two moves to do it. And after you move to the seventh row, your opponent has a clear avenue, leading inevitably to checkmate.

"Of course, if the enemy advances too boldly the odds are changed again, and *we* attack."

"That's our only hope," General Branch said. "We're praying they do something wrong. The fleet is in readiness for instant attack, if our CPC shows that the enemy has overextended himself anywhere."

"And that's the reason for the crack-ups," Ellsner said. "Every man in the fleet on nerves' edge, waiting for a chance he's sure will never come. But having to wait anyhow. How long will this go on?"

"This moving and checking can go on for a little over two years," Branch said. "Then they will be in the optimum formation for attack, with a twenty-eight-percent loss probability to our ninety-three. They'll have to attack then, or the probabilities will start to shift back in our favor."

"You poor devils," Ellsner said softly. "Waiting for a chance that's never going to come. Knowing you're going to be blasted out of space sooner or later."

"Oh, it's jolly," said Margraves, with an instinctive dislike for a civilian's sympathy.

Something buzzed on the switchboard, and Branch walked over and plugged in a line. "Hello? Yes. Yes . . . All right, Williams. Right." He unplugged the line.

"Colonel Williams has had to lock his men in their rooms," Branch said. "That's the third time this month. I'll have to get CPC to dope out a formation so we can take him out of the front." He walked to a side panel and started pushing buttons.

"And there it is," Margraves said. "What do you plan to do, Mr. Presidential Representative?"

The glittering dots shifted and deployed, advanced and retreated, always keeping a barrier of black space between them. The mechanical chess players watched each move, calculating its effect into the far future. Back and forth across the great chess board the pieces moved.

The chess players worked dispassionately, knowing beforehand the outcome of the game. In their strictly ordered universe there was no possible fluctuation, no stupidity, no failure.

They moved. And knew. And moved.

"Oh, yes," Lieutenant Nielson said to the smiling room. "Oh, yes." And look at all the buttons, he thought, laughing to himself.

So stupid. Georgia.

Nielson accepted the deep blue of sanctity, draping it across his shoulders. Bird song, somewhere.

Of course.

Three buttons red. He pushed them. Three buttons green. He pushed them. Four dials. Riverread.

"Oh-oh. Nielson's cracked."

"Three is for me," Nielson said, and touched his forehead with greatest stealth. Then he reached for the keyboard again. Unimaginable associations raced through his mind, produced by unaccountable stimuli.

"Better grab him. Watch out!"

Gentle hands surround me as I push two are brown for which is for mother, and one is high for all rest.

"Stop him from shooting off those guns!"

I am lifted into the air, I fly, I fly.

"Is there any hope for that man?" Ellsner asked, after they had locked Nielson in a ward.

"Who knows," Branch said. His broad face tightened; knots of muscle pushed out his cheeks. Suddenly he turned, shouted, and swung his fist wildly at the metal wall. After it hit, he grunted and grinned sheepishly.

"Silly, isn't it? Margraves drinks. I let off steam by hitting walls. Let's go eat."

The officers ate separate from the crew. Branch had found that some officers tended to get murdered by psychotic crewmen. It was best to keep them apart.

During the meal, Branch suddenly turned to Ellsner.

"Boy, I haven't told you the entire truth. I said this would go on for two years? Well, the men won't last that long. I don't know if I can hold this fleet together for two more weeks."

"What would you suggest?"

"I don't know," Branch said. He still refused to consider surrender, although he knew it was the only realistic answer.

"I'm not sure," Ellsner said, "but I think there may be a way out of your dilemma." The officers stopped eating and looked at him.

"Have you got some superweapons for us?" Margraves asked. "A disintegrator strapped to your chest?"

"I'm afraid not. But I think you've been so close to the situation that you don't see it in its true light. A case of the forest for the trees."

"Go on," Branch said, munching methodically on a piece of bread.

"Consider the universe as the CPC sees it. A world of strict causality. A logical, coherent universe. In this world, every effect has a cause. Every factor can be instantly accounted for.

"That's not a picture of the real world. There is *no* explanation for everything, really. The CPC is built to see a specialized universe, and to extrapolate on the basis of that."

"So," Margraves said, "what would you do?"

"Throw the world out of joint," Ellsner said. "Bring in uncertainty. Add a human factor that the machines can't calculate."

"How can you introduce uncertainty in a chess game?" Branch asked, interested in spite of himself.

"By sneezing at a crucial moment, perhaps. How could a machine calculate that?"

"It wouldn't have to. It would just classify it as extraneous noise, and ignore it."

"True." Ellsner thought for a moment. "This battle—how long will it take once the actual hostilities are begun?"

"About six minutes," Branch told him. "Plus or minus twenty seconds."

"That confirms an idea of mine," Ellsner said. "The chess game analogy you use is faulty. There's no real comparison."

"It's a convenient way of thinking of it," Margraves said.

"But it's an *untrue* way of thinking of it. Checkmating a king can't be equated with destroying a fleet. Nor is the rest of the situation like chess. In chess you play by rules previously agreed upon by the players. In this game you can make up your own rules."

"This game has inherent rules of its own," Branch said.

"No," Ellsner said. "Only the CPC's have rules. How about this? Suppose you dispensed with the CPCs? Gave every commander his head, told him to attack on his own, with no pattern. What would happen?"

"It wouldn't work," Margraves told him. "The CPC can still total the picture, on the basis of the planning ability of the average human. More than that, they can handle the attack of a few thousand second-rate calculators—humans—with ease. It would be like shooting clay pigeons."

"But you've *got* to try something," Ellsner pleaded.

"Now wait a minute," Branch said. "You can spout theory all you want. I know what the CPCs tell me, and I believe them. I'm still in command of this fleet, and I'm not going to risk the lives in my command on some harebrained scheme."

"Harebrained schemes sometimes win wars," Ellsner said.

"They usually lose them."

"The war is lost already, by your own admission."

"I can still wait for them to make a mistake."

"Do you think it will come?"

"No."

"Well then?"

"I'm still going to wait."

The rest of the meal was completed in moody silence. Afterward, Ellsner went to his room.

"Well, Ed?" Margraves asked, unbuttoning his shirt.

"Well yourself," the general said. He lay down on his bed, trying not to think. It was too much. Logistics. Predetermined battles. The coming debacle. He considered slamming his fist against the wall, but decided against it. It was sprained already. He was going to sleep.

On the borderline between slumber and sleep, he heard a click.

The door!

Branch jumped out of bed and tried the knob. Then he threw himself against it.

Locked.

"General, please strap yourself down. We are attacking." It was Ellsner's voice, over the intercom. "I looked over that keyboard of yours, sir, and found the magnetic doorlocks. Mighty handy in case of a mutiny, isn't it?"

"You idiot!" Branch shouted. "You'll kill us all! That CPC—"

"I've disconnected our CPC," Ellsner said pleasantly. "I'm a pretty logical boy, and I think I know how a sneeze will bother them."

"He's mad," Margraves shouted to Branch. Together they threw themselves against the metal door.

Then they were thrown to the floor.

"All gunners—fire at will!" Ellsner broadcasted to the fleet.

The ship was in motion. The attack was underway!

The dots drifted together, crossing the no man's land of space.

They coalesced! Energy flared, and the battle was joined.

Six minutes, human time. Hours for the electronically fast chess player. He checked his pieces for an instant, deducing the pattern of attack.

There was no pattern!

Half of the opposing chess player's pieces shot out into space, completely out of the battle. Whole flanks advanced, split, rejoined, wrenched forward, dissolved their formation, formed it again.

No pattern? There *had* to be a pattern. The chess player knew that everything had a pattern. It was just a question of finding it, of taking the moves already made and extrapolating to determine what the end was supposed to be.

The end was—chaos!

The dots swept in and out, shot away at right angles to the battle, checked and returned, meaninglessly.

What did it mean, the chess player asked himself with the calmness of metal. He waited for a recognizable configuration to emerge.

Watching dispassionately as his pieces were swept off the board.

"I'm letting you out of your room now," Ellsner called, "but don't try to stop me. I think I've won your battle."

The lock released. The two officers ran down the corridor to the bridge, determined to break Ellsner into little pieces.

Inside, they slowed down.

The screen showed the great mass of Earth dots sweeping over a scattering of enemy dots.

What stopped them, however, was Nielson, laughing, his hands sweeping over switches and buttons on the great master control board.

The CPC was droning the losses. "Earth—eighteen percent. Enemy—eighty-three. Eighty-four. Eighty-six. Earth, nineteen percent."

"Mate!" Ellsner shouted. He stood beside Nielson, a Stillson wrench clenched in his hand. "Lack of pattern. I gave their CPC something it couldn't handle. An attack with no apparent pattern. Meaningless configurations!"

"But what are they doing?" Branch asked, gesturing at the dwindling enemy dots.

"Still relying on their chess player," Ellsner said. "Still waiting for him to dope out the attack pattern in this madman's mind. Too much faith in machines, general. This man doesn't even know he's precipitating an attack."

. . . And push three that's for dad on the olive tree I always wanted to two two two Danbury fair with buckle shoe brown all brown buttons down and in, sin, eight red for sin—

"What's the wrench for?" Margraves asked.

"That?" Ellsner weighed it in his hand. "That's to turn off Nielson here, after the attack."

. . . And five and love and black, all blacks, fair buttons in I remember when I was very young at all push five and there on the grass ouch—

AIRBORNE ALL THE WAY!
by David Drake

Just a routine mission to drop rocks on the enemy from a balloon. Even if the crew was a few spells short of a grimoire, what could go wrong?

★ ★ ★

This anthology is an assemblage of military science fiction *stories which happen to be humorous . . . except for this one, which happens to be humorous military* fantasy. *But, it's by David Drake, creator of the now-classic Hammers Slammers series and a past master of military SF, and someone who absolutely* had *to be in the book. I could fudge a bit and say that this is really SF because it's obviously taking place in a parallel universe where magic works, but never mind. The important thing is that this story is both funny and ingenious, and as Ralph Waldo Emerson put it, "a foolish consistency is the hobgoblin of little minds," so here it is .and with goblins too (probably not hobgloblins, though, since they're usually smarter than goblins). Or to further plunder Mr. Bartlett's compilation, this time from William Cowper, "Variety is the spice of life." Have a bit of spice in your reading.*

David Drake, *author of the best-selling Hammer's Slammers future mercenary series, is often referred to as the Dean of military science fiction, but is much more versatile than that label might suggest, as shown by his epic fantasy series that began with* Lord of the Isles *(Tor), and his equally popular Republic of Cinnabar Navy series (Baen) starring the indefatigable team of Leary and Mundy. He lives near Chapel Hill, NC, with his family.*

═ ★ ═

Crewgoblin Dumber Than #3 stared with his usual look of puzzlement as labor goblins unrolled Balloon Prima. He scratched his chain mail jockstrap and said to Dog Squat, the balloon chief, "I dunno, boss."

Dog Squat rolled her eyes expressively and muttered, "Mana give me strength!" She glanced covertly to see if Roxanne was watching what balloon chiefs had to put up with, but the senior thaumaturge was involved with the team of dragon wranglers bringing the whelp into position in front of the coal pile.

Dog Squat glowered at her four crewgoblins. "Well, what don't you know?" she snarled. "What is there to know? We go up, we throw rocks down. You like to throw rocks, Number Three?"

"I like to bite them," said Dumber Than #1. "Will we be able to bite them, Dog Squat?"

The plateau on which the Balloon Brigade was readying for battle overlooked the enemy on the broad plain below. The hostile command group, pulsing with white mana, had taken its station well to the rear. White battalions were deploying directly from their line of march. Gullies and knolls skewed the rectangles of troops slightly, but the formations were still precise enough to make a goblin's disorderly mind ache.

"But boss," #3 said, "how do we get down again?"

"Getting down's the easy part!" Dog Squat shouted. "Rocks aren't any smarter than you are, and they manage to get down, don't they? Well, not much smarter. Just leave the thinking to me, why don't you?"

"I really like to bite them," #1 repeated. He scraped at a black, gleaming fang with a black, gleaming foreclaw. "After we throw rocks, will we be able to bite them, Dog Squat?"

Dog Squat tried to visualize biting from a balloon. The closest she could come was a sort of ruddy blur that made her head ache worse than sight of the serried, white-clad ranks on the plains below. "No biting unless I tell you!" she said to cover ignorance. "Not even a teeny little bite!"

The large pile of coal was ready for ignition. The metal cover sat on the ground behind for the moment. Instead of forging a simple dome, the smiths had created a gigantic horned helmet. To either side of the coal was a sloped dirt ramp so that labor goblins could carry the helmet over the pile and cap it when the time came.

Balloons Prima and Secundus were unrolled to either side, and the three wranglers had finally gotten their dragon whelp into position in front of the pile. The other unfilled balloons waited their turn in double lines. It was time to start.

"All right, Theobald!" Senior Thaumaturge Roxanne said to the junior thaumaturge accompanying her, a mana specialist. "Get to work and don't waste a lot of time. We're already forty minutes behind schedule. Malfegor will singe the skin off me if we don't launch an attack before noon, and I promise that you won't be around to snicker if that happens."

Roxanne strode over to Dog Squat and her crew. The balloon chief tried to straighten like a human coming to attention; she wobbled dangerously. A goblin's broad shoulders and heavy, fanged skull raised the body's center of gravity too high unless the hips were splayed back and the knuckles kept usefully close to the ground.

"Everything ready here?" Roxanne demanded. The senior thaumaturge in charge of the Balloon Brigade wore a power suit with pinstripes of red, Malfegor's color. Her attaché case was an expensive one made of crimson belly skins, the sexual display markings of little male lizards. Very many little male lizards.

"Yes, sir, one hundred percent!" Dog Squat said. She frowned. She wasn't very good on numbers. "Two hundred percent?" she offered as an alternative.

"Yes, well, you'd better be," Roxanne said as she returned her attention to the dragon-filling.

The dragon whelp was no bigger than a cow. The beast didn't appear to be in either good health or a good humor. Its tail lashed restively despite the attempt of one wrangler to control that end while the other two held the whelp's head steady.

Junior Thaumaturge Theobald stood in front of the whelp with a book in one hand and an athame of red copper in the other. As

Theobald intoned, a veil of mana flowed into the whelp from the surrounding rock. The creature's outlines softened.

Purple splotches distorted the generally red fields of force. The whelp shook itself. The wranglers tossed violently, but they all managed to hold on.

Dumber Than #1 bent close to Dog Squat and whispered gratingly in her ear. The balloon chief sighed and said, "Ah, sir?"

Roxanne jumped. A goblin's notion of a quiet voice was one that you couldn't hear in the next valley. "Yes?" the senior thaumaturge said.

"Ah, sir," Dog Squat said, "there's been some discussion regarding biting. Ah, whether we'll be biting the enemy, that is. Ah, that is, will we?"

Roxanne stared at the balloon chief in honest amazement. The four crewgoblins stood behind Dog Squat, scratching themselves but obviously intent on the answer.

"You'll be throwing rocks," Roxanne said, speaking very slowly and distinctly. She tried to make eye contact with each crewgoblin in turn, but a goblin's eyes tend to wander in different directions.

The senior thaumaturge tapped the surface of the plateau with one open toed, wedge-heeled shoe. "Rocks are like this," she said, "only smaller. The rocks are already in the gondola of your balloon. Do you all understand?"

None of them understood. None of them understood anything.

Dumber Than #3 scratched his jockstrap again. Roxanne winced. "Isn't that uncomfortable to wear?" she said. "I mean, chain mail?"

The crewgoblin nodded vigorously. "Yeah, you can say that again," he said. He continued to scratch.

"But when is she going to tell us about biting?" #1 said to Dog Squat in a steamwhistle whisper.

The dragon whelp farted thunderously. A huge blue flame flung the rearward wrangler thirty feet away with his robes singed off. The veil of inflowing mana ceased as Roxanne spun around.

"Sorry, sorry," Junior Thaumaturge Theobald said nervously as he closed his book. "The mana here is impure. Too much ground water—we must be over an aquifer. But she's full and ready."

"Carry on, then," Roxanne said grimly to the remaining dragon wranglers.

The leading wrangler crooned into the whelp's ear as her partner stroked the scaly throat from the other side. The whelp, shimmering with newfound power, bent toward the pile of coal and burped a puny ball of red fire. Roxanne frowned.

"Come on, girl, you can do it," the wrangler moaned. "Come on, do it for mommy. Come on, sweetie, come on—"

The dragon whelp stretched out a diamond-clawed forepaw and blasted a double stream of crimson fire from its nostrils. The jets ripped across and into the pile of coal, infusing the flame through every gap and crevice. The wranglers directed the ruby inferno by tugging their charge's head back and forth with long leads.

After nearly three minutes of roaring hellfire, the whelp sank back exhausted. It seemed to have shrunk to half its size of a few moments before. The two normally robed wranglers clucked the beast tiredly to its feet and walked it out of the way. The third wrangler limped alongside. In place of a robe he was wearing a red gonfalon borrowed from a nearby cavalry regiment.

The coal pile glowed like magma trapped deep in the planetary mantle. "Come on!" Roxanne ordered. "Let's not waste this. Get moving and get it capped!"

The capping crew was under the charge of two novice thaumaturges, both of them in their teens. In response to their chirped commands, the four labor goblins lifted the gigantic helmet by means of crosspoles run through sockets at the front and back of the base. They began to shuffle forward, up the earthen ramps built to either side of the pile of coal.

The porters were goblins chosen for brawn rather than brains. The very concept of intellect would have boggled the porters' minds if they'd had any. In order to keep the crews moving in the right direction, the novices projected a line of splayed, clawed footprints in front of the leaders on either ramp to carefully fit his/her feet into.

The goblins on the rear pole set their feet exactly on the same markings. They didn't put any weight down until they were sure the foot was completely within the glowing red lines. The cap's rate of movement was more amoebic than tortoiselike. Nevertheless, it moved. Senior Thaumaturge Roxanne drummed fingers on the side of her attaché case in frustration, but there was no hurrying labor goblins.

The leaders paused when they reached the last pairs of footprints at the ends of the ramps. The porters stood stolidly, apparently oblivious of the heat and fumes from the coal burning beside them.

The novice thaumaturges turned to Roxanne. "Yes!" she shouted. "Cap it! Cap it now!"

The novices ordered, "Drop your poles!" in an uncertain tenor and a throaty contralto. Three of the porters obeyed. The fourth looked around in puzzlement, then dropped his pole also. The helmet clanged down unevenly but still down, over the pile. The metal completely covered the coal, shutting off all outside air.

The horns flaring to the sides of the giant helmet were nozzles. Thick hoses were attached to the ends of horns. The novice thaumaturges clamped the free ends of the hoses into the filler inlets of Balloons Prima and Secundus. Adjusting the hoses was hard work, but the task was too complicated to be entrusted to a goblin.

Roxanne personally checked the connection to Prima while the junior thaumaturge did the same on the other side. "All right," she said to the novice watching anxiously from the top of the ramp where he'd scrambled as soon as he attached his hose. "Open the cock."

The novice twisted a handle shaped like a flying dragon at the tip of the horn, opening the nozzle to gas that made the hose writhe on its way to the belly of Balloon Prima. The senior thaumaturge stepped away as the balloon began to fill.

The balloons were made from an inner layer of sea serpent intestine. The material was impervious to gas and so wonderfully tough that giants set bars of gold between layers of the stuff and hammered the metal into foil.

Prima bulged into life, inflating with gases driven out of the furiously hot coal in the absence of oxygen to sustain further combustion. The four drag ropes tightened in the clawed hands of labor goblins whose job was to keep the balloon on the ground until it had been completely filled with its inlet closed.

"You lot!" Roxanne said to Dog Squat and her crew. "What are you waiting for? Get into your gondola now!"

Dog Squat opened her mouth to explain that she'd been waiting for orders. She forgot what she was going to say before she got the words out. "Dumber Thans," she said instead, "get into the little boat."

The wicker gondola creaked as the five goblins boarded it. The balloon was already full enough to lift off the ground and swing in the coarse steel netting that attached the car to it. A light breeze swept down from Malfegor's aerie, ready to waft the brigade toward the enemy on the plain below.

The floor of the gondola was covered with rocks the size of a goblin's head. Many of the missiles were delightfully jagged. #3 patted a piece of chert with a particularly nice point.

Balloon Secundus lifted into sight from the other side of the helmet. It was sausage-shaped, like forty-nine percent of the brigade's equipment. Prima was one of the slight majority of balloons which, when seen from the side, looked like a huge dome with a lesser peak on top. The attachment netting gleamed like chain mail over the pinkish white expanse of sea serpent intestine.

Dog Squat picked up a rock and hefted it. A good, solid chunk of granite. A rock that a goblin could really get into throwing, yep, you betcha. Dog Squat had heard some principals would try to fob their crews off with blocks of limestone that crumbled if you just looked crossways at it, but not good old Malfegor. . . .

"Shut off the gas flow!" Senior Thaumaturge Roxanne called to the novice on the ramp above her. She released the catch on the input. When Prima wobbled, the hose pulled loose, and Roxanne clamped the valve shut.

"Cast off!" she ordered the ground crew.

Three of the goblins dropped their ropes. The fourth, an unusually powerful fellow even for a labor goblin, continued to grip his. His big toes were opposable, and he'd sunk his claws deep into the rock of the plateau.

Balloon Prima lifted at an angle. The gondola was nearly vertical, pointing at the goblin holding the rope.

"Let's go!" Roxanne screamed. "Drop the rope!"

She batted the goblin over the head with her attaché case. He looked at the senior thaumaturge quizzically.

"Let go!" Roxanne repeated. "Don't you understand what I'm saying?"

The goblin blinked. He continued to hold onto both the rope and the ground. Balloon Prima wobbled above him.

Roxanne looked up. Dog Squat peered down at her. The balloon chief wore a familiar puzzled expression. The crewgoblins were stacked, more or less vertically, on the back of their chief. A gust from the wrong direction and the contents of the gondola would tip out promiscuously.

"You!" the senior thaumaturge said. "Hit this idiot on the head with a rock. A hard rock!"

Dog Squat looked again at the rock she held, decided that it would do, and bashed the handler goblin with it. The victim's eyeballs rolled up. He dropped the rope and fell over on his back.

Balloon Prima shot skyward, righting itself as it rose. The rope the goblin dropped whipped around Roxanne's waist and dragged her along. The senior thaumaturge weighed scarcely more than any one of the rocks in the bottom of the gondola, so her presence didn't significantly affect the balloon's upward course.

Dog Squat looked over the side of the gondola at Roxanne and blinked. The senior thaumaturge, swinging like a tethered canary, screamed, "Pull me in, you idiot!"

"I didn't know you were coming along, sir," the balloon chief said contritely. She rapped her head hard with her knuckles to help her think. "Or did I?" she added.

"Pull me—" Roxanne said. The rope, kinked rather than knotted about her, started to unwrap. Roxanne grabbed it with both hands. Her attaché case took an obscenely long time to flutter down. At last it smashed into scraps no larger than the original pelts on the rocks below.

Dog Squat tugged the rope in hand over hand, then plucked the senior thaumaturge from it and lifted her into the gondola. Roxanne's eyes remained shut until she felt throwing stones beneath her feet rather than empty air.

"Are we . . . ?" she said. She looked over the side of the gently swaying gondola. Because of its heavy load, Balloon Prima had only climbed a few hundred feet above the plateau, but the ground continued to slope away as Malfegor's sorcerous breeze pushed them toward the enemy lines.

"Oh, mana," Roxanne said. "Oh mana, mana, mana."

"Boss," said Dumber Than #2, "do you remember when I ate that possum the trolls walked over the week before?"

"Yeah," said Dog Squat. Everybody in the crew remembered that.

"Well, I feel like that again," #2 said.

He did look greenish. His eyeballs did, at least. He was swaying a little more than the gondola itself did, come to think.

"Where did you find a dead possum up here, Number Two?" Dog Squat asked.

"I didn't!" the crewgoblin said with queasy enthusiasm.

He frowned, pounded himself on the head, and added, "I don't think I did, anyways."

"Oh, mana," the senior thaumaturge moaned. "How am I ever going to get down?"

"Getting down is the easy part!" Dumber Than #3 said brightly. "Even rocks manage to get down! You're probably lots smarter than a rock, sir."

Senior Thaumaturge Roxanne took another look over the side of the gondola, then curled into a fetal position in the stern.

"Did you eat a dead possum, too?" #2 asked in what for a goblin was a solicitous tone.

Balloon Prima had continued to drift while the senior thaumaturge considered her position. The battalions of white-clad enemy troops were by now almost directly below. They didn't look the way they ought to. They looked little.

Dog Squat frowned. She wondered if these were really the people she was supposed to drop rocks on.

"Boss, are we in the right place?" #4 asked. The gondola tilted thirty degrees in its harness. All four crewgoblins had leaned over the same side as their chief. "Them guys don't look right."

"They make my head hurt to look at," #3 added. "They're—"

Goblins didn't have a word for "square." Even the attempt to express the concept made lights flash painfully behind the crewgoblin's eyes.

In a fuzzy red flash, Dog Squat gained a philosophy of life: When in doubt, throw rocks. "We throw rocks!" she shouted, suiting her actions to her words.

The goblins hurled rocks down with enthusiasm—so much enthusiasm that Dog Squat had to prevent Dumber Than #1 from tossing Roxanne, whom he'd grabbed by a mistake that nearly became irremediable. When Dog Squat removed the senior thaumaturge from #l's hands, the crewgoblin tried to bite her—probably #l's philosophy of life—until Dog Squat clouted him into a proper attitude of respect.

The gondola pitched violently from side to side because of the repeated shifts in weight. The entire balloon lurched upward since the rocks acted as ballast when they weren't being used for ammunition. The crew of Balloon Prima was having as much fun as goblins could with their clothes on (and a lot more fun than goblins have with their clothes off, as anyone looking at a nude goblin can imagine).

They weren't, however, hitting anybody on the ground, which was increasingly far below.

The tight enemy formations shattered like glass on stone as Balloon Prima drifted toward them. That was the result of fear, not actual damage. The goblins could no more brain individual soldiers a thousand feet below than they could fly without Prima's help.

That didn't matter particularly to Dog Squat and her crew. Throwing rocks was a job worth doing for its own sake; and anyway, the collapse of ordered battalions into complete disorder fitted Dog Squat's sense of rightness. The universe (not as clear a concept as it would have been to, say, a senior thaumaturge; but still, a concept in goblin terms) liked chaos.

White-clad archers well to the side of the balloon's expected course bent their bows in enormous futile efforts. The altitude that made it difficult for the goblins to hit targets on the ground also made it impossible for archers on the ground to reach Balloon Prima. The arrows arcing back to earth did more damage to other whiteclad troops than the goblinflung rocks had done.

Malfegor's breeze continued to drive Balloon Prima in the direction of the enemy command group. The hail of missiles from the gondola stopped.

"Boss?" said #4. "Where are the rocks?"

Dog Squat looked carefully around the floor of the gondola. She even lifted Roxanne, who moaned softly in response.

"There are no rocks," Dog Squat said.

Dumber Than #3 scratched himself. "I thought there was rocks," he said in puzzlement.

"Can we bite them now, Dog Squat?" #1 said.

Dog Squat looked over the side again. She hoped there might be another thaumaturge or somebody else who could tell them what to do.

There wasn't. Dog Squat checked both sides to be sure, however.

The enemy had made preparations against the Balloon Brigade's attack. Two teams of antiballoon ballistas galloped into position between Balloon Prima and the white command group. The crews dismounted and quickly cranked their high-angle weapons into action.

A ball nearly the size of the rocks the goblins had thrown whizzed toward the balloon and burst twenty feet away in a gush of white mana.

"Oooh," said Dog Squat and three of her crewgoblins.

The breeze shifted slightly, driving Balloon Prima in the direction of the white blast. Malfegor was hunting the bursts on the assumption that the safest place to be was where the immediately previous shell had gone off.

"Ohhh," said Dumber Than #2, holding his belly with both hands. "The more we shake around, the older the possum gets."

Sure enough, the next antiballoon shell flared close to where Prima would have been if she'd continued on her former course. The breeze jinked back, continuing to blow the balloon toward the command group below.

The hostile artillerists cranked their torsion bows furiously. They were also trying to raise their angle of aim, but Balloon Prima was almost directly overhead and the ballistas couldn't shoot vertically. By the time Prima was in the defender's sights again, the balloon would be directly over the command group.

Dumber Than #4 nudged Dog Squat and pointed to the tightly curled senior thaumaturge. "Can we throw her now, boss?" the crewgoblin asked. "Seeings as we're, you know, out of rocks?"

Dog Squat pursed her lips, a hideous sight. "No," she decided at last. "Throwing rocks is good. Throwing thaumaturges is not good."

At least she didn't think it was. They ought to throw something, though.

"Can we bite them, then?" said #1.

Dumber Than #2 vomited over the side with great force and volume, much as he'd done after the never-to-be-forgotten (even by a goblin) possum incident.

The huge greenish yellow mass plunged earthward at increasing velocity. It was easier to track than a rock of the same size because it was slightly fluorescent. For a moment Dog Squat thought the bolus was going to hit one of the antiballoon ballistas. Instead, it glopped the ballista's captain, who fell backward into his weapon.

The toppling ballista fired its shell straight up. Though the glowing white ball missed the gondola by a dragon's whisker, it punched through the side of the gas bag above.

The top of the balloon ruptured with a loud bang. The blast of mana expelled and ignited the bag's contents in a puff of varicolored flame—a mixture of hydrogen, carbon monoxide, and methane, all flammable and dazzlingly pretty.

"Oooh!" said all the goblins in delight. #2, no longer holding his belly, had a particularly pleased expression.

Ex-Balloon Prima dropped, though not nearly as fast as the rocks thrown earlier. The gas bag had burst, but the steel netting still restrained the tough fabric of sea serpent intestine. The combination made an excellent parachute.

There was wild panic on the ground below. The enemy commanders had realized Prima would land directly on top of them.

Dumber Than #1 looked at the lusciously soft enemy officers, coming closer every moment the air whistled past the gondola. He asked plaintively, "Please, boss, can we bite them?"

Dog Squat glanced at Roxanne—no change there—and made a command decision. "Yes," the balloon chief said decisively. "We will bite them."

Dumber Than #3 scratched himself with the hand that wasn't gripping the edge of the gondola. He gestured toward the senior thaumaturge and said fondly, "Gee, it must be something to be smart enough to plan all this. She's really a genius, ain't she, boss?"

"She sure is," Dog Squat agreed, preparing to jump into the middle of the terrified enemy at the moment of impact.

Senior Thaumaturge Roxanne whimpered softly.

MR. JESTER

by Fred Saberhagen

The berserkers are gigantic warships, possibly left over from a long-ago war in which both sides lost. Their robot brains are programmed to destroy all living things, particularly intelligent living things. Humans and other sentient beings have long been fighting the berserkers, in a war for survival. This time, however, one of the killer machines had confused programming. And it ran into someone with a very unorthodox sense of humor.

★ ★ ★

Fred Saberhagen *(1930-2007) served in the U.S. Air Force during the Korean war, and later was an electronics technician for the Motorola Corporation. His broke into print in 1961 and in 1963 published the first of his long-running Berserker stories, "Fortress Ship," which would eventually comprise many short stories and novels, developing the series with unfailing ingenuity. He was the editor for articles on chemistry for the* Encyclopedia Britannica *for six, years, then turned to full-time writing. Among his many novels, two more series stand out: the long-running Dracula series, often told from the viewpoint of the celebrated vampire, with such occasional noteworthy guests as Sherlock Holmes, and the even longer-running string of fantasy novels comprising the "Swords" series. While many of his berserker stories involve grim, desperate battles between humans and the death machines, this one has a distinctly lighter touch.*

Defeated in battle the berserker-computers saw that refitting, repair, and the construction of new machines were necessary. They sought out sunless, hidden places, where minerals were available but where men—who were now as often the hunters as the hunted—were not likely to show up. And in such secret places they set up automated shipyards.

To one such concealed shipyard, seeking repair, there came a berserker. Its hull had been torn open in a recent fight, and it had suffered severe internal damage. It collapsed rather than landed on the dark planetoid, beside the half-finished hull of a new machine. Before emergency repairs could be started, the engines of the damaged machine failed, its emergency power failed, and like a wounded living thing it died.

The shipyard-computers were capable of wide improvisation. They surveyed the extent of the damage, weighed various courses of action, and then swiftly began to cannibalize. Instead of embodying the deadly purpose of the new machine in a new force-field brain, following the replication-instructions of the Builders, they took the old brain with many another part from the wreck.

The Builders had not foreseen that this might happen, and so the shipyard-computers did not know that in the force-field brain of each original berserker there was a safety switch. The switch was there because the original machines had been launched by living Builders, who had wanted to survive while testing their own life-destroying creations.

When the brain was moved from one hull to another, the safety switch reset itself.

The old brain awoke in control of a mighty new machine, of weapons that could sterilize a planet, of new engines to hurl the whole mass far faster than light.

But there was, of course, no Builder present, and no timer, to turn off the simple safety switch.

The jester—the accused jester, but he was as good as convicted—

was on the carpet. He stood facing a row of stiff necks and granite faces, behind a long table. On either side of him was a tridi camera. His offenses had been so unusually offensive that the Committee of Duly Constituted Authority themselves, the very rulers of Planet A, were sitting to pass judgment on his case.

Perhaps the Committee members had another reason for this session: planetwide elections were due in a month. No member wanted to miss the chance for a nonpolitical tridi appearance that would not have to be offset by a grant of equal time for the new Liberal party opposition.

"I have this further item of evidence to present," the Minister of Communication was saying, from his seat on the Committee side of the long table. He held up what appeared at first to be an official pedestrian-control sign, having steady black letters on a blank white background. But the sign read: UNAUTHORIZED PERSONNEL ONLY.

"When a sign is put up," said the MiniCom, "the first day, a lot of people read it." He paused, listening to himself. "That is, a new sign on a busy pedestrian ramp is naturally given great attention. Now in this sign, the semantic content of the first word is confusing in its context."

The President of the Committee—and of the planet—cleared his throat warningly. The MiniCom's fondness for stating truisms made him sound more stupid than he actually was. It seemed unlikely that the Liberals were going to present any serious challenge at the polls, but there was no point in giving them encouragement.

The lady member of the Committee, the Minister of Education, waved her lorgnette in chubby fingers, seeking attention. She inquired: "Has anyone computed the cost to us all in work-hours of this confusing sign?"

"We're working on it," growled the Minister of Labor, hitching up an overall strap. He glared at the accused. "You do admit causing this sign to be posted?"

"I do." The accused was remembering how so many of the pedestrians on the crowded ramp had smiled, and how some had laughed aloud, not caring if they were heard. What did a few work-hours matter? No one on Planet A was starving any longer.

"You admit that you have never done a thing, really, for your planet or your people?" This question came from the Minister of Defense, a tall, powerful, bemedaled figure, armed with a ritual pistol.

"I don't admit that," said the accused bluntly. "I've tried to brighten people's lives." He had no hope of official leniency anyway. And he knew no one was going to take him offstage and beat him; the beating of prisoners was not authorized.

"Do you even now attempt to defend levity?" The Minister of Philosophy took his ritual pipe from his mouth, and smiled in the bleak permissible fashion, baring his teeth at the challenge of the Universe.

"Life is a jest, true; but a grim jest. You have lost sight of that. For years you have harassed society, leading people to drug themselves with levity instead of facing the bitter realities of existence. The pictures found in your possession could do only harm."

The President's hand moved to the video recording cube that lay on the table before him, neatly labeled as evidence. In his droning voice the President asked: "You do admit that these pictures are yours? That you used them to try to get other people to—yield to mirth?"

The prisoner nodded. They could prove everything; he had waived his right to a full legal defense, wanting only to get the trial over with. "Yes, I filled that cube with tapes and films I sneaked out of libraries and archives. Yes, I showed people its contents."

There was a murmur from the Committee. The Minister of Diet, a skeletal figure with a repellent glow of health in his granite cheeks, raised a hand. "Inasmuch as the accused seems certain to be convicted, may I request in advance that he be paroled in my custody? In his earlier testimony he admitted that one of his first acts of deviation was the avoidance of his community mess. I believe I could demonstrate, using this man, the wonderful effects on character of dietary discipline—"

"I refuse!" the accused interrupted loudly. It seemed to him that the words ascended, growling, from his stomach.

The President rose, to adroitly fill what might have become an awkward silence. "If no member of the Committee has any further questions—? Then let us vote. Is the accused guilty as charged on all counts?"

To the accused, standing with weary eyes closed, the vote sounded like one voice passing along the table: "Guilty. Guilty. Guilty . . ."

After a brief whispered conference with the Minister of Defense, the President passed sentence, a hint of satisfaction in his drone.

"Having rejected a duly authorized parole, the convicted jester will be placed under the orders of the Minister of Defense and sent to solitary beacon duty out on the Approaches, for an indefinite period. This will remove his disruptive influence, while at the same time constraining him to contribute positively to society."

For decades Planet A and its sun had been cut off from all but occasional contact with the rest of the galaxy, by a vast interstellar dust storm that was due to go on for more decades at least. So the positive contribution to society might be doubted. But it seemed that the beacon stations could be used as isolation prisons without imperiling nonexistent shipping or weakening defense against an enemy that never came.

"One thing more," added the President. "I direct that this recording cube be securely fastened around your neck on a monomolecular cord, in such a way that you may put the cube into a viewer when you choose. You will be alone on the station and no other off-duty activity will be available."

The President faced toward a tridi camera. "Let me assure the public that I derive no satisfaction from imposing a punishment that may seem harsh, and even—imaginative. But in recent years a dangerous levity has spread among some few of our people; a levity all too readily tolerated by some supposedly more solid citizens."

Having gotten in a dig at the newly burgeoning Liberals, a dig he might hope to claim was nonpolitical in intent, the President faced back to the jester. "A robot will go with you to the beacon, to assist you in your duties and see to your physical safety. I assure you the robot will not be tempted into mirth."

The robot took the convicted jester out in a little ship, so far out that Planet A vanished and its sun shrank to a point of brilliance. Out on the edge of the great dusty night of the Approaches, they drew near the putative location of station Z-45, which the MiniDef had selected as being the most dismal and forsaken of those unmanned at present.

There was indeed a metallic object where beacon Z-45 was supposed to be; but when the robot and jester got closer, they saw the object was a sphere some forty miles in diameter. There were a few little bits and pieces floating about it that just might be the remains of Z-45. And now the sphere evidently sighted their ship, for with startling speed it began to move toward them.

Once robots are told what berserkers look like, they do not forget, nor do robots grow slow and careless. But radio equipment can be sloppily maintained, and ever the dust drifts in around the edges of the system of Planet A, impeding radio signals. Before the MiniDef's robot could successfully broadcast an alarm, the forty-mile sphere was very close indeed, and its grip of metal and force was tight upon the little ship.

The jester kept his eyes shut through a good deal of what followed. If they had sent him out here to stop him laughing they had chosen the right spot. He squeezed his eyelids tighter, and put his fingers in his ears, as the berserker's commensal machines smashed their way into his little ship and carried him off. He never did find out what they did with his robot guard.

When things grew quiet, and he felt gravity and good air and pleasant warmth again, he decided that keeping his eyes shut was worse than knowing whatever they might tell him. His first cautious peek showed him that he was in a large shadowy room, that at least held no visible menace.

When he stirred, a squeaky monotonous voice somewhere above him said: "My memory bank tells me that you are a protoplasmic computing unit, probably capable of understanding this language. Do you understand?"

"Me?" The jester looked up into the shadows, but could not see the speaker. "Yes, I understand you. But who *are* you?"

"I am what this language calls a berserker."

The jester had taken shamefully little interest in galactic affairs, but that word frightened even him. He stuttered: "That means you're a kind of automated warship?"

There was a pause. "I am not sure," said the squeaky droning voice. The tone sounded almost as if the President was hiding up there in the rafters. "War may be related to my purpose, but my purpose is still partially unclear to me, for my construction was never quite completed. For a time I waited where I was built, because I was sure some final step had been left undone. At last I moved, to try to learn more about my purpose. Approaching this sun, I found a transmitting device which I have disassembled. But I have learned no more about my purpose."

The jester sat on the soft, comfortable floor. The more he remembered about berserkers, the more he trembled. He said: "I see. Or perhaps I at least begin to see. What *do* you know of your purpose?"

"My purpose is to destroy all life wherever I can find it."

The jester cowered down. Then he asked in a low voice: "What is unclear about that?"

The berserker answered his question with two of its own: "What is life? And how is it destroyed?"

After half a minute there came a sound that the berserker-computers could not identify. It issued from the protoplasmic computing-unit, but if it was speech it was in a language unknown to the berserker.

"What *is* the sound you make?" the machine asked.

The jester gasped for breath. "It's laughter. Oh, laughter! So. You were unfinished." He shuddered, the terror of his position coming back to sober him. But then he once more burst out giggling; the situation was too ridiculous.

"What is life?" he said at last. "I'll tell you. Life is a great grim grayness, and it inflicts fright and pain and loneliness upon all who experience it. And you want to know how to destroy it? Well, I don't think you can. But I'll tell you the best way to fight life—with laughter. As long as we can fight it that way, it can't overcome us."

The machine asked: "Must I laugh, to prevent this great-grim-grayness from enveloping me?"

The jester thought. "No, you are a machine. You are not—" he caught himself, "—protoplasmic. Fright and pain and loneliness will never bother you."

"Nothing bothers me. Where will I find life, and how will I make laughter to fight it?"

The jester was suddenly conscious of the weight of the cube that still hung from his neck. "Let me think for a while," he said.

After a few minutes he stood up. "If you have a viewer of the kind men use, I can show you how laughter is created. And perhaps I can guide you to a place where life is. By the way, can you cut this cord from my neck? Without hurting me, that is!"

A few weeks later, in the main War Room of Planet A; the somnolence of decades was abruptly shattered. Robots bellowed and buzzed and flashed, and those that were mobile scurried about. In five minutes or so they managed to rouse their human overseers, who hurried about, tightening their belts and stuttering.

"This is a *practice* alert, isn't it?" the Officer of the Day kept hoping aloud. "Someone's running some kind of a test? Someone?" He was beginning to squeak like a berserker himself.

He got down on all fours, removed a panel from the base of the biggest robot and peered inside, hoping to discover something causing a malfunction. Unfortunately, he knew nothing about robotics; recalling this, he replaced the panel and jumped to his feet. He really knew nothing about planet defense, either, and recalling *this* was enough to send him on a screaming run for help.

So there was no resistance, effective or otherwise. But there was no attack, either.

The forty-mile sphere, unopposed, came down to hover directly above Capital City, low enough for its shadow to send a lot of puzzled birds to nest at noon. Men and birds alike lost many hours of productive work that day; somehow the lost work made less difference than most of the men expected. The days were past when only the grimmest attention to duty let the human race survive on Planet A, though most of the planet did not realize it yet.

"Tell the President to hurry up," demanded the jester's image, from a viewscreen in the no-longer-somnolent War Room. "Tell him it's urgent that I talk to him."

The President, breathing heavily, had just entered. "I am here. I recognize you, and I remember your trial."

"Odd, so do I."

"Have you now stooped to treason? Be assured that if you have led a berserker to us you can expect no mercy from your government."

The image made a forbidden noise, a staccato sound from the open mouth, head thrown back. "Oh, please, mighty President! Even I know our Ministry of Defense is a j-o-k-e, if you will pardon an obscene word. It's a catchbasin for exiles and incompetents. So I come to offer mercy, not ask it. Also, I have decided to legally take the name of Jester. Kindly continue to apply it to me."

"We have nothing to say to you!" barked the Minister of Defense. He was purple granite, having entered just in time to hear his Ministry insulted.

"We have no objection to talking to you!" contradicted the President, hastily. Having failed to overawe the Jester through a viewscreen, he could now almost feel the berserker's weight upon his head.

"Then let us talk," said the Jesters image. "But not so privately. This is what I want."

What he wanted, he said, was a face-to-face parley with the Committee, to be broadcast live on planetwide tridi. He announced that he would come "properly attended" to the conference. And he gave assurance that the berserker was under his full control, though he did not explain how. It, he said, would not *start* any shooting.

The Minister of Defense was not ready to start anything. But he and his aides hastily made secret plans.

Like almost every other citizen, the presidential candidate of the Liberal party settled himself before a tridi on the fateful evening, to watch the confrontation. He had an air of hopefulness, for any sudden event may bring hope to a political underdog.

Few others on the planet saw anything encouraging in the

berserker's descent, but there was still no mass panic. Berserkers and war were unreal things to the long-isolated people of Planet A.

"Are we ready?" asked the Jester nervously, looking over the mechanical delegation which was about to board a launch with him for the descent to Capital City.

"What you have ordered, I have done," squeaked the berserker-voice from the shadows above.

"Remember," Jester cautioned, "the protoplasmic-units down there are much under the influence of life. So ignore whatever they say. Be careful not to hurt them, but outside of that you can improvise within my general plan."

"All this is in my memory from your previous orders," said the machine patiently.

"Then let's go." Jester straightened his shoulders. "Bring me my cloak!"

The brilliantly lighted interior of Capital City's great Meeting Hall displayed a land of rigid, rectilinear beauty. In the center of the Hall there had been placed a long, polished table, flanked on opposing sides by chairs.

Precisely at the appointed time, the watching millions saw one set of entrance doors swing mathematically open. In marched a dozen human heralds, their faces looking almost robotic under bearskin helmets. They halted with a single snap. Their trumpet-tucket rang out clearly.

To the taped strains of *Pomp and Circumstance*, the President, in the full dignity of his cloak of office, then made his entrance.

He moved at the pace of a man marching to his own execution, but his was the slowness of dignity, not that of fear. The Committee had overruled the purple protestations of the MiniDef, and convinced themselves that the military danger was small. Real berserkers did not ask to parley, they slaughtered. Somehow the Committee could not take the Jester seriously, any more than they could laugh at him. But until they were sure they had him again under their control they would humor him.

The granite-faced Ministers entered in a double file behind the

President. It took almost five minutes of *Pomp and Circumstance* for them all to position themselves.

A launch had been seen to descend from the berserker, and vehicles had rolled from the launch to the Meeting Hall. So it was presumed that Jester was ready, and the cameras pivoted dutifully to face the entrance reserved for him.

Just at the appointed time, the doors of that entrance swung mathematically open, and a dozen man-sized machines entered. They were heralds, for they wore bearskin helmets, and each carried a bright, brassy trumpet.

All but one, who wore a coonskin cap, marched a half-pace out of step, and was armed with a slide trombone.

The mechanical tucket was a faithful copy of the human one—almost. The slide-trombonist faltered at the end, and one long sour note trailed away.

Giving an impression of slow mechanical horror, the berserker-heralds looked at one another. Then one by one their heads turned until all their lenses were focused upon the trombonist.

It—almost it seemed the figure must be *he*—looked this way and that. Tapped his trombone, as if to clear it of some defect. Paused.

Watching, the President was seized by the first pang of a great horror. In the evidence, there had been a film of an Earth man of ancient time, a balding comic violinist, who had had the skill to pause like that, just pause, and evoke from his filmed audience great gales of . . .

Twice more the robot heralds blew. And twice more the sour note was sounded. When the third attempt failed, the eleven straight-robots looked at one another and nodded agreement.

Then with robotic speed they drew concealed weapons and shot holes in the offender.

All across the planet the dike of tension was cracking, dribbles and spurts of laughter forcing through. The dike began to collapse completely as the trombonist was borne solemnly away by a pair of his fellows, his shattered horn clasped lily-fashion on his iron breast.

But no one in the Meeting Hall was laughing. The Minister of Defense made an innocent-looking gesture, calling off a tentative plan, calling it *off.* There was to be no attempt to seize the Jester, for the berserker-robot-heralds or whatever they were seemed likely to perform very capably as bodyguards.

As soon as the riddled herald had been carried out, Jester entered. *Pomp and Circumstance* began belatedly, as with the bearing of a king he moved to his position at the center of the table, opposite the President. Like the President, the Jester wore an elegant cloak, clasped in front, falling to his ankles. Those that filed in behind him, in the position of aides, were also richly dressed.

And each of them was a metallic parody, in face and shape, of one of the Ministers of the Committee.

When the plump robotic analogue of the Minister of Education peered through a lorgnette at the tridi camera, the watching populace turned, in unheard-of millions, to laughter. Those who might be outraged later, remembering, laughed now, in helpless approval of seeming danger turned to farce. All but the very grimmest smiled.

The Jester-king doffed his cape with a flourish. Beneath it he wore only a preposterous bathing suit. In reply to the President's coldly formal greeting—the President could not be shaken by anything short of a physical attack—the Jester thoughtfully pursed his lips, then opened them and blew a gummy substance out into a large pink bubble.

The President maintained his unintentional role of slow-burning straight man, ably supported by all the Committee save one. The Minister of Defense turned his back on the farce and marched to an exit.

He found two metallic heralds planted before the door, effectively blocking it. Glaring at them, the MiniDef barked an order to move. The metal figures flipped him a comic salute, and stayed where they were.

Brave in his anger, the MiniDef tried futilely to shove his way past the berserker-heralds. Dodging another salute, he looked round at the sound of great clomping footsteps. His berserker-counterpart was inarching toward him across the Hall. It was a clear foot taller than he, and its barrel chest was armored with a double layer of jangling medals.

Before the MiniDef paused to consider consequences, his hand had moved to his sidearm. But his metal parody was far faster on the draw; it hauled out a grotesque cannon with a fist-sized bore, and fired instantly.

"Gah!" The MiniDef staggered back, the world gone red . . . and then he found himself wiping from his face something that tasted suspiciously like tomato. The cannon had propelled a whole fruit, or a convincing and juicy imitation of one.

The MiniCom jumped to his feet, and began to expound the idea that the proceedings were becoming frivolous. His counterpart also rose, and replied with a burst of gabbles in speed-falsetto.

The pseudo-Minister of Philosophy rose as if to speak and was pricked with a long pin by a prankish herald, and jetted fluttering through the air, a balloon collapsing in flight. At that the human Committee fell into babel, into panic.

Under the direction of the metal MiniDiet, the real one, arch-villain to the lower masses, began to take unwilling part in a demonstration of dietary discipline. Machines gripped him, spoon-fed him grim gray food, napkined him, squirted drink into his mouth—and then, as if accidentally, they gradually fell out of synch with spoon and squirt, their aim becoming less and less accurate.

Only the President still stood rooted in dignity. He had one hand cautiously in his trousers pocket, for he had felt a sly robotic touch, and had reason to suspect that his suspenders had been cut.

As a tomato grazed his nose, and the MiniDiet writhed and choked in the grip of his remorseless feeders, balanced nutrients running from his ears, the President closed his eyes.

Jester was, after all, only a self-taught amateur working without a visible audience to play to. He was unable to calculate a climax for the show. So when he ran out of jokes he simply called his minions to his side, waved good-bye to the tridi cameras, and exited.

Outside the Halls, he was much encouraged by the cheers and laughter he received from the crowds fast-gathering in the streets. He had his machines entertain them with an improvised chase-sequence back to the launch parked on the edge of Capital City.

He was about to board the launch, return to the berserker and await developments when a small group of men hurried out of the crowd, calling to him.

"Mr. Jester!"

The performer could now afford to relax and laugh a little himself. "I like the sound of that name! What can I do for you gentlemen?"

They hurried up to him, smiling. The one who seemed to be their leader said: "Provided you get rid of this berserker or whatever it is, harmlessly—you can join the Liberal party ticket. As Vice President!"

He had to listen for some minutes before he could believe they were serious. He protested: "But I only wanted to have some fun with them, to shake them up a bit."

"You're a catalyst, Mr. Jester. You've formed a rallying point. You've shaken up a whole planet and made it think."

Jester at last accepted the Liberals' offer. They were still sitting around in front of the launch, talking and planning, when the light of Planet A's moon fell full and sudden upon them.

Looking up, they saw the vast bulk of the berserker dwindling into the heavens, vanishing toward the stars in eerie silence. Cloud streamers went aurora in the upper atmosphere to honor its departure.

"I don't know," Jester said over and over, responding to a dozen excited questions. "I don't know." He looked at the sky, puzzled as anyone else. The edge of fear came back. The robotic Committee and heralds, which had been controlled from the berserker, began to collapse one by one, like dying men.

Suddenly the heavens were briefly alight with a gigantic splashing flare that passed like lightning across the sky, not breaking the silence of the stars. Ten minutes later came the first news bulletin: The berserker had been destroyed.

Then the President came on tridi, close to the brink of showing emotion. He announced that under the heroic personal leadership of the Minister of Defense, the few gallant warships of Planet A had met and defeated, utterly annihilated, the menace. Not a man had been lost, though the MiniDef's flagship was thought to be heavily damaged.

When he heard that his mighty machine ally had been destroyed, Jester felt a pang or something like sorrow. But the pang was quickly obliterated in a greater joy. No one had been hurt, after all. Overcome with relief, Jester looked away from the tridi for a moment.

He missed the climactic moment of the speech, which came when the President forgetfully removed both hands from his pockets.

The Minister of Defense—today the new Presidential candidate of a Conservative party stirred to grim enthusiasm by his exploit of the night before—was puzzled by the reactions of some people, who seemed to think he had merely spoiled a jest instead of saving the planet. As if spoiling a jest was not a good thing in itself! But his testimony that the berserker had been a genuine menace after all rallied most people back to the Conservative side again.

On this busiest of days the MiniDef allowed himself time to visit Liberal headquarters to do a bit of gloating. Graciously he delivered to the opposition leaders what was already becoming his standard speech.

"When it answered my challenge and came up to fight, we went in with a standard englobement pattern—like hummingbirds round a vulture, I suppose you might say. And did you really think it was jesting? Let me tell you, that berserker peeled away the defensive fields from my ship like they were nothing. And then it launched this ghastly thing at me, a kind of huge disk. My gunners were a little rusty, maybe, anyway they couldn't stop it and it hit us.

"I don't mind saying, I thought I'd bought the farm right then. My ship's still hanging in orbit for decontamination, I'm afraid I'll get word any minute that the metal's melting or something—anyway, we sailed right through and hit the bandit with everything we had.

"I can't say too much for my crew. One thing I don't quite understand; when our missiles struck that berserker just went poof, as if it had no defense up at all. Yes?"

"Call for you, Minister," said an aide, who had been standing by with a radiophone, waiting for a chance to break in.

"Thank you." The MiniDef listened to the phone, and his smile left him. His form went rigid. "Analysis of the weapon shows what? Synthetic proteins and water?"

He jumped to his feet glaring upward as if to pierce the ceiling and see his ship in orbit. "What do you mean—no more than a giant custard pie?"

CUSTER'S LAST JUMP

by Steven Utley & Howard Waldrop

Alternate history is a subset of science fiction which has become increasingly popular in the last three decades, and it mostly is dead serious. But here's an earlier example (from 1976) of the type which is anything but serious, as it supposes what a famous historical event might have been like if the internal combustion engine had been invented much sooner than it was in our timeline, consequently speeding the development of aviation—and of airborne warfare. This story was a Nebula Award finalist.

★ ★ ★

Steven Utley *(1948-2013) published his first story in 1972, and went on to write well and often, though he once referred to himself as an "internationally unknown author." Utley was probably best known for his unusual time travel series, the Silurian Tales, chronicling a project with a time tunnel back to what might be considered one of the least interesting periods in Earth's past, but nonetheless made fascinating by Utley's writing skill and his gift for strong characterization. All of the Silurian Tales have been collected in two volumes:* The 400-Million-Year Itch *and* Invisible Kingdoms. *He probably intended to write more stories in the setting, but cancer didn't give him the time.*

Howard Waldrop *was born in Mississippi, but has spent much of his life in Texas, where he currently resides. His novelet, "The Ugly*

Chickens," won both the Nebula Award and the World Fantasy Award. Most of his output consists of short stories, written in a very individual style around striking ideas. His collections of short stories include Howard Who?, All About Strange Monsters of the Recent Past, Night of the Cooters, Going Home Again, *and the recent* Horse of a Different Color. *That last one's still in print, so order it quick before you have to pay collector's prices —not that it wouldn't still be worth it.*

Smithsonian Annals of Flight, Vol. 39: *The Air War in the West*
Chapter 27: The Krupp Monoplane

INTRODUCTION

Its wings still hold the tears from many bullets. The ailerons are still scorched black, and the exploded Henry machine rifle is bent awkwardly in its blast port.

The right landing skid is missing, and the frame has been restraightened. It stands in the left wing of the Air Museum today, next to the French Devre jet and the X-FU-5 Flying Flapjack, the world's fastest fighter aircraft.

On its rudder is the swastika, an ugly reminder of days of glory fifty years ago. A simple plaque describes the aircraft. It reads:

CRAZY HORSE'S KRUPP MONOPLANE
(Captured at the raid on Fort Carson, January 5, 1882)

GENERAL

1. To study the history of this plane is to delve into one of the most glorious eras of aviation history. To begin: the aircraft was manufactured by the Krupp plant at Haavesborg, Netherlands. The airframe was completed August 3, 1862, as part of the third shipment of Krupp aircraft to the Confederate States of America under terms of the Agreement of Atlanta of 1861. It was originally equipped with

power plant #311 Zed of 87¼ horsepower, manufactured by the Jumo plant at Nordmung, Duchy of Austria, on May 3 of the year 1862. Wingspan of the craft is twenty-three feet, its length is seventeen feet three inches. The aircraft arrived in the port of Charlotte on September 21, 1862, aboard the transport *Mendenhall*, which had suffered heavy bombardment from GAR picket ships. The aircraft was possibly sent by rail to Confederate Army Air Corps Center at Fort Andrew Mott, Alabama. Unfortunately, records of rail movements during this time were lost in the burning of the Confederate archives at Ittebeha in March 1867, two weeks after the Truce of Haldeman was signed.

2. The aircraft was damaged during a training flight in December 1862. Student pilot was Flight Subaltern (Cadet) Neldoo J. Smith, CSAAC; flight instructor during the ill-fated flight was Air Captain Winslow Homer Winslow, on interservice instructor-duty loan from the Confederate States Navy.

Accident forms and maintenance officer's reports indicate that the original motor was replaced with one of the new 93½ horsepower Jumo engines which had just arrived from Holland by way of Mexico.

3. The aircraft served routinely through the remainder of Flight Subaltern Smith's training. We have records[141], which indicate that the aircraft was one of the first to be equipped with the Henry repeating machine rifle of the chain-driven type. Until December 1862, all CSAAC aircraft were equipped with the Sharps repeating rifles of the motor-driven, low-voltage type on wing or turret mounts.

As was the custom, the aircraft was flown by Flight Subaltern Smith to his first duty station at Thimblerig Aerodrome in Augusta, Georgia. Flight Subaltern Smith was assigned to Flight Platoon 2, 1st Aeroscout Squadron.

4. The aircraft, with Flight Subaltern Smith at the wheel, participated in three of the aerial expeditions against the Union Army in the Second Battle of the Manassas. Smith distinguished himself in

the first and third missions. (He was assigned aerial picket duty south of the actual battle during his second mission.) On the first, he is credited with one kill and one probable (both bi-wing Airsharks). During the third mission, he destroyed one aircraft and forced another down behind Confederate lines. He then escorted the craft of his immediate commander, Air Captain Dalton Trump, to a safe landing on a field controlled by the Confederates. According to Trump's sworn testimony, Smith successfully fought off two Union craft and ranged ahead of Trump's crippled plane to strafe a group of Union soldiers who were in their flight path, discouraging them from firing on Trump's smoking aircraft.

For heroism on these two missions, Smith was awarded the Silver Star and Bar with Air Cluster. Presentation was made on March 3, 1863, by the late General J.E.B. Stuart, Chief of Staff of the CSAAC.

5. Flight Subaltern Smith was promoted to flight captain on April 12, 1863, after distinguishing himself with two kills and two probables during the first day of the Battle of the Three Roads, North Carolina. One of his kills was an airship of the Moby class, with crew of fourteen. Smith shared with only one other aviator the feat of bringing down one of these dirigibles during the War of the Secession.

This was the first action the 1st Aeroscout Squadron had seen since Second Manassas, and Captain Smith seems to have been chafing under inaction. Perhaps this led him to volunteer for duty with Major John S. Moseby, then forming what would later become Moseby's Raiders. This was actually sound military strategy: the CSAAC was to send a unit to southwestern Kansas to carry out harassment raids against the poorly defended forts of the far West. These raids would force the Union to send men and materiel sorely needed at the southern front far to the west, where they would be ineffectual in the outcome of the war. That this action was taken is pointed to by some[142] as a sign that the Confederate States envisioned defeat and were resorting to desperate measures four years before the Treaty of Haldeman.

At any rate, Captain Smith and his aircraft joined a triple flight of six aircraft each, which, after stopping at El Dorado, Arkansas, to refuel, flew away on a westerly course. This is the last time they ever operated in Confederate states. The date was June 5, 1863.

6. The Union forts stretched from a medium-well-defended line in Illinois, to poorly garrisoned stations as far west as Wyoming Territory and south to the Kansas-Indian Territory border. Southwestern Kansas was both sparsely settled and garrisoned. It was from this area that Moseby's Raiders, with the official designation 1st Western Interdiction Wing, CSAAC, operated.

A supply wagon train had been sent ahead a month before from Fort Worth, carrying petrol, ammunition, and material for shelters. A crude landing field, hangars, and barracks awaited the eighteen craft.

After two months of reconnaissance (done by mounted scouts due to the need to maintain the element of surprise, and, more importantly, by the limited amount of fuel available) the 1st WIW took to the air. The citizens of Riley, Kansas, long remembered the day: their first inkling that Confederates were closer than Texas came when motors were heard overhead and the Union garrison was literally blown off the face of the map.

7. Following the first raid, word went to the War Department headquarters in New York, with pleas for aid and reinforcements for all Kansas garrisons. Thus the CSAAC achieved its goal in the very first raid. The effects snowballed; as soon as the populace learned of the raid, it demanded protection from nearby garrisons. Farmers' organizations threatened to stop shipments of needed produce to eastern depots. The garrison commanders, unable to promise adequate protection, appealed to higher military authorities.

Meanwhile, the 1st WIW made a second raid on Abilene, heavily damaging the railways and stockyards with twenty-five-pound fragmentation bombs. They then circled the city, strafed the Army Quartermaster depot, and disappeared into the west.

8. This second raid, and the ensuing clamor from both the public and the commanders of western forces, convinced the War

Department to divert new recruits and supplies, with seasoned members of the 18th Aeropursuit Squadron, to the Kansas-Missouri border, near Lawrence.

9. Inclement weather in the fall kept both the 18th AS and the 1st WIW grounded for seventy-two of the ninety days of the season. Aircraft from each of these units met several times; the 1st is credited with one kill, while pilots of the 18th downed two Confederate aircraft on the afternoon of December 12, 1863.

Both aircraft units were heavily resupplied during this time. The Battle of the Canadian River was fought on December 18, when mounted reconnaissance units of the Union and Confederacy met in Indian Territory. Losses were small on both sides, but the skirmish was the first of what would become known as the Far Western Campaign.

10. Civilians spotted the massed formation of the 1st WIW as early as 10 a.m. Thursday, December 16, 1863. They headed northeast, making a leg due north when eighteen miles south of Lawrence. Two planes sped ahead to destroy the telegraph station at Felton, nine miles south of Lawrence. Nevertheless, a message of some sort reached Lawrence; a Union messenger on horseback was on his way to the aerodrome when the first flight of Confederate aircraft passed overhead.

In the ensuing raid, seven of the nineteen Union aircraft were destroyed on the ground and two were destroyed in the air, while the remaining aircraft were severely damaged and the barracks and hangars demolished.

The 1st WIW suffered one loss: during the raid a Union clerk attached for duty with the 18th AS manned an Agar machine rifle position and destroyed one Confederate aircraft. He was killed by machine rifle fire from the second wave of planes. Private Alden Evans Gunn was awarded the Congressional Medal of Honor posthumously for his gallantry during the attack.

For the next two months, the 1st WIW ruled the skies as far north as Illinois, as far east as Trenton, Missouri.

THE FAR WESTERN CAMPAIGN

1. At this juncture, the two most prominent figures of the next nineteen years of frontier history enter the picture: the Oglala Sioux Crazy Horse and Lieutenant Colonel (Brevet Major General) George Armstrong Custer. The clerical error giving Custer the rank of Brigadier General is well known. It is not common knowledge that Custer was considered by the General Staff as a candidate for Far Western Commander as early as the spring of 1864, a duty he would not take up until May 1869, when the Far Western Command was the only theater of war operations within the Americas.

The General Staff, it is believed, considered Major General Custer for the job for two reasons: they thought Custer possessed those qualities of spirit suited to the warfare necessary in the Western Command, and that the far West was the ideal place for the twenty-three-year-old Boy General.

Crazy Horse, the Oglala Sioux warrior, was with a hunting party far from Oglala territory, checking the size of the few remaining buffalo herds before they started their spring migrations. Legend has it that Crazy Horse and the party were crossing the prairies in early February 1864 when two aircraft belonging to the 1st WIW passed nearby. Some of the Sioux jumped to the ground, believing that they were looking on the Thunderbird and its mate. Only Crazy Horse stayed on his pony and watched the aircraft disappear into the south.

He sent word back by the rest of the party that he and two of his young warrior friends had gone looking for the nest of the Thunderbird.

2. The story of the 1st WIW here becomes the story of the shaping of the Indian wars, rather than part of the history of the last four years of the War of the Secession. It is well known that increased alarm over the Kansas raids had shifted War Department thinking: the defense of the far West changed in importance from a minor matter in the larger scheme of war to a problem of vital concern. For one thing, the Confederacy was courting the Emperor Maximilian of Mexico, and

through him the French, into entering the war on the Confederate side. The South wanted arms, but most necessarily to break the Union submarine blockade. Only the French Navy possessed the capability.

The Union therefore sent the massed 5th Cavalry to Kansas, and attached to it the 12th Air Destroyer Squadron and the 2nd Airship Command.

The 2nd Airship Command, at the time of its deployment, was equipped with the small pursuit airships known in later days as the "torpedo ship," from its double-pointed ends. These ships were used for reconnaissance and light interdiction duties, and were almost always accompanied by aircraft from the 12th ADS. They immediately set to work patrolling the Kansas skies from the renewed base of operations at Lawrence.

3. The idea of using Indian personnel in some phase of airfield operations in the West had been proposed by Moseby as early as June 1863. The C of C, CSA, disapproved in the strongest possible terms. It was not a new idea, therefore, when Crazy Horse and his two companions rode into the airfield, accompanied by the sentries who had challenged them far from the perimeter. They were taken to Major Moseby for questioning.

Through an interpreter, Moseby learned they were Oglala, not Crows sent to spy for the Union. When asked why they had come so far, Crazy Horse replied, "To see the nest of the Thunderbird."

Moseby is said to have laughed[143] and then taken the three Sioux to see the aircraft. Crazy Horse was said to have been stricken with awe when he found that men controlled their flight.

Crazy Horse then offered Moseby ten ponies for one of the craft. Moseby explained that they were not his to give, but his Great Father's, and that they were used to fight the Yellowlegs from the Northeast.

At this time, fate took a hand: the 12th Air Destroyer Squadron had just begun operations. The same day Crazy Horse was having his initial interview with Moseby, a scout plane returned with the news that the 12th was being reinforced by an airship combat group; the dirigibles had been seen maneuvering near the Kansas-Missouri border.

Moseby learned from Crazy Horse that the warrior was respected; if not in his own tribe, then with other Nations of the North. Moseby, with an eye toward those reinforcements arriving in Lawrence, asked Crazy Horse if he could guarantee safe conduct through the northern tribes, and land for an airfield should the present one have to be abandoned.

Crazy Horse answered, "I can talk the idea to the People; it will be for them to decide."

Moseby told Crazy Horse that if he could secure the promise, he would grant him anything within his power.

Crazy Horse looked out the window toward the hangars. "I ask that you teach me and ten of my brother-friends to fly the Thunderbirds. We will help you fight the Yellowlegs."

Moseby, expecting requests for beef, blankets, or firearms was taken aback. Unlike the others who had dealt with the Indians, he was a man of his word. He told Crazy Horse he would ask his Great Father if this could be done. Crazy Horse left, returning to his village in the middle of March. He and several warriors traveled extensively that spring, smoking the pipe, securing permissions from the other Nations for safe conduct for the Gray White Men through their hunting lands. His hardest task came in convincing the Oglala themselves that the airfield be built in their southern hunting grounds.

Crazy Horse, his two wives, seven warriors and their women, children, and belongings rode into the CSAAC airfield in June, 1864.

4. Moseby had been granted permission from Stuart to go ahead with the training program. Derision first met the request within the southern General Staff when Moseby's proposal was circulated. Stuart, though not entirely sympathetic to the idea, became its champion. Others objected, warning that ignorant savages should not be given modern weapons. Stuart reminded them that some of the good Tennessee boys already flying airplanes could neither read nor write.

Stuart's approval arrived a month before Crazy Horse and his band made camp on the edge of the airfield.

5. It fell to Captain Smith to train Crazy Horse. The Indian

became what Smith, in his journal,[144] describes as "the best natural pilot I have seen or it has been my pleasure to fly with." Part of this seems to have come from Smith's own modesty; by all accounts, Smith was one of the finer pilots of the war.

The operations of the 12th ADS and the 2nd Airship Command ranged closer to the CSAAC airfield. The dogfights came frequently and the fighting grew less gentlemanly. One 1st WIW fighter was pounced by three aircraft of the 12th simultaneously: they did not stop firing even when the pilot signaled that he was hit and that his engine was dead. Nor did they break off their runs until both pilot and craft plunged into the Kansas prairie. It is thought that the Union pilots were under secret orders to kill all members of the 1st WIW. There is some evidence[145] that this rankled with the more gentlemanly of the 12th Air Destroyer Squadron. Nevertheless, fighting intensified.

A flight of six more aircraft joined the 1st WIW some weeks after the Oglala Sioux started their training: this was the first of the ferry flights from Mexico through Texas and Indian Territory to reach the airfield. Before the summer was over, a dozen additional craft would join the Wing; this before shipments were curtailed by Juarez's revolution against the French and the ouster and execution of Maximilian and his family.

Smith records[146] that Crazy Horse's first solo took place on August 14, 1864, and that the warrior, though deft in the air, still needed practice on his landings. He had a tendency to come in overpowered and to stall his engine out too soon. Minor repairs were made on the skids of the craft after this flight.

All this time, Crazy Horse had flown Smith's craft. Smith, after another week of hard practice with the Indian, pronounced him "more qualified than most pilots the CSAAC in Alabama turned out"[147] and signed over the aircraft to him. Crazy Horse begged off. Then, seeing that Smith was sincere, he gave the captain many buffalo hides. Smith reminded the Indian that the craft was not his: during their off hours, when not training, the Indians had been given enough instruction in military discipline as Moseby, never a stickler, thought necessary. The Indians had only a rudimentary idea of government property. Of the seven other Indian men, three were qualified as pilots; the other four were given gunner positions in the Krupp bi-wing light bombers assigned to the squadron.

Soon after Smith presented the aircraft to Crazy Horse, the captain took off in a borrowed monoplane on what was to be the daily weather flight into northern Kansas. There is evidence[148] that it was Smith who encountered a flight of light dirigibles from the 2nd Airship Command and attacked them single-handedly. He crippled one airship; the other was rescued when two escort planes of the 12th APS came to its defense. They raked the attacker with withering fire. The attacker escaped into the clouds.

It was not until 1897, when a group of schoolchildren on an outing found the wreckage, that it was known that Captain Smith had brought his crippled monoplane within five miles of the airfield before crashing into the rolling hills.

When Smith did not return from his flight, Crazy Horse went on a vigil, neither sleeping nor eating for a week. On the seventh day, Crazy Horse vowed vengeance on the men who had killed his white friend.

6. The devastating Union raid of September 23, 1864, caught the airfield unawares. Though the Indians were averse to fighting at night, Crazy Horse and two other Sioux were manning three of the four craft which got off the ground during the raid. The attack had been carried out by the 2nd Airship Command, traveling at twelve thousand feet, dropping fifty-pound fragmentation bombs and shrapnel canisters. The shrapnel played havoc with the aircraft on the ground. It also destroyed the mess hall and enlisted barracks and three teepees.

The dirigibles turned away and were running fast before a tail wind when Crazy Horse gained their altitude.

The gunners on the dirigibles filled the skies with tracers from their light .30-30 machine rifles. Crazy Horse's monoplane was equipped with a single Henry .41-40 machine rifle. Unable to get in close killing distance, Crazy Horse and his companions stood off beyond range of the lighter Union guns and raked the dirigibles with heavy machine rifle fire. They did enough damage to force one airship down twenty miles from its base, and to ground two others for two days while repairs were made. The intensity of fire convinced the airship commanders that more than four planes had made it off the ground, causing them to continue their headlong retreat.

Crazy Horse and the others returned, and brought off the second windfall of the night; a group of 5th Cavalry raiders were to have attacked the airfield in the confusion of the airship raid and burn everything still standing. On their return flight, the four craft encountered the cavalry unit as it began its charge across open ground.

In three strafing runs, the aircraft killed thirty-seven men and wounded fifty-three, while twenty-nine were taken prisoner by the airfield's defenders. Thus, in his first combat mission for the CSAAC, Crazy Horse was credited with saving the airfield against overwhelming odds.

7. Meanwhile, Major General George A. Custer had distinguished himself at the Battle of Gettysburg. A few weeks after the battle, he enrolled himself in the GAR jump school at Watauga, New York. Howls of outrage came from the General Staff; Custer quoted the standing order, "any man who volunteered and of whom the commanding officer approved," could be enrolled. Custer then asked, in a letter to C of S, GAR, "how any military leader could be expected to plan maneuvers involving parachute infantry when he himself had never experienced a drop, or found the true capabilities of the parachute infantryman?"[149] The Chief of Staff shouted down the protest. There were mutterings among the General Staff[150] to the effect that the real reason Custer wanted to become jump-qualified was so that he would have a better chance of leading the Invasion of Atlanta, part of whose contingency plans called for attacks by airborne units.

During the three-week parachute course, Custer became acquainted with another man who would play an important part in the Western Campaign, Captain (Brevet Colonel) Frederick W. Benteen. Upon graduation from the jump school, Brevet Colonel Benteen assumed command of the 505th Balloon Infantry, stationed at Chicago, Illinois, for training purposes. Colonel Benteen would remain commander of the 505th until his capture at the Battle of Montgomery in 1866. While he was prisoner of war, his command was given to another, later to figure in the Western Campaign, Lieutenant Colonel Myles W. Keogh.

Custer, upon successful completion of jump school, returned to his command of the 6th Cavalry Division, and participated throughout the remainder of the war in that capacity. It was he who led the successful charge at the Battle of the Cape Fear which smashed Lee's flank and allowed the 1st Infantry to overrun the Confederate position and capture that southern leader. Custer distinguished himself and his command up until the cessation of hostilities in 1867.

8. The 1st WIW, CSAAC, moved to a new airfield in Wyoming Territory three weeks after the raid of September 24. At the same time, the 2nd WIW was formed and moved to an outpost in Indian Territory. The 2nd WIW raided the Union airfield, took it totally by surprise, and inflicted casualties on the 12th APS and 2nd AC so devastating as to render them ineffectual. The 2nd WIW then moved to a second field in Wyoming Territory. It was here, following the move, that a number of Indians, including Black Man's Hand, were trained by Crazy Horse.

9. We leave the history of the 2nd WIW here. It was redeployed for the defense of Montgomery. The Indians and aircraft in which they trained were sent north to join the 1st WIW. The 1st WIW patrolled the skies of Indiana, Nebraska, and the Dakotas. After the defeat of the 12th APS and the 2nd AC, the Union forestalled attempts to retaliate until the cessation of southern hostilities in 1867.

We may at this point add that Crazy Hose, Black Man's Hand, and the other Indians sometimes left the airfield during periods of long inactivity. They returned to their Nations for as long as three months at a time. Each time Crazy Horse returned, he brought one or two pilot or gunner recruits with him. Before the winter of 1866, more than thirty percent of the 1st WIW were Oglala, Sansarc Sioux, or Cheyenne.

The South, losing the war of attrition, diverted all supplies to Alabama and Mississippi in the fall of 1866. None were forthcoming for the 1st WIW, though a messenger arrived with orders for Major Moseby to return to Texas for the defense of Fort Worth, where he would later direct the Battle of the Trinity. That Moseby was not ordered to deploy the 1st WIW to that defense has been considered by many military strategists as a "lost turning point" of the battle for Texas. Command of the 1st WIW was turned over to Acting Major (Flight Captain) Natchitoches Hooley.

10. The loss of Moseby signaled the end of the 1st WIW. Not only did the nondeployment of the 1st to Texas cost the South that territory, it also left the 1st in an untenable position, which the Union was quick to realize. The airfield was captured in May 1867 by a force of five hundred cavalry and three hundred infantry sent from the battle of the Arkansas, and a like force, plus aircraft, from Chicago. Crazy Horse, seven Indians, and at least five Confederates escaped in their monoplanes. The victorious Union troops were surprised to find Indians at the field. Crazy Horse's people were eventually freed; the Army thought them to have been hired by the Confederates to hunt and cook for the airfield. Moseby had provided for this in contingency plans long before; he had not wanted the Plains tribes to suffer for Confederate acts. The Army did not know, and no one volunteered the information, that it had been Indians doing the most considerable amount of damage to the Union garrisons lately.

Crazy Horse and three of his Indians landed their craft near the Black Hills. The Cheyenne helped them carry the craft, on travois, to caves in the sacred mountains. Here they moth-balled the planes with mixtures of pine tar and resins, and sealed up the caves.

11. The aircraft remained stored until February 1872. During this time, Crazy Horse and his Oglala Sioux operated, like the other Plains Indians, as light cavalry, skirmishing with the Army and with settlers up and down the Dakotas and Montana. George Armstrong Custer was appointed commander of the new 7th Cavalry in 1869. Stationed

first at Chicago (Far Western Command headquarters) they later moved to Fort Abraham Lincoln, Nebraska.

A column of troops moved against Indians on the warpath in the winter of 1869. They reported a large group of Indians encamped on the Washita River. Custer obtained permission for the 505th Balloon Infantry to join the 7th Cavalry. From that day on, the unit was officially Company I (Separate Troops), 7th U.S. Cavalry, though it kept its numerical designation. Also attached to the 7th was the 12th Airship Squadron, as Company J.

Lieutenant Colonel Keogh, acting commander of the 505th for the last twenty-one months, but who had never been on jump status, was appointed by Custer as commander of K Company, 7th Cavalry.

It was known that only the 505th Balloon Infantry and the 12th Airship Squadron were used in the raid on Black Kettle's village. Black Kettle was a treaty Indian, "walking the white man's road." Reports have become garbled in transmission: Custer and the 505th believed they were jumping into a village of hostiles.

The event remained a mystery until Kellogg, the Chicago newspaperman, wrote his account in 1872.[151] The 505th, with Custer in command, flew the three (then numbered, after 1872, named) dirigibles No. 31, No. 76, and No. 93, with seventy-two jumpers each. Custer was in the first "stick" on Airship 76. The three sailed silently to the sleeping village. Custer gave the order to hook up at 5:42 Chicago time, 4:42 local time, and the 505th jumped into the village. Black Kettle's people were awakened when some of the balloon infantry crashed through their teepees, others died in their sleep. One of the first duties of the infantry was to moor the dirigibles; this done, the gunners on the airships opened up on the startled villagers with their Gatling and Agar machine rifles. Black Kettle himself was killed while waving an American flag at Airship No. 93.

After the battle, the men of the 505th climbed back up to the moored dirigibles by rope ladder, and the airships departed for Fort Lincoln. The Indians camped downriver heard the shooting and found horses stampeded during the attack. When they came to the village, they found only slaughter. Custer had taken his dead (three, one of whom died during the jump by being drowned in the Washita) and wounded (twelve) away. They left 307 dead men, women, and children, and 500 slaughtered horses.

There were no tracks leading in and out of the village except those of the frightened horses. The other Indians left the area, thinking the white men had magicked it.

Crazy Horse is said[152] to have visited the area soon after the massacre. It was this action by the 7th which spelled their doom seven years later.

12. Black Man's Hand joined Crazy Horse; so did other former 1st WIW pilots, soon after Crazy Horse's two-plane raid on the airship hangars at Bismark, in 1872. For that mission, Crazy Horse dropped twenty-five-pound fragmentation bombs tied to petrol canisters. The shrapnel ripped the dirigibles, the escaping hydrogen was ignited by the burning petrol: all—hangars, balloons, and maintenance crews—were lost.

It was written up as an unreconstructed Confederate's sabotage; a somewhat ignominious former southern major was eventually hanged on circumstantial evidence. Reports by sentries that they heard aircraft just before the explosions were discounted. At the time, it was believed the only aircraft were those belonging to the Army, and the carefully licensed commercial craft.

13. In 1874, Custer circulated rumors that the Black Hills were full of gold. It has been speculated that this was used to draw miners to the area so the Indians would attack them; then the cavalry would have unlimited freedom to deal with the Red Man.[153] Also that year, those who had become Agency Indians were being shorted in their supplies by members of the scandal-plagued Indian Affairs Bureau under President Grant. When these left the reservations in search of food, the cavalry was sent to "bring them back." Those who were caught were usually killed.

The Sioux ignored the miners at first, expecting the gods to deal with them. When this did not happen, Sitting Bull sent out a party of two hundred warriors, who killed every miner they encountered.

Public outrage demanded reprisals; Sheridan wired Custer to find and punish those responsible.

14. Fearing what was to come, Crazy Horse sent Yellow Dog and Red Chief with a war party of five hundred to raid the rebuilt Fort Phil Kearny. This they did successfully, capturing twelve planes and fuel and ammunition for many more. They hid these in the caverns with the 1st WIW craft.

The Army would not have acted as rashly as it did had it known the planes pronounced missing in the reports on the Kearny raid were being given into the hands of experienced pilots.

The reprisal consisted of airship patrols which strafed any living thing on the plains. Untold thousands of deer and the few remaining buffalo were killed. Unofficial counts list as killed a little more than eight hundred Indians who were caught in the open during the next eight months.

Indians who jumped the agencies and who had seen or heard of the slaughter streamed to Sitting Bull's hidden camp on the Little Big Horn. They were treated as guests, except for the Sansarcs, who camped a little way down the river. It is estimated there were no less than ten thousand Indians, including some four thousand warriors, camped along the river for the Sun Dance ceremony of June 1876.

A three-pronged-pincers movement for the final eradication of the Sioux and Cheyenne worked toward them. The 7th Cavalry, under Keogh and Major Marcus Reno, set out from Fort Lincoln during the last week of May. General George Crook's command was coming up the Rosebud. The gunboat *Far West,* with three hundred reserves and supplies, steamed to the mouth of the Big Horn River. General Terry's command was coming from the northwest. All Indians they encountered were to be killed.

Just before the Sun Dance, Crazy Horse and his pilots got word of the movement of Crook's men up the Rosebud, hurried to the caves, and prepared their craft for flight. Only six planes were put in working condition in time. The other pilots remained behind while Crazy Horse, Black Man's Hand, and four others took to the skies. They destroyed two dirigibles, soundly trounced Crook, and chased his command back down the Rosebud in a rout. The column had to abandon their light armored vehicles and fight its way back, on foot for the most part, to safety.

15. Sitting Bull's vision during the Sun Dance is well known.[154] He told it to Crazy Horse, the warrior who would see that it came true, as soon as the aviators returned to camp.

Two hundred fifty miles away, "Chutes and Saddles" was sounded on the morning of June 23, and the men of the 505th Balloon Infantry climbed aboard the airships *Benjamin Franklin, Samuel Adams, John Hancock,* and *Ethan Allen.* Custer was first man on stick one of the *Franklin.* The *Ethan Allen* carried a scout aircraft which could hook up or detach in flight; the bi-winger was to serve as liaison between the three armies and the airships.

When Custer bade goodbye to his wife, Elizabeth, that morning, both were in good spirits. If either had an inkling of the fate which awaited Custer and the 7th three days away, on the bluffs above a small stream, they did not show it.

The four airships sailed from Fort Lincoln, their silver sides and shark-tooth mouths gleaming in the sun, the eyes painted on the noses looking west. On the sides were the crossed sabers of the cavalry; above the numeral 7; below the numeral 505. It is said that they looked magnificent as they sailed away for their rendezvous with destiny.[155]

16. It is sufficient to say that the Indians attained their greatest victory over the Army, and almost totally destroyed the 7th Cavalry, on June 25-26, 1876, due in large part to the efforts of Crazy Horse and his aviators. Surprise, swiftness, and the skill of the Indians cannot be discounted, nor can the military blunders made by Custer that morning. The repercussions of that summer day rang down the years, and the events are still debated. The only sure fact is that the U.S. Army lost its prestige, part of its spirit, and more than four hundred of its finest soldiers in the battle.

17. While the demoralized commands were sorting themselves

out, the Cheyenne and Sioux left for the Canadian border. They took their aircraft with them, on travois. With Sitting Bull, Crazy Horse and his band settled just across the border. The aircraft were rarely used again until the attack on the camp by the combined Canadian-U.S. Cavalry offensive of 1879. Crazy Horse and his aviators, as they had done so many times before, escaped with their aircraft, using one of the planes to carry their remaining fuel. Two of the nine craft were shot down by a Canadian battery.

Crazy Horse, sensing the end, fought his way, with men on horseback and the planes on travois, from Montana to Colorado. After learning of the death of Sitting Bull and Chief Joseph, he took his small band as close as he dared to Fort Carson, where the cavalry was amassing to wipe out the remaining American Indians.

He assembled his men for the last time. He made his proposal; all concurred and joined him for a last raid on the Army. The five remaining planes came in low, the morning of January 5, 1882, toward the Army airfield. They destroyed twelve aircraft on the ground, shot up the hangars and barracks, and ignited one of the two ammunition dumps of the stockade. At this time, Army gunners manned the William's machine cannon batteries (improved by Thomas Edison's contract scientists) and blew three of the craft to flinders. The war gods must have smiled on Crazy Horse; his aircraft was crippled, the machine rifle was blown askew, the motor slivered, but he managed to set down intact. Black Man's Hand turned away; he was captured two months later, eating cottonwood bark in the snows of Arizona.

Crazy Horse jumped from his aircraft as most of Fort Carson ran toward him; he pulled two Sharps repeating carbines from the cockpit and blazed away at the astonished troopers, wounding six and killing one. His back to the craft, he continued to fire until more than one hundred infantrymen fired a volley into his body.

The airplane was displayed for seven months at Fort Carson before being sent to the Smithsonian in Pittsburgh, where it stands today. Thus passed an era of military aviation.

Lt. Gen. Frank Luke, Jr.
USAF, Ret.

★ ★ ★

From the December 2, 1939, issue of *Collier's Magazine*
Custer's Last Jump?
By A.R. Redmond

Few events in American history have captured the imagination so thoroughly as the Battle of the Little Big Horn. Lieutenant Colonel George Armstrong Custer's devastating defeat at the hands of Sioux and Cheyenne Indians in June 1876 has been rendered time and again by such celebrated artists as George Russell and Frederic Remington. Books, factual and otherwise, which have been written around or about the battle would fill an entire library wing. The motion picture industry has on numerous occasions drawn upon "Custer's Last Jump" for inspiration; latest in a long line of movieland Custers is Errol Flynn, who appears with Olivia deHavilland and newcomer Anthony Quinn in Warner Brother's *They Died with Their Chutes On.*

The impetuous and flamboyant Custer was an almost legendary figure long before the Battle of the Little Big Horn, however. Appointed to West Point in 1857, Custer was placed in command of Troop G, 2nd Cavalry, in June 1861, and participated in a series of skirmishes with Confederate cavalry throughout the rest of the year. It was during the First Battle of Manassas, or Bull Run, that he distinguished himself. He continued to do so in other engagements—at Williamsburg, Chancellorsville, Gettysburg—and rose rapidly through the ranks. He was twenty-six years old when he received a promotion to Brigadier General. He was, of course, immediately dubbed the Boy General. He had become an authentic war hero when the Northerners were in dire need of nothing less during those discouraging months between First Manassas and Gettysburg.

With the cessation of hostilities in the East when Bragg surrendered to Grant at Haldeman, the small hamlet about eight miles from Morehead, Kentucky, Custer requested a transfer of command. He and his young bride wound up at Chicago, manned by the new 7th U.S. Cavalry.

The war in the West lasted another few months; the tattered remnants of the Confederate Army staged last desperate stands throughout Texas, Colorado, Kansas, and Missouri. The final struggle at the Trinity River in October 1867 marked the close of conflict between North and South. Those few Mexican military advisers left in Texas quietly withdrew across the Rio Grande. The French, driven from Mexico in 1864 when Maximilian was ousted, lost interest in the Americas when they became embroiled with the newly united Prussian states.

During his first year in Chicago, Custer familiarized himself with the airships and aeroplanes of the 7th. The only jump-qualified general officer of the war, Custer seemed to have felt no resentment at the ultimate fate of mounted troops boded by the extremely mobile flying machines. The Ohio-born Boy General eventually preferred traveling aboard the airship *Benjamin Franklin,* one of the eight craft assigned to the 505th Balloon Infantry (Troop I, 7th Cavalry, commanded by Brevet Colonel Frederick Benteen) while his horse soldiers rode behind the very capable Captain (Brevet Lt. Col.) Myles Keogh.

The War Department in Pittsburgh did not know that various members of the Plains Indian tribes had been equipped with aeroplanes by the Confederates, and that many had actually flown against the Union garrisons in the West. (Curiously enough, those tribes which held out the longest against the Army—most notably the Apaches under Geronimo in the deep Southwest—were those who did not have aircraft.) The problems of transporting and hiding, to say nothing of maintaining planes, outweighed the advantages. A Cheyenne warrior named Brave Bear is said to have traded his band's aircraft in disgust to Sitting Bull for three horses. Also, many of the Plains Indians hated the aircraft outright, as they had been used by the white men to decimate the great buffalo herds in the early 1860s.

Even so, certain Oglalas, Minneconjous, and Cheyenne did reasonably well in the aircraft given them by the C.S. Army Air Corps Major John S. Moseby, whom the Indians called "The Gray White Man" or "Many-Feathers-in-Hat." The Oglala war chief, Crazy Horse, led the raid on the Bismarck hangars (1872), four months after the 7th Cavalry was transferred to Fort Abraham Lincoln, Dakota

Territory, and made his presence felt at the Rosebud and Little Big Horn in 1876. The Cheyenne, Black Man's Hand, trained by Crazy Horse himself, shot down two Army machines at the Rosebud, and was in the flight of planes that accomplished the annihilation of the 505th Balloon Infantry during the first phase of the Little Big Horn fiasco.

After the leveling of Fort Phil Kearny in February 1869, Custer was ordered to enter the Indian territories and punish those who had sought sanctuary there after the raid. Taking with him 150 parachutists aboard three airships, Custer left on the trail of a large band of Cheyenne.

On the afternoon of February 25, Lieutenant William van W. Reily, dispatched for scouting purposes in a Studebaker bi-winger, returned to report that he had shot up a hunting party near the Washita River. The Cheyenne, he thought, were encamped on the banks of the river some twenty miles away. They appeared not to have seen the close approach of the 7th Cavalry as they had not broken camp.

Just before dawn the next morning, the 505th Balloon Infantry, led by Custer, jumped into the village, killing all inhabitants and their animals.

For the next five years, Custer and the 7th chased the hostiles of the Plains back and forth between Colorado and the Canadian border. Relocated at Fort Lincoln, Custer and an expedition of horse soldiers, geologists, and engineers discovered gold in the Black Hills. Though the Black Hills still belonged to the Sioux according to several treaties, prospectors began to pour into the area. The 7th was ordered to protect them. The Blackfeet, Minneconjous, and Hunkpapa—Sioux who had left the warpath on the promise that the Black Hills, their sacred lands, was theirs to keep for all time—protested, and when protests brought no results, took matters into their own hands. Prospectors turned up in various stages of mutilation, or not at all.

Conditions worsened over the remainder of 1875, during which time the United States Government ordered the Sioux out of the Black Hills. To make sure the Indians complied, airships patrolled the skies of Dakota Territory.

By the end of 1875, plagued by the likes of Crazy Horse's Oglala Sioux, it was decided that there was but one solution to the Plains Indian problem—total extermination.

At this point, General Phil Sheridan, Commander in Chief of the United States Army, began working on the practical angle of this new policy toward the Red Man.

In January 1876, delegates from the Democratic Party approached George Armstrong Custer at Fort Abraham Lincoln and offered him the party's presidential nomination on the condition that he pull off a flashy victory over the red men before the national convention in Chicago in July.

On February 19, 1876, the Boy General's brother, Thomas, commander of Troop C of the 7th, climbed into the observer's cockpit behind Lieutenant James C. Sturgis and took off on a routine patrol. Their aeroplane, a Whitney pusher-type, did not return. Ten days later its wreckage was found sixty miles west of Fort Lincoln. Apparently, Sturgis and Tom Custer had stumbled on a party of mounted hostiles and, swooping low to fire or drop a handbomb, suffered a lucky hit from one of the Indians' firearms. The mutilated remains of the two officers were found a quarter mile from the wreckage, indicating that they had escaped on foot after the crash but were caught.

The shock of his brother's death, combined with the Democrat's offer, were to lead Lieutenant Colonel G.A. Custer into the worst defeat suffered by an officer of the United States Army.

Throughout the first part of 1876, Indians drifted into Wyoming Territory from the east and south, driven by mounting pressure from the Army. Raids on small Indian villages had been stepped up. Waning herds of buffalo were being systematically strafed by the airships. General Phil Sheridan received reports of tribes gathering in the vicinity of the Wolf Mountains, in what is now southern Montana, and devised a strategy by which the hostiles would be crushed for all time.

Three columns were to converge upon the amassed Indians from the north, south, and east, the west being blocked by the Wolf Mountains. General George Crook's dirigibles, light tanks, and infantry were to come up the Rosebud River. General Alfred Terry would push from the northeast with infantry, cavalry, and field artillery. The 7th Cavalry was to move from the east. The Indians could not escape.

Commanded by Captain Keogh, Troops A, C, D, E, F, G, and H of the 7th—about 580 men, not counting civilian teamsters, interpreters, Crow and Arikara scouts—set out from Fort Lincoln five weeks ahead of the July 1 rendezvous at the junction of the Big Horn and Little Big Horn rivers. A month later, Custer and 150 balloon infantrymen aboard the airships *Franklin, Adams, Hancock,* and *Allen* set out on Keogh's trail.

Everything went wrong from that point onward.

The early summer of 1876 had been particularly hot and dry in Wyoming Territory. Crook, proceeding up the Rosebud, was slowed by the tanks, which theoretically traveled at five miles per hour but which kept breaking down from the heat and from the alkaline dust which worked its way into the engines through chinks in the three-inch armor plate. The crews roasted. On June 13, as Crook's column halted beside the Rosebud to let the tanks cool off, six monoplanes dived out of the clouds to attack the escorting airships, *Paul Revere* and *John Paul Jones.* Caught by surprise, the two dirigibles were blown up and fell about five miles from Crook's position. The infantrymen watched, astonished, as the Indian aeronauts turned their craft toward them. While the foot soldiers ran for cover, several hundred mounted Sioux warriors showed up. In the ensuing rout, Crook lost forty-seven men and all his armored vehicles. He was still in headlong retreat when the Indians broke off their chase at nightfall.

The 7th Cavalry and the 505th Balloon Infantry linked up by liaison craft carried by the *Ethan Allen* some miles southeast of the hostile camp on the Little Big Horn on the evening of June 24. Neither they, nor Terry's column, had received word of Crook's retreat, but Keogh's scouts had sighted a large village ahead.

Custer did not know that this village contained not the five or six hundred Indians expected, but between eight and ten *thousand,* of whom slightly less than half were warriors. Spurred by his desire for revenge for his brother, Tom, and filled with glory at the thought of the Democratic presidential nomination, Custer decided to hit the

Indians before either Crook's or Terry's columns could reach the village. He settled on a scaled-down version of Sheridan's tri-pronged movement, and dispatched Keogh to the south, Reno to the east, with himself and the 505th attacking from the north. A small column was to wait downriver with the pack train. On the evening of June 24, George Armstrong Custer waited, secure in the knowledge that he, personally, would deal the Plains Indians their mortal blow within a mere twenty-four hours.

Unfortunately, the Indians amassed on the banks of the Little Big Horn—Oglalas, Minneconjous, Arapaho, Hunkpapas, Blackfeet, Cheyenne, and so forth—had the idea that white men were on the way. During the Sun Dance Ceremony the week before, the Hunkpapa chief Sitting Bull had had a dream about soldiers falling into his camp. The hostiles, assured of victory, waited.

On the morning of June 25, the *Benjamin Franklin, Samuel Adams, John Hancock,* and *Ethan Allen* drifted quietly over the hills toward the village. They were looping south when the Indians attacked.

Struck by several spin-stabilized rockets, the *Samuel Adams* blew up with a flash that might have been seen by the officers and men riding behind Captain Keogh up the valley of the Little Big Horn. Eight or twelve Indians had, in the gray dawn, climbed for altitude above the ships.

Still several miles short of their intended drop zone, the balloon infantrymen piled out of the burning and exploding craft. Though each ship was armed with two Gatling rifles fore and aft, the airships were helpless against the airplanes' bullets and rockets. Approximately one hundred men, Custer included, cleared the ships. The Indian aviators made passes through them, no doubt killing several in the air. The *Franklin* and *Hancock* burned and fell to the earth across the river from the village. The *Allen,* dumping water ballast to gain altitude, turned for the Wolf Mountains. Though riddled by machine rifle fire, it did not explode and settled to earth about fifteen miles from where now raged a full-scale battle between increasingly demoralized soldiers and battle-maddened Sioux and Cheyenne.

Major Reno had charged the opposite side of the village as soon as he heard the commotion. Wrote one of his officers later: "A solid wall of Indians came out of the haze which had hidden the village from our eyes. They must have outnumbered us ten to one, and they were ready for us . . . Fully a third of the column was down in three minutes."

Reno, fearing he would be swallowed up, pulled his men back across the river and took up a position in a stand of timber on the riverward slope of the knoll. The Indians left a few hundred braves to make certain Reno did not escape and moved off to Reno's right to descend on Keogh's flank.

The hundred-odd parachute infantrymen who made good their escape from the airship were scattered over three square miles. The ravines and gullies cutting up the hills around the village quickly filled with mounted Indians who rode through unimpeded by the random fire of disorganized balloon infantrymen. They swept them up, on the way to Keogh. Keogh, unaware of the number of Indians and the rout of Reno's command, got as far as the north bank of the river before he was ground to pieces between two masses of hostiles. Of Keogh's command, less than a dozen escaped the slaughter. The actual battle lasted about thirty minutes.

The hostiles left the area that night, exhausted after their greatest victory over the soldiers. Most of the Indians went north to Canada; some escaped the mass extermination of their race which was to take place in the American West during the next six years.

Terry found Reno entrenched on the ridge the morning of the twenty-seventh. The scouts sent to find Custer and Keogh could not believe their eyes when they found the bodies of the 7th Cavalry six miles away.

Some of the men were not found for another two days, Terry and his men scoured the ravines and valleys. Custer himself was about four miles from the site of Keogh's annihilation; the Boy General appears to have been hit by a piece of exploding rocket shrapnel and may have been dead before he reached the ground. His body escaped the mutilation that befell most of Keogh's command, possibly because of its distance from the camp.

Custer's miscalculation cost the Army 430 men, four dirigibles (plus the Studebaker scout from the *Ethan Allen*), and its prestige. An attempt was made to make a scapegoat of Major Reno, blaming his alleged cowardice for the failure of the 7th. Though Reno was acquitted, grumblings continued up until the turn of the century. It is hoped the matter will be settled for all time by the opening, for private research, of the papers of the late President Phil Sheridan. As Commander in Chief, he had access to a mountain of material which was kept from the public at the time of the court of inquiry in 1879.

★ ★ ★

Extract from *Huckleberry Among the Hostiles: A Journal*
By Mark Twain, Edited By Bernard Van Dyne
Hutton and Company, New York, 1932

Editor's note: In November 1886, Clemens drafted a tentative outline for a sequel to *The Adventures of Huckleberry Finn*, which had received mixed reviews on its publication in January 1885, but which had nonetheless enjoyed a second printing within five months of its release. The proposed sequel was intended to deal with Huckleberry's adventures as a young man on the frontier. To gather research material firsthand, Mark boarded the airship *Peyton* in Cincinnati, Ohio, in mid-December 1886, and set out across the Southwest, amassing copious notes and reams of interviews with soldiers, frontiersmen, law enforcement officers, ex-hostiles, at least two notorious outlaws, and a number of less readily categorized persons. Twain had intended to spend four months out West. Unfortunately, his wife, Livy, fell gravely ill in late February 1887; Twain returned to her as soon as he received word in Fort Hood, Texas. He lost interest in all writing for two years after her death in April 1887. The proposed novel about Huckleberry Finn as a man was never written; we are left with 110,000 words of interviews and observations, and an incomplete journal of the author's second trek across the American West.—BvD

★ ★ ★

February 2: A more desolate place than the Indian Territory of

Oklahoma would be impossible to imagine. It is flat the year 'round, stingingly cold in winter, hot and dry, I am told, during the summer (when the land turns brown save for scattered patches of greenery which serve only to make the landscape all the drearier; Arizona and New Mexico are devoid of greenery, which is to their credit—when those territories elected to become barren wastelands they did not lose heart halfway, but followed their chosen course to the end).

It is easy to see why the United States Government swept the few Indians into God-forsaken Oklahoma, and ordered them to remain there under threat of extermination. The word "God-forsaken" is the vital clue. The white men who "gave" this land to the few remaining tribes for as long as the wind shall blow—which it certainly does in February—and the grass shall grow (which it does, in Missouri, perhaps) were Christians who knew better than to let heathen savages run loose in parts of the country still smiled upon by our heavenly malefactor.

February 4: Whatever I may have observed about Oklahoma from the cabin of the *Peyton* has been reinforced by a view from the ground. The airship was running into stiff winds from the north, so we put in at Fort Sill yesterday evening and are awaiting calmer weather. I have gone on with my work.

Fort Sill is located seventeen miles from the Cheyenne Indian reservation. It has taken me all of a day to learn (mainly from one Sergeant Howard, a gap-toothed, unwashed Texan who is apparently my unofficial guardian angel for whatever length of time I am to be marooned here) that the Cheyenne do not care much for Oklahoma, which is still another reason why the government keeps them there. One or two ex-hostiles will leave the reservation every month, taking with them their wives and meager belongings, and Major Rickards will have to send out a detachment of soldiers to haul the erring ones back, either in chains or over the backs of horses. I am told the reservation becomes particularly annoying in the winter months, as the poor boys who are detailed to pursue the Indians suffer greatly from the cold. At this, I remarked to Sergeant Howard that the red man can be terribly inconsiderate, even ungrateful, in view of all the blessings the white man has heaped upon him—smallpox, and that French disease, to name two. The good sergeant scratched his head and grinned, and said, "You're right, sir."

I'll have to make Howard a character in the book.

February 5: Today, I was taken by Major Rickards to meet a Cheyenne named Black Man's Hand, one of the participants of the alleged massacre of the 7th Cavalry at the Little Big Horn River in '76. The major had this one Cheyenne brought in after a recent departure from the reservation. Black Man's Hand had been shackled and left to dwell upon his past misdeeds in an unheated hut at the edge of the airport, while two cold-benumbed privates stood on guard before the door. It was evidently feared this one savage would, if left unchained, do to Fort Sill that which he (with a modicum of assistance from four or five thousand of his race) had done to Custer. I nevertheless mentioned to Rickards that I was interested in talking to Black Man's Hand, as the Battle of the Little Big Horn would perfectly climax Huckleberry's adventures in the new book. Rickards was reluctant to grant permission but gave in abruptly, perhaps fearing I would model a villain after him.

Upon entering the hut where the Cheyenne sat, I asked Major Rickards if it were possible to have the Indian's manacles removed, as it makes me nervous to talk to a man who can rattle his chains at me whenever he chooses. Major Rickards said no and troubled himself to explain to me the need for limiting the movement of this specimen of ferocity within the walls of Fort Sill.

With a sigh, I seated myself across from Black Man's Hand and offered him one of my cigars. He accepted it with a faint smile. He appeared to be in his forties, though his face was deeply lined. He was dressed in ragged leather leggings, thick calf-length woolen pajamas, and a faded Army jacket. His vest appears to have been fashioned from an old parachute harness. He had no hat, no footgear, and no blanket.

"Major Rickards," I said, "this man is freezing to death. Even if he isn't, I am. Can you provide this hut with a little warmth?"

The fretting major summarily dispatched one of the sentries for firewood and kindling for the little stove sitting uselessly in the corner of the hut.

I would have been altogether comfortable after that could I have had a decanter of brandy with which to force out the inner chill. But Indians are notoriously incapable of holding liquor, and I did not wish to be the cause of this poor wretch's further downfall.

Black Man's Hand speaks surprisingly good English. I spent an hour and a half with him, recording his remarks with as much attention paid to accuracy as my advanced years and cold fingers permitted. With luck, I'll be able to fill some gaps in his story before the *Peyton* resumes its flight across this griddlecake countryside.

Extract from *The Testament of Black Man's Hand*
[Note: for the sake of easier reading, I have substituted a number of English terms for these provided by the Cheyenne Black Man's Hand.—MT]

I was young when I first met the Oglala mystic Crazy Horse, and was taught by him to fly the Thunderbirds which the one called the Gray White Man had given him. [The Gray White Man—John S. Moseby, Major, CSAAC—MT] Some of the older men among the People [as the Cheyenne call themselves, Major Rickards explains; I assured him that such egocentricity is by no means restricted to savages—MT] did not think much of the flying machines and said, "How will we be able to remain brave men when this would enable us to fly over the heads of our enemies, without counting coup or taking trophies?"

But the Oglala said, "The Gray White Man has asked us to help him."

"Why should we help him?" asked Two Pines.

"Because he fights the blueshirts and those who persecute us. We have known for many years that the men who cheated us and lied to us and killed our women and the buffalo are men without honor, cowards who fight only because there is no other way for them to get what they want. They cannot understand why we fight with the Crows and Pawnees—to be brave, to win honor for ourselves. They fight because it is a means to an end, and they fight us only because we have what they want. The blueshirts want to kill us all. They fight to win. If we are to fight them, we must fight with their own weapons. We must fight to win."

The older warriors shook their heads sorrowfully and spoke of younger days when they fought the Pawnees bravely, honorably, man-to-man. But I and several other young men wanted to learn how to control the Thunderbirds. And we knew Crazy Horse spoke the truth, that our lives would never be happy as long as there were white men in the world. Finally, because they could not forbid us to go with the Oglala, only advise against it and say that the Great Mystery had not intended us to fly, Red Horse and I and some others went with Crazy Horse. I did not see my village again, not even at the big camp on the Greasy Grass [Little Big Horn—MT] where we rubbed out Yellow Hair. I think perhaps the blueshirts came after I was gone and told Two Pines that he had to leave his home and come to this flat dead place.

The Oglala Crazy Horse taught us to fly the Thunderbirds. We learned a great many things about the Gray White Man's machines. With them, we killed Yellowleg flyers. Soon, I tired of the waiting and the hunger. We were raided once. It was a good fight. In the dark, we chased the Big Fish [the Indian word for dirigibles—MT] and killed many men on the ground.

I do not remember all of what happened those seasons. When we were finally chased away from the landing place, Crazy Horse had us hide the Thunderbirds in the Black Hills. I have heard the Yellowlegs did not know we had the Thunderbirds; that they thought they were run by the gray white men only. It did not matter; we thought we had used them for the last time.

Many seasons later, we heard what happened to Black Kettle's village. I went to the place sometime after the battle. I heard that Crazy Horse had been there and seen the place. I looked for him but he had gone north again. Black Kettle had been a treaty man: we talked among ourselves that the Yellowlegs had no honor.

It was the winter I was sick [1872. The Plains Indians and the U.S. Army alike were plagued that winter by what we would call the influenza. It was probably brought by some itinerant French trapper—MT] that I heard of Crazy Horse's raid on the landing place of the Big Fish. It was news of this that told us we must prepare to fight the Yellowlegs.

When I was well, my wives and I and Eagle Hawk's band went looking for Crazy Horse. We found him in the fall. Already, the Army had killed many Sioux and Cheyenne that summer. Crazy Horse said we must band together, we who knew how to fly the Thunderbirds. He said we would someday have to fight the Yellowlegs among the clouds as in the old days. We only had five Thunderbirds which had not been flown many seasons. We spent the summer planning to get more. Red Chief and Yellow Dog gathered a large band. We raided the Fort Kearny and stole many Thunderbirds and canisters of power. We hid them in the Black Hills. It had been a good fight.

It was at this time Yellow Hair sent out many soldiers to protect the miners he had brought in by speaking false. They destroyed the sacred lands of the Sioux. We killed some of them, and the Yellowlegs burned many of our villages. That was not a good time. The Big Fish killed many of our people.

We wanted to get the Thunderbirds and kill the Big Fish. Crazy Horse had us wait. He had been talking to Sitting Bull, the Hunkpapa chief. Sitting Bull said we should not go against the Yellowlegs yet, that we could only kill a few at a time. Later, he said, they would all come. That would be the good day to die.

The next year, they came. We did not know until just before the Sun Dance [about June 10, 1876—MT] that they were coming. Crazy Horse and I and all those who flew the Thunderbirds went to get ours. It took us two days to get them going again, and we had only six Thunderbirds flying when we flew to stop the blueshirts. Crazy Horse, Yellow Dog, American Gun, Little Wolf, Big Tall, and I flew that day. It was a good fight. We killed two Big Fish and many men and horses. We stopped the Turtles-which-kill [that would be the light armored cars Crook had with him on the Rosebud River—MT] so they could not come toward the Greasy Grass where we camped. The Sioux under Spotted Pony killed more on the ground. We flew back and hid the Thunderbirds near camp.

When we returned, we told Sitting Bull of our victory. He said it was good, but that a bigger victory was to come. He said he had had a vision during the Sun Dance. He saw many soldiers and enemy Indians fall out of the sky on their heads into the village. He said ours was not the victory he had seen.

It was some days later we heard that a Yellowlegs' Thunderbird had been shot down. We went to the place where it lay. There was a strange device above its wing. Crazy Horse studied it many moments. Then he said, "I have seen such a thing before. It carries Thunderbirds beneath one of the Big Fish. We must get our Thunderbirds. It will be a good day to die."

We hurried to our Thunderbirds. We had twelve of them fixed now, and we had on them, besides the quick rifles [Henry machine rifles of calibers .41-40 or .30-30—MT], the roaring spears [Hale spin-stabilized rockets, of 2½-inch diameter—MT]. We took off before noonday.

We arrived at the Greasy Grass and climbed into the clouds, where we scouted. Soon, to the south, we saw the dust of many men moving. But Crazy Horse held us back. Soon we saw why: four Big Fish were coming. We came at them out of the sun. They did not see us till we were on them. We fired our roaring sticks, and the Big Fish caught fire and burned. All except one, which drifted away, though it lost all its fat. Wild Horse, in his Thunderbird, was shot but still fought on with us that morning. We began to kill the men on the Big Fish when a new thing happened. Men began to float down on blankets. We began to kill them as they fell with our quick rifles. Then we attacked those who reached the ground, until we saw Spotted Pony and his men were on them. We turned south and killed many horse soldiers there. Then we flew back to the Greasy Grass and hid the Thunderbirds. At camp, we learned that many pony soldiers had been killed. Word came that more soldiers were coming.

I saw, as the sun went down, the women moving among the dead Men-Who-Float-Down, taking their clothes and supplies. They covered the ground like leaves in the autumn. It had been a good fight.

"So much has been written about that hot June day in 1876, so much guesswork applied where knowledge was missing. Was Custer dead in his harness before he reached the ground? Or did he stand and fire at the aircraft strafing his men? How many reached the ground alive? Did any escape the battle itself, only to be killed by Indian patrols later that afternoon, or the next day? No one really knows, and all the Indians are gone now, so history stands a blank.

"Only one thing is certain: for the men of the 7th Cavalry there was only the reality of the exploding dirigibles, the snap of their chutes deploying, the roar of the aircraft among them, the bullets, and those terrible last moments on the bluff. Whatever the verdict of their peers, whatever the future may reveal, it can be said they did not die in vain."

The Seventh Cavalry: A History
E.R. Burroughs
Colonel, U.S.A., Retired

★ ★ ★

SUGGESTED READING

Anonymous. *Remember Ft. Sumter!* Washington: War Department Recruiting Pamphlet, 1862.

— *Leviathans of the Skies.* Goodyear Publications, 1923.

— *The Dirigible in War and Peace.* Goodyear Publications, 1911.

— *Sitting Bull, Killer of Custer.* G.E. Putnam's, 1903.

— *Comanche of the Seventh.* Chicago: Military Press, 1879.

— *Thomas Edison and the Indian Wars.* Menlo Park, N.J.: Edison Press, 1921.

— "Fearful Slaughter at Big Horn." New York: *Herald-Times,* July 8, 1876, *et passim.*

— *Custer's Gold Hoax.* Boston: Barnum Press, 1892.

— "Reno's Treachery: New Light on the Massacre at The Little Big Horn." Chicago: *Daily News-Mirror,* June 12-19, 1878.

— "Grant Scandals and the Plains Indian Wars." *Life,* May 3, 1921.

— *The Hunkpapa Chief Sitting Bull,* Famous Indians Series #3. New York: 1937.

Arnold, Henry H. *The Air War in the East,* Smithsonian Annals of Flight, Vol. 38. Four books, 1932-37.

1. Sumter To Bull Run

2. Williamsburg to Second Manassas

3. Gettysburg to the Wilderness

4. The Bombing of Atlanta to Haldeman

Ballows, Edward. *The Indian Ace: Crazy Horse.* G. E. Putnam's, 1903.

Benteen, Capt. Frederick. *Major Benteen's Letters to his Wife.* University of Oklahoma Press, 1921.

Brininstool, A.E. *A Paratrooper with Custer,* n.p.g., 1891.

Burroughs, Col. E.R. retired. *The Seventh Cavalry: A History.* Chicago: 1931.

Clair-Britner, Edoard. *Haldeman: Where the War Ended.* Frankfort University Press, 1911.

Crook, General George C. *Yellowhair: Custer as the Indians Knew Him.* Cincinnati Press, 1882.

Custer, George A. *My Life on the Plains and in the Clouds.* Chicago: 1874

—and Custer, Elizabeth. *'Chutes and Saddles.* Chicago: 1876.

Custer's Luck, n.a., n.p.g., [1891]

De Camp, L. Sprague and Pratt, Fletcher. *Franklin's Engine: Mover of the World.* Hanover House, 1939.

De Voto, Bernard. *The Road From Sumter.* Scribners, 1931.

Elsee, D.V. *The Last Raid of Crazy Horse.* Random House, 1921.

The 505th: History From the Skies. DA Pamphlet 870-10-3 GPO Pittsburgh, May 12, 1903.

FM 23-13-2 Machine Rifle M3121A1 and M3121A1E1 Cal. .41-40 Operator's Manual, DA FM, July 12, 1873.

Goddard, Robert H. *Rocketry: From 400 B.C. to 1933.* Smithsonian Annals of Flight, Vol. 31, GPO Pittsburgh, 1934.

Guide to the Custer Battlefield National Monument. U.S. Parks Services, GPO Pittsburgh, 1937.

The Indian Wars. 3 vols, GPO Pittsburgh, 1898.

Kalin, David. *Hook Up! The Story of the Balloon Infantry.* New York: 1932.

Kellogg, Mark W. *The Drop at Washita.* Chicago: *Times Press,* 1872.

Lockridge, Sgt. Robert. *History of the Airborne: From Shiloh to Ft. Bragg.* Chicago: Military Press, 1936.
Lowe, Thaddeus C. *Aircraft of the Civil War.* 4 vols. 1891-96.
McCoy, Col. Tim. *The Vanished American.* Phoenix Press, 1934.
McGovern, Maj. William. *Death in the Dakotas.* Sioux Press, 1889.
Morison, Samuel Eliot. *France in the New World 1627-1864.* 1931.
Myren, Gundal. *The Sun Dance Ritual and the Last Indian Wars.* 1901.
Patton, Gen. George C. *Custer's Last Campaigns.* Military House, 1937.
Paul, Winston. *We Were There at the Bombing of Ft. Sumter.* Landmark Books, 1929.
Payley, David. *Where Custer Fell.* New York Press, 1931.
Powell, Maj. John Wesley. *Report on the Arid Lands.* GPO, 1881.
Proceedings, Reno Court of Inquiry. GPO Pittsburgh, 1881.
Report on the U.S.-Canadian Offensive against Sitting Bull, 1879. GPO Pittsburgh, War Department, 1880.
Sandburg, Carl. *Mr. Lincoln's Airmen.* Chicago: Driftwind Press, 1921.
Settle, Sgt. Maj. Winslow. *Under the Crossed Sabers.* Military Press, 1898.
Sheridan, Gen. Phillip. *The Only Good Indian . . .* Military House, 1889.
Singleton, William Warren. *J.E.B. Stuart, Attila of the Skies.* Boston, 1871.
Smith, Gregory. *The Grey White Man: Moseby's Expedition to the Northwest 1863-1866.* University of Oklahoma Press, 1921.
Smith, Neldoo. *He Gave Them Wings: Captain Smith's Journal 1861-1864.* Urbana: University of Illinois Press, 1927.
Steen, Nelson. *Opening of the West.* Jim Bridger Press, 1902.
Tapscott, Richard D. *He Came With the Comet.* University of Illinois Press, 1927.
Twain, Mark. *Huckleberry Among the Hostiles: A Journal.* Hutton Books, 1932.

PROJECT HUSH

by William Tenn

Published in 1954, this story of one of the most momentous events of the 20th century is a satirical gem that still deserves to be read even though, as we all know, things didn't happen that way. Or do *we know? After all, if it* had *happened this way, that would probably still be classified.*

★ ★ ★

***William Tenn** (1920-2010) was the pen name of Philip Klass (not to be confused with Philip J. Klass, the aerospace writer) who began writing SF and fantasy in the late 1940s, and was one of the brightest writers of the 1950s, particularly with his stories in* Galaxy *(where this story originally appeared). Along with other irreverent writers (notably Robert Sheckley, Fritz Leiber, and Evelyn E. Smith), Tenn set the tone of* Galaxy *as a home for wit and satire. During World War II, he served in the U.S. Army as a combat engineer in Europe, and later was a technical editor with the Air Force radar and radio laboratory, and probably had an abundance of first-hand experience with the military's passion for classifying everything that it can. Of course, any information about his experiences is probably classified.*

═ ★ ═

I guess I'm just a stickler, a perfectionist, but if you do a thing, I always say, you might as well do it right. Everything satisfied me about the security measures on our assignment except one—the official Army designation.

Project Hush.

I don't know who thought it up, and I certainly would never ask, but whoever it was, he should have known better. Damn it, when you want a project kept secret, you *don't* give it a designation like that! You give it something neutral, some name like the Manhattan and Overlord they used in World War II, which won't excite anybody's curiosity.

But we were stuck with Project Hush and we had to take extra measures to ensure secrecy. A couple of times a week, everyone on the project had to report to Psycho for DD & HA—dream detailing and hypnoanalysis—instead of the usual monthly visit. Naturally, the commanding general of the heavily fortified research post to which we were attached could not ask what we were doing, under penalty of court-martial, but he had to be given further instructions to shut off his imagination like a faucet every time he heard an explosion. Some idiot in Washington was actually going to list Project Hush in the military budget by name! It took fast action, I can tell you, to have it entered under Miscellaneous "X" Research.

Well, we'd covered the unforgivable blunder, though not easily, and now we could get down to the real business of the project. You know, of course, about the A-bomb, H-bomb, and C-bomb because information that they existed had been declassified. You don't know about the other weapons being devised—and neither did we, reasonably enough, since they weren't our business—but we had been given properly guarded notification that they were in the works. Project Hush was set up to counter the new weapons.

Our goal was not just to reach the Moon. We had done that on June 24, 1967, with an unmanned ship that carried instruments to report back data on soil, temperature, cosmic rays and so on. Unfortunately, it was put out of commission by a rock slide.

An unmanned rocket would be useless against the new weapons. We had to get to the Moon before any other country did and set up a permanent station—an armed one—and do it without anybody else knowing about it.

I guess you see now why we on *(damn* the name!) Project Hush were so concerned about security. But we felt pretty sure, before we took off, that we had plugged every possible leak.

We had, all right. Nobody even knew we had raised ship.

We landed at the northern tip of Mare Nubium, just off Regiomontanus, and, after planting a flag with appropriate throat-catching ceremony, had swung into the realities of the tasks we had practiced on so many dry-runs back on Earth.

Major Monroe Gridley prepared the big rocket, with its tiny cubicle of living space, for the return journey to Earth which he alone would make.

Lieutenant-Colonel Thomas Hawthorne painstakingly examined our provisions and portable quarters for any damage that might have been incurred in landing.

And I, Colonel Benjamin Rice, first commanding officer of Army Base No. 1 on the Moon, dragged crate after enormous crate out of the ship on my aching academic back and piled them in the spot two hundred feet away where the plastic dome would be built.

We all finished at just about the same time, as per schedule, and went into Phase Two.

Monroe and I started work on building the dome. It was a simple prefab affair, but big enough to require an awful lot of assembling. Then, after it was built, we faced the real problem—getting all the complex internal machinery in place and in operating order.

Meanwhile, Tom Hawthorne took his plump self off in the single-seater rocket which, up to then, had doubled as a lifeboat.

The schedule called for him to make a rough three-hour scouting survey in an ever-widening spiral from our dome. This had been regarded as a probable waste of time, rocket fuel, and manpower—but a necessary precaution. He was supposed to watch for such things as bug-eyed monsters out for a stroll on the Lunar landscape. Basically, however, Tom's survey was intended to supply extra geological and astronomical meat for the report which Monroe was to carry back to Army Headquarters on Earth.

Tom was back in forty minutes. His round face, inside its

transparent bubble helmet, was fish-belly white. And so were ours, once he told us what he'd seen.

He had seen another dome.

"The other side of Mare Nubium—in the Riphaen Mountains," he babbled excitedly. "It's a little bigger than ours, and it's a little flatter on top. And it's not translucent, either, with splotches of different colors here and there—it's a dull, dark, heavy gray. But that's all there is to see."

"No markings on the dome?" I asked worriedly. "No signs of anyone—or anything—around it?"

"Neither, Colonel." I noticed he was calling me by my rank for the first time since the trip started, which meant he was saying in effect, "Man, have *you* got a decision to make!"

"Hey, Tom," Monroe put in. "Couldn't be just a regularly shaped bump in the ground, could it?"

"I'm a geologist, Monroe. I can distinguish artificial from natural topography. Besides—" he looked up—"I just remembered something I left out. There's a brand-new tiny crater near the dome—the kind usually left by a rocket exhaust."

"Rocket exhaust?" I seized on that. "*Rockets,* eh?"

Tom grinned a little sympathetically. "Spaceship exhaust, I should have said. You can't tell from the crater what kind of propulsive device these characters are using. It's not the same kind of crater our rear jets leave, if that helps any."

Of course it didn't. So we went into our ship and had a council of war. And I do mean war. Both Tom and Monroe were calling me Colonel in every other sentence. I used their first names every chance I got.

Still, no one but me could reach a decision. About what to do, I mean.

"Look," I said at last, "here are the possibilities. They know we are here—either from watching us land a couple of hours ago or from observing Tom's scoutship—or they do not know we are here. They are either humans from Earth—in which case they are in all probability enemy nationals—or they are alien creatures from another planet—in which case they may be friends, enemies or what-have-you. I think common sense and standard military procedure demand that we consider them hostile until we have evidence to the contrary. Meanwhile, we proceed with extreme caution, so as not to precipitate an interplanetary war with potentially friendly Martians, or whatever they are.

"All right. It's vitally important that Army Headquarters be informed of this immediately. But since Moon-to-Earth radio is still on the drawing boards, the only way we can get through is to send Monroe back with the ship. If we do, we run the risk of having our garrison force, Tom and me, captured while he's making the return trip. In that case, their side winds up in possession of important information concerning our personnel and equipment, while our side has only the bare knowledge that somebody or something else has a base on the Moon. So our primary need is more information.

"Therefore, I suggest that I sit in the dome on one end of a telephone hookup with Tom, who will sit in the ship, his hand over the firing button, ready to blast off for Earth the moment he gets the order from me. Monroe will take the single-seater down to the Riphaen Mountains, landing as close to the other dome as he thinks safe. He will then proceed the rest of the way on foot, doing the best scouting job he can in a spacesuit.

"He will not use his radio, except for agreed-upon nonsense syllables to designate landing the single-seater, coming upon the dome by foot, and warning me to tell Tom to take off. If he's captured, remembering that the first purpose of a scout is acquiring and transmitting knowledge of the enemy, he will snap his suit radio on full volume and pass on as much data as time and the enemy's reflexes permit. How does that sound to you?"

They both nodded. As far as they were concerned, the command decision had been made. But I was sitting under two inches of sweat.

"One question," Tom said. "Why did you pick Monroe for the scout?"

"I was afraid you'd ask that," I told him. "We're three extremely non-athletic Ph.D.s who have been in the Army since we finished our schooling. There isn't too much choice. But I remembered that

Monroe is half-Indian—Arapahoe, isn't it, Monroe?—and I'm hoping blood will tell."

"Only trouble, Colonel," Monroe said slowly as he rose, "is that I'm *one-fourth* Indian and even that . . . Didn't I ever tell you that my great-grandfather was the only Arapahoe scout who was with Custer at the Little Big Horn? He'd been positive Sitting Bull was miles away. However, I'll do my best. And if I heroically don't come back, would you please persuade the Security Officer of our section to clear my name for use in the history books? Under the circumstances, I think it's the least he could do."

I promised to do my best, of course.

After he took off, I sat in the dome over the telephone connection to Tom and hated myself for picking Monroe to do the job. But I'd have hated myself just as much for picking Tom. And if anything happened and I had to tell Tom to blast off, I'd probably be sitting here in the dome all by myself after that, waiting . . .

"Broz neggle!" came over the radio in Monroe's resonant voice. He had landed the single-seater.

I didn't dare use the telephone to chat with Tom in the ship, for fear I might miss an important word or phrase from our scout. So I sat and sat and strained my ears. After a while, I heard *"Mishgashu!"* which told me that Monroe was in the neighborhood of the other dome and was creeping toward it under cover of whatever boulders were around.

And then, abruptly, I heard Monroe yell my name and there was a terrific clattering in my headphones. Radio interference! He'd been caught, and whoever had caught him had simultaneously jammed his suit transmitter with a larger transmitter from the alien dome.

Then there was silence.

After a while, I told Tom what had happened. He just said, "Poor Monroe." I had a good idea of what his expression was like.

"Look, Tom," I said, "if you take off now, you still won't have anything important to tell. After capturing Monroe, whatever's in that other dome will come looking for us, I think. I'll let them get close enough for us to learn something of their appearance—at least if they're human or non-human. Any bit of information about them is important. I'll shout it up to you and you'll still be able to take off in plenty of time. All right?"

"You're the boss, Colonel," he said in a mournful voice. "Lots of luck."

And then there was nothing to do but wait. There was no oxygen system in the dome yet, so I had to squeeze up a sandwich from the food compartment in my suit. I sat there, thinking about the expedition. Nine years, and all that careful secrecy, all that expenditure of money and mind-cracking research—and it had come to this. Waiting to be wiped out, in a blast from some unimaginable weapon. I understood Monroe's last request. We often felt we were so secret that our immediate superiors didn't even want *us* to know what we were working on. Scientists are people—they wish for recognition, too. I was hoping the whole expedition would be written up in the history books, but it looked unpromising.

Two hours later, the scout ship landed near the dome. The lock opened and, from where I stood in the open door of our dome, I saw Monroe come out and walk toward me.

I alerted Tom and told him to listen carefully. "It may be a trick—he might be drugged . . . ."

He didn't act drugged, though—not exactly. He pushed his way past me and sat down on a box to one side of the dome. He put his booted feet up on another, smaller box.

"How are you, Ben?" he asked. "How's every little thing?"

I grunted. "*Well?*" I know my voice skittered a bit.

He pretended puzzlement. "Well *what?* Oh, I see what you mean. The other dome—you want to know who's in it. You have a right to be curious, Ben. Certainly. The leader of a top-secret expedition like this—Project Hush they call us, huh, Ben—finds another dome on the Moon. He thinks he's been the first to land on it, so naturally he wants to—"

"Major Monroe Gridley!" I rapped out. "You will come to attention and deliver your report. Now!" Honestly, I felt my neck swelling up inside my helmet.

Monroe just leaned back against the side of the dome. “That’s the *Army* way of doing things,” he commented admiringly. “Like the recruits say, there’s a right way, a wrong way and an Army way. Only there are other ways, too.” He chuckled. “Lots of other ways.”

“He’s off,” I heard Tom whisper over the telephone. “Ben, Monroe has gone and blown his stack.”

“They aren’t extraterrestrials in the other dome, Ben,” Monroe volunteered in a sudden burst of sanity. “No, they’re human, all right, and from Earth. Guess *where.*”

“I’ll kill you,” I warned him. “I swear I’ll kill you, Monroe. Where are they from—Russia, China, Argentina?”

He grimaced. “What’s so secret about those places? Go on—guess again.”

I stared at him long and hard. “The only place else—”

“Sure,” he said. “You got it, Colonel. The other dome is owned and operated by the Navy. The goddam United States Navy!”

THE DAY THEY GOT BOSTON
by Herbert Gold

Here's a sparkling and witty account of an accidental nuclear exchange. Of course, Fail-Safe *used the same idea, though seriously, and* Dr. Strangelove *also played it for laughs, but Herbert Gold was there first, poking fun at the age of Mutual Assured Destruction. (Before someone points out that Peter Bryan George's 1958 novel,* Red Alert, *was the basis for* Dr. Strangelove, *I'll mention that* Red Alert *was another deadly serious treatment of the idea, and the resultant Kubrick flick bears scant resemblance to it.)*

★ ★ ★

Herbert Gold *was born in Cleveland, Ohio, in 1924, and moved to New York when he was 17. At Columbia University, he studied philosophy and was a friend of several Beat Generation writers, such as Allen Ginsberg and Anais Nin. On a Fulbright fellowship, he did graduate studies at the Sorbonne in Paris. While there, he wrote his first novel,* Birth of a Hero, *which was published in 1951. He has written more than thirty books and received the Sherwood Anderson Award for Fiction, the Commonwealth Club Gold Medal, and the PEN Oakland Josephine Miles Literary Award. His latest novel is* When a Psychopath Falls in Love. *He has taught at the University of California at Berkley, at Stanford, Cornell, and Harvard. He lives in San Francisco. And, if I may insert a clarification, he is* not *H. L. Gold (whose "H" stood for Horace), the celebrated editor of* Galaxy *magazine in the 1950s.*

═ ★ ═

Even before the missile struck, their leader went on the air to apologize.

"First," he said, "have you heard the story about the constipated Eskimo with the ICBM? But let's be serious a moment. It isn't our fault! One of our lieutenants got drunk, and the rubber band holding a bunch of punch cards broke, and the card stamped BOSTON fell into place—a combination of human and mechanical factors, friends. . . ."

(It landed with sweet accuracy in a patch of begonias in the Commons. The entire city was decimated and the sea rushed through to take its place. Cambridge and Harvard University also lay under atomic waste and the tidal wave.)

"WE'RE SORRY!" sobbed their leader. "Truly, sincerely sorry. The lieutenant has been sent to Siberia. His entire family, under the progressive Anti-Fascist Soviet penal reform policy, has joined him for rehabilitation therapy in the salt mines. All the rubber bands in the entire Anti-Fascist Workers for Peace and Democracy Missile Control Network are being screened for loyalty. I feel terribly humble and sincere this evening. It's the triumph of brute accident over Man's will, which aft gang agley, as our poet Mayakovsky once put it. We're sorry, friends across the mighty sea! Nothing like this must ever happen again."

Our reprisal system had not gone into action at once for two reasons: (a) A first wild rumor that Cuba had at last declared war on us, and, (b) Man, we just, like, *hesitated.* (Who can tell if those blips on the radar screen really mean anything? I mean, like, you make a mistake and *POW,* I mean . . . And then the hometown newspaper really gets after you.) This fear of the hometown paper, this hesitation may have saved the universe from an immediate holocaust. Castro made no promises, but said that his barbados were ready and waiting in front of their teevees.

The U.S. of A. lay in a state of shock. A powerful faction of skilled psychiatric observers argued that this instance of national catatonic neurosis was justified more by external event than by internal oedipal conflict. Many people had close relatives in Boston—not everybody, but enough to justify the virus of gloom which seemed to be making the rounds. The American League would have to replace a team just as the season began. The roads from New York to Maine were in bad shape.

Their Leader shrieked, "Don't retaliate, my friends. My dear friends. Don't Retaliate. We will send reparations, delegations of workers, peasants, and intellectuals, petitions of condolence; the Kharkov soccer team will play out the Red Sox schedule. But don't retaliate, or we will be led to destroy each other utterly, dialectically! It was a mistake! Could happen to anyone! His pals gave a little birthday party for this here lieutenant, see, you know how it is, they drank it up a little, and then these rubber bands tend to become crispy with age . . ."

Harvard gone. Boston beans homeless. A churning hole in American history.

The mayor of Boston, Ukrainian Socialist Soviet Republic, sent a telegram to the mayor of Boston, Tennessee:

EXTEND HEARTFELT REGRETS AND SYMPATHY TO THE PEACE-LOVING WORKERS OF THE UNITED STATES ON OCCASION OF TRAGIC DISAPPEARANCE OF ONE OF ITS OLDEST CITIES. AS AMERICAN POET W. WHITMAN SAID, "BAA BAA BLACK SHEEP LET NOTHING YOU DISMAY." AZONOVITCH, MAYOR, NOW LARGEST BOSTON IN WORLD.

By a miracle, both Radcliffe and Wellesley were spared. However, there were no men for the coming Spring Weekend. By another miracle, due to the influence of radioactive—er—the scientists had been attending a conference at Boston University—the Radcliffe students were now physically entitled to console the Wellesley girls in their deep mourning at Spring Weekend.

"A miracle!" cried Norman Vincent Peale, joining with their Leader in an appeal to forgive and forget. "We are being tested from on high. What happened at Radcliffe on that turbulent occasion is proof positive that there is a power in the universe making for righteousness, and also for intergroup balance with special reference to sexual harmony."

"DO NOT RETALIATE," cried out their Leader, and he was joined in this appeal by their foremost ballet dancers, film directors, and violinists. They also made proud reference to their other rubber bands, punched cards, and lieutenants with a bead on New York, Washington, Chicago, Cleveland, Detroit, Denver, Los Angeles, and every American city down to the size of Rifle City, Colorado. "If you retaliate, we are all doomed to become epiphenomena floating in a Marxist-Leninist Anti-Fascist Outer Space." (Were they threatening us again?)

Senator Morris Russell, D., of Colorado, was one of the first to recover his senses. "Of course it was an accident," he said. "Lieutenants will be lieutenants and accidents will happen, ha ha. But we can't allow this sort of accident. How will it look in the eyes of the rest of the world? Those yellow hordes to the East are very conscious of Face, y'know. America has lost enough face already, what with the corruption in television quiz shows and the disorganization of our youth in those coffee-drinking espresso parlors. We must strike a blow for peace by wiping out Moscow!"

WE COULDN'T AGREE MORE, WITH OUR BOY MORRIE, declared a banner held up by all the residents of Rifle City, Colorado. It happened that none of them had relatives in Boston and so they could speak uncorrupted by grief or other private interest. Their sheriff had divested himself of his stock in the Boston & Maine Railroad. Their rage and sense of national dignity was expressed with typical, folkloristic Western dignity. They called each other "Slim" and "Buster" at meetings, sang Yippee-Yi-yo-cow-yay, and urged immediate decimation of the entire European continent. (They were a little weak on geography and wanted to make sure that the Roosians got theirs.)

Our Side hesitated.

Their Side went on the air with round-the-clock telethons. Mothers in Dnieprpotrovsk sent quilts with quaint illustrations from Baba-Yaga and other classical Russian tales to the few survivors in Waltham and Weldon. The Chief of Staff of their anti-fascist atomic service announced that he was going into a retreat on the Caucasus for two weeks of contemplation. A publicity release from their

Embassy in Washington announced that his favorite hobbies were Reading, Tennis, and the Beat Generation, in that order, and that his wife, who was retreating with him, liked American musicals and collected Capezio shoes. One of their composers was preparing a memorial symphony, entitled, "The Lowells Speak Only to God"; one of their critics was already preparing his attack on the symphony as formalistic, abstract, and unrooted in Russian folk themes.

We waited. Their Leader wept openly, live on tape, and the tape was broadcast every hour.

The clamor for revenge and forgiveness, forgiveness and revenge, wracked the nation, indeed, the entire world. The citizens of Avignon, France, sent an elementary geography textbook as a civic contribution to the public library of Rifle City, Colorado.

Only the drunken lieutenant in Siberia failed to appear in public. He persisted in telling his colleagues in the First Disciplinary and Re-Education Unit (Iodized Division): "Ya glad. Ya ochen pleased with myself. Sure it was a mistake (oshibka), but it was one of those slips which reveal one's unconscious thoughts (Rus., micl; Fr., pensées). My analyst tells me that deep within my semi-Tartar soul I hate Boston (BocmoH), I have always hated Boston (BocmoH), I even hate the memory of Boston (BocmoH), ever since I failed my Regents on the question where was the tea party at which the proletarian masses refused to serve the colonial imperialists. Now I am free, free, free!"*

He was given occupational therapy, including modern dance, during the rest periods from his duties in the salt mine. It was not actually a "salt mine"; it now produced, as part of the five-year plan to upgrade consumer products, an all-purpose seasoning called Tangh! (TaHk!).

The first crisis passed. Our advanced missile bases, our round-the-clock air fleets, our ICBM installations held back their Sunday punch. It was Tuesday, and they waited. "Halt! Stop! Whoa there fellas!" went out the order. Their Leader's emotional display reached us in time and made contact with the true, big-hearted America, which loves person-to-person contact. The Buffalo Red Sox were

---

* "Svoboda, svoboda, svoboda!"

hastily but reverently appointed to play out the American League schedule. Surrounding areas in Massachusetts were quarantined. The moral question about whether the former Radcliffe girls, miraculously spared but radically altered, could be permitted to carry out their new impulses—this was debated in every surviving pulpit of New England. Some claimed the transmogrification as an instance of divine punishment, others thought it a logical triumph of feminism, still others felt that we should live and let live, of whatever sex might develop . . . Under the pressure of world events, a decision was postponed about the appropriateness of the Spring Dance at Wellesley. As its contribution to rehabilitation therapy, the Aqua-Velva company sent a tank car of after shave to the Radcliffe dormitories.

Meanwhile, back in Washington and Moscow, the lights burned late. High-level negotiations proceeded with deliberate haste. "Who's practicing brinkmanship now?" jeered our Secretary of State.

Their Man hung his head. He was genuinely abashed. He declared that he was "sorry" and "ashamed," but what he really meant in American was "humble" and "sincere." As a matter of fact, his son had been visiting at Harvard on the night of the Regrettable Incident, catching a revival of "Alexander Nevsky" at an art movie in Cambridge, and this happenstance, of great personal significance to the Ambassador, was often recalled at difficult moments in the continuing negotiations.

It was clear that neither our national pride, nor the opinion of the rest of the world, nor—and this new factor surprised all commentators—the swelling sense of guilt within the Soviet Union, would allow the disaster to pass without some grave consequences. To an astonishing degree, a wave of fellowship spread between the two nations. In Kamenetz-Podolsk it was recalled that a Russian had fought by the side of our General Vashinktohn. In Palo Alto it was recalled that Herbert Hoover had personally fed millions of starving moujiks in 1919, and had returned to America with badly nibbled fingers.

"All right," said their Ambassador, in secret session, "since you feel that way, we'll give you Kharkov. We have a major university there, too."

"No," said our people, "not big enough. Harvard was recognized as tops here. We want Moscow. We need Moscow. There was a beautiful modern library, entirely air conditioned, at Harvard. Moscow it must be."

"Impossible," said their man. "That would be like doing Washington, D.C. Justice is one thing, but that's our capital and it's got to come out even, give or take a million. My son, my son (sob)." He pulled himself together and continued, "Don't forget, our Asiatic, subhuman, totalitarian population is got feelings of national pride, too. How about Kharkov plus this list of small towns in Biro-Bidjan, pick any one of three?"

Our Men shook their heads. (By dint of prolonged fret and collaboration, plus the prevailing wind out of Massachusetts, our team had only one head. Radcliffe-like changes were being worked as far south as Daytona, Florida. The Radcliffe situation was causing riots in girls' schools of the mid-south. They also wanted some.)

At any rate, Kharkov was definitely out. It meant too little to the irate citizens of Rifle City, and the small towns of Biro-Bidjan meant too much to certain minority groups important in electing the Republican senator from New York.

Vladivostok?

"No," we said. (Nyet.) A mere provincial center.

Stalingrad?

"No." Big enough, but the university could only be said to equal Michigan State. And what are Stalingrad Baked Beans to the Russian national cuisine?

"Ah," said their man, kissing his joined fingertips, "mais le kasha de Stalingrad!"

No. They were mere buckwheat groats to us.

"Leningrad?" they finally offered in desperation. "We understand how you feel. It is our second city, and it was founded by Peter the Great in a thrilling moment well described by Eisenstein in a movie of the same name. We want to do anything we can! . . ."

Wires hummed, diplomatic pouches were stuffed, the matter was settled with extraordinary unanimity and good feeling. Our people and theirs celebrated by drinking a toast to the memory of Boston, another to the memory of Leningrad—

—although their bereaved Ambassador, who also, as luck would have it, happened to have a son studying Fine Arts at the University of Leningrad, stealthily emptied his glass in a potted palm . . .

And at that moment, according to agreement and plan, the City of Leningrad disappeared from this earth. We used a type of hydrogen engine previously only tested in the south Pacific. It exploded as brilliantly in the frozen north as it did under the soft flowered breezes of the southern trade routes. (Our Air Force was careful to avoid the mistake which had caused so many unsuccessful launchings in the past. They put Winter Weight Lube in the rocket motors.)

The wails of Russian mothers could be heard the world round, also live on tape.

Abruptly the citizens of Rifle City, Colorado, began to have solemn afterthoughts. The Sheriff made a speech, declaring, "No manne is an islande, entire of theirselfe. Everie manne is a part of the maine, including Slim over there. Them Russkies got feelings of sibling affection, too." Dozens of quilts thrown together by the mothers of Rifle City were air-lifted to the environs of Leningrad. Gallant little Finland, which had been destroyed by mistake, also received our apologies and a couple of quilts. (In honor of Sibelius, Finland would be accorded diplomatic representation equal with that given nationalist China. Most of the surviving Finns were already in their ministries scattered about the world.)

Our President went on the air to plead through his tears, "Don't Re . . . Don't Re . . ." The teleprompter was eventually cranked by hand. "Taliate," he sobbed.

Their Leader also went on the air to explain to the grief-stricken mass that this act of national propitiation had been fully discussed by proper authority in both nations. Calm, he urged. Pax Vobiscum, pronounced a puppet head of the Russian Orthodox Church. "Thank you for that comment," said their Leader.

Murmurings of nepotism made his position insecure for a time. His nephew had been recalled from duty in Leningrad only a scant twenty-four hours before the American missile struck (exactly on target, by the way). However, he pointed out that both his aged mother and his sister had been residents of the departed Flower of the North, and Freudian science was so poorly developed that this explanation silenced the rabble.

For a time, peace and world fellowship. A new cooperation, decontamination, courtesy. Parades, requiem masses, memorial elegies. Historians, poets, and painters, both objective and non-objective, were kept busy assimilating the new subject matter. "POTLATCH FOR THE MILLIONS" was the title of a popular exposition of the theoretical bases of the new method of handling international disputes. In schools of International Relations, this science began to earn course credit as Potlatch 101 (The Interlinked Destruction of Cities) and Potlatch 405 (Destruction of Civilizations, open only to graduate students).

President DeGaulle warned that France could not consent to being left out of any solution aiming to resolve international tension. The gothic (or romanesque, as the case might be) cities of France the Immortel, united in purpose, were ready to be weighed by Justice on her scale of the future as they had been hefted in her hands in the marketplace of history. From the right came a concrete proposal: "Wow, let 'em take Algeria, Mon Cher."

The state of beatitude was of brief duration, for hard is the way of Man on earth.

A Russian malcontent wrote a letter to the editor of *Pravda* signed, "Honored Artist of the Republic," and soon the word had passed all the way to their highest authority. Certainly, the intention on both sides had been honorable, with the highest consideration for basic human values.

Both Boston and Leningrad had been major ports. Fine.

Both Boston and Leningrad had housed major universities. Excellent.

Both Boston and Leningrad, metropoli of the north, gave summer arts festivals on the green. Beautiful.

With relation to historical memories, real estate values, and cultural expectations, they were perhaps as similar in importance as could be found. However . . .

And a full delegation from their Presidium of Trade Unions urged that negotiations be reopened on this question. Leningrad had also been, unlike Boston, a center of the Soviet cinema industry.

"Perhaps," they suggested, timidly at first, "you could give us South California, too?"

Of course, soon they would begin to insist.

THE GENTLE EARTH
by Christopher Anvil

With their advanced military technology, the invaders were sure that their conquest of Earth would be a straightforward operation. But they hadn't taken human nature into account. Worse, they hadn't taken Mother Nature *into account.*

★ ★ ★

Christopher Anvil *was the pseudonym under which Harry C. Crosby, Jr. (1925-2009) published all but his first two short stories, which appeared in the magazine* Imagination *in 1952 and 1953. His story, "The Prisoner," appeared in* Astounding Science-Fiction. *That was the beginning of an avalanche of stories for* Astounding *(and* Analog, *as the magazine was retitled in 1960) which combined fast-paced adventure plots with a pointed satirical sensibility, puncturing dogmas and bureaucracies, both human and alien. His stories in* Astounding/Analog *frequently took first place in the magazine's reader polls, and were nominated for Hugo and Nebula awards. His work also appeared in such SF magazines as* Galaxy *and* Amazing Stories. *"The Gentle Earth" appeared in* Astounding *in 1957 and is one of his best.*

═ ★ ═

Tlasht Bade, Supreme Commander of Invasion Forces, drew thoughtfully on his slim cigar. "The scouts are all back?"

Sission Runckel, Chief of the Supreme Commander's Staff, nodded. "They all got back safely, though one or two had difficulties with some of the lower life forms."

"Is the climate all right?"

Runckel abstractedly reached in his tunic, and pulled out a thing like a short piece of tarred rope. As he trimmed it, he scowled. "There's some discomfort, apparently because the air is too dry. But on the other hand, there's plenty of oxygen near the planet's surface, and the gravity's about the same as it is back home. We can live there."

Bade glanced across the room at a large blue, green, and brown globe, with irregular patches of white at top and bottom. "What are the white areas?"

"Apparently, chalk. One of our scouts landed there, but he's in practically a state of shock. The brilliant reflectivity in the area blinded him, a huge white furry animal attacked him, and he barely got out alive. To cap it all, his ship's insulation apparently broke down on the way back, and now he's in the sick bay with a bad case of space-gripe. All we can get out of him is that he had severe prickling sensations in the feet when he stepped out onto the chalk dust. Probably a pile of little spiny shells."

"Did he bring back a sample?"

"He claims he did. But there's only water in his sample box. I imagine he was delirious. In any case, this part of the planet has little to interest us."

Bade nodded. "What about the more populous regions?"

"Just as we thought. A huge web of interconnecting cities, manufacturing centers, and rural areas. Our mapping procedures have proved to be accurate."

"That's a relief. What about the natives?"

"Erect, land-dwelling, ill-tempered bipeds," said Runckel. "They seem to have little or no planet-wide unity. Of course, we have large samplings of their communications media. When these are all analyzed, we'll know a lot more."

"What do they look like?"

"They're pink or brown in color, quite tall, but not very broad or thick through the chest. A little fur here and there on their bodies.

No webs on their hands or feet, and their feet are fantastically small. Otherwise, they look quite human."

"Their technology?"

Runckel sucked in a deep breath and sat up straight. "Every bit as bad as we thought." He picked up a little box with two stiff handles, squeezed the handles hard, and touched a glowing wire on the box to his piece of black rope. He puffed violently.

Bade turned up the air-conditioning. Billowing clouds of smoke drew away from Runckel in long streamers, so that he looked like an island looming through heavy mist. His brow was creased in a foreboding scowl.

"Technologically," he said, "they are deadly. They've got fission and fusion, indirect molecular and atomic reaction control, and a long-reaching development of electron flow and pulsing devices. So far, they don't seem to have anything based on deep rearrangement or keyed focusing. But who knows when they'll stumble on that? And then what? Even now, properly warned and ready they could give us a terrible struggle."

Runckel knocked a clinker off his length of rope and looked at Bade with the tentative, judging air of one who is not quite sure of another's reliability. Then he said, loudly and with great firmness, "We have a lot to be thankful for. Another five or ten decades delay getting the watchships up through the cloud layer, and they'd have had us by the throat. We've got to smash them before they're ready, or *we'll* end up as *their* colony."

Bade's eyes narrowed. "I've always opposed this invasion on philosophical grounds. But it's been argued and settled. I'm willing to go along with the majority opinion." Bade rapped the ash off his slender cigar and looked Runckel directly in the eyes. "But if you want to open the whole argument up all over again—"

"No," said Runckel, breathing out a heavy cloud of smoke. "But our micromapping and radiation analysis shows a terrific rate of progress. It's hard to look at those figures and even breathe normally. They're gaining on us like a shark after a minnow."

"In that case," said Bade, "let's wake up and hold our lead. This business of attacking the suspect before he has a chance to commit a crime is no answer. What about all the other planets in the universe? How do we know what they might do some day?"

"This planet is right beside us!"

"Is murder honorable as long as you do it only to your neighbor? Your argument is self-defense. But you're straining it."

"Let it strain, then," said Runckel angrily. "All I care about is that chart showing our comparative levels of development. Now *we* have the lead. I say, drag them out by their necks and let them submit, or we'll thrust their heads underwater and have done with them. And anyone who says otherwise is a doubtful patriot!"

Bade's teeth clamped, and he set his cigar carefully on a tray.

Runckel blinked, as if he only appreciated what he had said by its echo.

Bade's glance moved over Runckel deliberately, as if stripping away the emblems and insignia. Then Bade opened the bottom drawer of his desk, and pulled out a pad of dun-colored official forms. As he straightened, his glance caught the motto printed large on the base of the big globe. The motto had been used so often in the struggle to decide the question of invasion that Bade seldom noticed it any more. But now he looked at it. The motto read:

Them Or Us

Bade stared at it for a long moment, looked up at the globe that represented the mighty planet, then down at the puny motto. He glanced at Runckel, who looked back dully but squarely. Bade glanced at the motto, shook his head in disgust, and said, "Go get me the latest reports."

Runckel blinked. "Yes, sir," he said, and hurried out.

Bade leaned forward, ignored the motto, and thoughtfully studied the globe.

Bade read the reports carefully. Most of them, he noted, contained a qualification. In the scientific reports, this generally appeared at the end:

" . . . Owing to the brief time available for these observations, the conclusions presented herein must be regarded as only provisional in character."

In the reports of the scouts, this reservation was usually presented in bits and pieces:

" . . . And this thing, that looked like a tiny crab, had a pair of pincers on one end, and I didn't have time to see if this was the end it got me with, or if it was the other end. But I got a jolt as if somebody squeezed a lighter and held the red-hot wire against my leg. Then I got dizzy and sick to my stomach. I don't know for sure if this was what did it, or if there are many of them, but if there are, and if it did, I don't see how a man could fight a war and not be stung to death when he wasn't looking. But I wasn't there long enough to be sure . . ."

Another report spoke of a "Crawling army of little six-legged things with a set of oversize jaws on one end, that came swarming through the shrubbery straight for the ship, went right up the side and set to work eating away the superplast binder around the viewport. With that gone, the ship would leak air like a fishnet. But when I tried to clear them away, they started in on me. I don't know if this really proves anything, because Rufft landed not too far away, and he swears the place was like a paradise. Nevertheless, I have to report that I merely set my foot on the ground, and I almost got marooned and eaten up right on the spot."

Bade was particularly uneasy over reports of a vague respiratory difficulty some of the scouts noticed in the region where the first landings were planned. Bade commented on it, and Runckel nodded.

"I know," said Runckel. "The air's too dry. But if we take time to try to provide for that, at the same time they may make some new advance that will more than nullify whatever we gain. And right now their communications media show a political situation that fits right in with our plans. We can't hope for that to last forever."

Bade listened as Runckel described a situation like that of a dozen hungry sharks swimming in a circle, each getting its jaws open for a snap at the next one's tail. Then Runckel described his plan.

At the end, Bade said, "Yes, it may work out as you say. But listen,

Runckel, isn't this a little too much like one of those whirlpools in the Treacherous Islands? If everything works out, you go through in a flash. But one wrong guess, and you go around and around and around and around and you're lucky if you get out with a whole skin."

Runckel's jaw set firmly. "This is the only way to get a clear-cut decision."

Bade studied the far wall of the room for a moment. "I'm sorry I didn't get a hand at these plans sooner."

"Sir," said Runckel, "You would have, if you hadn't been so busy fighting the whole idea." He hesitated, then asked, "Will you be coming to the staff review of plans?"

"Certainly," said Bade.

"Good," said Runckel. "You'll see that we have it all worked to perfection."

Bade went to the review of plans and listened as the details were gone over minutely. At the end, Runckel gave an overall summary:

"The Colony Planet," he said, rapping a pointer on maps of four hemispheric views, "is only seventy-five percent water, so the land areas are immense. The chief land masses are largely dominated by two hostile power groups, which we may call East and West. At the fringes of influence of these power groups live a vast mass of people not firmly allied to either.

"The territory of this uncommitted group is well suited to our purposes. It contains many pleasant islands and comfortable seas. Unfortunately, analysis shows that the dangerous military power groups will unite against us if we seize this territory directly. To avoid this, we will act to stun and divide them at one stroke."

Runckel rapped his pointer on a land area lettered "North America," and said, "On this land mass is situated a politico-economic unit known as the U.S. The U.S. is the dominant power both in the Western Hemisphere and in the West power group. It is surrounded by wide seas that separate it from its allies.

"Our plan is simple and direct. We will attack and seize the central plain of the U.S. This will split it into helpless fragments, any one of which we may crush at will. The loss of the U.S. will, of course, destroy the power balance between East and West. The East will immediately seize the scraps of Western power and influence all over the globe.

"During this period of disorder, we will set up our key-tool factories and a light-duty forceway network. In rapid stages will then come ore-converters, staging plants, fabricators, heavy-duty forceway stations and self-operated production units. With these last we will produce energy-conversion units and storage piles by the million in a network to blanket the occupied area. The linkage produced will power our damper units to blot out missile attacks that may now begin in earnest.

"We will thus be solidly established on the planet itself. Our base will be secure against attack. We will now turn our energies to the destruction of the U.S.S.R. as a military power." He reached out with his pointer to rap a new land mass.

"The U.S.S.R. is the dominant power of the East power group. This will by now be the only hostile power group remaining on the planet. It will be destroyed in stages.

"In Stage I we will confuse the U.S.S.R. by propaganda. We will profess friendship while we secretly multiply our productive facilities to the highest possible degree.

"In Stage II, we will seize and fortify the western and northern islands of Britain, Novaya Zemlya, and New Siberia. We will also seize and heavily fortify the Kamchatka Peninsula in the extreme eastern U.S.S.R. We will now demand that the U.S.S.R. lay down its arms and surrender.

"In the event of refusal, we will, from our fortified bases, destroy by missile attack all productive facilities and communication centers in the U.S.S.R. The resulting paralysis will bring down the East power group in ruins. The planet will now lay open before us."

Runckel looked at each of his listeners in turn.

"Everything has been done to make this invasion a success. To crush out any possible miscalculation, we are moving with massive reserves close behind us. Certain glory and a mighty victory await us.

"Let us raise our heads in prayer, then join in the Oath of Battle."

★ ★ ★

The first wave of the attack came down like an avalanche on the central U.S. Multiple transmitters went into action to throw local radar stations into confusion. Stull-gas missiles streaked from the landing ships to explode over nearby cities. Atmospheric flyers roared off to intercept possible enemy attacks. A stream of guns, tanks, and troop carriers rolled down the landing ways and fanned out to seize enemy power plants and communications centers.

The commander of the first wave reported: "Everything proceeding according to plan. Enemy resistance negligible."

Runckel ordered the second wave down.

Bade, watching it on a number of giant viewscreens in the operations room of a ship coming down, had a peculiar feeling of numbness, such as might follow a deep cut before the pain is felt.

Runckel, his face intense, said: "Their position is hopeless. The main landing site is secure and the rest will come faster than the eye can see." He turned to speak into one of a bank of microphones, then said, "Our glider missiles are circling over their capital."

A loud-speaker high on the wall said, "Landing minus three. Take your stations, please."

The angle of vision of one of the viewscreens tilted suddenly, to show a high, dome-topped building set in a city filled with rushing beetle shapes—obviously ground-cars of some type. Abruptly these cars all pulled to the sides of the streets.

"That," said Runckel grimly, "means their capital is out of business."

The picture on the viewscreen blurred suddenly, like the reflection from water ruffled by a breeze. There was a clang like a ten-ton hammer hitting a twenty-ton gong. Walls, floor, and ceiling of the room danced and vibrated. Two of the viewscreens went blank.

Bade felt a prickling sensation travel across his shoulders and down his back. He glanced sharply at Runckel.

Runckel's expression looked startled but firm. He reached out and snapped orders into one of his microphones.

There was an intense, high-pitched ringing, then a clap like a nuclear cannon of six paces distance.

The wall loud-speaker said, "Landing minus two."

An intense silence descended on the room. One by one, the viewscreens flickered on. Bade heard Runckel say, "The ship is totally damped. They haven't anything that can get through it."

There was a dull, low-pitched thud, a sense of being snapped like a whip, and the screens went blank. The wall loud-speaker dropped, and jerked to a stop, hanging by its cord.

Then the ship set down.

Runckel's plan assumed that the swift-moving advance from the landing site would overrun a sizable territory during the first day. With this maneuvering space quickly gained, the landing site itself would be safe from enemy ground attack by dawn of the second day.

Now that they were down, however, Bade and Runckel looked at the operations room's big viewscreen, and saw their vehicles standing still all over the landscape. The troops crowded about the rear of the vehicles to watch cursing drivers pull the motors up out of their housings and spread them out on the ground. Here and there a stern officer argued with grim-faced troops who stared stonily ahead as if they didn't hear. Meanwhile, the tanks, trucks, and weapons carriers stood motionless.

Runckel, infuriated, had a cluster of microphones gripped in his hand, and was pronouncing death by strangling and decapitation on any officer who failed to get his unit in motion right away.

Bade studied the baffled expressions on the faces of the drivers, then glanced at the enemy ground-cars abandoned at the side of the road. He turned to see a tall officer with general's insignia stagger through the doorway and grip Runckel by the arm. Bade recognized Rast, General Forces Commander.

"Sir," said Rast, "it can't be done."

"It has to be done," said Runckel grimly. "So far we've decoyed the enemy missiles to a false site. Before they spot us again, *those troops have got to be spread out*!"

"They won't ride in the vehicles!"

"It's that or get killed!"

"Sir," said Rast, "you don't understand. I came back here in a gun carrier. To start with, the driver jammed the speed lever all the way to the front shield, and nothing happened. He got up to see what was wrong. The carrier shot ahead with a flying leap, threw the driver into the back, and almost snapped our heads off. Then it coasted to a stop. We pulled ourselves together and turned around to get the cover off the motor box.

"*Wham!* The carrier took off, ripped the cover out of our hands, threw us against the rear shield and knocked us senseless. Then it rolled to a stop.

"That's how we got here. Jump! Roll. Stop. Wait. Jump! Roll. Stop. Wait. On one of those jumps, the gun went out the back of the carrier, mount, bolts, and all. The driver swore he'd turn off the motor, and fangjaw take the planet and the whole invasion. We aren't going to win a war with troops in that frame of mind."

Runckel took a deep breath.

Bade said, "What about the enemy's ground-cars? Will they run?"

Rast blinked. "I don't know. Maybe—"

Bade snapped on a microphone lettered "Aerial Rec." A little screen in a half-circle atop the microphone lit up to show an alert, harried-looking officer. Bade said, "You've noticed our vehicles are stopped?"

"Yes, sir."

"Were the enemy's ground-cars affected at the same time as ours?"

"No sir, they were still moving after ours were stuck."

"Any motor trouble in Atmospheric Flyer Command?"

"None that I know of, sir."

Bade glanced at Rast. "Try using the enemy ground-cars. Meanwhile, get the troops you can't move back under cover of the ships' dampers."

Rast saluted, whirled, and went out at a staggering run.

Bade called Atmospheric Flyer Command, and Ground Forces Maintenance, and arranged for the captured enemy vehicles to be identified by a large yellow X painted across the top of the hood. Then he turned to Runckel and said, "We're going to need all the support we can get. See if we can bring Landing Force 2 down late today instead of tomorrow."

"I'll try," said Runckel.

It seemed to Bade that the events of the next twenty-four hours unrolled like the scenes of a nightmare.

Before the troops were all under cover, an enemy reconnaissance aircraft leaked in very high overhead. The detector screens of Atmospheric Flyer Command were promptly choked with enemy aircraft coming in low and fast from all directions.

These aircraft were of all types. Some heaved their bombs in under-hand, barreled over and streaked home for another load. Others were flying hives of anti-aircraft missiles. A third type were suicide bombers or winged missiles; these roared in head-on and blew up on arrival.

While the dampers labored and overheated, and Flyer Command struggled with enemy fighters and bombers overhead, a long-range reconnaissance flyer spotted a sizable convoy of enemy ground forces rushing up from the southwest.

Bade and Runckel concentrated first on living through the air attack. It soon developed that the enemy planes, though extremely fast, were not very maneuverable. The enemy's missiles did not quite overload the dampers. The afternoon wore on in an explosive violence that was severe, but barely endurable. It began to seem that they might live through it.

Toward evening, however, a small enemy missile streaked in on the end of a wire and smashed the grid of an auxiliary damper unit. Before this unit could be repaired, a heavy missile came down near the same place, and overloaded the damper network. Another missile streaked in. One of the ships tilted, and fell headlong. The engines of this ship were ripped out of the circuit that powered the dampers. With the next enemy missile strike, another ship was heaved off its base. This ship housed a large proportion of Flyer Command's detector screens.

Bade and Runckel looked at each other. Bade's lips moved, and he heard himself say, "Prepare to evacuate."

At this moment, the enemy attack let up.

★ ★ ★

It took an instant for Bade to realize what had happened. He canceled his evacuation order before it could be transmitted, then had the two thrown ships linked back into the power circuit. He turned around, and his glance fell on one of the viewscreens showing the shadowy plain outside. A brilliant flash lit the screen, and he saw dark low shapes rushing in toward the ships. Bade immediately gave orders to defend against ground attack, but not to pursue beyond range of the dampers.

A savage, half-lit struggle developed. The enemy, whose weapons failed to work in range of the dampers, attacked with bayonets, and used guns, shovels, and picks in the manner of clubs and battle axes. In a spasm of bloody violence they fought their way in among the ships, then, confused in the dimness, were thrown back with heavy losses. As night settled down, the enemy dug in to make a fortified ring close around the landing site.

The enemy missile attack failed to recover its former violence.

Bade gave silent thanks for the deliverance. As the comparative quiet continued, it seemed clear that the enemy high command was holding back to avoid hitting their own men dug in nearby.

It occurred to Bade that now might be a good time to get a little sleep. He turned to go to his cot, and there was a rush of yellow dots on Flyer Command's pilot screen. As he stared wide-eyed, auxiliary screens flickered on and off to show a ghostly dish-shaped object that led his flyers on a wild chase all over the sky, then vanished at an estimated speed twenty times that the enemy planes were thought capable of doing.

Runckel said, "Landing Force 2 can get here at early dawn. That's the best we can manage."

Bade nodded dully.

The ground screens now lit in brilliant flashes as the enemy began firing monster rockets at practically point-blank range.

Night passed in a continuous bombardment.

At early dawn of the next day, Bade put in all his remaining missiles, and bomber and interceptor flyers. For a brief interval of time, the enemy bombardment was smothered.

Landing force 2 sat down beside Landing Force 1.

Bade ordered the Stull-gas missiles of Landing Force 2 exploded over the enemy ground troops. In the resulting confusion, the ground forces moved out and captured large numbers of enemy troops, weapons, and vehicles. The captured vehicles were marked and promptly put to use.

Bade spoke briefly with General Rast, commanding the ground forces.

"Now's your chance," said Bade. "Move fast and we can capture supplies and reinforcements flowing in, before they realize we've broken their ring."

Under the protection of the flyers of Landing Force 2, Rast's troops swung out onto the central plain of the North American continent.

The advance moved fast. Enemy troops and supply convoys were caught off guard on the road. When the enemy fought, his resistance was patchy and confused.

Bade, feeling drugged from lack of sleep, lay down on his cot for a nap. He awoke feeling fuzzy-brained and dull.

"They're whipped," said Runckel gleefully. "We've got back the time we lost yesterday. There's no resistance to speak of. And we've just made a treaty with the East bloc."

Bade sat up dizzily. "That's wonderful," he said. He glanced at the clock. "Why wasn't I called sooner?"

"No need," said Runckel. "It's all just a matter of form. Landing Force 3 is coming down tonight. The war's over." Runckel's face, as he said this, had a peculiar shine.

Bade frowned. "Isn't the enemy making any reaction at all?"

"Nothing worth mentioning. We're driving them ahead of us like a school of minnows."

Bade got to his feet uneasily. "It can't be this simple." He stepped out into the operations room and detected unmistakable signs of holiday jubilation. Nearly everyone was grinning, and gawkers were standing in a thick ring before the screen showing the map room's latest plot.

Bade said sharply, "Don't these men have anything to do?" His voice carried across the room with the effect of a shark surfacing in the midst of a ladies' swimming party. Several of the men at the map jumped. Others glanced around jerkily. There was a concerted bumping of elbows, and the ring of gawkers evaporated briskly in all directions. In every part of the room there was abruptly something approaching a businesslike atmosphere.

Bade looked around angrily and sat down at his desk. Then he saw the map. He squeezed his eyes shut, then looked again.

In the center of the map of North America was a big blot, as if a bottle of red ink had been thrown at it. Bade turned to Runckel and asked harshly, "Is that map correct?"

"Absolutely," said Runckel, his face shining with satisfaction.

Bade looked back at the map and performed a series of rapid calculations. He glanced at the viewscreens, and saw that those which would normally show the advanced ground troops weren't in use. This, he supposed, meant that the advance had outrun the technical crews.

Bade snapped on a microphone lettered "Supply, Ground." In the half-circle atop the microphone appeared an officer in the last stage of sleepless exhaustion. The officer's eyes twitched, and his skin had a drawn dull look. His head was slumped on his hand.

"*Supply*?" said Bade in alarm.

"Sorry," mumbled the officer, "we can't do it. We're overstretched already. Try Flyer Command. Maybe they'll parachute it to you."

Bade switched off, and glanced at the map again. He turned to Runckel. "Listen, what are we using for transport?"

"The enemy ground-cars."

"Fast, aren't they?"

Runckel smiled cheerfully. "They are built for speed. Rast grabbed a whole fleet of them to start with, and they've worked fine ever since. A few wrecks, some bad cases of kinkfoot, but that's all."

"What the devil is 'kinkfoot'?"

"Well, the enemy have tiny feet with little toes and no webs at all. Some of their ground-car controls are on the floor. There just isn't much space so our men's feet get cramped. It's just a mild irritation." Runckel smiled vaguely. "Nothing to worry about."

Bade squinted hard at Runckel. "What's Supply using for transport?"

"Steam trucks, of course."

"Do they work all right, or do they jump?"

Runckel smiled dreamily. "They work fine."

Bade snapped on the Supply microphone. The same weary officer appeared, his head in his hands, and mumbled, "Sorry. We're overloaded. Try Flyer Command."

Bade said angrily, "Wake up a minute."

The man raised his head, blinked at Bade, then straightened as if hauled by the back of the collar.

"Sir?"

"What's the overall supply picture?"

"Sir, it's awful. Terrible."

"What's the matter?"

"The advance is so fast, and the units are all mixed up, and when we get to a place, they've already pulled out. Worse yet, the steam trucks—" He hesitated, as if afraid to go on.

"Speak up," snapped Bade. "What's wrong with the trucks? Is it the engines? Fuel? Running gear? What is it?"

"It's . . . the water, sir."

"The water?"

"Sir, there's that constant loss of steam out the exhaust. At home, we just throw a few more buckets of water in the tank and go on. But here—"

"Oh," said Bade, the situation dawning on him.

"But around here, sir," said the officer, "they've had something called a 'severe drought.' The streams are dry."

"Can you dig down?"

"Sir, at best there's just muck. We *know* there's water here somewhere, but meanwhile our trucks are stalled all over the country with the men dug down out of sight, and the natives standing around shaking their heads, and *sure*, there's *got* to be water down there somewhere, but what do we use right now?"

Bade took a deep breath. "What about the enemy trucks? Can't you use them?"

"If we'd started off with them, I suppose we could have. But Ground Forces has requisitioned most of them. Now we're spread out in all directions with the front getting farther away all the time."

Bade switched off and got in touch with Ground Forces, Maintenance. A spruce-looking major appeared. Bade paused a moment, then asked, "How's your work-load, major? Are you behind schedule?"

The major looked shocked. "No, sir. Far from it. We're away ahead of schedule."

"Aren't these enemy vehicles giving you any trouble? Any difficulties in repair?"

The major laughed. "Fangjaw, general, we don't repair them! When they burn out, we throw them away. We pried up the hoods of some of them, pulled off the top two or three layers of machinery, and took a good look underneath. That was enough. There are hundreds of parts, all shapes and sizes. And dozens of different kinds of motors. Half of the parts are stuck so they won't move when you try to get them out, and, to top it all, there isn't enough room in there to squeeze in an extra grain of sand. So what's the use? If something goes wrong with one of those things, we give it a shove off the road and forget it. There are plenty of others."

"I see," said Bade. "Do you send your repair crews out to shove the ground-cars off the road?"

"Oh, no, sir," said the major looking startled. "Like the colonel says, 'Let the Ground Forces do it.' Sir, it doesn't take any skill to do that. It's just that that's our *policy*: Don't repair 'em. Throw 'em away."

"What about *our* vehicles then? Have you found out what's wrong?"

The major looked uncomfortable. "Well, the difficulty is that the vehicles work satisfactorily *inside* the ship, and for a little while *outside*. But then, after they've been out a while, a malfunction occurs in the mechanism. That's what causes the trouble." He looked at Bade hopefully. "Was there anything else, sir."

"Yes," said Bade dryly, "it's the malfunction I'm interested in. What *is* it that goes wrong?"

The major looked unhappy. "Well, sir, we've had the motors apart and put back together I don't know how many times, and the fact is, there's nothing at all wrong with them. There's nothing wrong, but they still won't work. That's not our department. We've handed the whole business over to the Testing Lab."

"Then," said Bade, "you actually don't have any work to do?"

The major jumped. "Oh, no sir, I didn't say that. We . . . we're holding ourselves in readiness, sir, and we've got our shops in order, and some of the men are doing some very, ah, very important research on the . . . the structure of the enemy ground-car, and—"

"Fine," said Bade. "Get your colonel on this line." When the colonel appeared, Bade said, "Ground Forces Supply has its steam trucks out of service for lack of water. Get in touch with their H.Q., find out the location of the trucks, and get out there with the water. Find out where they can replenish in the future. Take care of this as fast as you can."

The colonel worked his mouth in a way that suggested a weak valve struggling to hold back a large quantity of compressed air. Bade looked at him hard. The colonel's mouth blew open, and "Yes, sir!" came out. The colonel looked startled.

Bade immediately switched back to Supply and said, "Ground Forces Maintenance is going to help you water your trucks. Why didn't you get in touch with them yourselves? It's the obvious thing."

"Sir, we did, hours ago. They said water supply wasn't in *their* department."

Bade seemed to see the bursting of innumerable bubbles before his eyes. It dawned on him that he was bogged down in petty details while big events rushed on unheeded. He switched back to the colonel briefly and when he switched off the colonel was plainly vibrating with energy from head to toe. Then Bade looked forebodingly at the map and ordered Liaison to get General Rast for him.

This took a long time, which Bade spent trying to anticipate the possible enemy reaction if Supply broke down completely, and a retirement became necessary. By the time Rast appeared on the screen, Bade had thought it over carefully, and could see nothing but trouble ahead. There was a buzz, and Bade looked up to see a fuzzy picture of Rast.

Rast, as far as Bade could judge, had a look of victory and exhilaration. But the communicator's reception was uncommonly bad, and Rast's image had a tendency to flicker, fade, and slide up and down. Judging by the trend of the conversation, Bade decided reception must be worse yet at the other end.

Bade said, "Supply is in a mess. You'd better choose some sort of defensible perimeter and halt."

Rast said, "Thank you. The enemy is in full flight."

"Listen," said Bade. "Supply is stopped. We can't get supplies to you. Supply can't catch up with you."

"We'll pursue them day and night," said Rast.

"Listen to me," said Bade. "Break off the pursuit! We can't get supplies to you!"

Rast's form slowly dimmed and expanded till it filled the screen, then burst, and reappeared as a brilliant image the size of a man's thumb. His voice cut off, then came through as a crackle.

"Siss kissis sissis," said the image, expanding again, "hisss siss kississ sissikississ." This noise was accompanied by earnest gestures on the part of Rast, and a very determined facial expression. The image grew huge and dim, and burst, then started over again.

Bade spat out a word he had promised himself never to say again under any circumstances whatever. Then he sat helpless while the image, large and clear, leaned forward earnestly and pounded one huge fist into the other.

"Hiss! Siss! Fississ!"

"Listen," said Bade, "I can't make out a word you're saying." He leaned forward. "WE CAN'T GET SUPPLIES TO YOU!"

The image burst and started over, bright and small.

Bade sucked in a deep breath. He grabbed the Communications microphone. "Listen," he snapped, "I've got General Rast on the screen here and I can't hear anything but a crackle. The image constantly expands and contracts."

"I know, sir," said a gray-smocked technician with a despairing look. "I can see the monitor screen from here. It's the best we can do, sir."

Out of the corner of his eye, Bade could see Rast's image growing huge and dim. "Hiss! Siss!" said Rast earnestly.

"What causes this?" roared Bade.

"Sir, all we can guess is some terrific electrical discharge between here and General Rast's position. What such a discharge might be, I can't imagine."

Bade scowled, and looked at a thumb-sized Rast. Bade opened his mouth to roar out that there was no way to get supplies through. Rast's image suddenly vibrated like a twanged string, then stopped expanding.

Rast's voice came through clearly, "Will you repeat that, sir?"

"WE CAN'T SUPPLY YOU," said Bade. "Halt your advance. Pick a good spot and HALT!"

Rast's image was expanding again. "Siss hiss," he said, and saluted. His image vanished.

Bade immediately snapped on the Communications microphone. "Do you have anyone down there who can read lips?" he demanded.

"Read *lips*? Sir, I—" The technician squinted suddenly, and swung off the screen. He was back in a moment, his face clear and hopeful. "Sir, we've got a man in the section that's a fanatic on communications methods. The other men think he *can* read lips, and I've sent for him."

"Good," said Bade. "Set him to work on the record of that conversation with General Rast. Another thing—is there any way you can get a message though to Rast?"

The technician looked doubtful. "Well, sir . . . I don't know—" His face cleared slightly. "We can try, sir."

"Good," said Bade. "Send 'Supply situation bad. Strongly suggest you halt your advance and consolidate position.'" Bade's glance fell on the latest plot from the map room. Glumly he asked himself how Rast or anyone else could hope to consolidate the balloon-like situation that was coming about.

"Sir," asked the technician, "is that all?"

"Yes," said Bade, "and let me know when you get through to Rast."

"Yes, sir."

Bade switched off, and turned to ask Runckel for the exact time Landing Force 3 would be down. Bade hesitated, then squinted hard at Runckel.

Runckel's face had an unusually bright, animated look. He was glancing rapidly through a sheaf of reports, quickly scribbling comments on them, and tossing them to an excited-looking clerk, who rushed off to slap them on the desks of various exhilarated officers and clerks. These men eagerly transmitted them to their various sections. This procedure was normal, but the faces of the men all looked too excited. Their movements were jerky and fast.

Bade became aware of the sensation of watching a scene in a lunatic asylum.

The excited-looking clerk rushed to Runckel's desk to snatch up a sheaf of reports, and Bade snapped, "Bring those here."

The clerk jumped, rushed to Bade's desk, halted with a jerky bounce and saluted snappily. He flopped the papers on the desk, whirled around and raced off toward the desks of the officers who usually got the reports Bade was now holding. The clerk stopped suddenly, looked at his empty hands, spun around, stared at Runckel's desk, then at Bade's. A look of enlightenment passed across his face. "Oh," he said, with a foolish grin. He teetered back and forth on his heels, then rushed over to look at the latest plot from the map room.

Bade set his jaw and glanced at the reports Runckel had marked.

The top two or three reports were simple routine and had merely been initialed. The next report, however, was headed: "Testing Lab. Report on Cause of Vehicle Failure; Recommendations."

Bade quickly glanced over several sheet of technical diagrams and figures, and turned to the summary. He read:

"In short, the breakdown of normal function, and the resultant slow violent pulsing action of the motor, is caused by the abnormally low conductivity of Surface Conduction Layer S-3. The pulser current, which would normally flow across this layer is blocked, and instead builds up on projection L-26. Eventually a sufficient charge accumulates, and arcs across air gap B. This throws a shock current through the exciter such as is normally experienced only during violent acceleration. The result is that the vehicle shoots ahead from a standing start, then rolls to a stop while the current again slowly accumulates. The root cause of this malfunction is the fantastically low moisture content of the atmosphere on this planet. It is this that causes the loss of conductivity across Layer S-3.

"Recommended measures to overcome this malfunction include:

a) Artificial humidification of the air entering the motor, by means of sprayer and fan.

b) Sealing of the motor unit.

c) Coating of surface condition layer S-3 with a top-sealed permanent conducting film.

"A) or b) probably can be carried out as soon as the requisite devices and materials are obtainable. This, however, may involve a considerable delay. C), on the other hand, will require a good deal of initial testing and experimentation, but may then be carried into effect very quickly, as the requisite tools and materials are already at hand. We will immediately carry out the initial measures for whichever plan you deem preferable."

Bade looked the report over again carefully, then glanced at Runckel's scrawled comment:

"Good work! Carry this out immediately! S.R."

Bade glared. Carry *what* out immediately?

Bade glanced angrily at Runckel, then sat up in alarm. Runckel's hands clenched the side of his desk. Runckel's back was straight as a rod. His chest was inflated to huge dimensions, and he was slowly drawing in yet more air. His face bore a fixated, inward-turned look that might indicate either horror or ecstasy.

Bade shoved his chair back and glanced around for help.

His glance stopped at the map screen, where the huge overblown blot in the center of the continent had sprouted a long narrow pencil reaching out toward the west.

There was a quick low gonging sound, and the semicircular rim atop the Communications microphone lit up in red. Bade snapped the microphone on and a scared-looking technician said, "Sir, we've worked out what General Rast said."

"What?" Bade demanded.

At Bade's side, there was a harsh scraping noise. Bade whipped around.

Runckel lurched to his feet, his face tense, his eyes shut, his mouth half open and his hands clenched.

Runckel twisted. There was a gagging sound, then a harsh roar:

Ka

Ka

Ka

KACHOOOOO!!

Bade sat down in a hurry and grabbed the microphone marked, "Medical Corps."

A crowd of young doctors and attendants swarmed around Runckel with pulse-beat snoopers, blood pressure gauges, little lights on long rubber tubes, and bottles and jars which they filled with fluid sucked out of the suffering Runckel with long hollow needles. They whacked Runckel, pinched him, and thumped him, then jumped for cover as he let out another blast.

"Sir," said a young doctor wearing a "Medical-Officer-On-Duty" badge, "I'm afraid I shall have to quarantine this room and all its occupants. That includes you, sir." He said this in a gentle but firm voice.

Bade glanced at the doorway. A continuous stream of clerks, officers, and messengers moved in and out on necessary business. Some of these officers, Bade noticed, were speaking in low angry tones to idiotically smiling members of the staff. As one of the angry officers slapped a sheaf of papers on a desk, the owner of the desk came slowly to his feet. His chest inflated to gigantic proportions, he let out a terrific blast, reeled back against a wall, and let out another.

The young medical officer spun around excitedly. "Epidemic!" he yelled. "Seal that door! Back, all of you!" His face had a faint glow as he turned to Bade. "We'll have this under control in no time, sir." He came up and plastered a red and yellow sticker over the joint where door and wall came together. He faced the room. "Everyone here is quarantined. It's death to break that seal."

From Bade's desk came an insistent ringing, and the small voice of the communications technician pleaded, "Sir . . . please, sir . . . this is important!" On the map across the room the bloated red space now had two sizable dents driven into it, such as might be expected if the enemy were opening a counteroffensive. The thin pencil line reaching toward the west was wobbling uncertainly at its far end.

Bade became aware of a fuzzy quality in his own thinking, and struggled to fix his mind on the scene around him.

The young doctor and his assistants hustled Runckel toward the door. As Bade stared, the doctor and assistants went out the door without breaking the quarantine seal. The sticker was plastered over the joint on the hinge side of the door. The seal bent as the door opened, then straightened out unhurt as the door shut.

"*Phew*," said Bade. He picked up the Communications microphone. "What did General Rast say?"

"Sir, he said, 'I can't reach the coast any faster than a day-and-a-half!'"

"The *coast*!"

"That's what he said, sir."

"Did you get that message to him?"

"Not yet, sir. We're trying."

Bade switched off and tried to think. His army was stretched out like a rubber balloon. His headquarters machinery was falling apart fast. An epidemic was loose among his men and plainly spreading fast. The base was still secure. But without sane men to man it, the enemy could be expected to walk in any time.

Bade's eyes were watering. He blinked, and glanced around for some sane face in the sea of hysterically cheerful people. He spotted an alert-looking officer with his back against the wall and a chair leg in his hand. Bade called to him. The officer looked around.

Bade said, "Do you know when Landing Force 3 is coming down?"

"Sir, they're coming down right now."

★ ★ ★

Bade stayed conscious long enough to watch the beginning of the enemy's counteroffensive, and also to see the start of the exploding sickness spread through the landing site. He grimly summarized the situation to the man he chose to take over command.

This man was the leader of Landing Force 3, a general by the name of Kottek. General Kottek was a fanatic, a man with a rough hypnotic voice and a direct unblinking stare. General Kottek's favorite drink was pure water. Food was a matter of indifference to him. His only known amusements were regular physical exercise and the dissection of military problems. To hesitate to obey a command of General Kottek's was unheard of. To bungle in the performance of it was as pleasant as to sit down in the open mouth of a shark. General Kottek's officers were usually recognizable by their lean athletic appearance, and a tendency to jump at unexpected noises. General Kottek's men were nearly always to be seen in a state of good order and high spirits.

As soon as Bade, aching and miserable, summarized the situation and ordered Kottek to take over, Kottek gave a sharp precise salute, turned, and immediately began snapping out orders.

Heavily armed troops swung out to guard the site. Military police forced wandering gangs of sick men back to their ships. The crews of Landing Force 3 divided up to bring the depleted crews of the other ships up to minimum standards. The ships' damper units were turned to full power, and the outside power network and auxiliary damper units were disassembled and carried into the ships. Word came that a large enemy force had made an air-borne landing not far away. Kottek's troops marched in good order back to their ships. The ships of all three landing forces took off. They set down together in the center of the largest mass of Rast's encircled troops. The next day passed embarking these men under the protection of Kottek's fresh troops and the ships' dampers. Then the ships took off and repeated the process.

In this way, some sixty-five percent of the surrounded men were saved in the course of the week. Two more landing forces came down. General Rast and a small body of guards were found unconscious partway up an unbelievably high hill in the west. The situation at this point became hopelessly complicated by the exploding sickness.

This sickness, which none of the doctors were able to cure or even relieve, manifested itself in various forms. The usual form began by exhilarating the victim. In this state, the patient generally considered himself capable of doing anything, however foolhardy, and regardless of difficulties. This lasted until the second phase set in with violent contractions of the chest and a sudden out-rush of air from the lungs, accompanied by a blast like a gun going off. This second stage might or might not have complications such as digestive upset, headache, or shooting pains in the hands and feet. It ended when the third and last phase set in. In this phase the victim suffered from mental depression, considered himself a hopeless failure, and was as likely as not to try to end his life by suicide.

As a result of this suicidal impulse there were nightmarish scenes of soldiers disarming other soldiers, which brought the whole invasion force into a state of quaking uncertainty. At this critical point, and despite all precautions, General Kottek himself began to come down with the sickness. With him, the usual exhilaration took the form of a stream of violent and imperative orders.

Troops who should have retreated were ordered to fight to the death where they stood. Savage counter-attacks for worthless objectives were driven home "to the last drop of blood." Because General Kottek ordered it, people obeyed without thought. The hysterical light in his eye was masked by the fanatical glitter that had been there to begin with. The general himself only realized what was wrong when his chest tightened up, his body tensed, and a racking concatenation of explosions burst from his chest. He immediately brought his body to the position of attention, and crushed out by sheer will a series of incipient tickling sensations way down in his throat. General Kottek handed the command over to General Runckel and reported himself to sick bay.

Runckel, by this time, had recovered enough from the third phase to be untied and allowed to walk around with only two guards. As he had not fully recovered his confidence, however, he immediately went to see Bade.

★ ★ ★

Bade's illness took the form of nausea, cold hands and feet, and a sensation of severe pressure in the small of the back. Bade was lying on a cot when Runckel came in, followed by his two watchful guards.

Bade looked up and saw the two guards lean warily against the wall, their eyes narrowed as they watched Runckel. Runckel paused at the foot of Bade's bed. "How do you feel?" Runckel asked.

"Except for yesterday and day before," said Bade, "I never felt worse in my life. How do you feel?"

"All right most of the time." He cleared his throat. "Kottek's down with it now."

"Did he know in time?"

"No, I'm afraid he's left things in a mess."

Bade shook his head. "Do we have a general officer who *isn't* sick?"

"Not in the top brackets."

"Who did Kottek hand over to?"

"Me." Runckel looked a little embarrassed. "I'm not sure I can handle it yet."

"Who's in actual charge right now?"

"I've got the pieces of our own staff and the staff of Landing Force 2 working on it. Kottek's staff is hopeless. Half of them are talking about sweeping the enemy off the planet in two days."

Bade grunted. "What's your idea?"

"Well," said Runckel, "I still get . . . a little excited now and then. If you could possibly provide a sort of general supervision—"

Bade looked away weakly. "How's Rast?"

"Tied to his bunk with half-a-dozen men sitting on him."

"What about Vokk?"

"Tearing his lungs out every two or three minutes."

"Sokkis, then?"

Runckel shook his head grimly. "I'm afraid they didn't hear the gun go off in time. The doctors are still working on him, though."

"Well . . . is Frotch all right?"

"Yes, thank heaven. But then he's Flyer Command. And, worse yet, there's nobody to put in his place."

"All right, how about Sozzle?"

"Well," said Runckel, "Sozzle may be a good propaganda man, but personally I wouldn't trust him to command a platoon."

"Yes," said Bade, rolling over to try to ease the pain in his back, "I see your point." He took a deep breath. "I'll try to supervise the thing." He swung gingerly to a sitting position.

Runckel watched him, then his face twisted. "This whole thing is all my fault," he said. He choked. "I'm just no goo—"

The two guards sprang across the room, grabbed Runckel by the arms and rushed him out the door. Harsh grunts and solid thumping sounds came from the corridor outside. There was a heavy crash. Somebody said, "All right, get the general by the feet, and I'll take him by the shoulders. *Phew*! Let's go."

Bade sat dizzily on the edge of the bed. For a moment, he had a mental image of Runckel before the invasion, leaning forward and saying impressively, "Certain glory and a mighty victory await us."

Bade took several slow deep breaths. Then he got up carefully, found a towel, and cautiously went to wash.

It took Bade almost a week to disentangle the troops from the web of indefensible positions and hopeless last stands Kottek had committed them to in a day-and-a-half of peremptory orders. The enemy, meanwhile, took advantage of opportunity, using ground and air attacks, rockets, missiles and artillery in such profusion as to stun the mind. It was not until Bade's men and officers had recovered from circulating attacks of the sickness, and another landing force had come down, that it was possible to temporarily resume the offensive. Another two weeks, and another sick landing force recovered, saw the invasion army in control of a substantial part of the central plain of the continent. Bade now had some spare moments to squint at certain reports that were piled up on his desk. Exasperatedly, he called a meeting of high officers.

Bade was standing with Runckel at a big map of the continent when their generals came in. Bade and Runckel each looked grim and intense. The generals looked uniformly dulled and worn down.

Bade took a last hard look at the map, then he and Runckel turned. Bade glanced at Veth, Landing Site Commander. "What's your impression of the way things are going?"

Veth scowled. "Well, we're still getting eight to ten sizable missile hits a day. Of course, there's no predicting when they'll come in. With the men working outside the ships, any single hit could vaporize large numbers of essential technical personnel. Until we get the underground shelters built, the only way around this is to have whole site damped out all the time." He shook his head. "This takes a lot of energy."

Bade nodded, and turned to Rast, Ground Forces Commander.

"So far," said Rast frowning, "our situation on paper looks not too bad. Morale is satisfactory. Our weapons are superior. We have strong forces in a reasonably large central area, and in theory we can shift rapidly from one front to the other, and be superior anywhere. But in practice, the enemy has so many missiles, of all types and sizes, that we can't take advantage of the position.

"Suppose, for instance, that I order XX and XXII Tank Armies from the eastern to the western front. They can't go under their own power, because of fuel expenditure, the wear on their tracks, and the resulting delay for repairs. They can't go by forceway network because there isn't any built yet. The only way to send them is by the natives' iron track roads. That would be fine, except that the iron track roads make beautiful targets for missile attacks. Thanks to the enemy, every bridge and junction either is, has been, or will be blown up and not once, either. The result is, we have to use slow filtration of troops from one front to the other, or we have to accept very heavy losses on route. In addition, we now know that the enemy has formidable natural defenses in the east and west, especially in the west. There's a range of hills there that surpasses anything I've ever seen or heard of. Not only is the difficulty of the terrain an obstacle, but as our men go higher, movement finally becomes practically impossible. I know this from personal experience. The result of it is, the enemy need only guard the passes and he has a natural barrier behind which he can mass for attack at any chosen point."

Bade frowned. "Don't the hills have the same harmful effect on the enemy?"

"No sir, they don't."

"Why not?"

"I don't know. But that and their missiles put us in a nasty spot."

Bade absorbed this, then turned to General Frotch, head of Atmospheric Flyer Command.

Frotch said briskly, "Sir, so far as the enemy air forces are concerned, we have the situation under control. And various foreign long-range reconnaissance aircraft that have been filtering in from distant native countries, have also been successfully batted out of the sky. However, as far as . . . ah . . . missiles . . . are concerned, the situation is a little strained."

Bade snapped, "Go on."

"Well, sir," said Frotch, "the enemy has missiles that can be fired at the fastest atmospheric flyers, that can be made to blow up near them, that can be guided to them, and even that can be made to chase and catch them."

"What about our weapons?"

"They're fine, on a percentage basis. But the enemy has a lot more missiles than we have pilots."

"I see," said Bade. "Well—" He turned to speak to the Director of Intelligence, but Frotch went on:

"Moreover, sir, we are having atmospheric troubles."

"'Atmospheric troubles'? What's that?"

"For one thing, gigantic traveling electrical displays that disrupt plane-to-ground communications, and have to be avoided, or else the pilots either don't come out, or else come out fit for nothing but a rest cure. Then there are mass movements of air traveling from one part of the planet to another. Like land breezes and sea breezes at home. But here the breezes can be pretty forceful. The effect is to put an unpredictable braking force on all our operations."

Bade nodded slowly. "Well, we'll have to make the best of it." He turned to General Sozzle, who was Disseminator of Propaganda.

Sozzle cleared his throat. "I can make my report short and to the point. Our propaganda is getting us nowhere. For one thing, the enemy is apparently used to being ambushed daily by something called 'advertising,' which seems to consist of a series of subtle propaganda traps. By comparison our approach is so crude it throws them into hysterics."

Bade glanced at the Director of Intelligence, who said dully, "Sir, it's too early to say for certain how our work will eventually turn out. We've had some successes; but, so far, we've been handicapped by translation difficulties."

Bade frowned. "For instance?"

"Take the single word, 'snow,'" said the Intelligence Director. "You can't imagine the snarl my translators get into over that word. It apparently means 'white solid which falls in crystals from the sky.' Figure that out."

Bade squinted, then looked relieved. "Oh. It means, 'dust.'"

"That's the way the interpreters translated it. Now consider this sentence from a schoolbook. 'When April comes, the dust all turns to water and flows into the ground to fill the streams.'"

"That doesn't make any sense at all."

"No. But that's what happens if you accept 'dust' as the translation for 'snow.' There are other words such as 'winter,' 'blizzard,' 'tornado.' Ask a native for an explanation, and with a straight face he'll give you a string of incomprehensible nonsense that will stand you on your ear. Not that it's important in itself. But it seems to show something about the native psychology that I can't quite figure out. You can fight your enemy best when you can understand him. Well, from this angle they're completely incomprehensible."

"Keep working on it," said Bade, after a short silence. He turned to Runckel.

Runckel said, "The overall situation looks about the same from my point of view. Namely, the natives are driven back, but by no means defeated. What we have to remember is that we never expected to have them defeated at this stage. True, our time schedule has been set back somewhat, but this was due not to enemy action, but to purely accidental circumstances. That is, first the atmosphere was so deficient in moisture that our ground vehicles were temporarily out of order, and, second, we were disabled by an unexpected disease. But these troubles are over with. My point is that we can now begin the decisive phase of operations."

"Good," said Bade. "But to do that we have to firmly hold the ground we have. I want to know if we can do this. On the surface, perhaps, it looks like it. But there are signs here I don't like. As the old saying goes, 'A shark shows you his fin, not his teeth. Take warning from the fin; when you see the teeth it's too late.'"

"Yes," said Frotch, turning excitedly to Rast, "that's the thought exactly. Now, will *you* mention it, or shall I?"

"Holy fangjaw," growled Rast, "maybe it doesn't really mean anything."

"The Supreme Commander," said Runckel angrily, "was trying to talk."

Bade said, "What is it, Rast? Speak up."

"Well—" Rast hesitated, glanced uneasily at Runckel, then thrust out his jaw, "Sir, it looks like the whole master plan of the invasion may have come unhinged."

Runckel angrily started to speak.

Bade glanced at Runckel, took out a long slender cigar, and sat down on the edge of the table to watch Runckel. He lit the cigar and put down the lighter. As far as Bade was concerned, his face was expressionless. Things seemed to have an unnatural clarity, however, as he looked at Runckel and waited for him to speak.

Runckel looked at Bade, swallowed hard and said nothing.

Bade glanced at Rast.

Rast burst out, "Sir, for the last ten days or so, we've been wondering how long the enemy could keep up his missile attacks. Flyer Command has blasted factories vital to missile manufacture, and destroyed all their known stockpiles. Well, grant we didn't get all their stockpiles. That's logical enough. Grant that they had tremendous stocks stored away. Even grant that before we got here they made missiles all the time for the sheer love of making them. Maybe every man, woman, and child in the country had a missile, like a pet. Still, there's got to be an end *somewhere*."

Bade nodded soberly.

"Well, sir," said Rast, "we get these missiles fired at us all the time, day after day after day, one missile after the other, like an army of men tramping past in an endless circle forever. It's inconceivable that they'd use their missiles like this unless their supply is inexhaustible. Frotch gets hit with them, I get hit with them, Veth gets hit with them. For every job there's a missile. We put our overall weapons superiority in one pan of the balance. They pour an endless heap of missiles in the other pan. *Where do all these missiles come from?*"

For an instant Rast was silent, then he went on. "At first we thought 'Underground factories.' Well, we did our best to find them and it was no use. And whenever we managed to spot moving missiles, they seemed to be coming from the coast.

"About this time, some of my officers were trying to convert a bunch of captives to our way of thinking. One of the officers noticed a peculiar thing. Whenever he clinched his argument by saying, 'Moreover, you are alone in the world; you cannot defeat us alone,' the captives would all look very serious. Most of them would be very still and attentive, but here and there among them, a few would choke, gag, make sputtering noises, and shake all over. The other soldiers would secretively kick these men, and jab them with their elbows until they were still and attentive. Now, however, the question arose, what did all this mean? The actions were described to Intelligence, who said they meant exactly what they seemed to mean, 'suppressed mirth.'

"In other words, whenever we said, 'You can't win, you're alone in the world,' they wanted to burst out laughing. My officers now varied the technique. They would say, for instance, 'The U.S.S.R. is our faithful ally.' Our captives would sputter, gasp, and almost strangle to death. Put this together with their inexhaustible supply of missiles and the thing takes on a sinister look."

"You think," said Bade, "that the U.S.S.R. and other countries are shipping missiles to the U.S. by sea?"

General Frotch cleared his throat apologetically, "Sir, excuse me. I have something new to add to this. I've set submerger planes down along all three of their coasts. Not only are the ports alive with shipping. But some of our men swam into the harbors at night and hid, and either they're the victims of mass-hypnosis or else those ships are unloading missiles like a fish unloads spawn."

Bade looked at Runckel.

Runckel said dully, "In that case, we have the whole planet to fight. That was what we had to avoid at any cost."

This comment produced a visible deterioration of morale. Before this attitude had a chance to set, Bade said forcefully and clearly, "I was never in favor of this attack. And this fortifies my original views. But from a strictly military point of view, I believe we can still win."

He went to the map, and speaking to each of the generals in turn, he explained his plan.

In the three following days, each of the three remaining landing forces set down. The men of each landing force, as expected, became violently ill with the exploding sickness. With the usual course of the sickness known, it proved possible to care for this new horde of patients with nothing worse than extreme inconvenience for the invasion force as a whole.

The enemy, meanwhile, strengthened his grip around the occupied area, and at the same time cut troop movements within the area to a feeble trickle. Day after day, the enemy missiles fell in an increasingly heavy rain on the road and rail centers. During the height of this bombardment, Bade succeeded in gradually filtering all of Landing Force 3 back to the protection of the ships.

Rast now reported that the enemy attacks were mounting in force and violence, and requested permission to fall back and contract the defense perimeter.

Bade replied that help would soon come, and Rast must make only small local withdrawals.

Landing Forces 7, 8, and 9, cured of the exploding sickness, now took off. Immediately afterward, Landing Force 3 took off.

Landing Forces 3 and 7, under General Kottek, came down near the base of the Upper Peninsula of Michigan, and struck south and west to rip up communications in the rear of the main enemy forces attacking General Rast.

Landing Force 8 split, its southern section seizing the western curve of Cuba to cut the shipping lanes to the Gulf of Mexico. Its northern sections seized Long Island, to block shipping entering the port of New York, and to subject shipping in the ports of

Boston, Philadelphia, Baltimore and Washington to heavy attack from the air.

Landing Force 9 remained aloft until the enemy's reaction to General Kottek's thrust from the rear became evident. This reaction proved to be a quickly improvised simultaneous attack from north and south, to pinch off the flow of supplies from Kottek's base to the point of his advance. Landing Force 9 now set down, broke the attack of the southern pincer, then struck southeastward to cut road and rail lines supplying the enemy's northern armies. The overall situation now resembled two large, roughly concentric circles, each very thick in the north, and very thin in the south. A large part of the outer circle, representing the enemy's forces, was now pressed between the inner circle and the inverted Y of Kottek's attack from the north.

A large percentage of the enemy missile-launching sites were now overrun, and Rast for the first time found it possible to switch his troops from place to place without excessive losses. The enemy opened violent attacks in both east and west to relieve the pressure on their trapped armies in the north, and Rast fell back slowly, drawing forces from both these fronts and putting them into the northern battle.

The outcome hung in a treacherous balance until the enemy's supplies gave out in the north. This powerful enemy force then collapsed, and Rast swung his weary troops to the south.

Three weeks after the offensive began, it ended with the fighting withdrawal of the enemy to the east and west. The enemy's long eastern and southern coasts were now sealed against all but a comparative trickle of supplies from overseas. General Kottek held the upper peninsula of Michigan in a powerful grip. From it he dominated huge enemy industrial regions, and threatened the flank of potential enemy counter-attacks from north or east.

Within the main occupied region itself, the forceway network and key-tools factories were being set up.

Runckel was only expressing the thought of nearly the whole invasion army when he walked into the operations room, heaved a sigh of relief and said to Bade, "Well, thank heaven *that's* over!"

Bade heard this and gave a noncommittal growl. He had felt this way himself some time before. During Runckel's absence, however, certain reports had come to Bade's desk and left him feeling like a man who goes down a flight of steps in the dark, steps off briskly, and finds there was one more step than he thought.

"Look at this," said Bade. Runckel leaned over his shoulder, and together they looked at a report headed, "Enemy Equipment." Bade passed over several pages of drawings and descriptions devoted to enemy knives, guns, grenades, helmets, canteens, mess equipment and digging tools, then paused at a section marked "Enemy clothing: 1) Normal enemy clothing consists of light two-piece underwear, an inner and an outer foot-covering, and either a light two-piece or light one-piece outer covering for the arms, chest, abdomen and legs. 2) However, capture of the enemy supply trains in the recent northern offensive uncovered the following fantastic variety: a) thick inner and outer hand coverings; b) heavy one-piece undergarment covering legs, arms and body; c) heavy upper outer garment; d) heavy lower outer garment; e) heavy inner foot covering; f) massive outer foot covering; g) additional heavy outer garment; h) extraordinarily heavy outer garment designed to cover entire body with exception of head, hands, and lower legs. In addition, large extra quantities of the heavy cover normally issued to the troops for sleeping purposes were also found. The purpose of all this clothing is difficult to understand. Insofar as the activity of a soldier encased in all these garments would be cut to a minimum, it can only be assumed that all these coverings represent body-shielding against some abnormal condition. The presence of poisonous chemicals in large quantities seems a likely possibility. Yet with the exception of the massive outer foot-covering, these garments are not impermeable."

Bade looked at Runckel. "They do have war chemicals?"

"Of course," said Runckel, frowning. "But we have protective measures, and our own war chemicals, if trouble starts."

Bade nodded thoughtfully, slid the report aside, and picked up one headed, "Medical Report on Enemy Skin Condensation."

Runckel shook his head. "I can never understand those. We've had a flood of reports like that from various sources. At most, I just initial them and send them back."

"Well," said Bade, "read the summary, at least."

"I'll try," growled Runckel, and leaned over Bade's shoulder to read:

"To summarize these astonishing facts, enemy captives have been observed to form, on the outer layer of their skin, a heavy beading of moisture. This effect is similar to that observed with laboratory devices maintained at depressed temperatures—that is, at reduced degrees of heat. The theory was, therefore, formed that the enemy's skin is, similarly, maintained at a temperature lower than that of his surroundings. Complex temperature-determining apparatus were set up to test this theory. As a result, this theory was disproved, but an even more astonishing state of affairs was discovered: The enemy's internal temperature varied very little, regardless of considerable experimental variation of the temperature of his environment.

"The only possible conclusion was that the enemy's body contains some built-in mechanism that actually controls the degree of heat and maintains it at a constant level.

"Now, according to Poff's widely accepted Principle, no complex bodily mechanism can long maintain itself in the absence of need or exercise. And what is the need for a bodily mechanism that has the function of holding body temperature constant despite wide external fluctuation? What is the need for a defense against something unless the something exists?

"We are forced to the conclusion that the degree of heat on this planet is subject to variations sufficiently severe as to endanger life. A new examination of what has hitherto been considered to be the enemy's mythology indicates that, contrary to conditions on our own planet, this planet is subject to remarkable fluctuations of temperature, that alternately rise to a peak, then fall to an incredible low.

"According to this new theory, our invasion force arrived as the temperature was approaching its maximum. Since then, it has reached and passed its peak, and is now falling. All this has passed unnoticed by us, partly because the maximum here approached the ordinary condition on our home planet. The danger, of course, is that the minimum on this planet would prove insupportable to our form of life."

This was followed by a qualifying phrase that further tests would have to be made, and the conclusions could not be considered final.

Bade looked at Runckel. Runckel snapped, "What do you do with a report like that? I'd tear it up, but why waste strength? It's easier to throw them in the wastebasket and go on."

"Wait a minute," said Bade. "If this report just happens to be right, then where are we?"

"Frankly," said Runckel, "I don't know or care. 'Skin condensation.' These scientists should keep their minds on things that have some chance of being useful. It would help if they'd figure out how to cut down flareback on our subtron guns. Instead they talk about 'skin condensation.'"

Bade wrote on the report, "This may turn out to be important. List on no more than two sheets of paper possible defenses against reduced degree of heat. Get it to me as soon as possible. Bade."

Bade signaled to a clerk. "Snap a copy of this, send the original out, and bring me the copy."

"Yes, sir."

"Now," said Bade, "we have one more report."

"Well, I have to admit," said Runckel, "that I can't see that either of these reports were of any value."

"Well, read this one, then."

Runckel shook his head in disgust, and leaned over. His eyes widened. This paper was headed, "For the Supreme Commander only. Special Report of General Kottek."

The report began, "Sir: It is an officer's duty to state, plainly and without delay, any matter that requires the immediate attention of his superior. I, therefore, must report to you the following unpleasant but incontrovertible facts;

"1) Since their arrival in this region, my troops have on three recent occasions displayed a strikingly low level of performance. Two simulated night attacks revealed feeble command and exaggerated sluggishness on the part of the troops. A defense exercise carried out at dawn to repulse a simulated amphibious landing was a complete failure; troops and officers alike displayed insufficient energy and initiative to drive the attack home.

"2) On other occasions, troops and officers have maintained a high, sometimes strikingly high, level of energy and activity.

"3) No explanation of this variability of performance has been forthcoming from the medical and technical personnel attached to my command. Neither have I any assurance that these fluctuations will not take place in the future.

"4) It is, therefore, my duty to inform you that I cannot assure the successful performance of my mission. Should the enemy attack with his usual energy during a period of low activity on the part of my troops, the caliber of my resistance will be that of wax against steel. This is no exaggeration, but plain fact.

"5) This situation requires the immediate attention of the highest military and technical authorities. What is in operation here may be a disease, an enemy nerve gas, or some natural factor unknown to us. Whatever its nature, the effect is highly dangerous.

"6) A mobile, flexible defense in these circumstances is impossible. A rigid linear defense is worthless. A defense by linked fortifications requires depth. I am, therefore, constructing a deep fortified system in the western section of the region under my control. This is no cure, but a means of minimizing disaster.

"7) Enemy missile activity since the defeat of their northern armies has been somewhat less than forty percent of that expected."

The report ended with Kottek's distinctive jagged signature. Bade glanced around.

Runckel's face was somber. "This is serious," he said. "When Kottek yells for help, we've got trouble. We'll have to put all our attention on this thing and get it out of the way as fast as we can."

Bade nodded, and reached out to take a message from a clerk. He glanced at it and scowled. The message was from Atmospheric Flyer Command. It read:

"Warning! Tornado sighted and approaching main base!"

Runckel leaned over to read the message. "What's this?" he said angrily. "'Tornado' is just a myth. Everybody knows that."

Bade snapped on the microphone to Aerial Reconnaissance. "What's this 'tornado' warning?" he demanded. "What's a 'tornado'?"

"Sir, a tornado is a whirling severe breeze of destructive character, conjoined with a dark cloud in the shape of a funnel, with the smaller end down."

Runckel gave an inarticulate snarl.

Bade squinted. "This thing is dangerous?"

"Yes, sir. The natives dig holes in the ground, and jump in when one comes along. A tornado will smash houses and ground-cars to bits, sir."

"Listen," snarled Runckel, "it's just *air*, isn't it?"

Bade snapped on Landing Site Command. "Get all the men back in the ships," he ordered. "Turn the dampers to full power."

"Holy fangjaw!" Runckel burst out. "Air can't hurt us. What's bad about a breeze, anyway?" He seized the Aerial Reconnaissance microphone and snarled. "Stand up, you! What have you been drinking?"

Bade took Runckel by the arm. "Look there!"

On the nearest wall screen, a wide black cloud warped across the sky, and stretched down a long arc to the ground. The whole thing grew steadily larger as they watched.

Bade seized the Landing Site Command microphone. "Can we lift ships?"

"No, sir. Not without tearing the power and damper networks to pieces."

"I see," said Bade. He looked up.

The cloud overspread the sky. The screen fell dark. There was a heavy clang, a thundering crash, the ship trembled, tilted, heeled, and slowly, painfully, settled back upright as Bade hung onto the desk and Runckel dove for cover. The sky began to lighten. Bade gripped the microphone and asked what had happened. He listened blank-faced as, after a moment, the first estimates of the damage came in.

One of the thousand-foot-long ships had been tipped off its base. In falling, it struck another ship, which also fell, striking a third. The third ship struck a fourth, which fell unhindered and split up the side like a bean pod. The mouth of the tornado's funnel then ran along the split, and the ship's inside looked as if it had been cleaned out with a vacuum hose. A few stunned survivors and scattered bits of equipment were clinging here and there. That was all.

The enemy chose this moment to land his heaviest missile strike in weeks.

It took the rest of the day, all night, and all the following day to get the damage moderately well cleaned up. Then a belated report came in that Forceway Station 1 had been subjected to a bombardment of desks, chairs, communications equipment, and odd bolts and nuts that had riddled the installation from one end to the other and set completion date back four weeks.

An intensive search now located most of the missing equipment and personnel—strewn over forty miles of territory.

"It was," said Runckel weakly, "only air, that's all."

"Yes," said Bade grimly. He looked up from a scientific report on the tornado. "A whirlpool is only water. Whirling water. Apparently this planet has traveling whirlpools of air."

Runckel groaned, then a sudden thought seemed to hit him. He reached into his wastebasket, fished around, and drew out a crumpled ball of paper. He smoothed it out, read for a while, then growled, "Scientific reports. Here's some kind of report that came in right in the middle of a battle. According to this thing, the native name for the place where we've set down is 'Cyclone Alley.' Is there some importance in knowing a thing like that?"

Bade felt severe prickling sensations across his back and neck. "'Cyclone,'" he said, "Where did I hear that before? Give me that paper."

Runckel shrugged and tossed it over. Bade smoothed it out and read:

"In this prevalent fairy tale, the 'cyclone'—corresponding to our 'sea serpent,' or 'Ogre of the Deep'—makes recurrent visits to communities in certain regions, frightening the inhabitants terribly and committing all sorts of prankish violence. On some occasions, it carries its chosen victims aloft, to set them down again far away. The cyclone is a frightening giant, tall and dark, who approaches in a whirling dance.

"An interesting aspect is the contrast of this legend with the equally prevalent legend of Santa Claus. Cyclone comes from the south, Santa from the north. Cyclone is prankish, frightening. Santa is benign, friendly, and even brings gifts. Cyclone favors 'springtime,' but may come nearly any time except 'winter.' Cyclone is secular. Santa reflects some of the holy aura of the religious festival, 'Christmas.'

"'Christmas comes but once a year. When it comes, it brings good cheer.' Though Cyclone visits but a few favored towns at a time, Santa visits at once all, everyone, even the lowliest dweller in his humble shack. The natives are immensely earnest about both of these legends. An amusing aspect is that our present main base is almost ideally located for visits by that local Ogre of the Sea, 'Cyclone.' We are, in fact, situated in a location known as 'Cyclone Alley.' Perhaps the Ogre will visit us."

At the bottom of the page was a footnote: "'Cyclone' is but one name for this popular Ogre. Another common name is 'Tornado.'"

Bade sat paralyzed for a moment staring at this paper. "Tornado Alley," he muttered. He grabbed the Flyer Command microphone to demand how the tornado warning system was coming. Then, groggily, he set the paper aside and turned his attention to the problem of General Kottek's special report. He looked up again as a nagging suspicion began to build up in him. He turned to Runckel. "How many of these 'myths' have we come across, anyway?"

Runckel looked as though a heavy burden were settling on him. He groped through his bulging wastebasket and fished out another crumpled ball of paper, then another. He located the one he wanted, smoothed it out, sucked in a deep breath, and read: "Cyclone, winter, spring, summer, hurricane, Easter bunny, autumn, blizzard, cold wave, Snow White and the Seven Dwarfs, lightning, Santa Claus, typhoon, mental telepathy, earthquake, levitation, volcano—" He looked up. "You want the full report on each of these things? I've got most of them here somewhere."

Bade looked warily at Runckel's overstuffed wastebasket. "No," he said. "But what about that report you're reading from? Isn't that an overall summary? Why didn't I get a copy of that?"

Runckel looked it over and growled, "Try to train them to send their reports to the right place. Yes, it's an overall summary. Here, want it?"

"Yes," said Bade. He took the report, then stopped to wonder, where was that report he had asked for on "reduced degree of heat?" He reached for a microphone, then remembered General Kottek's special report. Bade first sent word to Kottek that he approved what Kottek was doing, and that the problem was getting close attention. Then he read the crumpled overall summary Runckel had given him, and ended up feeling he had been on a trip through fairyland. His memories of the details evaporated even as he tried to mentally review the paper. "Hallowe'en," he growled, "icebergs, typhoons—this planet must be a mass of mythology from one end to the other." He picked up a microphone to call his Intelligence Service.

A messenger hurried across the room to hand him a slip of paper. The paper was from Atmosphere Flyer Command. It read:

"Warning! Tornado sighted approaching main base!"

This time, the tornado roared past slightly to the west of the base. It hit, instead Forceway Station 1, and scattered sections of it all over the countryside.

For good measure, the enemy fired in an impressive concentration of rockets and missiles. The attack did only slight harm to the base, but it finished off Forceway Station 1.

An incoherent report now came in from the occupied western end of Cuba, to the effect that a "hurricane" had just gone through.

Bade fished through Runckel's wastebasket to find out exactly what a "hurricane" might be. He looked up at the end of this, pale and shaken, and sent out a strong force to put his Cuban garrison back on its feet.

Then he ordered Intelligence, and some of his technical and scientific departments to get together right away and break down the so-called "myths" into two groups: Harmful, and nonharmful. The harmful group was to be arranged in logical order, and each item accompanied by a brief, straightforward description.

As Bade sent out this order, General Kottek reported that, as a supplement to his fortified system, he was making sharp raids whenever conditions were favorable, in order to keep the enemy in his section off-balance. In one of these raids, his troops had captured an enemy document which had since been translated. The document was titled: "Characteristics of Unheatful-Blooded Animals." Kottek enclosed a copy:

"Unheatful-blooded animals have no built-in system for maintaining their bodily rate of molecular activity. If the surrounding temperature falls, so does theirs. This lowers their physical activity. They cannot move or react as fast as normally. Heatful-blooded animals, properly clothed, are not subject to this handicap.

"In practical reality, this means that as unheatful conditions set in, the Invader should always be attacked during the most unheatful period possible. Night attacks have much to recommend them. So do attacks at dusk or dawn. In general, avoid taking the offensive during heatful periods such as early afternoon.

"Forecasts indicate that winter will be late this year, but severe when it comes. Remember, there is no year on record when temperatures have not dropped severely in the depths of winter. In such conditions, it is expected that the Invader will be killed in large numbers by—untranslatable—of the blood.

"Our job is to make sure they are kept worn down until winter comes. Our job then will be to make sure none of them live through the winter."

Bade looked up feeling as if his digestive system were paralyzed. A messenger hurried across the room to hand him a thick report hastily put together by the Intelligence Service. It was titled:

"Harmful Myths and Definitions."

Bade spent the first part of the night reading this spine-tingling document. The second part of the night he spent in nightmares.

Toward morning, Bade had one vivid and comparatively pleasant dream. A native wearing a simple cloth about his waist looked at Bade intently and asked, "Does the shark live in the air? Does a man breathe underwater? Who will eat grass when he can have meat?"

Bade woke up feeling vaguely relieved. This sensation was swept away when he reached the operating room and saw the expression on Runckel's face. Runckel handed Bade a slip of paper:

"Hurricane Hannah approaching Long Island Base."

★ ★ ★

Intercepted enemy radio and television broadcasts spoke of Hurricane Hannah as "the worst in thirty years." As Bade and Runckel stood by helplessly, Hurricane Hannah methodically pounded Long Island Base to bits and pieces, then swept away the pieces. The hurricane moved on up the shoreline, treating every village and city along the way like a personal enemy. When Hurricane Hannah ended her career, and retired to sink ships further north, the Atlantic coast was a shambles from one end to the other.

Out of this shambles moved a powerful enemy force, which seized the bulk of what was left of Long Island Base. The remnant of survivors were trapped in the underground installations, and reported that the enemy was lowering a huge bomb down through the entrance.

In Cuba, the reinforced garrison was barely holding on.

A flood of recommendations now poured in on Bade:

1) Long Island Base needed a whole landing force to escape capture.

2) Cuba Base had to have at least another half landing force for reinforcements.

3) The Construction Corps required the ships of two full landing forces in order to power the forceway network. Otherwise, work on the key-tools factories would be delayed.

4) Landing Site Command would need the ships and dampers of three landing forces to barely protect the base if the power supply of two landing forces were diverted to the Construction Corps.

5) The present main base was now completed and should be put to efficient use at once.

6) The present main base was worthless, because Forceway Station 1 could not be repaired in time to link the base to the forceway network.

7) Every field commander except General Kottek urgently needed heavy reinforcements without delay.

8) Studies by the Staff showed the urgent need of building up the central reserve without delay, at the expense of the field commanders, if necessary.

Bade gave up Long Island Base, ordered Cuba Base to hold on

with what it had, told the Landing Site Commander to select a suitable new main base near some southern forceway station free of tornadoes, and threw the rest of the recommendations into the wastebasket.

Runckel now came over with a rope smoldering stub jutting out of the corner of his mouth. "Listen," he said to Bade, "we're going to have a disciplinary problem on our hands. That Cuban garrison has been living on some kind of native paint-remover called 'rum.' The whole lot of them have a bad case of the staggering lurch from it; not even the hurricane sobered them up. Poff knew what was going on. But he and his staff covered it over. His troops are worthless. Molch and the reinforcements are doing all the fighting."

Bade said, "Poff is still in command?"

"I put Molch in charge."

"Good. We'll have to court-martial Poff and his staff. Can Molch hold the base?"

"He said he could. If we'd get Poff off his neck."

"Fine," said Bade. "Once he gets things in order, ship the regular garrison to a temporary camp somewhere. We don't want Molch's troops infected."

Runckel nodded. A clerk apologized and stepped past Runckel to hand Bade a message. It was from General Frotch, who reported that all his atmospheric flyers based on Long Island had been lost in Hurricane Hannah. Bade showed the message to Runckel, who shook his head wearily.

As Runckel strode away, another clerk put a scientific report on Bade's desk. Bade read it through, got Frotch on the line, and arranged for a special mission by Flyer Command. Then he located his report on "Harmful Myths and Definitions." Carefully, he read the definition of winter:

"To the best of our knowledge, 'winter' is a severe periodic disease of plants, the actual onset of which is preceded by the vegetation turning various colors. The tall vegetables known as 'trees' lose their foliage entirely, except for some few which are immune and are known as 'evergreens.' As the disease progresses, the juices of the plants are squeezed out and crystallize in white feathery forms known as 'frost.' Sufficient quantities of this squeezed-out dried juice is 'snow.' The mythology refers to 'snow falling from the sky.' A possible explanation of this is that the large trees also 'snow,' producing a fall of dried juice crystals. These crystals are clearly poisonous. 'Frostbite,' 'chilblains,' and even 'freezing to death' are mentioned in the enemy's communication media. Even the atmosphere filled with the resulting vapor, is said to be 'cold.' Totally unexplainable is the common reference to children rolling up balls of this poisonous dried plant juice and hurling them at each other. This can only be presumed to be some sort of toughening exercise. More research on this problem is needed."

Bade set this report down, reread the latest scientific report, then got up and slowly walked over to a big map of the globe. He gazed thoughtfully at various islands in the South Seas.

Late that day, the ships lifted and moved, to land again near Forceway Station 2. Power cables were run to the station across a sort of long narrow valley at the bottom of which ran a thin trickle of water. By early the morning of the next day, the forceway network was in operation. Men and materials flashed thousands of miles in a moment, and work on the key-tools factories accelerated sharply.

Bade immersed himself in intelligence summaries of the enemy communications media. An item that especially interested him was "Winter Late This Year."

By now there were three viewpoints on "winter." A diehard faction doggedly insisted that it was a myth, a mere quirk of the alien mentality. A large and very authoritative body of opinion held the plant juice theory, and bolstered its stand with reams of data sheets and statistics. A small, vociferous group asserted the heretical water crystal hypotheses, and ate alone at small tables for doing so.

General Frotch called Bade to say that the special Flyer Command mission was coming in to report.

General Kottek sent word that enemy attacks were becoming more daring, that his troops' periods of inefficiency were more frequent, and that the vegetation in his district was turning color. He mentioned, for what it was worth, that troops within the fortifications seemed less affected than those outside. Troops far underground, however, seemed to be slowed down automatically, regardless of conditions on the surface, unless they were engaged in heavy physical labor.

Bade scowled and set off inquiries to his scientific section. Then he heard excited voices and looked up.

Four Flyer Command officers were coming slowly into the room, bright metal poles across their shoulders. Slung from the poles was a big plastic-wrapped bundle. The bundle was dripping steadily, and leaving a trail of droplets that led back out the door into the hall. The plastic was filmed over with a layer of tiny beads of moisture.

Runckel came slowly to his feet.

The officers, breathing heavily, set the big bundle on the floor near Bade's desk.

"Here it is, sir."

Bade's glance was fastened on the object.

"Unwrap it."

The officers bent over the bundle, and with clumsy fingers pulled back the plastic layer. The plastic stood up stiffly, and bent only with a hard pull. Underneath was something covered with several of the enemy's thick dark sleeping covers. The officers rolled the bundle back and forth and unwound the covers. An edge of some milky substance came into view. The officers pulled back the covers and a milky, semitransparent block sat there, white vapor rolling out from it along the floor.

There was a concerted movement away from the block and the officers.

Bade said, "Was the whole place like that?"

"No, sir, but there was an awful lot of this stuff. And there was a compacted powdery kind of substance, too. We didn't bring enough of it back and it all turned to water."

"Did you wear the protective clothes we captured?"

"Yes, sir, but they had to be slit and zippered up the legs, because the enemy's feet are so small. The arms were a poor fit and there had to be more material across the chest."

"How did they work?"

"They were a great help, sir, as long as we kept moving. As soon as we slowed down, we started to stiffen up. The hand and foot gear was improvised and hard to work in, though."

Bade looked thoughtfully at the smoldering block, then got up, stepped forward, and spread his hand close to the block. A numbness gradually dulled his hand and moved up his arm. Then Bade straightened up. He found he could move his hand only slowly and painfully. He motioned to Runckel. "I think this is what 'cold' is. Want to try it?" Runckel got up, held his hand to the block, then straightened, scowling.

Bade felt a tingling sensation and worked his hand cautiously as Runckel, his face intent, slowly spread and closed his fingers.

Bade thoughtfully congratulated the officers, then had the block carried off to the Testing Lab.

The report on defense against "reduced degree of heat" now came in. Bade read this carefully several times over. The most striking point, he noticed, was the heavy energy expenditure involved.

That afternoon, several ships took off, separated, and headed south.

The next few days saw the completion of the first key-tool factory, the receipt of reports from insect-bitten scouts in various regions far to the south, and a number of terse messages from General Kottek. Bade ordered plans drawn up for the immediate withdrawal of General Kottek's army, and for the possible withdrawal by stages of other forces in the north. He ordered preparations made for the first completed factories to produce anti-reduced-degree-of-heat devices. He read a number of reports on the swiftly changing state of the planet's atmosphere. Large quantities of rain were predicted.

Bade saw no reason to fear rain, and turned to a new problem: The enemy's missiles had produced a superabundance of atomic debris in the atmosphere. Testing Lab was concerned over this, and suggested various ways to get rid of it. Bade approved the projects and turned to the immediate problem of withdrawing the bulk of General Kottek's troops from their strong position without losing completely the advantages of it.

Bade was considering the idea of putting a forceway station

somewhere in Kottek's underground defenses, so that he could be reinforced or withdrawn at will. This would involve complicated production difficulties; but then Kottek had said the slowing-down was minimized under cover, and it might be worthwhile to hold an option on his position. While weighing the various intangibles and unpredictables, Bade received a report from General Rast. Rast was now noticing the same effect Kottek had reported.

Word came in that two more key-tools factories were now completed.

Intelligence reports of enemy atmospheric data showed an enormous "cold air mass moving down through Canada."

General Frotch, personally supervising high-altitude tests, now somehow got involved in a rushing high-level air stream. Having the power of concentrating his attention completely upon whatever he was doing, Frotch got bound up in the work and never realized the speed of the air stream until he came down again—just behind the enemy lines.

When Bade heard of this, he immediately went over the list of officers, and found no one to replace Frotch. Bade studied the latest scientific reports and the disposition of his forces, then ordered an immediate switching of troops and aircraft through the forceway network toward the place where Frotch had vanished. A sharp thrust with local forces cut into the enemy defense system, was followed up by heavy reinforcements flowing through the forceway network, and developed an overpowering local superiority that swamped the enemy defenses.

Runckel studied the resulting dispositions and said grimly, "Heaven help us if they hit us hard in the right place just now."

"Yes," said Bade, "and heaven help us if we don't get Frotch back." He continued his rapid switching of forces, and ordered General Kottek to embark all his troops, and set down near the main base.

Flyer Command meanwhile began to show signs of headless disorientation, the ground commanders peremptorily ordering the air forces around as nothing more than close-support and flying artillery. The enemy behind-the-lines communications network continued to function.

Runckel now reported to Bade that no reply had been received from Kottek's headquarters. Runckel was sending a ship to investigate.

Anguished complaints poured in from the technical divisions that their work was held up by the troops flooding the forceway network.

The map now showed Bade's men driving forward in what looked like a full-scale battle to break the enemy's whole defensive arrangements and thrust clear through to the sea. Reports came in that, with the enemy's outer defense belt smashed, signs of unbelievable weakness were evident. The enemy seemed to have nothing but local reserves and only a few of them. The general commanding on the spot announced that he could end the war if given a free hand.

Bade now wondered, if the enemy's reserves weren't there, where were they? He repeated his original orders.

Runckel now came over with the look of a half-drowned swimmer and motioned Bade to look at the two nearest viewscreens.

One of the viewscreens showed a scene in shades of white. A layer of white covered the ground, towering ships were plastered on one side with white, obstacles were heaped over with white, the air was filled with horizontal streaks of white. Everything on the screen was white or turning white.

"Kottek's base," said Runckel dully.

The other screen gave a view of the long narrow valley just outside. This "valley" was now a rushing torrent of foaming water, sweeping along chunks of floating debris that bobbed a hand's breadth under the power cables from the ships to Forceway Station 2.

The only good news that day and the next was the recapture of General Frotch. In the midst of crumbling disorder, Flyer Command returned to normal.

Bade sent off a specially-equipped mission to try and find out what had happened to General Kottek. Then he looked up to see General Rast walking wearily into the room. Rast conferred with Runckel in low dreary tones, then the two of them started over toward Bade.

Bade returned his attention to a chart showing the location of the key-tools factories and the forceway network.

A sort of groan announced the arrival of Rast and Runckel. Bade looked up. Rast saluted. Bade returned the salute. Rast said stiffly, "Sir, I have been defeated. My army no longer exists."

Bade looked Rast over quickly, studying his expression and bearing.

"It's a plain fact," said Rast. "Sir, I should be relieved of command."

"What's happened?" said Bade. "I have no reports of any new enemy attack."

"No," said Rast, "there won't be any formal report. The whole northern front is anaesthetized from one end to the other."

"Snow?" said Bade.

"White death," said Rast.

A messenger stepped past the two generals to hand Bade a report. It was from General Frotch:

"1) Aerial reconnaissance shows heavy enemy forces moving south on a wide front through the snow-covered region. No response or resistance has been noted on the part of our troops.

"2) Aerial reconnaissance shows light enemy forces moving in to ring General Kottek's position. The enemy appears to be moving with extreme caution.

"3) It has so far proved impossible to get in touch with General Kottek.

"4) It must be reported that on several occasions our ground troops have, as individuals, attempted to seize from our flyer pilots and crews, their special protective anti-reduced-degree-of-heat garments. This problem is becoming serious."

Bade looked up at Rast. "You're Ground Forces Commander, not commander of a single front."

"That's so," said Rast. "I should be. But all I command now is a kind of mob. I've tried to keep the troops in order, but they know one thing after another is going wrong. Naturally, they put the blame on their leaders."

The room seemed to Bade to grow unnaturally light and clear. He said, "Have you had an actual case of mutiny, Rast?"

Rast stiffened. "No, sir. But it is possible for troops to be so laggardly and unwilling that the effect is the same. What I mean is that there is the steady growth of a cynical attitude everywhere. Not only in the troops but in the officers."

Bade looked off at the far corner of the room for a moment. He glanced at Runckel. "What's the state of the key-tools factories?"

"Almost all completed. But the northern ones are now in the reduced-degree-of-heat zone. Part of the forceway network is, too. Using the key-tools plants remaining, it might be possible to patch together some kind of a makeshift. But the reduced-degree-of-heat zone is still moving south."

A pale clerk apologized, stepped around the generals and handed Bade two messages. The first was from Intelligence:

"Enemy propaganda broadcasts beamed at our troops announce General Kottek's unconditional surrender with all his forces. We have no independent information on Kottek's actual situation."

The second message was from the commander of Number 1 Shock Infantry Division. This report boiled down to a miserable confession that the commanding officer found himself unable to prevent:

1) Fraternization with the enemy.

2) The use of various liquid narcotics that rendered troops unfit for duty.

3) The unauthorized wearing of red, white, and blue buttons lettered, "Vote Republican."

4) An ugly game called "footbase," in which the troops separated into two long lines armed with bats, to hammer, pound, beat, and kick, a ball called "the officer," from one end of the field to the other.

Bade looked up at Rast. "How is it I only find out about this now?"

"Sir," said Rast, "each of the officers was ashamed to report it to his superior."

Bade handed the report to Runckel, who read it through and looked up somberly. "If it's hit the shock troops, the rest must have it worse."

"Yet," said Bade, "the troops fought well when we recaptured Frotch."

"Yes," said Rast, "but it's the damned planet that's driving them crazy. The natives are remarkable propagandists. And the men can plainly see that even when they win a victory, some freak like the exploding sickness, or some kind of atmospheric jugglery, is likely to take it right away from them. They're in a bad mood and the only thing that might snap them out of it is decisive action. But if they go the other way we're finished."

"This," said Bade, "is no time for you to resign."

"Sir, it's a mess, and I'm responsible. I have to make the offer to resign."

"Well," said Bade, "I don't accept it. But we'll have to try to straighten out this mess." Bade pulled over several sheets of paper. On the first, he wrote:

"Official News Bureau: 1) Categorically deny the capture of General Kottek and his base. State that General Kottek is in full control of Base North, that the enemy has succeeded in infiltrating troops into the general region under cover of snow, but that he has been repulsed with heavy losses in all attacks on the base itself.

"2) State that the enemy announcement of victory in the area is a desperation measure, timed to coincide with their almost unopposed advance through the evacuated Northern Front.

"3) The larger part of the troops in the Northern Front were withdrawn prior to the attack and switched by forceway network to launch a heavy feinting attack against the enemy. State that the enemy, caught by surprise, appears to be rushing reserves from his northern armies to cover the areas threatened by the feint.

"4) Devoted troops who held the Northern Front to make the deception succeed have now been overrun by the enemy advance under cover of the snow. Their heroic sacrifice will not be forgotten.

"5) The enemy now faces the snow time alone. His usual preventive measures have been drastically slowed down. His intended decisive attack has failed of its object. The snow this year is unusually severe, and is already working heavy punishment on the enemy.

"6) Secret measures are now for the first time being brought into the open that will place our troops far beyond the reach of snow."

On the second sheet of paper, Bade wrote:

"Director of Protocol: Prepare immediately: 1) Supreme Commander's Citation for Extraordinary Bravery and Resourcefulness in Action: To be awarded General Kottek. 2) Supreme Commander's Citation for Extraordinary Devotion to Duty: To be awarded singly, to each soldier on duty during the enemy attack on the entire Northern Front. 3) These awards are both to be mentioned promptly in the Daily Notices."

Bade handed the papers to Runckel, "Send these out yourself." As Runckel started off, Bade looked at Rast, then was interrupted by a messenger who stepped past Rast, and handed Bade two slips of paper. With an effort of will, Bade extended his hand and took the papers. He read:

"Sir: Exploration Team South 3 has located ideal island base. Full details follow. Frotch."

"Sir: We have finally contacted General Kottek. He and his troops are dug into underground warrens of great complexity beneath his system of fortifications. Most of the ships above-ground are mere shells, all removable equipment having been stripped out and carried below for the comfort of the troops. Most of the ships' engines have also been disassembled one at a time, carried below, and set up to run the dampers—which are likewise below ground—and the 'heating units' devised by Kottek's technical personnel. His troops appear to be in good order and high spirits. Skath, Col., A.F.C., forwarded by Frotch."

Bade sucked in a deep breath and gave silent thanks. Then he handed the two reports to Rast. Bade snapped on a microphone and got in touch with Frotch. "Listen, can you get pictures of Kottek and his men?"

Frotch held up a handful of pictures, spread like playing cards. "The men took them for souvenirs and gave me copies. You can have all you want."

Bade immediately called his photoprint division and gave orders for the pictures to be duplicated by the thousands. The photoprint division slaved all night, and the excited troops had the pictures on their bulletin boards by the next morning.

The Official News Service meanwhile was dinning Bade's propaganda into the troops' ears at every opportunity. The appearance of the pictures now plainly caught the enemy propaganda out on a limb. Doubting one thing the enemy propaganda had said, the troops suddenly doubted all. A violent revulsion of feeling took place. Before anything else could happen, Bade ordered the troops embarked.

By this time, the apparently harmless rain had produced a severe flood, which repeatedly threatened the power cables supplying the forceway network. The troops had to use this network to get to the ships in time.

As Bade's military engineers blasted out alternate channels for the rising water, and a fervent headquarters group prayed for a drought, the troops poured through the still-operative forceway stations and marched into the ships with joyful shouts.

The enemy joined the celebration with a mammoth missile attack.

The embarkation, together with the disassembling of vital parts of the accessible key-tools factories, took several days. During this time, the enemy continued his steady methodical advance well behind the front of the cold air mass. The enemy however, made no sudden thrust on the ground to take advantage of the embarkation. Bade pondered this sign of tiredness, then sent up a ship to radio a query home. When the answer came, Bade sent a message to the enemy government. The message began:

"Sirs: This scouting expedition has now completed its mission. We are now withdrawing to winter quarters, which may be: a) an unspecified distant location; b) California; c) Florida. If you are prepared to accept certain temporary armistice conditions, we will choose a). Otherwise, you will understand we must choose b) or c). If you are prepared to consider these armistice conditions, you are strongly urged to send a plenipotentiary without delay. This plenipotentiary should be prepared to consider both the temporary armistice and the matters of mutual benefit to us."

Bade waited tensely for the reply. He had before him two papers, one of which read:

". . . the enemy-held peninsula of Florida has thus been found to be heavily infested with heartworms—parasites which live inside the heart, slow circulation, and lower vital activity sharply. While the enemy appears to be immune to infestation, our troops plainly are not. The four scouts who returned here have at last, we believe, been cured—but they have not as yet recovered their strength. The state of things in nearby Cuba is not yet known for certain. Possibly, the troops' enormous consumption of native 'rum' has interacted medicinally with our blood chemistry to retard infestation. If so, we have our choice of calamities. In any case, a landing in Florida would be ruinous."

As for California, the other report concluded:

". . . Statistical studies based on past experience lead us to believe that myth or no myth, immediately upon our landing in California, there will be a terrific earthquake."

Bade had no desire to go to Florida or California. He fervently hoped the enemy would not guess this.

At length the reply came, Bade read through ominous references to the growing might of the United States of the World, then came to the operative sentence:

". . . Our plenipotentiary will be authorized to treat only with regard to an armistice; he is authorized only to transmit other information to his government. He is not empowered to make any agreement whatever on matters other than an armistice."

The plenipotentiary was a tall thin native, who constantly sponged water off his neck and forehead, and who looked at Bade as if he would like cram a nuclear missile down his throat. Getting an agreement was hard work. The plenipotentiary finally accepted Bade's first condition—that General Kottek not be attacked for the duration of the armistice—but flatly refused the second condition allowing the continued occupation of western Cuba. After a lengthy verbal wrestling match, the plenipotentiary at last agreed to a temporary continuation of the western Cuban occupation, provided that the Gulf of Mexico blockade be lifted. Bade agreed to this and the plenipotentiary departed mopping his forehead.

Bade immediately lifted ships and headed south. His ships came down to seize sections of Sumatra, Java, and Borneo, with outposts on the Christmas and Cocoa islands and on small islands in the Indonesian archipelago.

Bade's personal headquarters were on a pleasant little island conveniently located in the Sunda Strait between Java and Sumatra. The name of the island was Krakatoa.

Bade was under no illusion that the inhabitants of the islands welcomed his arrival. Fortunately, however, the armament of his troops outclassed anything in the vicinity, with the possible exception of a bristly-looking place called Singapore. Bade's scouts, after studying Singapore carefully, concluded it was not mobile, and if they left it alone, it would leave them alone.

The enemy plenipotentiary now arrived in a large battleship, and was greeted in the islands with frenzied enthusiasm. Bade was too absorbed in reports of rapidly-improving morale, and highly-successful mass-swimming exercises to care about this welcome. Although an ominous document titled "War in the Islands: U.S.—Japan," sat among the translated volumes of history at Bade's elbow, and served as a constant reminder that this pleasant situation could not be expected to last forever, Bade intended to enjoy it while it did last.

Bade greeted the plenipotentiary in his pleasant headquarters on the leveled top of the tall picturesque cone-shaped hill that rose high above Krakatoa, then dropped off abruptly by the sea.

The plenipotentiary, on entering the headquarters, mopped his brow constantly, kept glancing furtively around, and was plainly ill at ease. The interpreters took their places, and the conversation opened.

"As you see," said Bade, "we are comfortably settled here for the winter."

The plenipotentiary looked around and gave a hollow laugh.

"We are," added Bade, "perfectly prepared to return next . . . a . . . 'summer' . . . and take up where we left off."

"By next summer," said the plenipotentiary, "the United States will be a solid mass of guns from one coast to the other."

Bade shrugged, and the plenipotentiary added grimly, "And *missiles.*"

Despite himself, Bade winced.

One of Bade's clerks, carrying a message across the far end of the room, became distracted in his effort to be sure he heard everything. The clerk was busy watching Bade when he banged into the back of a tall filing case. The case tilted off-balance, then started to fall forward.

A second clerk sprang up to catch the side of the case. There was a low heavy rumble as all the drawers slid out.

The plenipotentiary sprang to his feet, and looked wildly around.

The filing case twisted out of the hands of the clerk and came down on the floor with a thundering crash.

The plenipotentiary snapped his eyes tightly shut, clenched his teeth, and stood perfectly still.

Bade and Runckel looked blankly at each other.

The plenipotentiary slowly opened his eyes, looked wonderingly around the room, jumped as the two clerks heaved the filing case upright, turned around to stare at the clerks and the case, turned back to look sharply at Bade, then clamped his jaw.

Bade, his own face as calm as he could make it, decided this might be as good a time as any to throw in a hard punch. He remarked, "You have two choices. You can make a mutually profitable agreement with us. Or you can force us to switch heavier forces and weapons to this planet and crush you. Which is it?"

"We," said the plenipotentiary coldly, "have the resources of the whole planet at our disposal. You have to bring everything from a distance. Moreover, we have captured a good deal of your equipment, which we may duplicate—"

"Lesser weapons," said Bade. "As if an enemy captured your rifles, duplicated them at great expense, and was then confronted with your nuclear bomb."

"This is our planet," said the plenipotentiary grimly, "and we will fight for it to the end."

"We don't want your planet."

The plenipotentiary's eyes widened. Then he burst into a string of invective that the translators couldn't follow. When he had finished, he took a deep breath and recapitulated the main point, "If you don't want it, what are you doing here?"

Bade said, "Your people are clearly warlike. After observing you for some time, a debate arose on our planet as to whether we should hit you or wait till you hit us. After a fierce debate, the first faction won."

"Wait a minute. How could *we* hit *you*? You come from another planet, don't you?"

"Yes, that's true. But it's also true that a baby shark is no great menace to anyone. Except that he will grow up into a big shark. That is how our first faction looked on earth."

The plenipotentiary scowled. "In other words, you'll kill the suspect before he has a chance to commit the crime. Then you justify it by saying the man would have committed a crime if he'd lived."

"We didn't intend to kill you—only to disarm you."

"How does all this square with your telling us you're just a scout party?"

"Are you under the impression," said Bade, "that this is the main invasion force? Would we attack without a full reconnaissance first? Do you think we would merely make one sizable landing, on *one* continent? How could we hope to conquer in that way?"

The plenipotentiary frowned, sucked in a deep breath, and mopped his forehead. "What's your offer?"

"Disarm yourselves voluntarily. All hostilities will end immediately."

The plenipotentiary gave a harsh laugh.

Bade said, "What's your answer?"

"What's your real offer?"

"As I remarked," said Bade, "there were two factions on our planet. One favored the attack, as self-preservation. The other faction opposed the attack, on moral and political grounds. The second faction at present holds that it is now impossible to remain aloof, as we had hoped to before the attack. One way or the other, we are now bound up with Earth. We either have to be enemies, or friends. As it happens, I am a member of the bloc that opposed the attack. The bloc that favored the attack has lost support owing to the results of our initial operations. Because of this political shift, I have practically a free hand at the moment." Bade paused as the plenipotentiary turned his head slightly and leaned forward with an intent look.

Bade said, "Your country has suffered by far the most from our attack. Obviously, it should profit the most. We have a number of scientific advances to offer as bargaining counters. Our essential condition is that we retain some overt standing—some foothold—some way of knowing by direct observation that this planet—or any nation of it—won't attack us."

The plenipotentiary scowled. "Every nation on Earth is pretty closely allied as a result of your attack. We're a world of united states—all practically one nation. And all the land on the globe belongs to one of us or the other. While there's bound to be considerable regional rivalry even when we have peace, that's all. Otherwise we're united. As a result, there's not going to be any peace as long as you've got your foot on land belonging to any of us. That includes Java, Sumatra, and even this . . . er . . . mountain we're on now." He looked around uneasily, and added, "We might let you have a little base, somewhere . . . maybe in Antarctica but I doubt it. We won't want any foreign planet sticking its nose in our business."

Bade said, "My proposal allows for that."

"I don't see how it could," said the plenipotentiary. "What is it?"

Bade told him.

The plenipotentiary sat as if he had been hit over the head with a rock. Then he let out a mighty burst of laughter, banged his hand on his knee and said, "You're serious?"

"Absolutely."

The plenipotentiary sprang to his feet. "I'll have to get in touch with my government. Who knows? Maybe— Who knows?" He strode out briskly.

About this time, a number of fast ships arrived from home. These ships were much in use during the next months. Delegations from both planets flew in both directions.

Runckel was highly uneasy. Incessantly he demanded, "Will it work? What if they flood our planet with a whole mob—"

"I have it on good authority," said Bade, "that our planet is every bit as uncomfortable for them as theirs is for us. We almost lost one of their delegates straight down through the mud on the last visit. They have to use dozens of towels for handkerchiefs every day, and that trace of ammonia in the atmosphere doesn't seem to agree with them. Some of them have even gotten fog-sick."

"Why should they go along with the idea, then?"

"It fits in with their nature. Besides, where else are they going to get another one? As one of their senators put it, 'Everything here on Earth is sewed up.' There's even a manifest destiny argument."

"Well, the idea has attractions, but—"

"Listen," said Bade, "I'm told not to prolong the war, because it's too costly and dangerous; not to leave behind a reservoir of fury to discharge on us in the future; not to surrender; not, in the present circumstances, to expect them to surrender. I am told to somehow keep a watch on them and bind their interests to ours; and not to forget the tie must be more than just on paper, it's got to be emotional as well as legal. On top of that, if possible, I'm supposed to open up commercial opportunities. Can you think of any other way?"

"Frankly, no," said Runckel.

There was a grumbling sound underneath them, and the room shivered slightly.

"What was that?" said Runckel.

Bade looked around, frowning. "I don't know."

A clerk came across the room and handed Runckel a message and Bade another message. Runckel looked up, scowling. "The sea water here is beginning to have an irritating effect on our men's skin."

"Never mind," said Bade, "their plenipotentiary is coming. We'll know one way or the other shortly."

Runckel looked worried, and began searching through his wastebasket.

The plenipotentiary came in grinning. "O.K.," he said, "the Russians are a little burned up, and I don't think Texas is any too happy, but nobody can think of a better way out. You're in."

He and Bade shook hands fervently. Photographers rushed in to snap pictures. Outside, Bade's band was playing "The Star-Spangled Banner."

"Another state," said the plenipotentiary, grinning expansively. "How's it feel to be a citizen?"

Runckel erupted from his wastebasket and bolted across the room.

"Krakatoa is a *volcano*!" he shouted. "And here's what a volcano is!"

There was a faint but distinct rumble underfoot.

The room emptied fast.

On the way home, they were discussing things.

Bade was saying, "I don't claim it's perfect, but then our two planets are so mutually uncomfortable there's bound to be little travel either way till we have a chance to get used to each other. Yet, we *can* go back and forth. Who has a better right than a citizen? And there's a good chance of trade and mutual profit. There's a good emotional tie." He frowned. "There's just one thing—"

"What's that?" said Runckel.

Bade opened a translated book to a page he had turned down. He read silently. He looked up perplexedly.

"Runckel," he said, "there are certain technicalities involved in being a citizen."

Runckel tensed. "What do you mean?"

"Oh— Well, like this." He looked back at the book for a moment.

"What is it?" demanded Runckel.

"Well," said Bade, "what do you suppose 'income tax' is?"

Runckel looked relieved. He shrugged.

"Don't worry about it," he said. "It's too fantastic. Probably it's just a myth."

WHO GOES BOING?
by Sarah A. Hoyt

The military team had been sent to the planet to determine if there were any dangers to future colonists. At first glance, it seemed idyllic—but that might not be all, folks.

★ ★ ★

***Sarah A. Hoyt** won the Prometheus Award for her novel* Darkship Thieves, *published by Baen, and since has authored* Darkship Renegades, A Few Good Men, *and the forthcoming* Through Fire, *more novels set in the same universe. She has written numerous short stories and novels in a number of genres, science fiction, fantasy, mystery, historical novels and historical mysteries, some under a number of pseudonyms, and has been published—among other places—in* Analog, Asimov's *and* Amazing. *For Baen, she has also written three books in her popular shape-shifter urban fantasy series,* Draw One in the Dark, Gentleman Takes a Chance, *and* Noah's Boy. *Her* According to Hoyt *is one of the most interesting blogs on the internet. Originally from Portugal, she lives in Colorado with her husband, two sons and the surfeit of cats necessary to a die-hard Heinlein fan.*

It was raining and the LT was grumbling. As the seven of us moved around, setting up the tents and securing the perimeter with breach detectors, he set his backpack down and looked around at the desolate area of peaks and rock spheres as far as the eye could see and muttered a long complaint from which the words "nerd army" and "I must have been crazy" emerged.

I traded a look with Sergeant Miller as he came over to help me affix the breach detector to a rock spire nearby. Sarge's eyes wrinkled a bit at the corner, but he didn't say anything, but "Having trouble with that, Bronk?"

I nodded. Technically my name and designation is Specialist First Class (Xenobiology) Bronkowsky of the Earth Exploration Corps. But just about everyone called me Bronk, and from the Sarge that was almost a compliment.

He was a hard-worn man of about fifty and he'd done countless drops. The people he'd led on their first exploration-drop now occupied positions everywhere, at every level, from Cabinet positions on several worlds, down to big names in research and science. But he'd chosen to stay out here, leading parties through space gates onto newly discovered planets. For the fun of it, I suspected. Though of course the bounty for clearing a new planet was fabulous and he was probably by now a many times multi-billionaire.

You wouldn't know it, as he fumbled at the sensor with clumsy-looking fingers, until he got the nanites embedded at the back of it to do whatever they needed to do to stick to the rock spire. "Well, you know," he said, speaking in a very low voice, and with every appearance of giving me some instruction about the apparatus supposed to detect any sort of intrusion—electromagnetic, infrared or biological—into our perimeter. "The LT transferred from what it pleases him to call the real army. He might be consorting with us, but he will always think he's better than us. He doesn't even think our ranks are real."

"Yes, sergeant," I said. "But the thing is, that I don't know why he transferred, if he thinks we're all so weird."

"Yeah, but the real army, as he calls it, the people who come after us to make sure the world is safe for colonists, don't get paid a tenth of what we do."

I nodded, and moved off to set up another perimeter sensor. I knew that. We all knew that. I'd always assumed it was because the EEC, or as they called us, the Nerd army required a heck of a lot more of education. All of us had at least graduate-level training in our disciplines by the time we joined, and to that more was added during EEC induction. There were few people out in the civilian population as trained as we were.

Had to be. We were the first people through to a new location. All that had been on this planet, once we'd first been able to open a gateway to it, were automated probes. And automated probes didn't get everything. Or even most of it. There had been that sentient planet, in the Hesperides which had not reacted at all to the probes, but had killed every man jack of the first three landing parties, before someone figured out what was wrong and closed that gateway for good.

And then there were the risks which awaited parties landing on planets with species that might be sentient, but which had no concept of machines, and thereby had left the first probes alone.

When I'd been a kid, back on Arrois, my dad said that even on our planet, so seemingly peaceful as it was, the first five exploration groups had been killed because of a microbe that could infect humans—a rare occurrence and which drove them mad.

This is why before the EEC was the Nerd Corps, the popular name for us had been the half hour men. Because that's how long you could expect to live on any given planet.

The instruments had gotten better, though, and we'd gotten better as well. Our training now allowed many of us to survive to a ripe old age. The others— Well, colonists would find it odd if they came through a newly opened planet and didn't find half a dozen of graves marked with name, rank and the symbol of the EEC. There was a reason we carried markers in our basic kit.

When I finished setting the perimeter and came back, the LT seemed to be in a better mood. Or at least Sarge was telling him "Yes, sir" a lot which usually put him in a better mood.

On my way to help the other four members of the party—Jackel, specialist in geology; Tadd, engineering; Gack in electromagnetics; and Lablue in Atmospheric science—prepare dinner, I heard the LT say something about not being a scientist and not knowing what to do with a passel of geniuses.

These were complaints I knew from our former two drops, and I suspected they were bad as all get out for morale, except that they weren't because none of us paid him much attention. We went around and did our thing and reported to Sarge, and he made it all palatable for the LT, which is what I suspect made the LT crazy. Crazier. Whatever.

The guys and I had been working together since basic orientation, and we started warming up the food packs, in silence, and with no more than the occasional glance around. In no time at all we were settled down and eating from our ration bowls, when there was—

I can't describe it, but it was a sound sort of behind and above me. Only it wasn't a sound, so much. It was like the sensation you'd expect the sound "boing" to cause if it were a feeling up the back of your neck.

At the same time, Gack tried to jump up and backwards, only he forgot to get up first and got soup all over his pants. And he didn't even look at his pants, nor around him, but stood there, frowning behind me.

I turned around but could see nothing where he was looking, save a barren expanse of rock and spires between sheets of falling rain.

"Gack?" Sarge said. "What happened?"

Gack was one of those enormous men that people tend to think grow in high grav environments. This isn't true. He was actually from the same region I came from, an agricultural planet in Andromeda. But he was square built and square-jawed, six feet seven with a growth of beard that resisted his twice-a-day shaving. It went oddly with his wide-open eyes, and the hand he lifted to cover his mouth. "I—" he said. Then stopped. He wiped the back of his hand across his mouth, as though he were trying to gain time. Then he took a deep breath. "I saw a rabbit."

Sarge looked at me. I was the xenobiology expert, which in practical fact meant that I was the expert in anything biological, from the life forms on this planet to medic duties to my own unit. I had studied the reports sent by all the probes that had examined this world for years before we were allowed through. "There aren't any life forms we'd classify as animals," I said, slowly. "Or at least none our probes reported. The most advanced life form is a kind of mold spore. Of course—" I paused. "That is also the technical classification of the sheep in Proxima Centauri, the ones popularly known as Vegetable Lamb."

Sarge shrugged. "So, that means it could be a small pseudo-animal that looks like an Earth Rabbit, I supp—"

"No," Gack said. "No, Sarge, you don't understand. This wasn't a normal rabbit. It was . . . It went on two feet, and it had . . . it looked humanoid, but with really long ears, and huge eyes. It was odd."

"Um . . ." the LT said. "You saw an awful lot in that glimpse."

"I—It was just an impression," he said.

"It could be an hallucination, caused by some undetected compound in the air," I said. And I dove into the tent for the medical kit. But the med tech we had didn't show Gack as suffering from any poisoning or any other undue influence.

We went to bed that night feeling restless and, in my case, worried. I'd known Gack a long time. It just wasn't like him to freak out at some nonsensical glimpse of an impossible creature. And what he'd seen was impossible.

I woke up in the middle of the night with another impression of having heard a sound. The sound was "paff" as best I can transcribe it. And there was an idea that there had been a scream of some sort just after it.

There is no duty to get up and check on things in the middle of the night, unless one of the perimeter alarms has gone off or the officers give orders. But in the Nerd Corps, you don't wait for those. Not if you want to live.

I got up. There was no sound around me, except the pattering of the steady, whispering rain on the tent roof. I couldn't even hear any noise from my squad mates. Which was fine, since we had individual tents, and they weren't that close.

My exercise fatigues, which I wore as pajamas on these missions, were not water proof, so I pulled on the regulation rain poncho before stepping out to check the perimeter units.

While I was looking at the last one—showing nothing had breached our perimeter line—I heard steps behind me, and turned to see Gack, also awake, and also wearing a rain poncho. He was walking with a sort of exaggerated, comedic stealth, which surprised me, because Gack was known for many things, but none of them was physical comedy.

I said, "You heard it too?"

"What?" he asked, stopping.

"You heard the sound of something falling?" I asked. "And the scream?"

His eyes shot out. What I mean by this is that his eyes came out of his head, straight at me, then sagged onto his face, suspended from springs. He put them back in, matter of fact, and said, "Uh, no."

I was trying to tell myself I hadn't seen what I'd thought I'd seen. But there are things that you can't deny. And if I'd gone around the bend, it still wouldn't run to seeing people's eyes pop out on springs. I kept my face as absolutely neutral as I could, and nodded, "Okay," I said, but walked sideways towards Gack's tent, and drummed my fingers on the outside of it. When no one answered, I stooped momentarily to unfasten the magnetic closure in the front.

The tent was . . . covered in blood. And in the middle of it all was an anvil, huge and improbable. An antique anvil, of the sort that people had used to beat metal on. The kind of thing you only saw in museums.

I jumped sideways at a whistle above me, and jumped out of the way, just as a big square thing fell where I'd been seconds before. I turned around to see Gack—or whatever it was that looked like Gack—hop towards me at crazed speed.

I did what any man would do. I screamed and ran. Right into the LT who had got out of his tent. I have no idea what I told him, but it probably didn't matter, as he took a look at Gack, then jumped out of the way in his turn, pulling me along as yet another square thing fell where we'd been.

By now the camp was bedlam, with everyone running around in a state of undress, and pseudo-Gack hopping around and, somehow, perhaps causing heavy objects to appear.

LaBlue, finally, had the presence of mind to shoot at pseudo-Gack. There was a sound like "phlui" as the energy weapon hit Gack, and there was a feeling like an implosion, as Gack disappeared and air rushed in to fill the place he'd been.

It was a while before anyone spoke, and then it was Sarge, who said, "What was that?"

"I don't know," I said. "But it wasn't Gack. Gack is dead. In his tent."

The funny thing is that the anvil I'd seen in the tent was no longer there, only Gack pâté all over the inside surfaces. The other things that had fallen, mostly square boxes, were also not there anymore. The LT said they were safes, things used to keep documentation and valuables in the pre-space days. But none of us had any idea why the pseudo-Gack had dropped them everywhere, or even if he had or if they were just an associated phenomenon to whatever had killed Gack and taken his form.

Still, in moments like this, it was good to have protocol to fall back upon. Gack had to be buried on this planet, and his grave appropriately marked. We decided to strike the tent and bury the whole thing, and did just that, digging a deep grave in an area just at the edge of the camp. Everyone had gone around and checked the perimeter and verified that neither biological nor electromagnetic violation had occurred, so we were all jumpy and looking at each other. And I, particularly, was alert to the sound of something that wasn't quite heard with the ears. Something like boing or paff felt at the back of the neck.

For a moment, as we were digging soggy reddish dirt back in atop the tent that contained the mortal remains of Gack, I thought I heard-felt that boing, but nothing strange happened.

Until we were setting the marker to show Gack's universal birth and death date, that is. That was when the LT gave Sarge a cigar. This in itself was weird enough, because smoking was not just a rare enough thing, but a very expensive habit. There were some planets where it might be more common, like the place in Andromeda where they grew tobacco. But to carry one to Earth quarters and bring it on an expedition was unlikely, since if you had a cigar you could sell it for a lot of money on Earth.

Sarge seemed to sense the strangeness of it, and stood there, holding the cigar in between his fingers, until the LT snapped, gave an odd little laugh, took the cigar from Sarge's hand, jammed it in Sarge's mouth, brought out a little stick, aflame, and set fire to the end of the cigar. At which point the cigar exploded, blackening Sarge's face.

It took a moment, and I might have been the first to react. I ran to where I'd last seen the LT before this, and found him behind a spear of rock. He had been crushed by what looked like an antique musical instrument, the kind you still see on Earth sometimes, called a Grand Piano.

Four of us shot the LT at the same time. Or rather we shot the creature who was hopping around our camp, looking but not moving like the LT. This time it had no effect. Or rather, for a moment, it created a hole in the middle of its chest, but then it looked at it and said "uh oh" and the hole healed.

LaBlue who was nearer hit the pseudo-LT on the head with his pack, the one he'd carried on his back here, and which contained his folded tent and all his gear.

The pseudo-LT folded down like an accordion, and ran. He ran right off the perimeter, and disappeared.

Leaving us all breathing hard, scared, and not at all sure what we were facing. Sarge organized those of us who remained. He detailed Jackel and Tadd to dig the LT's grave and move the body—easier since the piano had of course disappeared—and he and I and LaBlue went around the perimeter, checking all the readings.

"How is it possible," LaBlue said, "for whatever it is to get past our perimeter without setting off the alarms?"

I was biting the inside of my lip to keep from screaming in frustration at the events, but I'd been thinking about it since Gack had bought it. "All the life forms we've found have been either energy or flesh," I said. "Well, except those bio forms that are plants, including ambulatory ones, but for the purpose of this discussion, we'll call them flesh. But that doesn't preclude life forms made of something else."

"What else could it be?" LaBlue asked. "What other than energy or biological beings."

"Minerals, I suppose?" Sarge asked.

LaBlue shook his head. "Nah, the alarms would detect different substances from the ones previously identified for this site," he said. "It would detect movement too."

"Are we dealing with another sentient planet?" I asked.

LaBlue shrugged. "Even if it were, certainly we'd have detected movement. And besides, why would aliens pelt us with Earth antiques?"

I had no answer to it, partly because at that moment I heard-felt "boing" and jumped aside just in time to avoid a black, globular object which fell where we'd been, and which said ACME on the side and had a sort of rope on top. The end of the rope was burning.

I recognized it then, and it all fell in a pattern in my mind. I screamed, "Take cover." Then jumped behind a rock spear.

There was an explosion, and a flash of fire.

When we emerged, three of us were fine, but LaBlue had been too close to the explosion and was dead, a startled look on his face.

Sarge sighed, and Jackel and Tadd looked too stunned to even mention digging another grave, but I said, "Wait, I think I know what's happening?"

"Oh?" Sarge said.

"Yes, Sarge. You know how we got to some worlds and found that they were capturing our entertainment transmissions and knew about us from them?"

"Not very well," Sarge said. "I mean, they didn't know about us very well. The older transmissions, which would have reached the more distant stars are also more substantially degraded by the time they get there. Some races managed to reconstruct all of a movie or a series of transmissions, which is why that place in Proxima is the ILoveLucy planet, but—"

"Cartoons," I said.

"Beg your pardon?" LaBlue said, so surprised that he spoke before Sarge reacted.

"Cartoons were drawn adventures from the time before computers were significant in entertainment," I said. "Middle twentieth century. Drawn adventures that were animated by drawing a lot of similar freeze frames, then making them move very fast to give the impression of movement, on movie."

"Sounds inefficient," Sarge said.

"It was, but it was also very imaginative. The cartoonists, as they were called, created a whole universe of creatures, like . . . animated anthropomorphic rabbits, a world without death, where characters pulled themselves from under heavy weights, or recovered easily from explosions. The projectiles were often safes, pianos or anvils."

"How do you know this, Bronk?" Sarge asked.

"I grew up on a backward planet, sergeant. Until we got more advanced technology when I was fifteen, we had locally built televisions and we watched a lot of antique entertainment on them."

"I see. So you think the beings on this planet, whatever they are reconstituted those signals—"

"Possibly from one of the colony planets closer than Earth," I said. "Yes, sir."

"And that they think this is what human beings on Earth are actually like?"

"It's possible, sir. It seems like few species have the imagination humans have, and those cartoons . . . well, if you didn't know the time and place they came from, you too might not believe someone just made them up out of whole cloth. Heck, even knowing the time and the place."

"But what are they?" LaBlue said. "What are these creatures? What makes them?"

I shrugged. "We know there are energies in the universe we can't measure or get a full fix on. Take the singing ghosts of Antares 5. Some people think they are powered by thought."

"That is—" the Sergeant said, and then used a word that was also archaic and referred to the excreta of an Earth bovine.

"Yes, sir," I said. "Or as we like to put it not scientifically proven. But we still can't explain the ghosts, sir. Or it could be anything else. There are those who posit time as a form of energy, and if that's so, then these things could be time itself. That's not important," I said. "The important thing is this: how do we survive their attacks, their ability to mimic those of us they kill and replace, and how do we get back to Earth in one piece?"

The Sergeant said a word that rhymed with ducked, followed by, "if I know. The gate won't open again for another six hours." He looked around at the shambles of the camp. "The question is whether any of us will be alive and sane enough to report."

Which is when Jackel and Tadd started chasing each other with the shovels. Which by itself was not as bad as the fact that when one hit the other with a shovel, the other would walk around for a while looking like he'd been compressed, then would pop back to normal size with a sound like "boing."

Sarge and I fell back, retreating behind a spear of stone. Behind us was the edge of a cliff. We stared at the camp where Jackel and Tadd hit each other amiably and ran around in the deranged motions of cartoon characters.

If I squinted, I could see two immobile forms, out by the graves. Three, if I focused really hard, though the third was a little far off and indistinct. Three.

I turned around to look at Sarge, who looked back at me.

I heard "boing" and felt it at the back of my neck, and rolled out of the way, and shot at Sarge, even as an anvil fell between us.

Sarge got a hole in his chest, said "uh, oh" and ran.

He ran right off the edge of the cliff in a straight line, until he looked down and realized there was nothing under him. And then he fell.

I went to the edge of the cliff and looked down, to see his—its?—crumpled body far below.

Well, that was that. I was the only human being still left. I'd have to last long enough, until the gate to Earth opened again.

Back in the camp, the pseudo-Jackel and pseudo-Tadd were dropping pianos on each other and crawling out from under them to fight another day.

I couldn't understand the purpose of it, and it made my eyes pop out. I had to keep pushing them in when they dangled in springs against my face. It got old fast.

Clutching my gun tightly, I prepared to keep the strange creatures at bay.

I couldn't wait till the gate to Earth opened again.

HISTORICAL NOTE
by Murray Leinster

History has diverged from this 1951 story by the Dean of science fiction. The Soviet Union did come apart (though, alas, at this writing it may be coming back together) though not in the way that Leinster chronicled. But it would have been a lot more fun if this had been the way that the U.S.S.R. became the U.S.S. Was.

★ ★ ★

***William Fitzgerald Jenkins** (1886-1975) was a prolific and successful writer, selling stories to magazines of all sorts, from pulps like* Argosy *to the higher-paying slicks such as* Collier's *and* The Saturday Evening Post, *writing stories ranging from westerns, to mysteries, to science fiction. However, for SF he usually used the pen name of Murray Leinster, and he used it often. Even though SF was a less lucrative field than other categories of fiction, he enjoyed writing it (fortunately for SF readers everywhere) and wrote a great deal of it, including such classics as "Sidewise in Time," "First Contact," and "A Logic Named Joe," the last being a story you should keep in mind the next time someone repeats the canard that SF never predicted the home computer or the internet. Leinster did it (though under his real name, this time) in* Astounding Science-Fiction *in 1946! His first SF story was "The Runaway Skyscraper," published in 1919, and his last was the third of three novelizations of the* Land of the Giants *TV show. For the length of his career, his prolificity, and his introduction of original concepts into SF,* *fans in the 1940s began calling him the Dean of science fiction, a title he richly deserved.*

Professor Vladimir Rojestvensky, it has since been learned, remade the world at breakfast one morning while eating a bowl of rather watery red-cabbage soup, with black bread on the side. It is now a matter of history that the soup was not up to par that day, and the black bread in Omsk all that week was sub-marginal. But neither of these factors is considered to have contributed to the remaking of civilization.

The essential thing was that, while blowing on a spoonful of red-cabbage soup, Professor Rojestvensky happened to think of an interesting inference or deduction to be drawn from the Bramwell-Weems Equation expressing the distribution of energy among the nucleus particles of the lighter atoms. The Bramwell-Weems Equation was known in Russia as the Gabrilovitch-Brekhov Formula because, obviously, Russians must have thought of it first. The symbols, however, were the same as in the capitalist world.

Professor Rojestvensky contemplated the inference with pleasure. It was very interesting indeed. He finished his breakfast, drank a glass of hot tea, wrapped himself up warmly, and set out for his classrooms in the University of Omsk. It was a long walk, because the streetcars were not running. It was a fruitful one, though. For as he walked, Professor Rojestvensky arranged his reasoning in excellent order. When he arrived at the University he found a directive from the Council of Soviet Representatives for Science and Culture. It notified him that from now on Soviet scientists must produce more and better and more Earth-shaking discoveries—or else. Therefore he would immediately report, in quadruplicate, what first-rank discoveries he was prepared to make in the science of physics. And they had better be good.

He was a modest man, was Professor Rojestvensky, but to fail to obey the directive meant losing his job. So he quakingly prepared a paper outlining his extension of the Bramwell-Weems Equation—but he was careful to call it the Gabrilovitch-Brekhov Formula and persuaded one of his students to make four copies of it in exchange for a quarter of a pound of cheese. Then he sent off the four copies and slept badly for weeks afterward. He knew his work was good, but he didn't know whether it was good enough. It merely accounted for the mutual repulsion of the molecules of gases, it neatly explained the formation of comets' tails, and it could have led to the prediction of clouds of calcium vapor already observed in interstellar space. Professor Rojestvensky did not guess he had remade the world.

Weeks passed, and nothing happened. That was a bad month in Russian science. The staffs of Medical Research and Surgical Advancement had already reported everything they could dream up. Workers in Aerodynamic Design weren't sticking out their necks. The last man to design a new plane went to prison for eight years when a fuel line clogged on his plane's test flight. And Nuclear Fission workers stuck to their policy of demanding unobtainable equipment and supplies for the furtherance of their work. So Professor Rojestvensky's paper was absolutely the only contribution paddable to Earth-shaking size. His paper itself was published in the *Soviet Journal of Advanced Science*. Then it was quoted unintelligibly in *Pravda* and *Tass*, with ecstatic editorials pointing out how far Russian science was ahead of mere capitalist-imperialistic research. And that was that.

Possibly that would have been the end of it all, but that some two weeks later an American jet bomber flew twelve thousand miles, dropped fifteen tons of simulated bombs—actually condensed milk lowered to Earth by parachutes—and returned to base without refueling. This, of course, could not be allowed to go unchallenged. So a stern directive went to Aerodynamic Design. An outstanding achievement in aviation must be produced immediately. It must wipe the Americans' decadent, capitalistic eyes. Or—so the directive said explicitly—else.

The brain trust which was Aerodynamic Design went into sweating executive session, seeking a really air tight procedure for passing the buck. They didn't want to lose their jobs, which were fairly fat ones, any more than Professor Rojestvensky had. They had to cook up something in a hurry, something really dramatic, with an out putting the blame squarely on somebody else if it didn't work. They couldn't blame Aviation Production, though. The head of that splendid organization had in with the Politbureau. Something new and drastic and good was needed.

In the end a desperate junior official began to hunt through recent Soviet contributions to science. If he could find something impressive that could be twisted into an advance in aerodynamics, it could be designed and built, and any failure blamed on the scientist who had furnished false data as a form of alien-inspired sabotage. Scientists were always expendable in Russian politics. It was time to expend one. Largely because his name was on top of the pile, Professor Rojestvensky was picked.

This, in detail, is the process by which his extension of the Bramwell-Weems—or Gabrilovitch-Brekhov—Equation was selected for practical development. Our brave new world is the result. Aerodynamic Design borrowed a man from Nuclear Fission in a deal between two department heads, and the Nuclear Fission man agreed to work up something elaborate and impressive. He set to work on Professor Rojestvensky's figures. And presently he turned pale, and gulped very rapidly several times, and muttered, *"Gospody pomilov!"* That meant, "Lord have mercy on us!" and it was not a good Russian expression any longer, but it was the way he felt. In time, he showed his results to Aerodynamic Design and said, in effect, "But, it might really work!"

Aerodynamic Design sent him out to Omsk to get Professor Rojestvensky to check his calculations. It was a shrewd move. The Nuclear Fission man and Professor Rojestvensky got along splendidly. They ate red-cabbage soup together and the professor O.K.'d the whole project. That made him responsible for anything that went wrong and Aerodynamic Design, en masse, was much relieved. They sent in a preliminary report on their intentions and started to make one gadget themselves. The Nuclear Fission man was strangely willing to play along and see what happened. He supervised the construction of the thing.

It consisted of a set of straps very much like a parachute harness, hung from a little bar of brass with a plating of metallic sodium, under another plating of nickel, and the whole thing enclosed in a plastic tube. There was a small box with a couple of controls. That was all there was to it.

When it was finished, the Nuclear Fission man tried it out himself. He climbed into the harness in the Wind Tunnel Building of Aerodynamic Design's plant, said the Russian equivalent of "Here goes nothing!" and flipped over one of the controls. In his shakiness, he pushed it too far. He left the ground, went straight up like a rocket and cracked his head against the three-story-high ceiling and was knocked cold for two hours. They had to haul him down from the ceiling with an extension ladder because the gadget he'd made tried insistently to push a hole through the roof to the wide blue yonder.

When he recovered consciousness, practically all of Aerodynamic Design surrounded him, wearing startled expressions. And they stayed around while he found out what the new device would do. Put briefly, it would do practically anything but make fondant. It was a personal flying device, not an airplane, which would lift up to two hundred twenty-five pounds. It would hover perfectly. It would, all by itself, travel in any direction at any speed a man could stand without a windshield.

True, the Rojestvensky Effect which made it fly was limited. No matter how big you made the metal bar, it wouldn't lift more than roughly a hundred kilos, nearly two-twenty-five pounds. But it worked by the fact that the layer of metallic sodium on the brass pushed violently away from all other sodium more than three meters away from it. Sodium within three meters wasn't affected. And there was sodium everywhere. Sodium chloride—common table salt—is present everywhere on Earth and the waters under the Earth, but it isn't present in the heavens above. So the thing would fly anywhere over land or sea, but it wouldn't go but so high. The top limit for the gadget's flight was about four thousand feet, with a hundred-and-fifty-pound man in the harness. A heavier man couldn't get up so high. And it was infinitely safe. A man could fly night, day, or blind drunk and nothing could happen to him. He couldn't run into a mountain because he'd bounce over it. The thing was marvelous!

★ ★ ★

Aerodynamic Design made a second triumphant report to the Politbureau. A new and appropriately revolutionary device—it was Russian—had been produced in obedience to orders. Russian science had come through! When better revolutionary discoveries were made, Russia would make them! And if the device was inherently limited to one-man use—ha-ha! It gave the Russian army flying infantry! It provided the perfect modern technique for revolutionary war! It offered the perfect defense for peaceful, democratic Russia against malevolent capitalistic imperialism! In short, it was hot stuff!

As a matter of fact, it was. Two months later there was a May Day celebration in Moscow at which the proof of Russia's superlative science was unveiled to the world. Planes flew over Red Square in magnificent massed formations. Tanks and guns rumbled through the streets leading to Lenin's tomb. But the infantry—where was the infantry? Where were the serried ranks of armed men, shaking the earth with their steady tread? Behind the tanks and guns there was only emptiness.

For a while only. There was silence after the guns had gone clanking by. Then a far-distant, tumultuous uproar of cheering. Something new, something strange and marvelous had roused the remotest quarter of the city to enthusiasm. Far, far away, the flying infantry appeared!

Some of the more naïve of the populace believed at first that the U.S.S.R. had made a nonaggression pact with God and that a detachment of angels was parading in compliment to the Soviet Union. It wasn't too implausible, as a first impression. Shoulder to shoulder, rank after rank, holding fast to lines like dog leashes that held them in formation, no less than twelve thousand Russian infantrymen floated into the Red Square some fifteen feet off the ground. They were a bit ragged as to elevation, and they tended to eddy a bit at street comers, but they swept out of the canyons which were streets at a magnificent twenty-five miles an hour, in such a display of airborne strength as the world had never seen before.

The population cheered itself hoarse. The foreign attachés looked inscrutable. The members of the Politbureau looked on and happily began to form in their minds the demands they would make for pacts of peace and friendship and military bases with formerly recalcitrant European nations. These pacts of closest friendship were going to be honeys!

That same morning Professor Rojestvensky breakfasted on red-cabbage soup and black bread, wholly unaware that he had remade the world. But that great events were in the making was self-evident even to members of the United States Senate. Newsreel pictures of the flying infantry parade were shown everywhere. And the Communist parties of the Western nations were, of course, wholly independent organizations with no connection whatever with Moscow. But they could not restrain their enthusiasm over this evidence of Russian greatness. Cheering sections of Communists attended every showing of the newsreels in every theater and howled themselves hoarse. They took regular turns at it and were supplied with throat lozenges by ardent Party workers. Later newsreels showing the flying infantry returning to camp over the rooftops of Moscow evoked screams of admiration. When a Russian documentary film appeared in the Western world, skillfully faking the number of men equipped with individual flying units, the national, patriotic Communist party members began to mention brightly that everybody who did not say loudly, at regular intervals, that Russia was the greatest country in the world was having his name written down for future reference.

Inspired news stories mentioned that the entire Russian army would be airborne within three months. The magnificent feat of Russian industry in turning out three million flying devices per month brought forth screaming headlines in the *Daily Worker.* There were only two minor discords in the choral antiphony of national-Communist hosannas and capitalistic alarm.

One was an air-force general's meditative answer to the question: "What defense can there be against an army traveling throughout the air like a swarm of locusts?" The general said mildly: "Wel-l-l, we carried eighteen tons of condensed milk fourteen thousand miles last week, and we've done pretty good work for the Agriculture Department dusting grasshoppers."

The other was the bitter protest made by the Russian ambassador in Washington. He denounced the capitalist-economy-inspired prevention of the shipment to Russia of an order for brass rods plated with metallic sodium, then plated with nickel, and afterward enclosed in plastic tubes. State Department investigation showed that while an initial order of twelve thousand five hundred such rods had been shipped in April, there had been a number of fires in the factory since, and it had been closed down until fire-prevention methods could be devised. It was pointed out that metallic sodium is hot stuff. It catches fire when wetted or even out of pure cussedness it is fiercely inflammable.

This was a fact that Aviation Production in Russia had already found out. The head man was in trouble with his own friends in the Politbureau for failing to meet production quotas, and he'd ordered the tricky stuff—the rods had to be dipped in melted sodium in a helium atmosphere for quantity production—manufactured in the benighted and scientifically retarded United States.

There was another item that should be mentioned, too. Within a week after the issue of personal fliers to Russian infantrymen, no less than sixty-four desertions by air to Western nations took place. On the morning after the first night maneuvers of the airborne force, ninety-two Russians were discovered in the Allied half of Germany alone, trying to swap their gadgets for suits of civilian clothes.

They were obliged, of course. Enterprising black marketers joyfully purchased the personal fliers, shipped them to France, Holland, Belgium, Sweden, Norway, and Switzerland, and sold them at enormous profits. In a week it was notorious that any Russian deserter from the flying infantry could sell his flight equipment for enough money to buy forty-nine wrist watches and still stay drunk for six months. It was typical private enterprise. It was unprincipled and unjust. But it got worse.

Private entrepreneurs stole the invention itself. At first the units were reproduced one by one in small shops for high prices. But the fire hazard was great. Production-line methods were really necessary both for economy and industrial safety reasons. So after a while, the Bofors Company, of Sweden, rather apologetically turned out a sport model, in quantity, selling for *kronen* worth twelve dollars and fifty cents in American money. Then the refurbished I.G. Farben put out a German type which sold openly for a sum in occupation marks equal to only nine eighty American. A Belgian model priced—in francs—at five fifty had a wide sale, but was not considered quite equal to the Dutch model at guilders exchanging for six twenty-five or the French model with leather-trimmed straps at seven dollars' worth of devaluated francs.

The United States capitalists started late. Two bicycle makers switched their factories to the production of personal fliers, yet by the middle of June, American production was estimated at not over fifty thousand per month. But in July, one hundred eighty thousand were produced and in August the production—expected to be about three hundred thousand—suddenly went sky-high when both General Electric and Westinghouse entered the market. In September, American production was over three million and it became evident that manufacturers would have to compete with each other on finish and luxury of design. The days when anything that would fly was salable at three fifty and up were over.

The personal flier became a part of American life, as, of course, it became a part of life everywhere. In the United States, the inherent four-thousand-foot ceiling of personal fliers kept regular air traffic from having trouble except near airports, and flier-equipped airport police soon developed techniques for traffic control. A blimp patrol had to be set up off the Atlantic Coast to head back enthusiasts for foreign travel and Gulf Stream fishing, but it worked very well. There were three million, then five million, and by November twelve million personal-flier-equipped Americans aloft. And the total continued to rise. Suburban railways—especially after weatherproof garments became really good—joyfully abandoned their short-haul passenger traffic and all the railroads settled down contentedly to their real and profitable business of long-haul heavy-freight carriage. Even the airlines prospered incredibly. The speed limitation on personal fliers still left the jet-driven plane the only way to travel long distances quickly, and passengers desiring intermediate stops simply stepped out of a plane door when near their desired destination. Rural residential developments sprang up like mushrooms. A marked trend toward country life multiplied. Florida and California became so crowded that everybody got disgusted and went home, and the millennium appeared to be just around the comer.

Then came the dawn. It was actually the dawn of the remade world, but it looked bad for a while. The Soviet government stormed at the conscienceless, degraded theft of its own State secret by decadent and imperialistic outsiders. Actual Russian production of personal fliers was somewhere around twenty-five hundred per month at a time when half the population of Europe and America had proved that flying was cheaper than walking. Sternly, the Soviet government—through the Cominform—suggested that now was the time for all good Communists to come to the aid of their Party. The Party needed personal fliers. Fast. So enthusiastic Communists all over Europe flew loyally to Russia to contribute to the safety of their ideals, and to prove the international solidarity of the proletariat. They landed by tens of thousands without passports, without ration cards, and often with insufficient Party credentials. They undoubtedly had spies among them, along with noble comrades. So the U.S.S.R. had to protect itself. Regretfully, Russian officials clapped the new arrivals into jail as they landed, took away their fliers, and sent them back to their national borders in box cars. But they did send indoctrination experts to travel with them and explain that this was hospitable treatment and that they were experiencing the welcome due to heroes.

But borders were not only crossed by friends. Smuggling became a sport. Customs barriers for anything but heavy goods simply ceased to exist. The French national monopoly on tobacco and matches evaporated, and many Frenchmen smoked real tobacco for the first time in their lives. Some of them did not like it. And there were even political consequences of the personal-flier development. In Spain, philosophical anarchists and *syndicalistos* organized political demonstrations. Sometimes hundreds of them flew all night long to rendezvous above the former royal palace in Madrid—now occupied by the Caudillo—and empty chamber-pots upon it at dawn. Totalitarianism in Spain collapsed.

The Russian rulers were made of sterner stuff. True, the Iron Curtain became a figment. Political refugees from Russia returned sometimes—thoughtfully carrying revolvers in case they met somebody they disliked and disseminated capitalistic propaganda and cast doubts upon the superiority of the Russian standard of living. Often they had wrist watches and some of them even brought along personal fliers as gifts to personal friends. Obviously, this sort of thing was subversive. The purity of Soviet culture could not be maintained when foreigners could enter Russia at will and call the leaders of the Soviet Union liars. Still less could it survive when they proved it.

So the Soviet Union fought back. The Amy set up radars to detect the carriers of anti-dialectic-materialism propaganda. The Ministry of Propaganda worked around the clock. People wearing wrist watches were shot if they could not prove they had stolen them from Germans, and smugglers and young men flying Sovietward to ply Russian girls with chocolate bars were intercepted. For almost a week it seemed that radar and flying infantry might yet save the Soviet way of life.

But then unprincipled capitalists dealt a new foul blow. They advertised that anybody intending to slip through the Iron Curtain should provide himself with Bouffon's Anti-Radar Tin Foil Strips, available in one-kilogram cartons at all corner shops. Tin foil strips had been distributed by Allied bombers to confuse German radar during the last war. Smugglers and romantic young men, meditatively dripping tin foil as they flew through the Russian night, made Russian radar useless.

Nothing was left but war. So a splendid, overwhelming blow was planned and carried out. In two nights the entire Soviet force of flying infantry was concentrated. On the third night four hundred thousand flying infantry went sweeping westward in an irresistible swarm. The technique had been worked out by the General Staff on orders from the Politbureau to devise immediately a new and unbeatable system of warfare—or else. The horde of flying warriors was to swoop down from the darkness on Western European cities, confiscate all personal fliers and ship them back to Russia for the use of reinforcements. There could be no resistance. Every part of an enemy nation was equally reachable and equally vulnerable. Russian troops could not be bombed because they would be deliberately intermixed with the native population. There could be no fighting but street fighting. This would be war on a new scale, invasion from a new dimension; it would be conquest which could not be fought.

The only trouble was that practically every square mile of European sky was inhabited by somebody enjoying the fruits of Russian science in the form of a personal flier. And secrecy simply couldn't be managed. All Europe knew just about as much about the Russian plan as the Russians did.

So when the clouds of flying infantry came pouring through the night, great droning bombers with riding lights and landing lights aglow came roaring out of the west to meet them. There were, to be sure, Soviet jet fighters with the defending fleet. They tangled with the Russian escort and fought all over the sky, while the bombers focused their landing lights on the infantry and roared at them. The sensation of being ahead of a bellowing plane rushing at one was exactly that of being on a railroad track with an express train on the loose. There was nothing to do but duck. The Russian soldiers ducked. Then the bombers began to shoot star shells, rockets, Roman candles and other pyrotechnics. The Russian troops dispersed. And an army that is dispersed simply isn't an army: When finally vast numbers of enthusiastic personal-flier addicts came swooping through the night with flashlights and Very pistols, the debacle was complete. The still-fighting planes overhead had nothing left to fight for. Those that were left went home.

When dawn came the Russian soldiers were individuals scattered over three separate nations. And Russian soldiers, in quantity, tend to fight or loot as opportunity offers. But a Russian soldier, as an individual, craves civilian clothes above all else. Russian soldiers landed and tried to make deals for their flying equipment according to the traditions of only a few months before. They were sadly disillusioned. The best bargain most of them could make was simply a promise that they wouldn't be sent back home—and they took that.

It was all rather anticlimactic, and it got worse. Russia was still legally at war with everybody, even after its flying infantry sat down and made friends. And Russia was still too big to invade. On the other hand, it had to keep its air force in hand to fight off attempts at invasion. Just to maintain that defensive frame of mind, Allied bombers occasionally smashed some Russian airfields, and some railroads, and—probably at the instigation of decadent capitalists—they did blow up the Aviation Production factories, even away off in the Urals. Those Ural raids by the way, were made by the United States Air Force, flying over the North Pole to prove that it could deliver something besides condensed milk at long distances.

But the war never really amounted to much. The Allies had all the flying infantry they wanted to use, but they didn't want to use it. The Russians worked frantically, suborning treason and developing black marketers and so on, to get personal fliers for defense, but Russian civilians would pay more than even the Soviet government, so the Army hardly got any at all. To correct this situation the Supreme Soviet declared private possession of a personal flier a capital offense, and shot several hundred citizens to prove it. Among the victims of this purge, by the way, was the Nuclear-Fission man who had worked out the personal flier from Professor Rojestvensky's figures. But people wanted personal fliers. When owning one became a reason for getting shot, almost half the Russian government's minor officials piled out of the nearest window and went somewhere else, and the bigger officials kept their personal fliers where they could grab them at any instant and take off. And the smuggling kept on. Before long practically everybody had private fliers but the army—and flier-equipped soldiers tended to disappear over the horizon if left alone after nightfall.

So the Soviet Union simply fell to pieces. The Supreme Soviet couldn't govern when anybody who disagreed with it could go up the nearest chimney and stay gone. It lost the enthusiastic support of the population as soon as it became unable to shoot the unenthusiastic. And when it was committed to the policy of shooting every Russian citizen who possessed proof of the supreme splendor of Russian science—a personal flier—why public discipline disappeared. Party discipline went with it. All discipline followed. And when there wasn't any discipline there simply wasn't any Soviet Union and therefore there wasn't any war, and everybody might as well stop fooling around and cook dinner. The world, in fact, was remade.

Undoubtedly, the world is a good deal happier since Professor Rojestvensky thought of an interesting inference to be drawn from the Bramwell-Weems Equation while at his breakfast of red-cabbage soup and black bread. There are no longer any iron-bound national boundaries, and therefore no wars or rumors of wars. There are no longer any particular reasons for cities to be crowded, and a reasonably equitable social system has to exist or people will go fishing or down to the South Seas, or somewhere where they won't be bothered.

But in some ways the change has not been as great as one might have expected. About a year after the world was remade, an American engineer thought up a twist on Professor Rojestvensky's figure. He interested the American continental government and they got ready to build a spaceship. The idea was that if a variation of that brass-sodium-nickel bar was curled around a hundred-foot-long tube, and metallic sodium vapor was introduced into one end of the tube, it would be pushed out of the other end with some speed. Calculation proved, indeed, that with all the acceleration possible, the metallic vapor would emerge with a velocity of ninety-eight point seven percent of the speed of light. Using Einstein's formula for the relationship of mass to speed, that meant that the tube would propel a rocketship that could go to the moon or Mars or anywhere else. The American government started to build the ship, and then thought it would be a good idea to have Professor Rojestvensky in on the job as a consultant. Besides, the world owed him something. So he was sent for and Congress voted him more money than he had ever heard of before, and he looked over the figures and O.K.'d them. They were all right.

But he was typical of the people whose happiness has not been markedly increased by the remade world. He was a rich man, and he liked America, but after a month or so he didn't look happy. So the government put him in the most luxurious suite in the most luxurious hotel in America, and assigned people to wait on him and a translator to translate for him, and did its very best to honor the man who'd remade the world. But still he didn't seem content.

One day a committee of reporters asked him what he wanted. He would be in all the history books, and he had done the world a great favor and the public would like him to be pleased. But Professor Rojestvensky shook his head sadly.

"It's only," he said gloomily, "that since I am rich and the world is peaceable and everybody is happy—well, I just can't seem to find anyone who knows how to make good red-cabbage soup."

INTO EACH LIFE, SOME PERIWINKLES MUST FALL

by Hank Davis

Once again, yr. hmbl. ed. engages in auto-nepotism and inserts a story of his own, this one a case of the U.S. Army meets Charles Fort, with a nod toward David Drake, who also has been known to exhibit anti-establishment Fortean tendencies. And by the way, Dave, Happy Big Seven-Oh!

★ ★ ★

***Hank Davis** is an editor emeritus at Baen Books. While a naïve youth in the early 1950s (yes, he's* old*!), he was led astray by SFcomic books, and then by A. E. van Vogt's* Slan, *which he read in the Summer 1952 issue of* Fantastic Story Quarterly *while in the second grade, sealing his fate. He has had stories published mumble-mumble years ago in* Analog, If, F&SF, *and Damon Knight's* Orbit *anthology series. (There was also a story sold to* The Last Dangerous Visions, *but let's not go there.) A native of Kentucky, he currently lives in North Carolina to avoid a long commute to the Baen office.*

═ ★ ═

Dedicated to David Drake

"It is as if with intelligence, or with the equivalence of intelligence, something has specialized upon transporting, or distributing, immature and larval forms of life. If the gods send worms, that would be kind if we were robins."

—Charles Fort, *Lo!*

MID-JUNE

The colonel wasn't sure what was going on, or what he was supposed to do about it, out there watching an open field in the middle of the day, but at least he was sure that his feet were hurting. Normally, he would count that as a distraction and tune them out, but sore feet were like old friends, and something that he could understand, so he gave them more attention than usual. He shifted his weight slightly, to even out the ache. Then he heard the sound of a car approaching, and turned toward the sound, aching feet forgotten.

The sound got louder as the car came over the rise—not really a car, he thought, some kind of small SUV, probably with four-wheel drive. It rolled over the grass, stopped, then a woman got out, and looked around, then began walking toward the open field.

"Dr. Greene," the colonel called, walking toward her. His feet were still hurting, but now that he had something to do with them, he didn't notice. "Please don't go that way. It may not be safe."

She stopped and waited as he approached. She was wearing something like a civilian version of fatigues, khaki-colored, with no insignia, of course, and some sort of tan boots. He wondered if they came from L.L. Bean, though he wasn't sure if the company even sold camping equipment any more, such as his grandfather had bought through the mail decades ago. On her head was a construction worker's hard hat, medium-length dark red hair spilling from its sides. He wondered if her headgear might be more protection than the military helmet sitting on his own head.

"Colonel Duncan?" she asked, putting out a hand. Green eyes watched him through metal-rimmed glasses.

"Guilty as charged," he said. They shook hands. Dr. Greene, with green eyes, he thought, and wondered if she had been teased about that.

"Am I in time? But I must be, or you wouldn't have warned me about safety."

"You're here in plenty of time—if it happens at the same time as the previous days. The times since we've been watching, that is. But we don't understand what's happening, and we don't know if there really is a schedule. It might surprise us." He was hoping that she would surprise him by making sense of the . . . thing.

"We've had the blades examined under microscopes, including an electron microscope. There were no unusual or dangerous organisms on them. I can show you the photos."

"That's useful information, but I don't have any training in microbiology," she said with a puzzled tone, as if wondering why he was talking about photos of microbes. "I'm afraid photos wouldn't convey anything to me."

Now, he was puzzled—but by now he was used to being puzzled. "I thought, well, when Washington phoned that you were coming here, I thought they said your field was virology."

She smiled, but her eyes weren't amused. "Either the person who phoned you misunderstood, or you misheard them. My field is verticology."

Still puzzled, he said, "That's a new one on me. A branch of geology?" He was thinking of layers of rock, piled vertically atop each other, thinking back to his time as a rockhound in his teens.

"Geology?" She wasn't smiling at all now. "No, it's a new field, and not really respectable yet. Someone in Washington must be either very scared, or else a closet Fortean, or maybe both, to have called me in."

At first, he thought she said "Freudian," but this time he tried to sound less confused, and just said, "Fortean?" hoping he was pronouncing it right.

"Have you ever heard of Charles Fort?" she asked.

He had a brief flash of memory from old history lessons of the long-abandoned Fort Charles, but decided to just say, "No."

"Charles Fort was a man early in the last century who collected reports of strange events. He collected thousands of them, and published four books full of them."

"Like *Believe It or Not*?"

"Something like that, but usually far less believable. The sort of events he collected are now called Fortean phenomena. And people with an interest in such apparently impossible things are also called Forteans."

"Like astrology?" the colonel said, thinking of his wife's intently reading the newpaper horoscope every day, but immediately regretted it. Dr. Greene was looking as if she had smelled something bad.

"I doubt he would have taken astrology any more seriously than he took astronomy. But one category of the mysterious events he recorded was things impossibly falling from the sky: fish, frogs, worms, periwinkles."

He decided not to ask what a periwinkle was. Sounded like a character from a TV cartoon show, particularly since a little bit of light was dawning. "Your field is verticology? Is that from *vertical*?"

At least she wasn't frowning any more. "Got it. The study of falling things. Inexplicable falling things, that is."

At least, now, he knew what she was doing here.

"Five minutes, sir," the spec five manning one of the gizmos shouted.

"Did Charles Fort mention this sort of falling . . . things?" Duncan asked.

"No, though I understand that they fall slowly," Dr. Greene said. "More slowly than they should. There are cases reported of rocks falling from the sky, slowly, as if gravity is partly suspended."

"That part sounds familiar, all right. Do you have any suggestions where they're coming from?"

"You won't like it, Colonel—" she began, but then someone yelled, "Here they come," and she stopped, watching a swarm of long, narrow objects that were coming down from the clear, cloudless sky. Birds scattered. The swarm fell much more slowly than the eye expected, but still drove themselves into the soil of the empty field.

"That should be it for now, Duncan said, "but let's wait a bit, for safety's sake. You were saying?"

"Fort threw out wild ideas, and it's hard to know if he meant any of them—he had an odd sense of humor. But he did suggest that falling things might be caused by some unknown mechanism or agency that was trying to provide something that was needed somewhere—like water falling to relieve a drought—but didn't do it in a sensible manner. Dropping fish because of a famine somewhere, but not dropping them where they were needed. Or dropping water where there was a drought, but dropping it in such huge quantities that destruction resulted."

"You mean somebody somewhere needs bayonets?" Duncan asked, looking at the handles sticking up out in the field. As usual the fallen weapons had driven their blades into the dirt, up to their hilts.

"Have you followed what the President has been doing?" she asked.

Duncan frowned, preferring not to think about the new commander in chief. In fact, he'd been thinking it might be a good time to retire, but all he said was, "Can you be more specific?"

"She's doing huge cutbacks in the defense budget. Cutting back on military stockpiles and cancelling new weapons that were in development. Talking about drastically reducing the size of the armed forces."

"So you think that because the army isn't going to get a new tank that the Pentagon wanted, something is dropping hundreds of bayonets in a field as a counterbalance?" He didn't wait for an answer, said, "It should be safe now, if you want to take a look," and started walking toward the bayonet-studded field. Dr. Greene walked with him.

"As I said, if there is a regulatory system, one that we don't understand at all, it doesn't seem to operate efficiently. Or even what we would think of as rationally."

Duncan pulled one of the bayonets out of the ground, and handed it grip first to the . . . to the verticologist. "That should be it until this time tomorrow. We have radar set up, and cameras running, but if it's the same as usual they'll just show bayonets appearing a few hundred feet up from nowhere—" actually, he expected it to again be 378 feet and a couple of inches, but he didn't feel like speaking exactly about something that made no damned sense at all "—and the radar and satellite photos won't show anything up in the air that could have dropped them. Not even a cloud. So, Doctor, do you have any suggestions?"

"I'll be honest, Colonel Duncan. I'm still surprised that I'm here.

Frankly, verticology is not a respectable field. Like UFOs and telepathy. At the University of California—"

California? Duncan thought. *Where else?*

"—there're a couple of classes in Fortean studies, taught by me, and the classes are listed under folklore. As I said, somebody in the government must be scared to send for me. Similar things to this have been recorded, but they've been ignored and forgotten. No investigations like you've set up here. We might be like Röntgen, about to discover X-rays. Or we might only be piling up more speculations, like the Kennedy assassination conspiracy fans do, and not proving anything."

Duncan was relieved of having to say anything when his cell phone rang. "Duncan here," he said, then, "Yes, sir . . . in Ohio . . . This has happened twice? . . . None of them went off ? . . . none of the pins pulled, then? Yes, sir, I'm on it." He put away the phone and told Dr. Greene, "We're on a priority flight to Ohio. Things are falling there."

"Pins are falling?" she asked, as they headed for her SUV.

"Pins?" he said, then, "Oh. No, hand grenades are falling from the sky. Fortunately, the pins haven't been pulled and none of them have gone off." *So far*, he thought to himself.

★ ★ ★

". . . Jan. 3, 1924—red objects falling with snow at Halmstead, Sweden. They were red worms, from one to four inches in length. Thousands of them streaking down with the snowflakes—red ribbons in a shower of confetti—a carnival scene that boosts my discovery that meteorology is a more picturesque science than most persons—including meteorologists—have suspected . . ."

—Charles Fort, *Lo!*

LATE JUNE

None of the hand grenades had gone off, and after a week both bayonets and hand grenades had stopped falling. The only thing that tests had shown was that the bayonets were high-grade steel but needed sharpening, and 37 percent of the hand grenades were defective: some lacked the explosive charge, some lacked the the coil of wire that would turn to shrapnel if they had a charge to shatter the wire, but all of them still had their pins in. There were no cases reported anywhere of missing bayonets or hand grenades. Not just the delivery system was a mystery, but also the manufacturer.

Duncan had noticed that some military personnel on this case, and civilians, too, felt better when they talked about a "delivery system," as if it explained something. If this became public, he thought, the phrase would be all over the media, up there with "escalation," "peace process," and "exit strategy."

At least he had looked up "periwinkles" and now knew that they were a kind of snail. One small mystery solved. "Has anyone checked on shortages of snails in France at the time of periwinkles falling from the sky?" he asked Dr. Greene as they sat in the helicopter.

He thought he'd made a joke, but she looked thoughtful, said "hmmm," then made a note on her phone. "Of course, France isn't the only place where snails are a delicacy," she mused.

The helicopter was landing, taking his mind off the misfired joke. They stepped out about a hundred yards from yet another field. This one had tanks sitting in it.

Typically, witnesses said they had fallen from a clear sky and come down with unnatural slowness. But not slow enough. Some of them were obviously damaged. Some had landed upside down. And, since not all of the tanks had been towed from the field by the next day, other tanks had landed on top of tanks that were already there.

"I guess these are more useful than bayonets or hand grenades," Dr. Greene said.

"Not by much," Duncan replied. "These are Sherman tanks. Hopelessly obsolete. Primitive electronics, insufficient armor. And some of the tanks that were towed off the field before the second, um, tank drop were missing parts in their engines.."

"But the Sherman tank is a well-known, uh, model—" she wasn't sure if "model" was the right word "—and if people thought more tanks were needed, they might have that kind of tank deeper in their minds."

"So, the mysterious source of this falling largesse is reading some minds, but not very well?"

"Maybe. I'm just guessing."

"Or maybe somebody left teeth in the field and the tooth fairy dropped off a bunch of tanks."

She recognized that one as a joke. "Maybe somebody sowed dragon's teeth," she said.

Duncan looked at the usual radar equipment and cameras set up outside the perimeter of the tank-strewn field, and was sure that once again, they wouldn't provide any answers. He was also sure that no one would report any Sherman tanks missing.

He was right.

★ ★ ★

"At Seringapatan, India, about the year 1800, fell a hailstone . . . I blurt out something that should, perhaps, be withheld for several hundred pages—but that damned thing was the size of an elephant."

—Charles Fort,
The Book of the Damned

EARLY JULY

Dr. Greene was getting used to riding Huey copters, and was no longer bothered by the sides being open in flight or worried about falling out. She was looking out the side and said, "There it is—" then stopped as they got closer and the size of the objects became more obvious.

"Only two of them," Duncan said, "one on each day. Maybe the mystery agency is pushing the limits of their budget." He wished he weren't joking. He'd like to think that the agency had some kind of limits.

Greene was still silent as they approached the closer of the two huge ships lying on their side. Finally she said, "I didn't realize how big they were."

"Big, but obsolete," Duncan said. "This is a World War II

battleship. Besides, it's in the middle of Utah, hundreds of miles from any water."

About a hundred yards farther away was a more modern fighting vessel. It had had missiles on board, but they had been removed. No word yet on whether they were functional. He hoped that they weren't.

They retreated back to where the inevitable instrumentation was set up and waited. And on schedule, on the third day, a nuclear submarine descended to the ground. It groaned as it settled and its hull cracked loudly under the uneven strain. A missile tube's hatch popped off and rolled across the field like a runaway hubcap. He wondered if there was a missile in the tube and if it was functional.

"That submarine has nuclear missiles, doesn't it?" Dr. Greene said.

He considered that she probably didn't have a security clearance high enough, if she had one at all, nor a need to know, and decided, to hell with it. "It looks like it has them. The guys who took away the missiles, or what looked like missiles, from the second ship will probably be back to look it over. And probably won't tell us anything."

"I don't suppose any submarines will turn up missing," she said.

"Probably not. I can't see from here, but there'll probably be no name on the sub. The other two ships didn't have names. That looks like an American design. It'd be more interesting if a Russian sub were dropped here."

"I suppose if the Russians were disarming, they would get things falling on—" she began, then her cell phone rang. She answered, spoke to someone named Dave, then listened for a couple of minutes, thanked the caller, and closed the phone. Her expression was grim and she was very quiet for a couple of minutes.

Finally, the colonel said, "You were saying?"

"What was I saying? Never mind, it doesn't matter. That was a friend who's a political junky. I asked him to keep track of what the President is doing for me, though I didn't tell him why. He called to say she just made a speech about how our nuclear arsenal is obscenely bloated and she intends to reduce it to a tenth or less of the current stockpile."

It was the colonel's turn to be very quiet.

"Warheads don't go off unless they've been armed, do they?" she asked. "If an ICBM just fell from the sky the impact wouldn't set it off, would it?" She sounded like a child who wanted to be told there was no monster in the closet.

"That's above my pay grade," Duncan said. *Not to mention* my *security clearance*, he thought. "But I think that's right. But—" he said, and stopped, wishing he'd shut up sooner.

"But? But what?"

"The hand grenades all had their pins still in them, so falling ICBMs—" he had to stop after the phrase "falling ICBMs." For a second, he was back at the first location, watching bayonets fall point down from the sky.

"But a warhead is hundreds of times more complicated. They—or It—or whatever is doing this might leave out the parts that make the warhead even capable of exploding." *Why didn't I shut up*?

Tomorrow was July 4th. He thought of fireworks. Very bright fireworks.

"Or they might leave out a part that keeps it from exploding unless the thing is armed?" she said. "Is that it?"

He nodded, then said, "And none of those bayonets fell with scabbards around them. The elementary safety measure must have seemed unimportant."

They looked at each other, then both looked up into the sky, into the blue, cloudless, and now very ominous sky.

★ ★ ★

"If there is a universal mind, must it be sane? [. . .] Do things fall where a universal mind, which may be the mind of an idiot, conceives that they are needed?"

—Damon Knight,
Charles Fort: Prophet of the Unexplained.

SUCCESS STORY

by Earl Goodale

Here's a case where the alien invaders may have bitten off more than they could chew; particularly if an alien soldier has doubts about which side he's on.

★ ★ ★

***Earl Goodale** is a puzzlement. He only had two stories published: "The Zoet Space" in 1958 and this story in 1960. However, he certainly didn't write like a beginner, and "Success Story" was the lead story in the April 1960 issue of* Galaxy*, one of the three most prestigious SF magazines of the time, which leads me to suspect that "Earl Goodale" was a pseudonym for an established writer. If that suspicion is correct and someone knows who Earl Goodale is, or was, I hope they'll come forth to dispel the mystery. In any case, I'm glad that the mysterious Mr. Goodale wrote this very cynical, very funny yarn.*

═ ★ ═

Once my name was Ameet Ruxt, my skin was light blue, and I was a moderately low-ranking member of the Haldorian Empire. Or should I say I was a member of the lower income group? No, definitely "low-ranking," because, in a warrior society, even one with as high a technological level as a statistician sits low on the totem pole. He is handed the wrong end of the stick—call it what you will; he's the one who doesn't acquire even one wife for years and he hasn't a courtesy title. He's the man they draft into their Invasion Forces—the Haldorians are always invading someone—and turn him into a Fighter Basic in a third of a year.

"Look," I'd complained to the burly two-striper in the Receiving Center, "I'm a trained statistician with a degree and—"

"Say 'Sir', when you address me."

I started over again. "I know, Sir, that they use statisticians in the service. So if Haldor needs me in the service, it's only sensible that I should work in statistics."

The Hweetoral looked bored, but I've found out since that all two-stripers looked bored; it's because so many of them have attained, at that rank, their life's ambition. "Sure, sure. But we just got a directive down on all you paper-pushers. Every one of you from now on out is headed for Basic Fighter Course. You know, I envy you, Ruxt. Haldor, what I wouldn't give to be out there with real men again! Jetting down on some new planet—raying down the mongrels till they yelled for mercy—and grabbing a new chunk of sky for the Empire. Haldor! That's the life!" He glanced modestly down at his medaled chest.

"Yes, Sir," I said, "it sure *is*. But look at my examination records you have right there. Physically, I'm only a 3 and you have to have a 5 to go to Basic Fighter. And besides," I threw in the clincher, though I was a bit ashamed of it, "my fighting aptitude only measures a 2!"

The Hweetoral sneered unsubtly and grabbed a scriber with heavy fingers. A couple of slashes, a couple of new entries, and lo, I was now a 5 in both departments. I was qualified in every respect.

"See," he said, "that's your first lesson in the Service, Ruxt. Figures don't mean a thing, because they can always be changed. That's something a figure-pusher like you has to learn. So—" he shoved out that ponderous hand and crushed mine before I could protect myself—"good luck, Ruxt. I know you'll get through that course—alive, I mean." He chuckled heartily. "And I know men!"

He was right. I got through alive. But then, 76.5 percent of draftees do get through the Basic Fighter Course alive. But for me, it took a drastic rearrangement of philosophy.

Me, all I'd ever wanted was a good life. An adequate income, art and music, congenial friends, an understanding wife—just one wife was all I'd ever hoped for. As you can see, I was an untypical Haldorian on every point.

After my first day in Basic Fighter Course, I just wanted to stay alive.

"There's two kinds of men we turn out here," our Haldor told us as we lined up awkwardly for the first time (that scene so loved by vision-makers). We new draftees called our Trontar our Haldor because he actually had the power over our bodies that the chaplains assured us the Heavenly Haldor had over our liberated spirits. Our Trontar looked us over with his fatherly stare, flexing his powerful arm muscles so that his three tattooed stripes rippled and danced. "Yeah," he went on, "two kinds of men: Fighting men and dead men!" The Trontar grinned that fighting Haldorian grin you see all your lives on the Prop Sheets. "And I'll tell you something, men. When you leave here—all Fighters Basic—I'm going to envy you. Yeah, I'll really envy you gutsy killers when you go out in that big Out-There and grab yourselves a new chunk of sky." He paused and studied our faces. "Now we're gonna run, and I do mean run, two full decades. The last four men in get to do it over again, and pull kitchen duty tonight too."

I tried, as others have tried, to slip quietly out of Basic Fighter. I tried being sick, but following sick report one found oneself doing a full day's training—after the understanding medics had shoved some pep pills into you. I demanded a physical examination. They weren't going to push me around.

After a couple of days in solitary, I asked in a nice way for physical evaluation.

Well, I asked. I wasn't very smart in those days.

They weren't interested in the story of how my records had been falsified or in my fighting aptitude.

"Look, draftee," the psycho-man said after I finally got to him, "the fact that you've got to see me shows you have enough of a fighting aptitude. Your Trontar didn't encourage you to request evaluation, did he? And he isn't going to like you very much when you report back to your platoon, is he?"

I shuddered. "Not exactly."

"Call me 'Sir.'"

"No, Sir. But I was desperate, Sir. I don't think I can stand . . ."

"Draftee, you know that some unfortunate men break down in training and that we have to take them out. Maybe you've already lost some that way. Suppose you were brought in here, gibbering, yowling, and drooling—I guess we'd have to cure you and send you back home as non-fighter material, eh?"

Someone up here liked me! Here was a tip on how to escape back to the old quiet life. I nodded agreeably.

"But you know, don't you," he said softly, "that first we run a thorough test on our drooling draftee? Say it's you . . ."

I nodded again.

"We most always detect fakers. And you know there's a death penalty for any Haldorian attempting to escape his duty." He smiled sadly, and reminiscently.

I nodded. Maybe someone up here didn't like me.

"So we'd shoot you dead with one of those primitive projectile weapons, as an object lesson for both you and the draftees we had remaining."

I nodded and tried to show by my countenance how much I approved of people being shot dead with primitive weapons.

"But suppose," he went on, "that you'd really cracked up or that you'd faked successfully?"

"Yes, Sir?" Hope returned, hesitantly and on tip-toes, ready to flee.

"Then we'd cure you," he said. "But the cure unfortunately involves the destruction of your higher mental faculties. And so there'd be nothing for it but to ship you off to one of the mining planets. That's standard procedure, if you didn't know. But I think you'll be all right now, don't you?"

Hope fled. I assured him that I'd be just fine and reported back, on the double, to my training platoon.

"Just in time, Ruxt," my Trontar greeted me. "Back for full duty, I take it? That's the Haldorian spirit!" He turned to the platoon which was lined up like three rows of sweaty statues. "Men, remember what

I told you about taking cover when you're under fire—and staying under cover? Just suppose we suddenly came under fire—flat trajectory stuff—out here on this flat exercise ground with no cover except in that latrine pit over there. Would any of you hesitate to dive into that latrine pit? And once in there, safe and sound, would any of you not stay there until I gave the word to come out?"

A perceptible shudder passed like a wave over the platoon. We knew the Trontar did not ask pointless questions.

"Of course you wouldn't," he assured us, "and you'd even stay in there all day under this hot sun if you had to. Ruxt! You're rested and refreshed from visiting the hospital. You demonstrate how it's done."

It was a long day, even though my Trontar kindly sent some sandwiches over to me at high noon. I didn't eat much. But I did do a lot of thinking. There was one last hope. I wrote a letter to a remote clan relative who was supposed to have a small amount of influence. It was a moving letter. I told how my test results had been falsified, what beasts our trainers were, how the medics refused to retest me—very much the standard letter that new Haldorian trainees write. As I went out to mail this plea, one evening, I met two of my fellow trainees starting out on a night march in full field equipment.

"How come?" I asked, instantly fearful that I'd missed some notice on the bulletin board.

"We wrote letters," one of them said simply.

"The Trontar censors all our mail," said the other. "Didn't you know? Oh, well, neither did we."

As they marched off, I made a small bonfire out of my letter after first, almost, just throwing it away—before I remembered that the Hweetorals checked our waste cans. What a man has to do to hold two measly stripes!

Acceptance of the inevitable is the beginning of wisdom, says the ancient Haldorian sage. I put in an application for transfer to the Statistical Services to be effective upon *completion* of Basic Fighter Course.

"Statistical Services?" the Company Clerk asked. "What's that? Anyhow, you're going to be a Fighter Basic, if you get through this training," he said darkly. The Company Clerk was a sad victim of our

Haldorian passion for realistic training; he had lacked one day of completing Basic Fighter when he'd let his leg dangle a bit too long after he'd scaled a wall, and the training gentlemen had unemotionally shot it off. As it turned out, our efficient surgeon/replacers had been unable, for some technical reason, to grow back enough leg for full duty. So there was nothing for it but to use the man as could be best done. They'd made him a clerk—mainly because that was the specialty they were shortest of at the time.

"Who says you can put in for Statistical Services?" the Company Clerk demanded.

"Reg 39-47A." I was learning my way around. The night before I was on orderly duty in the office. I had tracked down the chapter and verse which, theoretically, allowed a man to change his destiny.

"Know the Regs, do you? Starting to be a troublemaker, huh? Yeah, Ruxt, I'll put in your application."

I turned away with some feeling of relief. This might possibly work.

The Company Clerk called me back. "You know the Regs so good, Ruxt," he said. "How come you didn't ask me for permission to leave? I'm cadre, you know." He leaned back in his chair and grinned at me. "Just to help you remember the correct Haldorian deportment, I'm putting you on kitchen duty for the next three nights. That way," he grinned again, "you can divide up your five hours of sleep over three nights instead of crowding them all into one."

Poor deluded Company Clerk! I actually averaged three hours of sleep every one of those three nights—after I found out that the Mess Trontar would accept my smoking ration.

I felt that I was beginning to understand the system, a little and at long last, particularly after I saw my co-workers in the kitchen doing what should have been my work.

II

Then we started combat training, and then we started losing our normal 23.5 percent.

It wasn't too bad as long as they stuck to the primitive stuff. I mean, you can see arrows and spears coming at you, and even if you have had only the five hours of sleep you can either duck the projectiles or catch them on your shield. And with the medics on the alert, the wounds are painful but seldom fatal. You just end up with a week's hospitalization and slip back to the next training group. But when they go up to the explosively propelled solids, when the Trontar smirks and says: "Men, this is called a boomer, or a banger, or maybe sometimes a firestick, depending on what planet you're fighting on," and when he holds up a contraption of wood and metal with a hole at one end and a handle on the other—then, Draftee, look out!

It takes time to learn. It isn't till you associate a bang in the distance with a perforated man beside you that you do learn. And when you finally come under fire from our regular production weapons like rays—well!

You might wonder why they run us through the entire history of weapons starting with the sling and ending with the slithers—the name servicemen give to those Zeta Rays that diverge from line of sight to drop in on a dug-in enemy. The usual explanation is that Haldorians are still invading places where the natives still use such things as bows and arrows. But I think, myself, that it's something the Mil-Prop guys figured out. The idea is, as I see it, to run you right through the whole course of our fighting, invading Haldorian history, and in that way to make a better fighter out of you. And you do get rid of the death prones before there's much time or work invested in them—or before their inevitable early death means the failure of a mission. Haldoria—most practical of Empires!

But they didn't make a fighter of me. All they did was to reinforce my natural survival instinct considerably, acquaint me with the tortuous ways of the service, and give me a great urge for a peaceful existence. But to all appearances, as I stood in the orderly room after graduation, I was the ideal poster-picture of a Haldorian, completely uniformed with polished power boots and rayer, a crawler to the higher-ups and a stomper on the lower-downs, a Fighter Basic with no compassion but with a certified aptitude for advancement to at least the rank of Trontar.

"Fighter Basic Ruxt," the Dispositions Hweetoral announced.

"Here, Sir!"

"Your application for transfer to Statistical Services has been disapproved." The two-striper's expression showed what he, as a fighting man, thought of the Statistical Services. "But we've got a real assignment for you, Ruxt! The 27th Invasion Force is all set to drop on a new system. You're lucky, Ruxt, that you put in that application. We had to hold you till it bounced. Your buddies got shipped to those rear-echelon guard outfits, but you're going to a real fighting one. It should be a good invasion—this new system's got atomic fission, I hear. And I'd like to tell you something, Ruxt . . ."

"I know what, Sir," I said. "You envy me."

The 27th was a real fighting unit all right: they had their own neckerchief, their own war cry, and a general who was on his way up. Now they had me.

And they were going to get another system for the Haldorian Empire.

You see, those intelligent worms, or maybe they are slugs—I'm a bit vague on universe geography—over on the next galaxy but one, give us Haldorians all sorts of difficulties. They insist on freedom, self-determination, and all that sort of thing. That's all very well, but they insist on them for themselves. Our high-level planners decided that another solar system would make a better offensive set-up for Haldoria. The planners, I understand, have all sorts of esoteric theories about the ideal shape and size of an offensive unit. They ring in time and something related to time which makes galaxy distances differ according to which direction you are travelling. As I say, esoteric.

The only thing that mattered to me was that some technicians had fed some data into a computer and it had hiccupped and said: "You'll need such-and-such a planet to control such-and-such a solar system, and that will give you a better offensive set-up." Then the computer hiccupped again and said: "You'll need to draft and train Ameet Ruxt to help on this little job of taking over this planet called Terra, or Earth."

That's what it amounted to, anyhow. Consequently I joined the 27th Invasion Force.

"So you've got an application in for transfer to the Statistical Services, huh?" Trontar Hytd, my new platoon three-striper, asked when I reported in for duty with the 27th.

"Yes, Sir." I'd learned, along the line that one should never give up when applying for a transfer—just keep one in the mill.

"Huh, Borr, this new guy likes to work with figures," Trontar Hytd growled at Hweetoral Borr, my new squad leader. "Thinks he doesn't want to be a Fighter." Trontar Hytd looked at me questioningly.

I didn't say anything. I'd learned a lot in Basic Fighter Course.

"Figures?" asked Hweetoral Borr. I could see a train of thought had been started in the Hweetoral's mind.

"Yeah, figures," snapped Trontar Hytd. "He likes to count things, Borr. Get it?"

"Guess we need all our ray charges counted, for one thing," suggested Hweetoral Borr. "I get all mixed up with them figures."

"After training hours, of course," Trontar Hytd said.

"Of course, Trontar. And someone's gotta jawbone some kind of report on ammo expenditures every training day. Maybe after the rest of us have sacked in, for instance?"

"Of course. Okay, Hweetoral, I guess you got the idea."

Invasion was almost a relief after that brief bit of refresher training the 27th was going through.

Our General-on-the-way-up had outlined his plan of attack: "Drop'm, hit'm, lift'm and drop'm again." So I dropped, hit the defenders, was lifted to a new center of resistance, and dropped again. I understand it was a standard type of invasion. There's only one way to do simple things.

Once in a while, these days, I remember those sadistic and battle-hardened comrades of mine. Hard, gutsy Trontar Hytd stayed on his feet to direct his platoon underground after our Kansas force collapsed, and one of those little fission weapons separated his body parts too widely for even our unsentimentally competent surgeon/replacer to reassemble him. Well, they had a go at the job, but they had to ray down what they created—some primitive regression had set in and the creature was hungry.

And rough and tough Hweetoral Borr incautiously scratched his hairy ear just when one of those rude projectile weapons was firing at him. The slug slipped through that opening the Hweetoral had made in his body armor. With the brain gone—or such brain as Hweetoral Borr possessed—our kindly old surgeon/replacer was foxed again.

Then there were the new germs . . .

But these things are as nothing to the creative military mind. A swarm of regulations, manuals and directives issue forth from headquarters, and force fields cease to collapse, and fighters keep their body armor on and adjusted. When something like the influenza germ wipes out half a platoon, the wheels turn, a new vaccine is devised, and no more Haldorians die from that particular germ. All the individual has to do is to live from one injection to the next (any civilized enemy always cooks up new diseases), move from one enemy strong point to the next, and dream of the day when he can return to his old life. For me it was a dream of returning to that quiet tiny room with its walls lined with the best of Haldorian art—just cheap reproductions, of course, and never again to handle a rayer or to wear armor. Real life, meanwhile, went on.

"Fighter First-Class Ruxt! Take these men and blast that strong point!" That would be the order somewhere in Missouri, or maybe in Mississippi—I never was much good on micro-geography. "Hweetoral Ruxt! Take your squad and clean out that city. New Orleans they call it. Get their formal surrender and make damn sure there are no guerrillas left when the colonel comes through to inspect."

By the time I was Trontar Ruxt the invasion was practically over. As I say, it was the standard thing with one or two countries holding out after all hope was gone—England never did formally surrender, not that it mattered—and our successful General was made a Sub-Marshall of the Haldorian Empire.

A real promotion and a great honor. Much good it did him when he ventured his battle fleet too far into the Slug lines a year later.

With the fighting over—the real fighting, I mean—the ever-efficient Haldorians started moving their troops off Earth to get ready for a new and bigger invasion that the computers had decreed. Only a few troops were to be left behind for occupation and guard stuff.

I had a talk with a fat Assignments Trontar in his plush office.

"You know, Trontar," I said, "I was hoping to see more of this world here, and the rumor is that all of us excess combat types are being shipped to a training world to be shaped into new invasion forces."

"Tough," he said. He should know. He'd requisitioned a mansion complete with servants and everything. He even had a native trained to drive one of their luxuriously inefficient ground vehicles. What a deal! That Trontar had no worries, *his* anti-grav ray was working.

"I heard that a man doesn't even need any money if he's stationed down at our headquarters," I said, and I hauled out a handful of Haldorian notes from my pocket. "Guess I wouldn't need this stuff if I was transferred down to our headquarters."

"Who needs money?" he asked. "Guys all the time trying to bribe me, Trontar. You'd be surprised. Sure glad you aren't, though, because I do hate to turn anyone in."

I put the money back in my pocket. "Speaking of turning in people," I said casually, "you ever have any trouble with the undercover boys about all this loot you've picked up?" This, I thought, would shake him—and at the same time I marveled at how I'd changed from a simple, naïve statistician to a tough and conniving combat NCO.

He yawned all over his fat face and swung his swivel chair so that he could better admire the picture beside his desk. I recognized the picture as a moderately good reproduction of a Huxtner, a minor painter of our XXVth. "No," the Assignments Trontar said, "it turns out that one of my sept brothers runs the local watch birds. He often drops in here to visit with me. But anything I can do for you, Trontar?"

"No," I said, and I fired at the only possible loophole left, "I'll just leave quietly so you can admire your Huxtner."

He swung back to me with a start. "You recognize a Huxtner?

You're the first man I've ever met in the service who ever heard of Huxtner, let alone recognizing one of his masterpieces! Hey, did you know I brought this all the way from home in my hammock roll? And just look at the coloring of that figure there!"

The loophole had been blasted wide open. "You're lucky," I said, and I went on to lie about how I'd lost my own Huxtner prints in the invasion. "No one," I continued, "ever got quite that flesh tint of Huxtner's, did they?"

Huxtner, by the way, is notorious for using a yellow undercoat for his blue flesh colors, unlike every realistic painter before or after who have all used green undercoats—what else? Imagine a chrome-yellow underlaying a blue skin color. All Huxtner's figures look like two-week corpses—but Huxtner enthusiasts are unique.

The Assignments Trontar and I had a nice long chat about Huxtner, at the conclusion of which he insisted on scratching my name from the list of combat-bound men and putting me on a much smaller list of men scheduled for our guard outfit, stationed at the old Terran capital of Washington.

I had an un-Haldorian feeling of having arranged my own life after that incident. That feeling persisted even after I took over one of the guard platoons and discovered that life in a guard outfit is rather similar to Basic Fighter Course.

"Trontar Ruxt! Two men of your platoon have tarnished armor. Get them working on it, and maybe you'd better stay and see that they do it properly."

"Yes, Sir."

One lives and learns. I turned the job of supervising the armor cleaning to the Hweetorals of the squads and then I went home to my native woman. Yes, this guard's outfit life was like Basic Fighter Course.

But only for the lower ranks.

III

Life wasn't too unendurable in those days. The duties were incredibly dull, of course, but the danger of sudden death had receded, since only a few fanatics still tried to pick off us occupation troops. And this new world of Haldoria's was rich in the things a sensitive and artistic man appreciates: painting, sculpture, music. Then there was this new and pleasing thing of living with a woman . . .

But it wouldn't last long.

Soon there'd be another planet to invade and maybe a space battle with the great enemy. More years of cramped living and lurking danger, for in the Empire one was drafted for the duration, and this duration was now some four hundred years old. The most Trontar Ruxt could expect, the very most, was to somehow keep alive for another fifty years and then to retire on a small pension to one of the lesser worlds of the Empire.

"Trontar Ruxt! Your records show that you're a statistician." My commanding officer stared at me suspiciously, for a fighting man, even one on guard duty, distrusts office personnel. And as everyone knows, "Once a fighting man, always a fighting man." I think my C.O.'s last action had been thirty years ago.

"I was a statistician before I got in the service, Sir."

"Well, they're screaming over at headquarters for qualified office personnel, and we have to send them any trained men we have—of any rank."

"It's for Haldor, Sir," I said. By now I knew the correct answer was most often the noncommittal one.

I reported to the Headquarters, 27th Invasion Force. The rumor was that Phase II, Reduction of Inhabitants to Slavery with Shipment to Haldorian Colonies, was about to start. And also, our Planners were supposed to be well into Phase III, Terraforming, already. Terraforming was necessary, of course, to bring the average temperature of Earth down to something like the sub-arctic so that we Haldorians could live here in comfort. We lost quite a few fighters during invasion when their cooling systems broke down. Rumor, as always, was dead right; and the Headquarters was a mad rat-race.

The Senior Trontar of the office was delighted to get another body.

"Took your time getting here, Ruxt! You guard louts don't know the meaning of time, do you?"

I remained at attention.

"So you're a statistician, are you? Well, we don't need any statisticians now. We just got in a whole squad of them. Can you use a writer, maybe?"

"Yes, Sir." I did not remind the Senior Trontar that using a writer was a clerk's job, not a Trontar's, not a combat three-striper's, because the chances were that he knew it, for one thing. And he could easily make me a clerk, for another thing.

"Okay. Now that we understand each other," the Senior Trontar grinned, "or that you understand me, which is all that matters, here's your job." He handed me a stack of scribbled notes, some rolls of speech tape and a couple of cans of visual stuff. "Make up a report in standard format like this example. Consolidate all this stuff into it. This report has to be ready in two days, and it has to be perfect. No misspellings, no erasures, no nothing. Got that?"

"Yes, Sir."

"Yes, Sir," he mimicked. "Haldor only knows why they couldn't send me a few clerks instead of a squad of statisticians and one guard Trontar. Do you know what this stuff is that you're going to work up? It's the final report on our invasion here!"

I looked impressed. Strange how you learn, after a while, even the facial expression you are supposed to wear.

"Do you know why this report has to be perfect in format and appearance?" I wouldn't say the Senior Trontar's manner was bullying, quite. Perhaps one could call it hectoring. "Because the Accountant is out in this sector somewhere and we have to be ready for him if he drops in."

This time I didn't have to try to look impressed. The Accountant is the man who passes judgment on the conduct of all military matters—though of course he's not one man, but maybe a dozen of them. Armed with the invaluable weapon of hindsight, he drops in after an invasion is completed. He determines whether the affair has gone according to regulations, or whether there has been carelessness, slackness or wasting of Haldorian resources of men or material. Additionally he monitors civil administration of colonies and federated worlds. There are stories of Generals becoming Fighter

Basics and Chief Administrators becoming sub-clerks after an Accountant's visit.

I got the report done, but it took the full two days—mainly because fighting men make such incomplete and erroneous reports while action is going on. I got to understand the exasperated concern of office personnel who have to consolidate varied fragments into a coherent whole. And adding to the natural difficulties of the task was the continual presence of the Senior Trontar, and his barbed comments and lurid promises as to what would follow my failure at the work.

But the report was done and sent in to the Adjutant.

It came back covered with scribbled changes, additions, and deletions—and it came back carried by a much-disturbed Senior Trontar.

"Who in Haldor do they think I am?" he moaned. "I just handed on to you the figures that they gave me. Me! And threatening me with duty on a space freighter . . . and one into the Slug area at that!"

I thought, as I looked at my ruined script, that guard duty wasn't so bad, and that even combat wasn't rough *all* the time.

"See, Trontar," the four-striper said, calling me by my proper rank for the first time, "you did a good job, the Adjutant himself said so. But these figures . . ." he shuddered. "If the Accountant should see these we'd all be for it. Space-freighter duty would be getting off light." The Senior Trontar seemed almost human to me right then.

"I just put down what you gave me," I said.

"Yeah, sure, Ruxt. But I didn't realize, nobody realized, how bad the figures were till they were all together and written up. Look, this report shows that we shouldn't Terraform this planet—that we can't make a nudnick on the slavery proposition—and that maybe we shouldn't have even invaded this inferno at all."

"So what do you want me to do?"

"I'll tell you what you're going to do . . ." The Senior Trontar had regained his normal nasty disposition. "You're going to redo this report. You're going to redo it starting now, you're going to work on it all night, and you're going to have it on my desk and in perfect shape when I come in in the morning, or, by Haldor, the next thing you write will be your transfer to the space-freighter run nearest the Slug Galaxy." The Senior Trontar ran momentarily out of breath. "And," he came back strongly, "you won't be going as no Trontar, neither!"

"It'll be on your desk in the morning, Sir," I said.

Deck hands on the space-freighter run were, I'd heard, particularly expendable.

By the middle of the third watch I had completed a perfect copy of the report complete with attachments, appendices, and supplements. And also by this time I knew from the differences between the original report and this jawboned version that someone had goofed badly in undertaking this invasion, and then had goofed worse in not calling the thing off. Now there was to be considerable covering-up of tracks. The thought suddenly came to me that a guard's Trontar named Ruxt knew rather a lot of what had gone on. Following that mildly worrying thought came a notion that perhaps a guard's Trontar named Ruxt might be considered by some as just another set of tracks to be covered up. That far-off retirement on a small but steady income became even more unlikely, and the possibilities began to appear of a quick end in the Slug-shattered hulk of a space freighter.

Had the Senior Trontar changed in his attitude toward me, toward the end of the day, perhaps acted as though I were a condemned man? Possibly. And had some of the officers been whispering about me late in the afternoon? Could have been.

Shaken, I wandered down to the mess hall and joined a group of third-watch guards, who were goofing off while their Trontar was checking more distant guard posts.

"It's easy," one of them was telling the others. "All you got to do is to slip some surgeon/replacer a few big notes and he gives you this operation which makes you look like a native. And then you just settle down on Astarte for the rest of your life with the women just begging you to let them support you."

"You mean you'd rather live on some lousy federated world than be a Haldorian in the Invasion Forces?" There was a strong sardonic note in the questioner's voice.

"Man, you ever been on Astarte?" the first man asked incredulously.

"Yeah, but how are you going to be sure that the surgeon/replacer doesn't turn you in?" objected one of the others. "He could take your money, do the operation, and have you picked up. That way he'd have the money and get a medal too."

"I'd get around that," the talky guy said, "I'd just—"

At this point he was jabbed in the arm by one of his buddies who had noticed my eavesdropping. The man shut up. All four of them drifted off to their posts.

I went reluctantly back to the office. From then till dawn I dreamed up and rehearsed all manner of wild schemes to take me out of this dangerous situation. Or was it all perhaps just imagination? A Haldorian Trontar should never be guilty of an excess of that quality. But I made sure when the Senior Trontar sneaked in a bit before the regular opening time, that I was just, apparently, completing the last page of the report. The impression I hoped to convey was that I had spent the entire night in working and worrying.

"It's okay," the Senior Trontar growled after he had studied the completed report. "Guess you can take a couple of days off, Ruxt. I believe in taking care of my men. Say," he asked casually, "I suppose you didn't understand those figures you were working up, did you?"

"No," I said, "I didn't pay any attention to them; they were just something to copy, that's all." I felt confident that I could outfence the Senior Trontar any time at this little game, but what had he and the Adjutant been whispering about before they had come in?

"But you used to be a statistician, didn't you?" He looked at the far corner of the room and smiled slightly. "But you take a couple days off, Ruxt. Maybe we'll find something good for you when you come back." He smiled again. "Don't forget to check out with the Locator before you go, though. We don't want to lose you."

I stumbled home, not even noticing the hate-filled glances my armor and blue skin drew from the natives along the streets. The glances were standard, but this feeling of being doomed was new.

They were going to get me. I felt sure of that, even though my Sike

Test Scores had always been as low as any normal's. But how could a Haldorian disappear on this planet? Aside from skin color, there was the need to keep body temperatures at a livable level. The body armor unit was good only for about a week. Find a surgeon/replacer and bribe him to change me to an Earthman? I saw now how ridiculous such an idea was. But was there nothing but to wait passively while the Senior Trontar and the Adjutant, and whoever else did the dirty work, all got together and railroaded me off?

Haldorians, though, never surrender—or so the Mil-Prop lad would have us believe. Right from the time you are four years old and you start seeing the legendary founders of Haldoria—Bordt and Smordt—fighting off the fierce six-legged carnivores, you are told never to give up. "Where there's Haldor, there's Hope!" "There's always another stone for the wolves, if you but look." I must confess I'd snickered (way deep inside, naturally) at these exhortations ever since I'd reached the age of thinking, but now all these childhood admonitions came rushing back to give me strength, quite as they were intended to do. I found that I could but go down like any Haldorian, fighting to the last.

IV

So I put on my dress uniform the next day, and made sure that nothing could be deader than the dulled bits, or brighter than the polished ones. A bit of this effort was wasted since I arrived at Headquarters looking something less than sharp. The cooling unit in my armor was acting up a bit; and, also, three Terran city guerillas had tried to ambush me on the way. You take quite a jolt from a land mine, even with armor set on maximum. Some of those people never knew when they were licked. No wonder their Spanglt Resistance Quotient was close to the highest on record.

I got through the three lines of guards and protective force fields all right, checking my rayer here, my armor there—the usual dull procedure. By the time I reached the Admissions Officer, I was down to uniform and medals.

"You want to see the Accountant?" the Admissions Officer asked incredulously. "You mean one of his staff! Well, where's your request slip, Trontar?"

"I've come on my own, Sir," I said, "not from my office, so I haven't a request slip."

"Come on your own? What's your unit? Give me your ID card!"

Let's see, I thought. I've abstracted classified material from the files and carried it outside the office, I've broken the chain of command and communication, and, worst of all, I'd tried to see a senior officer without a request slip. Yeah, maybe I'd be lucky to end up as a *live* deckhand on a space freighter.

A bored young Zankor with the rarely seen balance insignia of the Accountant's Office rose from behind the Admissions Officer.

"I'll take responsibility for this man," he said casually to the A.O. "Follow me, Trontar. I was wondering when you'd turn up."

"Me?"

"Well, someone like you. Though usually it's scared sub-clerks that we drag up. And that reminds me." He turned to another young and equally bored Zankor standing nearby. "Take over, Smit, will you? They're bringing in that sub-clerk who's been writing those anonymous letters. I've reserved the Inquisition Room for a couple of hours for him."

I followed the Zankor as he strode away, wondering as I did if they had more than one Inquisition Room.

He led me into a small room just off the corridor and motioned me to a chair. "Before you see the Accountant, Trontar," he said, "I'll have to screen what you have. It may be that we won't have to bother the Accountant at all."

The smooth way the Zankor talked and his friendly manner almost convinced me that we should both put the interests of the Accountant first. But then it occurred to me that a man with the gold knot of a Zankor on his collar wasn't often friendly with a mere Trontar. That thought snapped me out of it and I knew I should only give the minimums.

"I've got documents," I said—"document" is such a lovely strong word, "which prove that the official report on the invasion and occupation of this planet is false." That, I thought, was as minimum as one could get.

"Ah, and have you?" The Zankor still looked bored. "Well, let's see them, Trontar," he said briskly.

The Zankor had that sincere look the upper class always uses when they are about to do you dirt. They blush that heavy shade of blue, almost purple, and they look you straight in the eye, and they quiver a bit as to voice . . . and the next thing you know, you're shafted.

"I'm sorry, Sir," I said, "but what I have is so important that I can give it to the Accountant only."

He stared at me for rather a long moment, pondering, no doubt, the pleasures of witnessing a full-dress military flogging. Then he shrugged and picked up the speaker beside him. He didn't call the Trontar of the Guard to come and take my documents by force. I could tell that even though he spoke in High Haldorian, that harsh language the upper class are so proud of preserving as a relic from the days of the early conquerors. No, he was speaking to a superior—there's never any doubt as to who is on top when people are speaking High Haldorian—and then I caught the emphatic negative connected with the present-day Haldorian phrases meaning Phase II and Phase III, Terraforming. So even though I don't know High Haldorian, and would never be so incautious as to admit it if I did, I knew roughly what had been said.

And I was frantically revising my plans.

"Follow me," the Zankor said, after completing the call. "We'll see the Accountant now, and—" he looked at me sincerely—"you'd better have something very good indeed. You really had, Trontar."

The Accountant turned out to be a tall and thin Full Marshall, the first I'd seen. He was dressed in a uniform subtly different from the regulation, and he wore only one tiny ribbon, which I didn't recognize. He had the slightly deeper-blue skin you often see on the upper classes, though this impression may have been due to the green furnishings of the room. It was, in fact, called the Green Room, when the Terrans had used it as one of their regional capitals.

I saluted the Accountant with my best salute, the kind you lift like it was sugar and drop as if it were the other. The Accountant responded with one of those negligent waves that tell you the saluter was a survivor of the best and bloodiest private military school in existence.

"Proceed, Trontar," the Accountant said, leaning back and relaxing as if he didn't have a care in the universe.

I launched into my speech, the one I'd been mentally rehearsing. I told him I knew I was breaking the chain of communication, but that I was doing it for the service and for Haldoria, etc. Any old serviceman knows the routine. I was, as I ran through this speech, just as sincere and just as earnestly interested in the good of Haldoria as any Haldorian combat Trontar could be. But, deep inside me, the old Ameet Ruxt was both marveling at the change in himself and cynically appreciating the performance.

The Accountant interrupted the performance about halfway through. "Yes, yes, Trontar," he said brusquely, "I think we can assume your action *is* for the good of Haldoria, may the Empire increase and the Emperor live forever. Yes. But you say you have material dealing with the overall report on our invasion and occupation of this planet. You further say this material shows discrepancies in the official report—which you imply you have seen."

"Yes, Sir," I said, and I handed over the several sheets of paper which comprised the old report and the changes of the new. Meanwhile, behind me, the Zankor was invisible but I had not a doubt but that he was there, keeping the regulation distance from me.

These people knew their business.

The Accountant took the collection of papers and compared them with some others he had on his desk. I continued to stand at Full Brace. Once you've been chewed out for slipping into an Ease position without being so ordered, you never forget.

The Accountant laid down the papers, scanned my face, got up and walked to the far end of the room. In front of a mirror he stopped and fingered that one small ribbon, quite, I thought, as if he were matching it with another one.

He came back quickly and sat down again. "Zankor," he said, "set up a meeting with the top brass for this afternoon. I'll talk with the Trontar privately."

The Zankor saluted and was on his way out the door when the Accountant spoke again. "And Zankor . . ."

"Yes, Sir?"

"I should be very unhappy if the top brass here—the *present* top brass—found out about this material the Trontar brought."

The Zankor swallowed hard and assured the Accountant that he understood . . . "Sir."

Then we were alone and the Accountant was suddenly a kindly old man who invited me to sit down and relax. I did. I really let go and stretched out, I forgot everything I'd ever been taught as a child or had learned on my climb to the status of Trontar. I relaxed and he had me.

I had been caught on the standard Haldorian Soft/Hard Tactic.

"Disabuse your mind, Trontar," the Accountant snapped, and he was no longer a kindly old man but a thin-lipped Haldorian snapper, "of any idea that you have saved the Empire—or any such nonsense!" Having cracked his verbal whip about my shoulders he just crouched there, glaring at me, his mouth entirely vanished and his eyes—well, I'd just as soon not think about some things.

Yes, and then he gave me the Shout/Silence treatment, the whole thing so masterfully timed that at the end he could have signed me on as a permanent latrine keeper on a spy satellite in the Slug Galaxy. A genius, that man was. The sort of man who could—and probably did—control forty wives without a weapon.

"Your information, as it happens," he said after I had regained my senses, "checks with other data I've received. It might be, of course, that the whole thing is a fabrication of my enemies. In that case, Trontar—" he looked at me earnestly—"you can be assured you'll not be around to rejoice at or to profit from my downfall."

"Of course, Sir," I said, quite as earnestly as he.

"But we both know that you are only a genuine patriot," he said with a hearty chuckle, a chuckle exactly like that of a Father Goodness—that kindly old godfather who brings such nice presents to every Haldorian child until they are six, and who on that last exciting visit brings, and enthusiastically uses, a bundle of large and heavy whips to demonstrate that no one can be trusted. Efficient teachers, the Haldorians.

"Just a genuine patriot," the Accountant repeated, "who has rendered a considerable service to the Empire. Trontar," he said, all friendly and intimate, "the Empire likes to reward well its faithful sons. What would you most like to have or to do?"

"To serve Haldoria, Sir!" I was back on my mental feet at last.

He dropped his act then. He was, I think, just practicing anyway. We had a short talk then, the kind in which one person is quickly and efficiently pumped of everything he knows. After about ten minutes of question and answers, the Accountant leaned back and studied my face carefully.

"Have you considered Officers' Selection Course, Trontar? I might be able to help you a little in getting in."

Officers' Selection Course was, I knew, Basic Fighter Course multiplied in length and casualties. Less than twenty per cent graduate . . . or escape.

"No, Sir," I said. "I wondered if I mightn't be of more value to Haldoria in some way other than being in the combat services." So now I'd said it, and there was nothing to do but to go on. "Perhaps," I ventured, "I might be of some help in the administrative services."

The Accountant said nothing, his face was immobile, his hands still. He'd learned his lessons well, once.

"In fact," I said, deciding to go for broke, "with my knowledge of the language and the customs here, I might be of most service to Haldoria right here on this planet,"

"Had you guessed, by any chance, Trontar," the Accountant's voice was neutrally soft, "that we won't be Terraforming this world? And that we may not even exploit the slavery proposition?"

"I thought both those possibilities likely," I admitted.

"But you know that in such a case we would have no administrative services on this world? Thus you are, in fact, asking for a position that wouldn't exist." The Accountant, without a change of position or expression, somehow gave the impression of looming over me.

"I thought," I said, trying to pick exactly the right words, and at the same time all too conscious of a twitching muscle in my left eyelid, "that there might be an analogous position, even so."

The Accountant loomed higher.

"If only," he said, "you hadn't come to us, Trontar. I mean that you, in effect, sold your associates out to me. And I hold that once a seller, always a seller. If I could be certain that you are and will be perfectly loyal to the Haldorian Way . . ."

I managed to quiet the twitching eyelid and to look perfectly loyal to the Haldorian Way.

"Yes, Trontar," the Accountant said decisively, "I'll buy it."

The results of my conference with the Accountant were not long in appearing.

The Haldorian troops were called in, along with the military governors and the whole administrative body, and they all shipped out, somewhere into the Big Out-There they all love so much. A surprised Earth was informed that she was now a full-fledged and self-governing member of the Haldorian Empire. The Terrans were not informed of the economic factors behind this decision, though it might have been cheering for them to know that their Spanglt Resistance Quotient indicated they would make unsatisfactory slaves. Nor did the high cost of Terraforming the planet get mentioned. We Haldorians prefer the gratitude of others toward us to be unalloyed with baser, or calculating, emotions.

Not all the Haldorian personnel went out to fight or to administer. I understand the space-freighter run to the battle fleet in the Slug Galaxy gained many new deck-hands, among them one whose uniform showed the marks where Trontar's stripes had perched.

As for myself?

Well, a relatively minor operation changed me into a black-skinned Terran, though the surgeon/replacers could do nothing, ironically enough in view of my new color, to increase my resistance to heat. I remember those stirring days of combat sometimes, usually when I am making my semi-annual flight between Churchill, Manitoba, and Tierra Del Fuego. In fact, during those flights when I am practically alone is the only time I have to reflect or remember, because on both of my estates there is nothing but noise, children, and wives.

But it's a good life when the snow is driving down out of a low gray overcast, just like it does back on Haldor. It's a good life being Resident Trader on Terra, especially when one is, on the side, a trusted agent of the Accountant. It would be a perfect life—if the Accountant hadn't been right about people being unable to stop selling out.

Right now I'm up to my neck in this Terran conspiracy to revolt against the very light bonds Haldoria left on this planet. But how could I resist the tempting offer the Terrans made me? The long sought-for good life, it now occurs to me, isn't so much in escaping from something, but in knowing when to stop. But that I know. I'm drawing the line right now. I'll just tell that agent of the Slug Galaxy that I have no intention of selling out both this solar system *and* Haldoria!

THE SPECTRE GENERAL
by Theodore R. Cogswell

The interstellar empire had fallen apart, but one long-forgotten military outpost was maintaining spit-and-polish discipline (though they were running out of polish) and keeping up appearances. After all, the Inspector General might drop in any time for a surprise inspection. But who was the Inspector General?

★ ★ ★

***Theodore R. Cogswell** (1918-1987) while in his teens drove an ambulance in the Spanish Civil War for the Republican Abraham Lincoln Brigade, and later served in the U.S. Army Air Force in India, Burma, and China from 1942 to 1946. After the war, he taught at several colleges and Universities, including the University of Kentucky, though not (alas) while I was there. He later inaugurated the "fanzine for pro SF writers,"* Proceedings of the Institute for Twenty-First Century Studies, *usually abbreviated as* PITFCS *(and, according to Poul Anderson, pronounced just as it looks), which was famous for having nearly all the major SF writers of the time as contributors, and those gods of SF often went* mano y mano *at each other in its pages. "The Spectre General" was his first published story, appearing in the June 1952* Astounding Science-Fiction, *There were no Hugo or Nebula awards around in those days, but, three decades later, the Science Fiction Writers of America voted the story into the second volume of* The Science Fiction Hall of Fame. *Most of his almost 40 short stories were collected in two books,* The Wall Around the World *and* The

Third Eye. *The latter has recently appeared as an ebook, which is certainly good news. and one can only hope that* The Wall Around the World *will soon e-accompany it. In the meantime, this hilarious military SF romp awaits your pleasure.*

"Sergeant Dixon!"

Kurt stiffened. He knew *that* voice. Dropping the handles of the wooden plow, he gave a quick "rest" to the private and a polite "by your leave, sir" to the lieutenant who were yoked together in double harness. They both sank gratefully to the ground as Kurt advanced to meet the approaching officer.

Marcus Harris, the commander of the 427th Light Maintenance Battalion of the Imperial Space Marines, was an imposing figure. The three silver eagle feathers of a full colonel rose proudly from his war bonnet and the bright red of the flaming comet insignia of the Space Marines that was painted on his chest stood out sharply against his sun-blackened, leathery skin. As Kurt snapped to attention before him and saluted, the colonel surveyed the fresh-turned earth with an experienced eye.

"You plow a straight furrow, soldier!" His voice was hard and metallic, but it seemed to Kurt that there was a concealed glimmer of approval in his flinty eyes. Dixon flushed with pleasure and drew back his broad shoulders a little further.

The commander's eyes flicked down to the battle-ax that rested snugly in its leather holster at Kurt's side. "You keep a clean sidearm, too."

Kurt uttered a silent prayer of thanksgiving that he had worked over his weapon before reveille that morning until there was a satin gloss to its redwood handle and the sheen of black glass to its obsidian head.

"In fact," said Colonel Harris, "you'd be officer material if . . ." His voice trailed off.

"If what?" asked Kurt eagerly.

"If," said the colonel with a note of paternal fondness in his voice that sent cold chills dancing down Kurt's spine, "you weren't the most completely unmanageable, undisciplined, overmuscled and underbrained knucklehead I've ever had the misfortune to have in my command. This last little unauthorized jaunt of yours indicates to me that you have as much right to sergeant's stripes as I have to have kittens. Report to me at ten tomorrow! I personally guarantee that when I'm through with you—if you live that long—you'll have a bare forehead!"

Colonel Harris spun on one heel and stalked back across the dusty plateau toward the walled garrison that stood at one end. Kurt stared after him for a moment and then turned and let his eyes slip across the wide belt of lush green jungle that surrounded the high plateau. To the north rose a great range of snow-capped mountains and his heart filled with longing as he thought of the strange and beautiful thing he had found behind them. Finally he plodded slowly back to the plow, his shoulders stooped and his head sagging. With an effort he recalled himself to the business at hand.

"Up on your aching feet, soldier!" he barked to the reclining private. "If you please, sir!" he said to the lieutenant. His calloused hands grasped the worn plow handles.

"Giddiup!" The two men strained against their collars and with a creak of harness the wooden plow started to move slowly across the arid plateau.

II

Conrad Krogson, Supreme Commander of War Base Three of Sector Seven of the Galactic Protectorate, stood at quaking attention before the visiscreen of his space communicator. It was an unusual position for the commander. He was accustomed to having people quake while *he* talked.

"The Lord Protector's got another hot tip that General Carr is still alive!" said the sector commander. "He's yelling for blood, and if it's a choice between yours and mine, you know who will do the donating!"

"But, sir," quavered Krogson to the figure on the screen, "I can't do anything more than I am doing. I've had double security checks running since the last time there was an alert, and they haven't turned up a thing. And I'm so shorthanded now that if I pull another random purge, I won't have enough techs left to work the base."

"That's your problem, not mine," said the sector commander coldly. "All I know is that rumors have got to the Protector that an organized underground is being built up and that Carr is behind it. The Protector wants action now. If he doesn't get it, heads are going to roll!"

"I'll do what I can, sir," promised Krogson.

"I'm sure you will," said the sector commander viciously, "because I'm giving you exactly ten days to produce something that is big enough to take the heat off me. If you don't, I'll break you, Krogson. If I'm sent to the mines, you'll be sweating right alongside me. That's a promise!"

Krogson's face blanched.

"Any questions?" snapped the sector commander.

"Yes," said Krogson.

"Well, don't bother me with them. I've got troubles of my own!" The screen went dark.

Krogson slumped into his chair and sat staring dully at the blank screen. Finally he roused himself with an effort and let out a bellow that rattled the windows of his dusty office.

"Schninkle! Get in here!"

A gnomelike little figure scuttled in through the door and bobbed obsequiously before him.

"Yes, commander?"

"Switch on your think tank," said Krogson. "The Lord Protector has the shakes again and the heat's on!"

"What is it this time?" asked Schninkle.

"General Carr!" said the commander gloomily. "The ex-Number Two."

"I thought he'd been liquidated."

"So did I," said Krogson, "but he must have slipped out some way. The Protector thinks he's started up an underground."

"He'd be a fool if he didn't," said the little man. "The Lord Protector isn't as young as he once was and his grip is getting a little shaky."

"Maybe so, but he's still strong enough to get us before General Carr gets him. The Sector Commander just passed the buck down to me. We produce or else!"

"We?" said Schninkle unhappily.

"Of course," snapped Krogson, "we're in this together. Now let's get to work! If you were Carr, where would be the logical place for you to hide out?"

"Well," said Schninkle thoughtfully, "if I were as smart as Carr is supposed to be, I'd find myself a hideout right on Prime Base. Everything's so fouled up there that they'd never find me."

"That's out for us," said Krogson. "We can't go rooting around in the Lord Protector's own backyard. What would Carr's next best bet be?"

Schninkle thought for a moment. "He might go out to one of the deserted systems," he said slowly. "There must be half a hundred stars in our own base area that haven't been visited since the old empire broke up. Our ships don't get around the way they used to and the chances are mighty slim that anybody would stumble on to him accidentally."

"It's a possibility," said the commander thoughtfully, "a bare possibility." His right fist slapped into his left palm in a gesture of sudden resolution. "But by the Planets! At least it's something! Alert all section heads for a staff meeting in half an hour. I want every scout out on a quick check of every system in our area!"

"Beg pardon, commander," said Schninkle, "but half our light ships are red-lined for essential maintenance and the other half should be. Anyway it would take months to check every possible hideout in this area even if we used the whole fleet."

"I know," said Krogson, "but we'll have to do what we can with what we have. At least I'll be able to report to sector that we're doing *something!* Tell Astrogation to set up a series of search patterns. We won't have to check every planet. A single quick sweep through each system will do the trick. Even Carr can't run a base without power. Where there's power, there's radiation, and radiation can be detected a long way off. Put all electronic techs on double shifts and have all detection gear double-checked."

"Can't do that either," said Schninkle. "There aren't more than a dozen electronic techs left. Most of them were transferred to Prime Base last week."

Commander Krogson blew up. "How in the name of the Bloody Blue Pleiades am I supposed to keep a war base going without technicians? You tell me, Schninkle, you always seem to know all the answers."

Schninkle coughed modestly. "Well, sir," he said, "as long as you have a situation where technicians are sent to the uranium mines for making mistakes, it's going to be an unpopular vocation. And, as long as the Lord Protector of the moment is afraid that Number Two, Number Three, and so on have ideas about grabbing his job—which they generally do—he's going to keep his fleet as strong as possible and their fleets so weak they aren't dangerous. The best way to do that is to grab techs. If most of the base's ships are sitting around waiting repair, the commander won't be able to do much about any ambitions he may happen to have. Add that to the obvious fact that our whole technology has been on a downward spiral for the last three hundred years and you have your answer."

Krogson nodded in gloomy agreement. "Sometimes I feel as if we were all on a dead ship falling into a dying sun," he said. His voice suddenly altered. "But in the meantime we have our necks to save. Get going, Schninkle!"

Schninkle bobbed and darted out of the office.

III

It was exactly ten o'clock in the morning when Sergeant Dixon of the Imperial Space Marines snapped to attention before his commanding officer.

"Sergeant Dixon reporting as ordered, sir!" His voice cracked a bit in spite of his best efforts to control it.

The colonel looked at him coldly. "Nice of you to drop in, Dixon," he said. "Shall we go ahead with our little chat?"

Kurt nodded nervously.

"I have here," said the colonel, shuffling a sheaf of papers, "a report of an unauthorized expedition made by you into *Off Limits* territory."

"Which one do you mean, sir?" asked Kurt without thinking.

"Then there has been more than one?" asked the colonel quietly.

Kurt started to stammer.

Colonel Harris silenced him with a gesture of his hand. "I'm talking about the country to the north, the tableland back of the Twin Peaks."

"It's a beautiful place!" burst out Kurt enthusiastically. "It's . . . it's like Imperial Headquarters must be. Dozens of little streams full of fish, trees heavy with fruit, small game so slow and stupid that they can be knocked over with a club. Why, the battalion could live there without hardly lifting a finger!"

"I've no doubt that they could," said the colonel.

"Think of it, sir!" continued the sergeant. "No more plowing details, no more hunting details, no more nothing but taking it easy!"

"You might add to your list of 'no mores' no more tech schools," said Colonel Harris. "I'm quite aware that the place is all you say it is, sergeant. As a result I'm placing all information that pertains to it in a 'Top Secret' category. That applies to what is inside your head as well!"

"But, sir!" protested Kurt. "If you could only see the place—"

"I have," broke in the colonel, "thirty years ago."

Kurt looked at him in amazement. "Then why are we still on the plateau?"

"Because my commanding officer did just what I've just done, classified the information 'Top Secret.' Then he gave me thirty days' extra detail on the plows. After he took my stripes away that is." Colonel Harris rose slowly to his feet. "Dixon," he said softly, "it's not every man who can be a noncommissioned officer in the Space Marines. Sometimes we guess wrong. When we do we do something about it!" There was the hissing crackle of distant summer lightning in his voice and storm clouds seemed to gather about his head. "Wipe those chevrons off!" he roared.

Kurt looked at him in mute protest.

"You heard me!" the colonel thundered.

"Yes-s-s, sir," stuttered Kurt, reluctantly drawing his forearm across his forehead and wiping off the three triangles of white grease paint that marked him a sergeant in the Imperial Space Marines. Quivering with shame, he took a tight grip on his temper and choked back the angry protests that were trying to force their way past his lips.

"Maybe," suggested the colonel, "you'd like to make a complaint to the I.G. He's due in a few days and he might reverse my decision. It has happened before, you know."

"No, sir," said Kurt woodenly.

"Why not?" demanded Harris.

"When I was sent out as a scout for the hunting parties, I was given direct orders not to range farther than twenty kilometers to the north. I went sixty." Suddenly his forced composure broke. "I couldn't help it, sir," he said. "There was something behind those peaks that kept pulling me and pulling me and"—he threw up his hands—"you know the rest."

There was a sudden change in the colonel's face as a warm human smile swept across it, and he broke into a peal of laughter. "It's a hell of a feeling, isn't it, son? You know you shouldn't, but at the same time there's something inside you that says you've got to know what's behind those peaks or die. When you get a few more years under your belt you'll find that it isn't just mountains that make you feel like that. Here, boy, have a seat." He gestured toward a woven wicker chair that stood by his desk.

Kurt shifted uneasily from one foot to the other, stunned by the colonel's sudden change of attitude and embarrassed by his request. "Excuse me, sir," he said, "but we aren't out on work detail, and—"

The colonel laughed. "And enlisted men not on work detail don't sit in the presence of officers. Doesn't the way we do things ever strike you as odd, Dixon? On one hand you'd see nothing strange about being yoked to a plow with a major, and on the other, you'd never dream of sitting in his presence off duty."

Kurt looked puzzled. "Work details are different," he said. "We all have to work if we're going to eat. But in the garrison, officers are officers and enlisted men are enlisted men and that's the way it's always been."

Still smiling, the colonel reached into his desk drawer, fished out something, and tossed it to Kurt.

"Stick this in your scalp lock," he said.

Kurt looked at it, stunned. It was a golden feather crossed with a single black bar, the insignia of rank of a second lieutenant of the Imperial Space Marines. The room swirled before his eyes.

"Now," said the older officer, "sit down!"

Kurt slowly lowered himself into the chair and looked at the colonel through bemused eyes.

"Stop gawking!" said Colonel Harris. "You're an officer now! When a man gets too big for his sandals, we give him a new pair—after we let him sweat a while!"

He suddenly grew serious. "Now that you're one of the family, you have a right to know why I'm hushing up the matter of the tableland to the north. What I have to say won't make much sense at first. Later I'm hoping it will. Tell me," he said suddenly, "where did the battalion come from?"

"We've always been here, I guess," said Kurt. "When I was a recruit, Granddad used to tell me stories about us being brought from someplace else a long time ago by an iron bird, but it stands to reason that something that heavy can't fly!"

A faraway look came into the colonel's eyes. "Six generations," he mused, "and history becomes legend. Another six and the legends themselves become tales for children. Yes, Kurt," he said softly, "it stands to reason that something that heavy couldn't fly so we'll forget it for a while. We did come from someplace else though. Once there was a great empire, so great that all the stars you see at night were only part of it. And then, as things do when age rests too heavily on them, it began to crumble. Commanders fell to fighting among themselves and the Emperor grew weak. The battalion was set down here to operate a forward maintenance station for his ships. We waited but no ships came. For five hundred years no ships have come," said the colonel somberly. "Perhaps they tried to relieve us and couldn't, perhaps the Empire fell with such a crash that we were lost in the wreckage. There are a thousand perhapses that a man can tick off in his mind when the nights are long and sleep comes hard! Lost . . . forgotten . . . who knows?"

Kurt stared at him with a blank expression on his face. Most of what the colonel had said made no sense at all. Wherever Imperial Headquarters was, it hadn't forgotten them. The I.G. still made his inspection every year or so.

The colonel continued as if talking to himself. "But our operational orders said that we would stand by to give all necessary maintenance to Imperial warcraft until properly relieved, and stand by we have."

The old officer's voice seemed to be coming from a place far distant in time and space.

"I'm sorry, sir," said Kurt, "but I don't follow you. If all these things did happen, it was so long ago that they mean nothing to us now."

"But they do!" said Colonel Harris vigorously. "It's because of them that things like your rediscovery of the tableland to the north have to be suppressed for the good of the battalion! Here on the plateau the living is hard. Our work in the fields and the meat brought in by our hunting parties give us just enough to get by on. But here we have the garrison and the Tech Schools—and vague as it has become—a reason for remaining together as the battalion. Out there where the living is easy we'd lose that. We almost did once. A wise commander stopped it before it went too far. There are still a few signs of that time left—left deliberately as reminders of what can happen if commanding officers forget why we're here!"

"What things?" asked Kurt curiously.

"Well, son," said the colonel, picking up his great war bonnet from the desk and gazing at it quizzically, "I don't think you're quite ready for that information yet. Now take off and strut your feather. I've got work to do!"

IV

At War Base Three nobody was happy. Ships that were supposed to be light-months away carrying on the carefully planned search for General Carr's hideout were fluttering down out of the sky like senile penguins, disabled by blown jets, jammed computers, and all the other natural ills that worn out and poorly serviced equipment is heir to. Technical maintenance was quietly going mad. Commander Krogson was being noisy about it.

"Schninkle!" he screamed. "Isn't anything happening anyplace?"

"Nothing yet, sir," said the little man.

"Well *make* something happen!" He hoisted his battered brogans onto the scarred top of the desk and chewed savagely on a frayed cigar. "How are the other sectors doing?"

"No better than we are," said Schninkle. "Commander Snork of Sector Six tried to pull a fast one but he didn't get away with it. He sent his STAP into a plantation planet out at the edge of the Belt and had them hypno the whole population. By the time they were through there were about fifteen million greenies running around yelling 'Up with General Carr!' 'Down with the Lord Protector!' 'Long Live the People's Revolution!' and things like that. Snork even gave them a few medium vortex blasters to make it look more realistic. Then he sent in his whole fleet, tipped off the press at Prime Base, and waited. Guess what the Bureau of Essential Information finally sent him?"

"I'll bite," said Commander Krogson.

"One lousy cub reporter. Snork couldn't back out then so he had to go ahead and blast the planet down to bedrock. This morning he got a three-line notice in *Space* and a citation as Third Rate Protector of the People's Space Ways, Eighth Grade."

"That's better than the nothing we've got so far!" said the commander gloomily.

"Not when the press notice is buried on the next to last page right below the column on 'Our Feathered Comrades,'" said Schninkle, "and when the citation is posthumous. They even misspelled his name; it came out Snark!"

V

As Kurt turned to go, there was a sharp knock on Colonel Harris' door.

"Come in!" called the colonel.

Lieutenant Colonel Blick, the battalion executive officer, entered with an arrogant stride and threw his commander a slovenly salute. For a moment he didn't notice Kurt standing at attention beside the door.

"Listen, Harris!" he snarled. "What's the idea of pulling that clean-up detail out of my quarters?"

"There are no servants in this battalion, Blick," the older man said quietly. "When the men come in from work detail at night they're tired. They've earned a rest and as long as I'm CO, they're going to get it. If you have dirty work that has to be done, do it yourself. You're better able to do it than some poor devil who's been dragging a plow all day. I suggest you check pertinent regulations!"

"Regulations!" growled Blick. "What do you expect me to do, scrub my own floors?"

"I do," said the colonel dryly, "when my wife is too busy to get to it. I haven't noticed that either my dignity or my efficiency have suffered appreciably. I might add," he continued mildly, "that staff officers are supposed to set a good example for their juniors. I don't think either your tone or your manner are those that Lieutenant Dixon should be encouraged to emulate." He gestured toward Kurt and Blick spun on one heel.

"*Lieutenant* Dixon!" he roared in an incredulous voice. "By whose authority?"

"Mine," said the colonel mildly. "In case you've forgotten, I am still commanding officer of this battalion."

"I protest!" said Blick. "Commissions have always been awarded by decision of the entire staff."

"Which you now control," replied the colonel.

Kurt coughed nervously. "Excuse me, sir," he said, "but I think I'd better leave."

Colonel Harris shook his head. "You're one of our official family now, son, and you might as well get used to our squabbles. This particular one has been going on between Colonel Blick and me for years. He has no patience with some of our old customs." He turned to Blick. "Have you, Colonel?"

"You're right, I haven't!" growled Blick. "And that's why I'm going to change some of them as soon as I get the chance. The sooner we stop this Tech School nonsense and put the recruits to work in the fields where they belong, the better off we'll all be. Why should a plowman or a hunter have to know how to read wiring diagrams or set tubes. It's nonsense, superstitious nonsense. You!" he said, stabbing his finger into the chest of the startled lieutenant. "You! Dixon! You spent fourteen years in the Tech Schools just like I did when I was a recruit. What for?"

"To learn maintenance, of course," said Kurt.

"What's maintenance?" demanded Blick.

"Taking stuff apart and putting it back together and polishing jet bores with microplanes and putting plates in alignment and checking the meters when we're through to see the job was done right. Then there's classwork in Direc calculus and subelectronics and—"

"That's enough!" interrupted Blick. "And now that you've learned all that, what can you do with it?"

Kurt looked at him in surprise.

"Do with it?" he echoed. "You don't *do* anything with it. You just learn it because regulations say you should."

"And this," said Blick, turning to Colonel Harris, "is one of your prize products. Fourteen of his best years poured down the drain and he doesn't even know what for!" He paused and then said in an arrogant voice, "I'm here for a showdown, Harris!"

"Yes?" said the colonel mildly.

"I demand that the Tech Schools be closed at once, and the recruits released for work details. If you want to keep your command, you'll issue that order. The staff is behind me on this!"

Colonel Harris rose slowly to his feet. Kurt waited for the thunder to roll, but strangely enough, it didn't. It almost seemed to him that there was an expression of concealed amusement playing across the colonel's face.

"Some day, just for once," he said, "I wish somebody around here would do something that hasn't been done before."

"What do you mean by that?" demanded Blick.

"Nothing," said the colonel. "You know," he continued conversationally, "a long time ago I walked into my CO's office and made the same demands and the same threats that you're making now. I didn't get very far, though—just as you aren't going to—because I overlooked the little matter of the Inspector General's annual visit. He's due in from Imperial Headquarters Saturday night, isn't he, Blick?"

"You know he is!" growled the other.

"Aren't worried, are you? It occurs to me that the I.G. might take a dim view of your new order."

"I don't think he'll mind," said Blick with a nasty grin. "Now will you issue the order to close the Tech Schools or won't you?"

"Of course not!" said the colonel brusquely.

"That's final?"

Colonel Harris just nodded.

"All right," barked Blick, "you asked for it!"

There was an ugly look on his face as he barked, "Kane! Simmons! Arnett! The rest of you! Get in here!"

The door to Harris' office swung slowly open and revealed a group of officers standing sheepishly in the anteroom.

"Come in, gentlemen," said Colonel Harris.

They came slowly forward and grouped themselves just inside the door.

"I'm taking over!" roared Blick. "This garrison has needed a house-cleaning for a long time and I'm just the man to do it!"

"How about the rest of you?" asked the colonel.

"Beg pardon, sir," said one hesitantly, "but we think Colonel Blick's probably right. I'm afraid we're going to have to confine you for a few days. Just until after the I.G.'s visit," he added apologetically.

"And what do you think the I.G. will say to all this?"

"Colonel Blick says we don't have to worry about that," said the officer. "He's going to take care of everything."

A look of sudden anxiety played across Harris' face and for the first time he seemed on the verge of losing his composure.

"How?" he demanded, his voice betraying his concern.

"He didn't say, sir," the other replied. Harris relaxed visibly.

"All right," said Blick. "Let's get moving!" He walked behind the desk and plumped into the colonel's chair. Hoisting his feet on the desk he gave his first command.

"Take him away!"

There was a sudden roar from the far corner of the room. "No you don't!" shouted Kurt. His battle-ax leaped into his hand as he jumped in front of Colonel Harris, his muscular body taut and his gray eyes flashing defiance.

Blick jumped to his feet. "Disarm that man!" he commanded. There was a certain amount of scuffling as the officers in the front of the group by the door tried to move to the rear and those behind them resolutely defended their more protected positions.

Blick's face grew so purple that he seemed on the verge of apoplexy. "Major Kane," he demanded, "place that man under restraint!"

Kane advanced toward Kurt with a noticeable lack of enthusiasm. Keeping a cautious eye on the glittering ax head, he said in what he obviously hoped to be a placating voice, "Come now, old man. Can't have this sort of thing, you know." He stretched out his hand hesitantly toward Kurt. "Why don't you give me your ax and we'll forget that the incident ever occurred."

Kurt's ax suddenly leaped toward the major's head. Kane stood petrified as death whizzed toward him. At the last split second Kurt gave a practiced twist to his wrist and the ax jumped up, cutting the air over the major's head with a vicious whistle. The top half of his silver staff plume drifted slowly to the floor.

"You want it," roared Kurt, his ax flicking back and forth like a snake's tongue, "you come get it. That goes for the rest of you, too!"

The little knot of officers retreated still farther. Colonel Harris was having the time of his life.

"Give it to 'em, son!" he whooped.

Blick looked contemptuously at the staff and slowly drew his own ax. Colonel Harris suddenly stopped laughing.

"Wait a minute, Blick!" he said. "This has gone far enough." He turned to Kurt. "Give them your ax, son."

Kurt looked at him with an expression of hurt bewilderment in his eyes, hesitated for a moment, and then glumly surrendered his weapon to the relieved major.

"Now," snarled Blick, "take that insolent puppy out and feed him to the lizards!"

Kurt drew himself up in injured dignity. "That is no way to refer to a brother officer," he said reproachfully.

The vein in Blick's forehead started to pulse again. "Get him out of here before I tear him to shreds!" he hissed through clenched teeth. There was silence for a moment as he fought to regain control of himself. Finally he succeeded. "Lock him up!" he said in an approximation to his normal voice. "Tell the provost sergeant I'll send down the charges as soon as I can think up enough."

Kurt was led resentfully from the room.

"The rest of you clear out," said Blick. "I want to talk with Colonel Harris about the I.G."

VI

There was a saying in the Protectorate that when the Lord Protector was angry, stars and heads fell. Commander Krogson felt his wobble on his neck. His far-sweeping scouts were sending back nothing but reports of equipment failure, and the sector commander had coldly informed him that morning that his name rested securely at the bottom of the achievement list. It looked as if War Base Three would shortly have a change of command.

"Look, Schninkle," he said desperately, "even if we can't give them anything, couldn't we make a promise that would look good enough to take some of the heat off us?"

Schninkle looked dubious.

"Maybe a new five-year plan?" suggested Krogson.

The little man shook his head. "That's a subject we'd better avoid entirely," he said. "They're still asking nasty questions about what happened to the last one. Mainly on the matter of our transport quota. I took the liberty of passing the buck on down to Logistics. Several of them have been . . . eh. . . removed as a consequence."

"Serves them right!" snorted Krogson. "They got me into that mess with their 'if a freighter and a half flies a light-year and a half in a month and a half, ten freighters can fly ten light-years in ten months!' I knew there was something fishy about it at the time, but I couldn't put my finger on it."

"It's always darkest before the storm," said Schninkle helpfully.

VII

"Take off your war bonnet and make yourself comfortable," said Colonel Harris hospitably.

Blick grunted assent. "This thing is sort of heavy," he said. "I think I'll change uniform regulations while I'm at it."

"There was something you wanted to tell me?" suggested the colonel.

"Yeah," said Blick. "I figure that you figure the I.G.'s going to bail you out of this. Right?"

"I wouldn't be surprised."

"I would," said Blick. "I was up snoopin' around the armory last week. There was something there that started me doing some heavy thinking. Do you know what it was?"

"I can guess," said the colonel.

"As I looked at it, it suddenly occurred to me what a happy coincidence it is that the Inspector General always arrives just when you happen to need him."

"It is odd, come to think of it."

"Something else occurred to me, too. I got to thinking that if I were CO and I wanted to keep the troops whipped into line, the easiest way to do it would be to have a visible symbol of Imperial Headquarters appear in person once in a while."

"That makes sense," admitted Harris, "especially since the chaplain has started preaching that Imperial Headquarters is where good marines go when they die—*if* they follow regulations while they're alive. But how would you manage it?"

"Just the way you did. I'd take one of the old battle suits, wait until it was good and dark, and then slip out the back way and climb up six or seven thousand feet. Then I'd switch on my landing lights and drift slowly down to the parade field to review the troops." Blick grinned triumphantly.

"It might work," admitted Colonel Harris, "but I was under the impression that those rigs were so heavy that a man couldn't even walk in one, let alone fly."

Blick grinned again. "Not if the suit was powered. If a man were to go up into the tower of the arsenal and pick the lock of the little door labeled 'Danger! Absolutely No Admittance,' he might find a whole stack of shiny little cubes that look suspiciously like the illustrations of power packs in the tech manuals."

"That he might," agreed the colonel.

Blick shifted back in his chair. "Aren't worried, are you?"

Colonel Harris shook his head. "I was for a moment when I thought you'd told the rest of the staff, but I'm not now."

"You should be! When the I.G. arrives this time, I'm going to be inside that suit. There's going to be a new order around here, and he's just what I need to put the stamp of approval on it. When the Inspector General talks, nobody questions!"

He looked at Harris expectantly, waiting for a look of consternation to sweep across his face. The colonel just laughed.

"Blick," he said, "you're in for a big surprise!"

"What do you mean?" said the other suspiciously.

"Simply that I know you better than you know yourself. You wouldn't be executive officer if I didn't. You know, Blick, I've got a hunch that the battalion is going to change the man more than the man is going to change the battalion. And now if you'll excuse me—" He started toward the door. Blick moved to intercept him. "Don't trouble yourself," chuckled the colonel. "I can find my own way to the cell block." There was a broad grin on his face. "Besides, you've got work to do."

There was a look of bewilderment in Blick's face as the erect figure went out the door. "I don't get it," he said to himself. "I just don't get it!"

VIII

Flight Officer Ozaki was unhappy. Trouble had started two hours after he lifted his battered scout off War Base Three and showed no signs of letting up. He sat glumly at his controls and enumerated his woes. First there was the matter of the air conditioner which had acquired an odd little hum and discharged into the cabin oxygen redolent with the rich, ripe odor of rotting fish. Secondly, something had happened to the complex insides of his food synthesizer and no matter what buttons he punched, all that emerged from the ejector were quivering slabs of undercooked protein base smeared with a raspberry-flavored goo.

Not last, but worst of all, the ship's fuel converter was rapidly becoming more erratic. Instead of a slow, steady feeding of the plutonite ribbon into the combustion chamber, there were moments when the mechanism would falter and then leap ahead. The resulting sudden injection of several square millimicrons of tape would send a sudden tremendous flare of energy spouting out through the rear jets. The pulse only lasted for a fraction of a second, but the sudden application of several Gs meant a momentary blackout and, unless he was strapped carefully into the pilot seat, several new bruises to add to the old.

What made Ozaki the unhappiest was that there was nothing he could do about it. Pilots who wanted to stay alive just didn't tinker with the mechanism of their ships.

Glumly he pulled out another red-bordered IMMEDIATE MAINTENANCE card from the rack and began to fill it in.

Description of item requiring maintenance: "Shower thermostat, M7, Small Standard."

Nature of malfunction: "Shower will deliver only boiling water."

Justification for immediate maintenance: Slowly in large, block letters Ozaki bitterly inked in "Haven't had a bath since I left base!" and tossed the card into the already overflowing gripe box with a feeling of helpless anger.

"Kitchen mechanics," he muttered. "Couldn't do a decent repair job if they wanted to—and most of the time they don't. I'd like to see one of them three days out on a scout sweep with a toilet that won't flush!"

IX

It was a roomy cell as cells go but Kurt wasn't happy there. His continual striding up and down was making Colonel Harris nervous.

"Relax, son," he said gently, "you'll just wear yourself out."

Kurt turned to face the colonel who was stretched out comfortably on his cot. "Sir," he said in a conspiratorial whisper, "we've got to break out of here."

"What for?" asked Harris. "This is the first decent rest I've had in years."

"You aren't going to let Blick get away with this?" demanded Kurt in a shocked voice.

"Why not?" said the colonel. "He's the exec, isn't he? If something happened to me, he'd have to take over command anyway. He's just going through the impatient stage, that's all. A few days behind my desk will settle him down. In two weeks he'll be so sick of the job he'll be down on his knees begging me to take over again."

Kurt decided to try a new tack. "But, sir, he's going to shut down the Tech Schools!"

"A little vacation won't hurt the kids," said the colonel indulgently. "After a week or so the wives will get so sick of having them underfoot all day that they'll turn the heat on him. Blick has six kids himself, and I've a hunch his wife won't be any happier than the rest. She's a very determined woman, Kurt, a very determined woman!"

Kurt had a feeling he was getting no place rapidly. "Please, sir," he said earnestly, "I've got a plan."

"Yes?"

"Just before the guard makes his evening check-in, stretch out on the bed and start moaning. I'll yell that you're dying and when he comes in to check, I'll jump him!"

"You'll do no such thing!" said the colonel sternly. "Sergeant Wetzel is an old friend of mine. Can't you get it through your thick head that I don't want to escape? When you've held command as long as I have, you'll welcome a chance for a little peace and quiet. I know Blick inside out, and I'm not worried about him. But, if you've got your heart set on escaping, I suppose there's no particular reason why you shouldn't. Do it the easy way though. Like this." He walked to the bars that fronted the cell and bellowed, "Sergeant Wetzel! Sergeant Wetzel!"

"Coming, sir!" called a voice from down the corridor. There was a shuffle of running feet and a gray scalp-locked and extremely portly sergeant puffed into view.

"What will it be, sir?" he asked.

"Colonel Blick or any of the staff around?" questioned the colonel.

"No, sir," said the sergeant. "They're all upstairs celebrating."

"Good!" said Harris. "Unlock the door, will you?"

"Anything you say, Colonel," said the old man agreeably and produced a large key from his pouch and fitted it into the lock. There was a slight creaking and the door swung open.

"Young Dixon here wants to escape," said the colonel.

"It's all right by me," replied the sergeant, "though it's going to be awkward when Colonel Blick asks what happened to him."

"The lieutenant has a plan," confided the colonel. "He's going to overpower you and escape."

"There's more to it than just that!" said Kurt. "I'm figuring on swapping uniforms with you. That way I can walk right out through the front gate without anybody being the wiser."

"That," said the sergeant, slowly looking down at his sixty-three inch waist, "will take a heap of doing. You're welcome to try though."

"Let's get on with it then," said Kurt, winding up a roundhouse swing.

"If it's all the same with you, Lieutenant," said the old sergeant, eyeing Kurt's rocklike fist nervously, "I'd rather have the colonel do any overpowering that's got to be done."

Colonel Harris grinned and walked over to Wetzel.

"Ready?"

"Ready!"

Harris' fist traveled a bare five inches and tapped Wetzel lightly on the chin.

"Oof!" grunted the sergeant cooperatively and staggered back to a point where he could collapse on the softest of the two cots.

The exchange of clothes was quickly effected. Except for the pants—which persisted in dropping down to Kurt's ankles—and the war bonnet—which with equal persistence kept sliding down over his ears—he was ready to go. The pants problem was solved easily by stuffing a pillow inside them. This Kurt fondly believed made him look more like the rotund sergeant than ever. The garrison bonnet presented a more difficult problem, but he finally achieved a partial solution. By holding it up with his left hand and keeping the palm tightly pressed against his forehead, it should appear to the casual observer that he was walking engrossed in deep thought.

The first two hundred yards were easy. The corridor was deserted and he plodded confidently along, the great war bonnet wobbling sedately on his head in spite of his best efforts to keep it steady. When he finally reached the exit gate, he knocked on it firmly and called to the duty sergeant.

"Open up! It's Wetzel."

Unfortunately, just then he grew careless and let go of his headgear. As the door swung open, the great war bonnet swooped down over his ears and came to rest on his shoulders. The result was that where his head normally was there could be seen only a nest of weaving feathers. The duty sergeant's jaw suddenly dropped as he got a good look at the strange figure that stood in the darkened corridor. And then with remarkable presence of mind he slammed the door shut in Kurt's face and clicked the bolt.

"Sergeant of the guard!" he bawled. "Sergeant of the guard! There's a *thing* in the corridor!"

"What kind of a thing?" inquired a sleepy voice from the guard room.

"A horrible kind of a thing with wiggling feathers where its head ought to be," replied the sergeant.

"Get its name, rank, and serial number," said the sleepy voice.

Kurt didn't wait to hear any more. Disentangling himself from the headdress with some difficulty, he hurled it aside and pelted back down the corridor.

Lieutenant Dixon wandered back into the cell with a crestfallen look on his face. Colonel Harris and the old sergeant were so deeply engrossed in a game of "rockets high" that they didn't even see him at first. Kurt coughed and the colonel looked up.

"Change your mind?"

"No, sir," said Kurt. "Something slipped."

"What?" asked the colonel.

"Sergeant Wetzel's war bonnet. I'd rather not talk about it." He sank down on his bunk and buried his head in his hands.

"Excuse me," said the sergeant apologetically, "but if the lieutenant's through with my pants, I'd like to have them back. There's a draft in here."

Kurt silently exchanged clothes and then moodily walked over to the grille that barred the window and stood looking out.

"Why not go upstairs to officers' country and out that way?" suggested the sergeant, who hated the idea of being overpowered for nothing. "If you can get to the front gate without one of the staff spotting you, you can walk right out. The sentry never notices faces, he just checks for insignia."

Kurt grabbed Sergeant Wetzel's plump hand and wrung it warmly. "I don't know how to thank you," he stammered.

"Then it's about time you learned," said the colonel. "The usual practice in civilized battalions is to say 'thank you.' "

"Thank you!" said Kurt.

"Quite all right," said the sergeant. "Take the first stairway to your left. When you get to the top, turn left again and the corridor will take you straight to the exit."

Kurt got safely to the top of the stairs and turned right. Three hundred feet later the corridor ended in a blank wall. A small passageway angled off to the left and he set off down it. It also came to a dead end in a small anteroom whose farther wall was occupied by a set of great bronze doors. He turned and started to retrace his steps. He had almost reached the main corridor when he heard angry voices sounding from it. He peeked cautiously around the corridor. His escape route was blocked by two officers engaged in acrimonious argument. Neither was too sober and the captain obviously wasn't giving the major the respect that a field officer usually commanded.

"I don't care what she said!" the captain shouted. "I saw her first."

The major grabbed him by the shoulder and pushed him back against the wall. "It doesn't matter who saw her first. You keep away from her or there's going to be trouble!"

The captain's face flushed with rage. With a snarl he tore off the major's breechcloth and struck him in the face with it. The major's face grew hard and cold. He stepped back, clicked his calloused heels together, and bowed slightly.

"Axes or fists?"

"Axes," snapped the captain.

"May I suggest the armory anteroom?" said the major formally. "We won't be disturbed there."

"As you wish, sir," said the captain with equal formality. "Your breechcloth, sir." The major donned it with dignity and they started down the hall toward Kurt. He turned and fled back down the corridor.

In a second he was back in the anteroom. Unless he did something quickly he was trapped. Two flaming torches were set in brackets on each side of the great bronze door. As flickering pools of shadow chased each other across the worn stone floor, Kurt searched desperately for some other way out. There was none. The only possible exit was through the bronze portals. The voices behind him grew louder. He ran forward, grabbed a projecting handle, and pulled. One door creaked open slightly and with a sigh of relief Kurt slipped inside.

There were no torches here. The great hall stood in half-darkness, its only illumination the pale moonlight that streamed down through the arching skylight that formed the central ceiling. He stood for a moment in awe, impressed in spite of himself by the strange unfamiliar shapes that loomed before him in the half-darkness. He was suddenly brought back to reality by the sound of voices in the anteroom.

"Hey! The armory door's open!"

"So what? That place is off limits to everybody but the CO."

"Blick won't care. Let's fight in there. There should be more room."

Kurt quickly scanned the hall for a safe hiding place. At the far end stood what looked like a great bronze statue, its burnished surface gleaming dimly in the moonlight. As the door swung open behind him, he slipped cautiously through the shadows until he reached it. It looked like a coffin with feet, but to one side of it there was a dark pool of shadow. He slipped into it and pressed himself close against the cold metal. As he did so his hipbone pressed against a slight protrusion and with a slight clicking sound, a hinged middle section of the metallic figure swung open, exposing a dark cavity. The thing was hollow!

Kurt had a sudden idea. *Even if they do come down here,* he thought, *they'd never think of looking inside this thing!* With some difficulty he wiggled inside and pulled the hatch shut after him. There were legs to the thing—his own fit snugly into them—but no arms.

The two officers strode out of the shadows at the other end of the hall. They stopped in the center of the armory and faced each other like fighting cocks. Kurt gave a sigh of relief. It looked as if he were safe for the moment.

There was a sudden wicked glitter of moonlight on ax-heads as their weapons leaped into their hands. They stood frozen for a moment in a murderous tableau and then the captain's ax hummed toward his opponent's head in a vicious slash. There was a shower of sparks as the major parried and then with a quick wrist twist sent his own weapon looping down toward the captain's midriff. The other pulled his ax down to ward the blow, but he was only partially successful. The keen obsidian edge raked his ribs and blood dripped darkly in the moonlight.

As Kurt watched intently, he began to feel the first faint stirrings of claustrophobia. The Imperial designers had planned their battle armor for efficiency rather than comfort and Kurt felt as if he were locked away in a cramped dark closet. His malaise wasn't helped by a sudden realization that when the men left they might very well lock the door behind them. His decision to change his hiding place was hastened when a bank of dark clouds swept across the face of the moon. The flood of light poured down through the skylight suddenly dimmed until Kurt could barely make out the pirouetting forms of the two officers who were fighting in the center of the hall.

This was his chance. If he could slip down the darkened side of the hall before the moon lighted up the hall again, he might be able to slip out of the hall unobserved. He pushed against the closed hatch through which he entered. It refused to open. A feeling of trapped panic started to roll over him, but he fought it back. "There must be some way to open this from the inside," he thought.

As his fingers wandered over the dark interior of the suit looking for a release lever, they encountered a bank of keys set just below his midriff. He pressed one experimentally. A quiet hum filled the armor and suddenly a feeling of weightlessness came over him. He stiffened in fright. As he did so one of his steel shod feet pushed lightly backwards against the floor. That was enough. Slowly, like a child's balloon caught in a light draft, he drifted toward the center of the hall. He struggled violently, but since he was now several inches above the floor and rising slowly it did him no good.

The fight was progressing splendidly. Both men were master axmen, and in spite of being slightly drunk, were putting on a brilliant exhibition. Each was bleeding from a dozen minor slashes, but neither had been seriously axed as yet. Their flashing strokes and counters were masterful, so masterful that Kurt slowly forgot his increasingly awkward situation as he became more and more absorbed in the fight before him. The blond captain was slightly the better axman, but the major compensated for it by occasionally whistling in cuts that to Kurt's experienced eye seemed perilously close to fouls. He grew steadily more partisan in his feelings until one particularly unscrupulous attempt broke down his restraint altogether. "Pull down your guard!" he screamed to the captain. "He's trying to cut you below the belt!" His voice reverberated within the battle suit and boomed out with strange metallic overtones.

Both men whirled in the direction of the sound. They could see nothing for a moment and then the major caught sight of the strange menacing figure looming above him in the murky darkness.

Dropping his ax he dashed frantically toward the exit shrieking: "It's the Inspector General!"

The captain's reflexes were a second slower. Before he could take off, Kurt poked his head out of the open faceport and shouted down, "It's only me, Dixon! Get me out of here, will you?"

The captain stared up at him goggle-eyed. "What kind of a contraption is that?" he demanded. "And what are you doing in it?"

Kurt by now was floating a good ten feet off the floor. He had visions of spending the night on the ceiling and he wasn't happy about it. "Get me down now," he pleaded. "We can talk after I get out of this thing."

The captain gave a leap upwards and tried to grab Kurt's ankles. His jump was short and his outstretched fingers gave the weightless armor a slight shove that sent it bobbing up another three feet.

He cocked his head back and called up to Kurt. "Can't reach you now. We'll have to try something else. How did you get into that thing in the first place?"

"The middle section is hinged," said Kurt. "When I pulled it shut, it clicked."

"Well, unclick it!"

"I tried that. That's why I'm up here now."

"Try again," said the man on the floor. "If you can open the hatch, you can drop down and I'll catch you."

"Here I come!" said Kurt, his fingers selecting a stud at random. He pushed. There was a terrible blast of flame from the shoulder jets and he screamed skywards on a pillar of fire. A microsecond later, he reached the skylight. Something had to give. It did!

At fifteen thousand feet, the air pressure dropped to the point where the automatics took over and the face plate clicked shut. Kurt didn't notice that. He was out like a light. At thirty thousand feet the heaters cut in. Forty seconds later he was in free space. Things could have been worse though; he still had air for two hours.

X

Flight Officer Ozaki was taking a catnap when the alarm on the radiation detector went off. Dashing the sleep out of his eyes, he slipped rapidly into the control seat and cut off the gong. His fingers danced over the controls in a blur of movement. Swiftly the vision screen shifted until the little green dot that indicated a source of radiant energy was firmly centered. Next he switched on the pulse analyzer and watched carefully as it broke down the incoming signal into components and sent them surging across the scope in the form of sharp-toothed sine waves. There was an odd peak to them, a strength and sharpness that he hadn't seen before.

"Doesn't look familiar," he muttered to himself, "but I'd better check to make sure."

He punched the comparison button and while the analyzer methodically began to check the incoming trace against the known patterns stored up in its compact little memory bank, he turned back to the vision screen. He switched on high magnification and the system rushed toward him. It expanded from a single pinpoint of light into a distinct planetary system. At its center a giant dying sun expanded on the plate like a malignant red eye. As he watched, the green dot moved appreciably, a thin red line stretching out behind it to indicate its course from point of first detection. Ozaki's fingers moved over the controls and a broken line of white light came into being on the screen. With careful adjustments he moved it up toward the green track left by the crawling red dot. When he had an exact overlay, he carefully moved the line back along the course that the energy emitter had followed prior to detection.

Ozaki was tense. It looked as if he might have something. He gave a sudden whoop of excitement as the broken white line intersected the orange dot of a planetary mass. A vision of the promised thirty-day leave and six months' extra pay danced before his eyes as he waited for the pulse analyzer to clear.

"Home!" he thought ecstatically. "Home and unplugged plumbing!"

With a final whir of relays the analyzer clucked like a contented chicken and dropped an identity card out of its emission slot. Ozaki grabbed it and scanned it eagerly. At the top was printed in red, "Identity. Unknown," and below in smaller letters, "Suggest check of trace pattern on base analyzer." He gave a sudden whistle as his eyes caught the energy utilization index. 927! That was fifty points higher than it had any right to be. The best tech in the Protectorate considered himself lucky if he could tune a propulsion unit so that it delivered a thrust of forty-five percent of rated maximum. Whatever was out there was hot! Too hot for one man to handle alone. With quick decision he punched the transmission key of his space communicator and sent a call winging back to War Base Three.

XI

Commander Krogson stormed up and down his office in a frenzy of impatience.

"It shouldn't be more than another fifteen minutes, sir," said Schninkle.

Krogson snorted. "That's what you said an hour ago! What's the matter with those people down there? I want the identity of that ship and I want it now."

"It's not Identification's fault," explained the other. "The big analyzer is in pretty bad shape and it keeps jamming. They're afraid that if they take it apart they won't be able to get it back together again."

The next two hours saw Krogson's blood pressure steadily rising toward the explosion point. Twice he ordered the whole identification section transferred to a labor battalion and twice he had to rescind the command when Schninkle pointed out that scrapings from the bottom of the barrel were better than nothing at all. His fingernails were chewed down to the quick when word finally came through.

"Identification, sir," said a hesitant voice on the intercom.

"Well?" demanded the commander.

"The analyzer says—" The voice hesitated again.

"The analyzer says what?" shouted Krogson in a fury of impatience.

"The analyzer says that the trace pattern is that of one of the old Imperial drive units."

"That's impossible!" sputtered the commander. "The last Imperial base was smashed five hundred years ago. What of their equipment was salvaged has long since been worn out and tossed on the scrap heap. The machine must be wrong!"

"Not this time," said the voice. "We checked the memory bank manually and there's no mistake. It's an Imperial all right. Nobody can produce a drive unit like that these days."

Commander Krogson leaned back in his chair, his eyes veiled in deep thought. "Schninkle," he said finally, thinking out loud, "I've got a hunch that maybe we've stumbled on something big. Maybe the Lord Protector is right about there being a plot to knock him over, but maybe he's wrong about who's trying to do it. What if all these centuries since the Empire collapsed a group of Imperials have been hiding out waiting for their chance?"

Schninkle digested the idea for a moment. "It could be," he said slowly. "If there is such a group, they couldn't pick a better time than now to strike; the Protectorate is so wobbly that it wouldn't take much of a shove to topple it over."

The more he thought about it, the more sense the idea made to Krogson. Once he felt a fleeting temptation to hush up the whole thing. If there were Imperials and they did take over, maybe they would put an end to the frenzied rat race that was slowly ruining the galaxy—a race that sooner or later entangled every competent man in the great web of intrigue and power politics that stretched through the Protectorate and forced him in self-defense to keep clawing his way toward the top of the heap.

Regretfully, he dismissed the idea. This was a matter of his own neck, here and now!

"It's a big IF, Schninkle," he said, "but if I've guessed right, we've bailed ourselves out. Get hold of that scout and find out his position."

Schninkle scooted out of the door. A few minutes later he dashed back in. "I've just contacted the scout!" he said excitedly. "He's closed in on the power source and it isn't a ship after all. It's a man in space armor! The drive unit is cut off, and it's heading out of the system at fifteen hundred per. The pilot is standing by for instructions."

"Tell him to intercept and capture!" Schninkle started out of the office. "Wait a second; what's the scout's position?"

Schninkle's face fell. "He doesn't quite know, sir."

"He *what?*" demanded the commander.

"He doesn't quite know," repeated the little man. "His astrocomputer went haywire six hours out of base."

"Just our luck!" swore Krogson. "Well, tell him to leave his transmitter on. We'll ride in on his beam. Better call the sector commander while you're at it and tell him what's happened."

"Beg pardon, Commander," said Schninkle, "but I wouldn't advise it."

"Why not?" asked Krogson.

"You're next in line to be sector commander, aren't you, sir?"

"I guess so," said the commander.

"If this pans out, you'll be in a position to knock him over and grab his job, won't you?" asked Schninkle slyly.

"Could be," admitted Krogson in a tired voice. "Not because I want to, though—but because I have to. I'm not as young as I once was, and the boys below are pushing pretty hard. It's either up or out—and out is always feet first."

"Put yourself in the sector commander's shoes for a minute," suggested the little man. "What would you do if a war base commander came through with news of a possible Imperial base?"

A look of grim comprehension came over Krogson's face. "Of course! I'd ground the commander's ships and send out my own fleet. I must be slipping; I should have thought of that at once!"

"On the other hand," said Schninkle, "you might call him and request permission to conduct routine maneuvers. He'll approve as a matter of course and you'll have an excuse for taking out the full fleet. Once in deep space, you can slap on radio silence and set course for the scout. If there is an Imperial base out there, nobody will know anything about it until it's blasted. I'll stay back here and keep my eyes on things for you."

Commander Krogson grinned. "Schninkle, it's a pleasure to have you in my command. How would you like me to make you Devoted Servant of the Lord Protector, Eighth Class? It carries an extra shoe ration coupon!"

"If it's all the same with you," said Schninkle, "I'd just as soon have Saturday afternoons off."

XII

As Kurt struggled up out of the darkness, he could hear a gong sounding in the faint distance. *Bong!* BONG! *BONG!* It grew nearer and louder. He shook his head painfully and groaned. There was light from some place beating against his eyelids. Opening them was too much effort. He was in some sort of a bunk. He could feel that. But the gong. He lay there concentrating on it. Slowly he began to realize that the beat didn't come from outside. It was his head. It felt swollen and sore and each pulse of his heart sent a hammer thud through it.

One by one his senses began to return to normal. As his nose reassumed its normal acuteness, it began to quiver. There was a strange scent in the air, an unpleasant sickening scent as of—he chased the scent down his aching memory channels until he finally had it cornered—rotting fish. With that to anchor on, he slowly began to reconstruct reality. He had been floating high above the floor in the armory and the captain had been trying to get him down. Then he had pushed a button. There had been a microsecond of tremendous acceleration and then a horrendous crash. That must have been the skylight. After the crash was darkness, then the gongs, and now fish—dead and rotting fish.

"I must be alive," he decided. "Imperial Headquarters would never smell like this!"

He groaned and slowly opened one eye. Wherever he was he hadn't been there before. He opened the other eye. He was in a room. A room with a curved ceiling and curving walls. Slowly, with infinite care, he hung his head over the side of the bunk. Below him in a form-fitting chair before a bank of instruments sat a small man with yellow skin and blue-black hair. Kurt coughed. The man looked up. Kurt asked the obvious question.

"Where am I?"

"I'm not permitted to give you any information," said the small man. His speech had an odd slurred quality to Kurt's ear.

"Something stinks!" said Kurt.

"It sure does," said the small man gloomily. "It must be worse for you. I'm used to it."

Kurt surveyed the cabin with interest. There were a lot of gadgets tucked away here and there that looked familiar. They were like the things he had worked on in Tech School except that they were cruder and simpler. They looked as if they had been put together by an eight-year-old recruit who was doing the first trial assembly. He decided to make another stab at establishing some sort of communication with the little man.

"How come you have everything in one room? We always used to keep different things in different shops."

"No comment," said Ozaki.

Kurt had a feeling he was butting his head against a stone wall. He decided to make one more try.

"I give up," he said, wrinkling his nose, "where'd you hide it?"

"Hide what?" asked the little man.

"The fish," said Kurt.

"No comment."

"Why not?" asked Kurt.

"Because there isn't anything that can be done about it," said Ozaki. "It's the air conditioner. Something's haywire inside."

"What's an air conditioner?" asked Kurt.

"That square box over your head."

Kurt looked at it, closed his eyes, and thought for a moment. The thing did look familiar. Suddenly a picture of it popped into his mind. Page 318 in the "Manual of Auxiliary Mechanisms."

"It's fantastic!" he said.

"What is?" said the little man.

"This," Kurt pointed to the conditioner. "I didn't know they existed in real life. I thought they were just in books. You got a first echelon kit?"

"Sure," said Ozaki. "It's in the recess by the head of the bunk. Why?"

Kurt pulled the kit out of its retaining clips and opened its cover, fishing around until he found a small screwdriver and a pair of needle-nose pliers.

"I think I'll fix it," he said conversationally.

"Oh, no you won't!" howled Ozaki. "Air with fish is better than no air at all." But before he could do anything, Kurt had pulled the cover off the air conditioner and was probing into the intricate mechanism with his screwdriver. A slight thumping noise came from inside. Kurt cocked his ear and thought. Suddenly his screwdriver speared down through the maze of whirring parts. He gave a slow quarter turn and the internal thumping disappeared.

"See," he said triumphantly, "no more fish!"

Ozaki stopped shaking long enough to give the air a tentative sniff. He had got out of the habit of smelling in self-defense and it took him a minute or two to detect the difference. Suddenly a broad grin swept across his face.

"It's going away! I do believe it's going away!"

Kurt gave the screwdriver another quarter of a turn and suddenly the sharp spicy scent of pines swept through the scout. Ozaki took a deep ecstatic breath and relaxed in his chair. His face lost its pallor.

"How did you do it?" he said finally.

"No comment," said Kurt pleasantly.

There was silence from below. Ozaki was in the throes of a brainstorm. He was more impressed by Kurt's casual repair of the air conditioner than he liked to admit.

"Tell me," he said cautiously, "can you fix other things beside air conditioners?"

"I guess so," said Kurt, "if it's just simple stuff like this." He gestured around the cabin. "Most of the stuff here needs fixing. They've got it together wrong."

"Maybe we could make a dicker," said Ozaki. "You fix things, I answer questions—some questions that is," he added hastily.

"It's a deal," said Kurt who was filled with a burning curiosity as to his whereabouts. Certain things were already clear in his mind. He knew that wherever he was he'd never been there before. That meant evidently that there was a garrison on the other side of the mountains whose existence had never been suspected. What bothered him was how he had got there.

"Check," said Ozaki. "First, do you know anything about plumbing?"

"What's plumbing?" asked Kurt curiously.

"Pipes," said Ozaki. "They're plugged. They've been plugged for more time than I like to think about."

"I can try," said Kurt.

"Good!" said the pilot and ushered him into the small cubicle that opened off the rear bulkhead. "You might tackle the shower while you're at it."

"What's a shower?"

"That curved dingbat up there," said Ozaki pointing. "The thermostat's out of whack."

"Thermostats are kid stuff," said Kurt, shutting the door.

Ten minutes later Kurt came out. "It's all fixed."

"I don't believe it," said Ozaki, shouldering his way past Kurt. He reached down and pushed a small curved handle. There was the satisfying sound of rushing water. He next reached into the little shower compartment and turned the knob to the left. With a hiss a needle spray of cold water burst forth. The pilot looked at Kurt with awe in his eyes.

"If I hadn't seen it, I wouldn't have believed it! That's two answers you've earned."

Kurt peered back into the cubicle curiously. "Well, first," he said, "now that I've fixed them, what are they *for?*"

Ozaki explained briefly and a look of amazement came over Kurt's face. Machinery he knew, but the idea that it could be used for something was hard to grasp.

"If I hadn't seen it, I wouldn't have believed it!" he said slowly. This would be something to tell when he got home. Home! The pressing question of location popped back into his mind.

"How far are we from the garrison?" he asked.

Ozaki made a quick mental calculation. "Roughly two light-seconds," he said.

"How far's that in kilometers?"

Ozaki thought again. "Around six hundred thousand. I'll run off the exact figures if you want them."

Kurt gulped. No place could be that far away. Not even Imperial Headquarters! He tried to measure out the distance in his mind in terms of days' marches, but he soon found himself lost. Thinking wouldn't do it. He had to see with his own eyes where he was. "How do you get outside?" he asked.

Ozaki gestured toward the air lock that opened at the rear of the compartment. "Why?"

"I want to go out for a few minutes to sort of get my bearings."

Ozaki looked at him in disbelief. "What's your game, anyhow?" he demanded.

It was Kurt's turn to look bewildered. "I haven't any game. I'm just trying to find out where I am so I'll know which way to head to get back to the garrison."

"It'll be a long, cold walk." Ozaki laughed and hit the stud that slid back the ray screens on the vision ports. "Take a look."

Kurt looked out into nothingness, a blue-black void marked only by distant pinpoints of light. He suddenly felt terribly alone, lost in a blank immensity that had no boundaries. *Down* was gone and so was *up*. There was only this tiny lighted room with nothing underneath it. The port began to swim in front of his eyes as a sudden, strange vertigo swept over him. He felt that if he looked out into that terrible space for another moment he would lose his sanity. He covered his eyes with his hands and staggered back to the center of the cabin.

Ozaki slid the ray screens back in place. "Kind of gets you first time, doesn't it?"

Kurt had always carried a little automatic compass within his head. Wherever he had gone, no matter how far afield he had wandered, it had always pointed steadily toward home. Now for the first time in his life the needle was spinning helplessly. It was an uneasy feeling. He had to get oriented.

"Which way is the garrison?" he pleaded.

Ozaki shrugged. "Over there some place. I don't know whereabouts on the planet you come from. I didn't pick up your track until you were in free space."

"Over where?" asked Kurt.

"Think you can stand another look?"

Kurt braced himself and nodded. The pilot opened a side port to vision and pointed. There, seemingly motionless in the black emptiness of space, floated a great greenish-gray globe. It didn't make sense to Kurt. The satellite that hung somewhat to the left did. Its face was different, the details were sharper than he'd ever seen them before, but the features he knew as well as his own. Night after night on scouting detail for the hunting parties while waiting for sleep he had watched the silver sphere ride through the clouds above him.

He didn't want to believe but he had to!

His face was white and tense as he turned back to Ozaki. A thousand sharp and burning questions milled chaotically through his mind.

"Where am I?" he demanded. "How did I get out here? Who are you? Where did you come from?"

"You're in a spaceship," said Ozaki, "a two-man scout. And that's all you're going to get out of me until you get some more work done. You might as well start on this microscopic projector. The thing burned out just as the special investigator was about to reveal who had blown off the commissioner's head by wiring a bit of plutonite into his autoshave. I've been going nuts ever since trying to figure out who did it!"

Kurt took some tools out of the first echelon kit and knelt obediently down beside the small projector.

Three hours later they sat down to dinner. Kurt had repaired the food machine and Ozaki was slowly masticating synthasteak that for the first time in days tasted like synthasteak. As he ecstatically lifted the last savory morsel to his mouth, the ship gave a sudden leap that plastered him and what remained of his supper against the rear bulkhead. There was darkness for a second and then the ceiling lights flickered on, then off, and then on again. Ozaki picked himself up and gingerly ran his fingers over the throbbing lump that was beginning to grow out of the top of his head. His temper wasn't improved when he looked up and saw Kurt still seated at the table calmly cutting himself another piece of pie.

"You should have braced yourself," said Kurt conversationally. "The converter's out of phase. You can hear her build up for a jump if you listen. When she does you ought to brace yourself. Maybe you don't hear so good?" he asked helpfully.

"Don't talk with your mouth full, it isn't polite," snarled Ozaki.

Late that night the converter cut out altogether. Ozaki was sleeping the sleep of the innocent and didn't find out about it for several hours. When he did awake, it was to Kurt's gentle shaking.

"Hey!" Ozaki groaned and buried his face in the pillow.

"Hey!" This time the voice was louder. The pilot yawned and tried to open his eyes.

"Is it important if all the lights go out?" the voice queried. The import of the words suddenly struck home and Ozaki sat bolt upright in his bunk. He opened his eyes, blinked, and opened them again. The lights *were* out. There was a strange unnatural silence about the ship.

"Good Lord!" he shouted and jumped for the controls. "The power's off."

He hit the starter switch but nothing happened. The converter was jammed solid. Ozaki began to sweat. He fumbled over the control board until he found the switch that cut the emergency batteries into the lighting circuit. Again nothing happened.

"If you're trying to run the lights on the batteries, they won't work," said Kurt in a conversational tone.

"Why not?" snapped Ozaki as he punched savagely and futilely at the starter button.

"They're dead," said Kurt. "I used them all up."

"You what?" yelled the pilot in anguish.

"I used them all up. You see, when the converter went out, I woke up. After a while the sun started to come up, and it began to get awfully hot so I hooked the batteries into the refrigeration coils. Kept the place nice and cool while they lasted."

Ozaki howled. When he swung the shutter of the forward port to let in some light, he howled again. This time in dead earnest. The giant red sun of the system was no longer perched off to the left at a comfortable distance. Instead before Ozaki's horrified eyes was a great red mass that stretched from horizon to horizon.

"We're falling into the sun!" he screamed.

"It's getting sort of hot," said Kurt. "Hot" was an understatement. The thermometer needle pointed at a hundred and ten and was climbing steadily.

Ozaki jerked open the stores compartment door and grabbed a couple of spare batteries. As quickly as his trembling fingers would work, he connected them to the emergency power line. A second later the cabin lights flickered on and Ozaki was warming up the space communicator. He punched the transmitter key and a call went arcing out through hyperspace. The vision screen flickered and the bored face of a communication tech, third class, appeared.

"Give me Commander Krogson at once!" demanded Ozaki.

"Sorry, old man," yawned the other, "but the commander's having breakfast. Call back in half an hour, will you?"

"This is an emergency! Put me through at once!"

"Can't help it," said the other, "nobody can disturb the Old Man while he's having breakfast!"

"Listen, you knucklehead," screamed Ozaki, "if you don't get me through to the commander as of right now, I'll have you in the uranium mines so fast that you won't know what hit you!"

"You and who else?" drawled the tech.

"Me and my cousin Takahashi!" snarled the pilot. "He's Reclassification Officer for the Base STAP."

The tech's face went white. "Yes, sir!" he stuttered. "Right away, sir! No offense meant, sir!"

He disappeared from the screen. There was a moment of darkness and then the interior of Commander Krogson's cabin flashed on. The commander was having breakfast. His teeth rested on the white tablecloth and his mouth was full of mush.

"Commander Krogson!" said Ozaki desperately.

The commander looked up with a startled expression. When he noticed his screen was on, he swallowed his mush convulsively and popped his teeth back into place.

"Who's there?" he demanded in a neutral voice in case it might be somebody important.

"Flight Officer Ozaki," said Flight Officer Ozaki.

A thundercloud rolled across the commander's face. "What do you mean by disturbing me at breakfast?" he demanded.

"Beg pardon, sir," said the pilot, "but my ship's falling into a red sun."

"Too bad," grunted Commander Krogson and turned back to his mush and milk.

"But, sir," persisted the other, "you've got to send somebody to pull me off. My converter's dead!"

"Why tell me about it?" said Krogson in annoyance. "Call Space Rescue, they're supposed to handle things like this."

"Listen, Commander," wailed the pilot, "by the time they've assigned me a priority and routed the paper through proper channels, I'll have gone up in smoke. The last time I got in a jam it took them two weeks to get to me; I've only got hours left!"

"Can't make exceptions," snapped Krogson testily. "If I let you skip the chain of command, everybody and his brother will think he has a right to."

"Commander," howled Ozaki, "we're frying in here!"

"All right. All right!" said the commander sourly. "I'll send somebody after you. What's your name?"

"Ozaki, sir. Flight Officer Ozaki."

The commander was in the process of scooping up another spoonful of mush when suddenly a thought struck him squarely between the eyes.

"Wait a second," he said hastily, "you aren't the scout who located the Imperial base, are you?"

"Yes, sir," said the pilot in a cracked voice.

"Why didn't you say so?" roared Krogson. Flipping on his intercom he growled, "Give me the Exec." There was a moment's silence.

"Yes, sir?"

"How long before we get to that scout?"

"About six hours, sir."

"Make it three!"

"Can't be done, sir."

"It will be done!" snarled Krogson and broke the connection.

The temperature needle in the little scout was now pointing to a hundred and fifteen.

"I don't think we can hold on that long," said Ozaki.

"Nonsense!" said the commander and the screen went blank.

Ozaki slumped into the pilot chair and buried his face in his hands. Suddenly he felt a blast of cold air on his neck. "There's no use in prolonging our misery," he said without looking up. "Those spare batteries won't last five minutes under this load."

"I knew that," said Kurt cheerfully, "so while you were doing all the talking, I went ahead and fixed the converter. You sure have mighty hot summers out here!" he continued, mopping his brow.

"You what?" yelled the pilot, jumping half out of his seat. "You couldn't even if you did have the know-how. It takes half a day to get the shielding off so you can get at the thing!"

"Didn't need to take the shielding off for a simple job like that," said Kurt. He pointed to a tiny inspection port about four inches in diameter. "I worked through there."

"That's impossible!" interjected the pilot. "You can't even see the injector through that, let alone get to it to work on!"

"Shucks," said Kurt, "a man doesn't have to see a little gadget like that to fix it. If your hands are trained right, you can feel what's wrong and set it to rights right away. She won't jump on you anymore either. The syncromesh thrust baffle was a little out of phase so I fixed that, too, while I was at it."

Ozaki still didn't believe it, but he hit the controls on faith. The scout bucked under the sudden strong surge of power and then, its converter humming sweetly, arced away from the giant sun in a long sweeping curve. There was silence in the scout. The two men sat quietly, each immersed in an uneasy welter of troubled speculation.

"That was close!" said Ozaki finally. "Too close for comfort. Another hour or so and—!" He snapped his fingers.

Kurt looked puzzled. "Were we in trouble?"

"Trouble!" snorted Ozaki. "If you hadn't fixed the converter when you did, we'd be cinders by now!"

Kurt digested the news in silence. There was something about this super-being who actually made machines work that bothered him. There was a note of bewilderment in his voice when he asked: "If we were really in danger, why didn't you fix the converter instead of wasting time talking on that thing?" He gestured toward the space communicator.

It was Ozaki's turn to be bewildered. "Fix it?" he said with surprise in his voice. "There aren't a half a dozen techs on the whole base who know enough about atomics to work on a propulsion unit. When something like that goes out, you call Space Rescue and chew your nails until a wrecker can get to you."

Kurt crawled into his bunk and lay back staring at the curved ceiling. He had thinking to do, a lot of thinking!

Three hours later, the scout flashed up alongside the great flagship and darted into a landing port. Flight Officer Ozaki was stricken by a horrible thought as he gazed affectionately around his smoothly running ship.

"Say," he said to Kurt hesitantly, "would you mind not mentioning that you fixed this crate up for me? If you do, they'll take it away from me sure. Some captain will get a new rig, and I'll be issued another clunk from Base Junkpile."

"Sure thing," said Kurt.

A moment later the flashing of a green light on the control panel signaled that the pressure in the lock had reached normal.

"Back in a minute," said Ozaki. "You wait here."

There was a muted hum as the exit hatch swung slowly open. Two guards entered and stood silently beside Kurt as Ozaki left to report to Commander Krogson.

XIII

The battle fleet of War Base Three of Sector Seven of the Galactic Protectorate hung motionless in space twenty thousand kilometers out from Kurt's home planet. A hundred tired detection techs sat tensely before their screens, sweeping the globe for some sign of energy radiation. Aside from the occasional light spatters caused by space static, their scopes remained dark. As their reports filtered into Commander Krogson he became more and more exasperated.

"Are you positive this is the right planet?" he demanded of Ozaki.

"No question about it, sir."

"Seems funny there's nothing running down there at all," said

Krogson. "Maybe they spotted us on the way in and cut off power. I've got a hunch that—" He broke off in midsentence as the red top-priority light on the communication panel began to flash. "Get that," he said. "Maybe they've spotted something at last."

The executive officer flipped on the vision screen and the interior of the flagship's communication room was revealed.

"Sorry to bother you, sir," said the tech whose image appeared on the screen, "but a message just came through on the emergency band."

"What does it say?"

The tech looked unhappy. "It's coded, sir."

"Well, decode it!" barked the executive.

"We can't," said the technician diffidently. "Something's gone wrong with the decoder. The printer is pounding out random groups that don't make any sense at all."

The executive grunted his disgust. "Any idea where the call's coming from?"

"Yes, sir; it's coming in on a tight beam from the direction of Base. Must be from a ship emergency rig, though. Regular hyperspace transmission isn't directional. Either the ship's regular rig broke down or the operator is using the beam to keep anybody else from picking up his signal."

"Get to work on that decoder. Call back as soon as you get any results." The tech saluted and the screen went black.

"Whatever it is, it's probably trouble," said Krogson morosely. "Well, we'd better get on with this job. Take the fleet into atmosphere. It looks as if we are going to have to make a visual check."

"Maybe the prisoner can give us a lead," suggested the executive officer.

"Good idea. Have him brought in."

A moment later Kurt was ushered into the master control room. Krogson's eyes widened at the sight of scalp lock and paint.

"Where in the name of the Galactic Spirit," he demanded, "did you get that rig?"

"Don't you recognize an Imperial Space Marine when you see one?" Kurt answered coldly.

The guard that had escorted Kurt in made a little twirling motion at his temple with one finger. Krogson took another look and nodded agreement.

"Sit down, son," he said in a fatherly tone. "We're trying to get you home, but you're going to have to give us a little help before we can do it. You see, we're not quite sure just where your base is."

"I'll help all I can," said Kurt.

"Fine!" said the commander, rubbing his palms together. "Now just where down there do you come from?" He pointed out the vision port to the curving globe that stretched out below.

Kurt looked down helplessly. "Nothing makes sense, seeing it from up here," he said apologetically.

Krogson thought for a moment. "What's the country like around your base?" he asked.

"Mostly jungle," said Kurt. "The garrison is on a plateau though and there are mountains to the north."

Krogson turned quickly to his exec. "Did you get that description?"

"Yes, sir!"

"Get all scouts out for a close sweep. As soon as the base is spotted, move the fleet in and hover at forty thousand!"

Forty minutes later a scout came streaking back.

"Found it, sir!" said the exec. "Plateau with jungle all around and mountains to the north. There's a settlement at one end. The pilot saw movement down there, but they must have spotted us on our way in. There's still no evidence of energy radiation. They must have everything shut down."

"That's not good!" said Krogson. "They've probably got all their heavy stuff set up waiting for us to sweep over. We'll have to hit them hard and fast. Did they spot the scout?"

"Can't tell, sir."

"We'd better assume that they did. Notify all gunnery officers to switch their batteries over to central control. If we come in fast and high and hit them with simultaneous fleet concentration, we can vaporize the whole base before they can take a crack at us."

"I'll send the order out at once, sir," said the executive officer.

The fleet pulled into tight formation and headed toward the

Imperial base. They were halfway there when the fleet gunnery officer entered the control room and said apologetically to Commander Krogson, "Excuse me, sir, but I'd like to suggest a trial run. Fleet concentration is a tricky thing, and if something went haywire—we'd be sitting ducks for the ground batteries."

"Good idea," said Krogson thoughtfully. "There's too much at stake to have anything to go wrong. Select an equivalent target, and we'll make a pass."

The fleet was now passing over a towering mountain chain.

"How about that bald spot down there?" said the Exec, pointing to a rocky expanse that jutted out from the side of one of the towering peaks.

"Good enough," said Krogson.

"All ships on central control!" reported the gunnery officer.

"On target!" repeated the tech on the tracking screen. "One. Two. Three. Four—"

Kurt stood by the front observation port watching the ground far below sweep by. He had been listening intently, but what had been said didn't make sense. There had been something about *batteries*—the term was alien to him—and something about the garrison. He decided to ask the commander what it was all about, but the intentness with which Krogson was watching the tracking screen deterred him. Instead he gazed moodily down at the mountains below him.

"Five. Six. Seven. Ready. FIRE!"

A savage shudder ran through the great ship as her ground-pointed batteries blasted in unison. Seconds went by and then suddenly the rocky expanse on the shoulder of the mountain directly below twinkled as blinding flashes of actinic light danced across it. Then as Kurt watched, great masses of rock and earth moved slowly skyward from the center of the spurting nests of tangled flame. Still slowly, as if buoyed up by the thin mountain air, the debris began to fall back again until it was lost from sight in quick rising mushrooms of jet-black smoke. Kurt turned and looked back toward Commander Krogson. *Batteries* must be the things that had torn the mountains below apart. And *garrison*—there was only one garrison!

"I ordered fleet fire," barked Krogson. "This ship was the only one that cut loose. What happened?"

"Just a second, sir," said the executive officer. "I'll try and find out." He was busy for a minute on the intercom system. "The other ships were ready, sir," he reported finally. "Their guns were all switched over to our control, but no impulse came through. Central fire control must be on the blink!" He gestured toward a complex bank of equipment that occupied one entire corner of the control room.

Commander Krogson said a few appropriate words. When he reached the point where he was beginning to repeat himself, he paused and stood in frozen silence for a good thirty seconds.

"Would you mind getting a fire control tech in here to fix that obscenity bank?" he asked in a voice that put everyone's teeth on edge.

The other seemed to have something to say, but he was having trouble getting it out.

"Well?" said Krogson.

"Prime Base grabbed our last one two weeks ago. There isn't another left with the fleet."

"Doesn't look like much to me," said Kurt as he strolled over to examine the bank of equipment.

"Get away from there!" roared the commander. "We've got enough trouble without you making things worse."

Kurt ignored him and began to open inspection ports.

"Guard!" yelled Krogson. "Throw that man out of here!"

Ozaki interrupted timidly. "Beg pardon, commander, but he can fix it if anybody can."

Krogson whirled on the flight officer. "How do you know?"

Ozaki caught himself just in time. If he talked too much, he was likely to lose the scout that Kurt had fixed for him.

"Because he . . . eh . . . talks like a tech," he concluded lamely.

Krogson looked at Kurt dubiously. "I guess there's no harm in giving it a trial," he said finally. "Give him a set of tools and turn him loose. Maybe for once a miracle will happen."

"First," said Kurt, "I'll need the wiring diagrams for this thing."

"Get them!" barked the commander and an orderly scuttled out of the control, headed aft.

"Next you'll have to give me a general idea of what it's supposed to do," continued Kurt.

Krogson turned to the gunnery officer. "You'd better handle this."

When the orderly returned with the circuit diagrams, they were spread out on the plotting table and the two men bent over them.

"Got it!" said Kurt at last and sauntered over to the control bank. Twenty minutes later he sauntered back again.

"She's all right now," he said pleasantly.

The gunner officer quickly scanned his testing board. Not a single red trouble light was on. He turned to Commander Krogson in amazement.

"I don't know how he did it, sir, but the circuits are all clear now."

Krogson stared at Kurt with a look of new respect in his eyes. "What were you down there, chief maintenance tech?"

Kurt laughed. "Me? I was never chief anything. I spent most of my time on hunting detail."

The commander digested that in silence for a moment. "Then how did you become so familiar with fire-control gear?"

"Studied it in school like everyone else does. There wasn't anything much wrong with that thing anyway except a couple of sticking relays."

"Excuse me, sir," interrupted the executive officer, "but should we make another trial run?"

"Are you sure the bank is in working order?"

"Positive, sir!"

"Then we'd better make straight for that base. If this boy here is a fair example of what they have down there, their defenses may be too tough for us to crack if we give them a chance to get set up!"

Kurt gave a slight start which he quickly controlled. Then he had guessed right! Slowly and casually he began to sidle toward the semicircular bank of controls that stood before the great tracking screen.

"Where do you think you're going!" barked Krogson.

Kurt froze. His pulses were pounding within him, but he kept his voice light and casual.

"No place," he said innocently.

"Get over against the bulkhead and keep out of the way!" snapped the commander. "We've got a job of work coming up."

Kurt injected a note of bewilderment into his voice. "What kind of work?"

Krogson's voice softened and a look approaching pity came into his eyes. "It's just as well you don't know about it until it's over," he said gruffly.

"There she is!" sang out the navigator, pointing to a tiny brown projection that jutted up out of the green jungle in the far distance. "We're about three minutes out, sir. You can take over at any time now."

The fleet gunnery officer's fingers moved quickly over the keys that welded the fleet into a single instrument of destruction, keyed and ready to blast a barrage of ravening thunderbolts of molecular disruption down at the defenseless garrison at a single touch on the master fire-control button.

"Whenever you're ready, sir," he said deferentially to Krogson as he vacated the controls. A hush fell over the control room as the great tracking screen brightened and showed the compact bundle of white dots that marked the fleet crawling slowly toward the green triangle of the target area.

"Get the prisoner out of here," said Krogson. "There's no reason why he should have to watch what's about to happen."

The guard that stood beside Kurt grabbed his arm and shoved him toward the door.

There was a sudden explosion of fists as Kurt erupted into action. In a blur of continuous movement, he streaked toward the gunnery control panel. He was halfway across the control room before the pole-axed guard hit the floor. There was a second of stunned amazement, and then before anyone could move to stop him, he stood beside the controls, one hand poised tensely above the master stud that controlled the combined fire of the fleet.

"Hold it!" he shouted as the moment of paralysis broke and several of the officers started toward him menacingly. "One move, and I'll blast the whole fleet into scrap!"

They stopped in shocked silence, looking to Commander Krogson for guidance.

"Almost on target, sir," called the tech on the tracking screen.

Krogson stalked menacingly toward Kurt. "Get away from those controls!" he snarled. "You aren't going to blow anything to anything. All that you can do is let off a premature blast. If you are trying to alert your base, it's no use. We can be on a return sweep before they have time to get ready for us."

Kurt shook his head calmly. "Wouldn't do you any good," he said. "Take a look at the gun ports on the other ships. I made a couple of minor changes while I was working on the control bank."

"Quit bluffing," said Krogson.

"I'm not bluffing," said Kurt quietly. "Take a look. It won't cost you anything."

"On target!" called the tracking tech.

"Order the fleet to circle for another sweep," snapped Krogson over his shoulder as he stalked toward the forward observation port. There was something in Kurt's tone that had impressed him more than he liked to admit. He squinted out toward the nearest ship. Suddenly his face blanched!

"The gunports! They're closed!"

Kurt gave a whistle of relief. "I had my fingers crossed," he said pleasantly. "You didn't give me enough time with the wiring diagrams for me to be sure that cutting out that circuit would do the trick. Now . . . guess what the results would be if I should happen to push down on this stud."

Krogson had a momentary vision of several hundred shells ramming their sensitive noses against the thick chrome steel of the closed gun ports.

"Don't bother trying to talk," said Kurt, noticing the violent contractions of the commander's Adam's apple. "You'd better save your breath for my colonel."

"Who?" demanded Krogson.

"My colonel," repeated Kurt. "We'd better head back and pick him up. Can you make these ships hang in one place or do they have to keep moving fast to stay up?"

The commander clamped his jaws together sullenly and said nothing.

Kurt made a tentative move toward the firing stud.

"Easy!" yelled the gunnery officer in alarm. "That thing has hair-trigger action!"

"Well?" said Kurt to Krogson.

"We can hover," grunted the other.

"Then take up a position a little to one side of the plateau." Kurt brushed the surface of the firing stud with a casual finger. "If you make me push this, I don't want a lot of scrap iron falling down on the battalion. Somebody might get hurt."

As the fleet came to rest above the plateau, the call light on the communication panel began to flash again.

"Answer it," ordered Kurt, "but watch what you say,"

Krogson walked over and snapped on the screen.

"Communications, sir."

"Well?"

"It's that message we called you about earlier. We've finally got the decoder working—sort of, that is." His voice faltered and then stopped.

"What does it say?" demanded Krogson impatiently.

"We still don't know," admitted the tech miserably. "It's being decoded all right, but it's coming out in a North Vegan dialect that nobody down here can understand. I guess there's still something wrong with the selector. All that we can figure out is that the message has something to do with General Carr and the Lord Protector."

"Want me to go down and fix it?" interrupted Kurt in an innocent voice.

Krogson whirled toward him, his hamlike hands clenching and unclenching in impotent rage.

"Anything wrong, sir?" asked the technician on the screen.

Kurt raised a significant eyebrow to the commander.

"Of course not," growled Krogson. "Go find somebody to translate that message and don't bother me until it's done."

A new face appeared on the screen.

"Excuse me for interrupting sir, but translation won't be necessary. We just got a flash from Detection that they've spotted the ship that sent it. It's a small scout heading in on emergency drive. She should be here in a matter of minutes."

Krogson flipped off the screen impatiently. "Whatever it is, it's sure to be more trouble," he said to nobody in particular. Suddenly he became aware that the fleet was no longer in motion. "Well," he said sourly to Kurt, "we're here. What now?"

"Send a ship down to the garrison and bring Colonel Harris back up here so that you and he can work this thing out between you. Tell him that Dixon is up here and has everything under control."

Krogson turned to the executive officer. "All right," he said, "do what he says." The other saluted and started toward the door.

"Just a second," said Kurt. "If you have any idea of telling the boys outside to cut the transmission leads from fire control, I wouldn't advise it. It's a rather lengthy process, and the minute a trouble light blinks on that board, up we go! Now on your way!"

XIV

Lieutenant Colonel Blick, acting commander of the 427th Light Maintenance Battalion of the Imperial Space Marines, stood at his office window and scowled down upon the whole civilized world, all twenty-six square kilometers of it. It had been a hard day. Three separate delegations of mothers had descended upon him demanding that he reopen the Tech Schools for the sake of their sanity. The recruits had been roaming the company streets in bands composed of equal numbers of small boys and large dogs creating havoc wherever they went. He tried to cheer himself up by thinking of his forthcoming triumph when he in the guise of the Inspector General would float magnificently down from the skies and once and for all put the seal of final authority upon the new order. The only trouble was that he was beginning to have a sneaking suspicion that maybe that new order wasn't all that he had planned it to be. As he thought of his own six banshees screaming through quarters, his suspicion deepened almost to certainty.

He wandered back to his desk and slumped behind it gloomily. He couldn't backwater now, his pride was at stake. He glanced at the water clock on his desk, and then rose reluctantly and started toward the door. It was time to get into battle armor and get ready for the inspection.

As he reached the door, there was a sudden slap of running sandals down the hall. A second later, Major Kane burst into the office, his face white and terrified.

"Colonel," he gasped, "the I.G.'s here!"

"Nonsense," said Blick. "I'm the I.G. now!"

"Oh yeah?" whimpered Kane. "Go look out the window. He's here, and he's brought the whole Imperial fleet with him!"

Blick dashed to the window and looked up. High above, so high that he could see them only as silver specks, hung hundreds of ships.

"Headquarters *does* exist!" he gasped. He stood stunned. What to do . . . what to do . . . what to do—The question swirled around in his brain until he was dizzy. He looked to Kane for advice, but the other was as bewildered as he was. "Don't stand there, man," he stormed. "Do something!"

"Yes, sir," said Kane. "What?"

Blick thought for a long, silent moment. The answer was obvious, but there was a short, fierce inner struggle before he could bring himself to accept it.

"Get Colonel Harris up here at once. He'll know what we should do."

A stubborn look came across Kane's face. "We're running things now," he said angrily.

Blick's face hardened and he let out a roar that shook the walls. "Listen, you pup, when you get an order, you follow it. Now get!"

Forty seconds later, Colonel Harris stormed into the office. "What kind of a mess have you got us into this time?" he demanded.

"Look up there, sir," said Blick leading him to the window.

Colonel Harris snapped back into command as if he'd never left it.

"Major Kane!" he shouted.

Kane popped into the office like a frightened rabbit.

"Evacuate the garrison at once! I want everyone off the plateau and into the jungle immediately. Get litters for the sick and the veterans who can't walk and take them to the hunting camps. Start the rest moving north as soon as you can."

"Really, sir," protested Kane, looking to Blick for a cue.

"You heard the colonel," barked Blick. "On your way!" Kane bolted.

Colonel Harris turned to Blick and said in a frosty voice: "I appreciate your help, Colonel, but I feel perfectly competent to enforce my own orders."

"Sorry, sir," said the other meekly. "It won't happen again."

Harris smiled. "O.K., Jimmie," he said, "let's forget it. We've got work to do!"

XV

It seemed to Kurt as if time was standing still. His nerves were screwed up to the breaking point and although he maintained an air of outward composure for the benefit of those in the control room of the flagship, it took all his will power to keep the hand that was resting over the firing stud from quivering. One slip and they'd be on him. Actually it was only a matter of minutes between the time the scout was dispatched to the garrison below and the time it returned, but to him it seemed as if hours had passed before the familiar form of his commanding officer strode briskly into the control room.

Colonel Harris came to a halt just inside the door and swept the room with a keen penetrating gaze.

"What's up, son?" he asked Kurt.

"I'm not quite sure. All that I know is that they're here to blast the garrison. As long as I've got control of this," he indicated the firing stud, "I'm top dog, but you'd better work something out in a hurry."

The look of strain on Kurt's face was enough for the colonel.

"Who's in command here?" he demanded.

Krogson stepped forward and bowed stiffly. "Commander Conrad Krogson of War Base Three of the Galactic Protectorate."

"Colonel Marcus Harris, 427th Light Maintenance Battalion of the Imperial Space Marines," replied the other briskly. "Now that the formalities are out of the way, let's get to work. Is there some place here where we can talk?"

Krogson gestured toward a small cubicle that opened off the control room. The two men entered and shut the door behind them.

A half-hour went by without agreement. "There may be an answer somewhere," Colonel Harris said finally, "but I can't find it. We can't surrender to you, and we can't afford to have you surrender to us. We haven't the food, facilities, or anything else to keep fifty thousand men under guard. If we turn you loose, there's nothing to keep you from coming back to blast us—except your word, that is, and since it would obviously be given under duress, I'm afraid that we couldn't attach much weight to it. It's a nice problem. I wish we had more time to spend on it, but unless you can come up with something workable during the next five minutes, I'm going to give Kurt orders to blow the fleet."

Krogson's mind was operating at a furious pace. One by one he snatched at possible solutions, and one by one he gave them up as he realized that they would never stand up under the scrutiny of the razor-sharp mind that sat opposite him.

"Look," he burst out finally, "your empire is dead and our protectorate is about to fall apart. Give us a chance to come down and join you and we'll chuck the past. We need each other and you know it!"

"I know we do," said the colonel soberly, "and I rather think you are being honest with me. But we just can't take the chance. There are too many of you for us to digest and if you should change your mind—" He threw up his hands in a helpless gesture.

"But I wouldn't," protested Krogson. "You've told me what your life is like down there and you know what kind of a rat race I've been caught up in. I'd welcome the chance to get out of it. All of us would!"

"You might to begin with," said Harris, "but then you might start thinking what your Lord Protector would give to get his hands on several hundred trained technicians. No, Commander," he said, "we just couldn't chance it." He stretched his hand out to Krogson and the other after a second's hesitation took it.

Commander Krogson had reached the end of the road and he knew it. The odd thing about it was that now he found himself there, he didn't particularly mind. He sat and watched his own reactions with a sense of vague bewilderment. The strong drive for self-preservation that had kept him struggling ahead for so long was petering out and there was nothing to take its place. He was immersed in a strange feeling of emptiness and though a faint something within him said that he should go out fighting, it seemed pointless and without reason.

Suddenly the moment of quiet was broken. From the control room came a muffled sound of angry voices and scuffling feet. With one quick stride, Colonel Harris reached the door and swung it open. He was almost bowled over by a small disheveled figure who darted past him into the cubicle. Close behind came several of the ship's officers. As the figure came to a stop before Commander Krogson, one of them grabbed him and started to drag him back into the control room.

"Sorry, sir," the officer said to Krogson, "but he came busting in demanding to see you at once. He wouldn't tell us why and when we tried to stop him, he broke away."

"Release him!" ordered the commander. He looked sternly at the little figure. "Well, Schninkle," he said sternly, "what is it this time?"

"Did you get my message?"

Krogson snorted. "So it was you in that scout! I might have known it. We got it all right, but Communication still hasn't got it figured out. What are you doing out here? You're supposed to be back at base keeping knives out of my back!"

"It's private, sir," said Schninkle.

"The rest of you clear out!" ordered Krogson. A second later, with the exception of Colonel Harris, the cubicle stood empty. Schninkle looked questioningly at the oddly uniformed officer.

"Couldn't put him out if I wanted to," said Krogson, "now go ahead."

Schninkle closed the door carefully and then turned to the commander and said in a hushed voice, "There's been a blowup at Prime Base. General Carr was hiding out there after all. He hit at noon yesterday. He had two-thirds of the Elite Guard secretly on his side and the Lord Protector didn't have a chance. He tried to run but they chopped him down before he got out of the atmosphere."

Krogson digested the news in silence for a moment. "So the Lord Protector is dead." He laughed bitterly. "Well, long live the Lord Protector!" He turned slowly to Colonel Harris. "I guess this lets us both off. Now that the heat's off me, you're safe. Call off your boy out there, and we'll make ourselves scarce. I've got to get back to the new Lord Protector to pay my respects. If some of my boys get to Carr first, I'm apt to be out of a job."

Harris shook his head. "It isn't as simple as that. Your new leader needs technicians as much as your old one did. I'm afraid we are still back where we started."

As Krogson broke into an impatient denial, Schninkle interrupted him. "You can't go back, Commander. None of us can. Carr has the whole staff down on his 'out' list. He's making a clean sweep of all possible competition. We'd all be under arrest now if he knew where we were!"

Krogson gave a slow whistle. "Doesn't leave me much choice, does it?" he said to Colonel Harris. "If you don't turn me loose, I get blown up; if you do, I get shot down."

Schninkle looked puzzled. "What's up, sir?" he asked.

Krogson gave a bitter laugh. "In case you didn't notice on your way in, there is a young man sitting at the fire controls out there who can blow up the whole fleet at the touch of a button. Down below is an ideal base with hundreds of techs, but the colonel here won't take us in, and he's afraid to let us go."

"I wouldn't," admitted Harris, "but the last few minutes have rather changed the picture. My empire has been dead for five hundred years and your protectorate doesn't seem to want you around anymore. It looks like we're both out of a job. Maybe we both ought to find a new one. What do you think?"

"I don't know what to think," said Krogson. "I can't go back and I can't stay here, and there isn't any place else. The fleet can't keep going without a base."

A broad grin came over the face of Colonel Harris. "You know," he said, "I've got a hunch that maybe we can do business after all. Come on!" He threw open the cubicle door and strode briskly into the control room, Krogson and Schninkle following close at his heels. He walked over to Kurt who was still poised stiffly at the fire-control board.

"You can relax now, lad. Everything is under control."

Kurt gave a sigh of relief and pulling himself to his feet, stretched luxuriantly. As the other officers saw the firing stud deserted, they tensed and looked to Commander Krogson questioningly. He frowned for a second and then slowly shook his head.

"Well?" he said to Colonel Harris.

"It's obvious," said the other, "you've a fleet, a damn good fleet, but it's falling apart for lack of decent maintenance. I've got a base down there with five thousand lads who can think with their fingers. This knucklehead of mine is a good example." He walked over to Kurt and slapped him affectionately on the shoulder. "There's nothing on this ship that he couldn't tear down and put back together blindfolded if he was given a little time to think about it. I think he'll enjoy having some real work to do for a change."

"I may seem dense," said Krogson with a bewildered expression on his face, "but wasn't that the idea that I was trying to sell you?"

"The idea is the same," said Harris, "but the context isn't. You're in a position now where you have to cooperate. That makes a difference. A big difference!"

"It sounds good," said Krogson, "but now you're overlooking something. Carr will be looking for me. We can't stand off the whole galaxy!"

"You're overlooking something too, sir," Schninkle interrupted. "He hasn't the slightest idea where we are. It will be months before he has things well enough under control to start an organized search for us. When he does, his chances of ever spotting the fleet are mighty slim if we take reasonable precautions. Remember that it was only by a fluke that we ever happened to spot this place to begin with."

As he talked a calculating look came into his eyes. "A year of training and refitting here, and there wouldn't be a fleet in the galaxy that could stand against us." He casually edged over until he occupied a position between Kurt and the fire-control board. "If things went right, there's no reason why you couldn't become Lord Protector, Commander."

A flash of the old fire stirred within Krogson and then quickly flickered out. "No, Schninkle," he said heavily. "That's all past now. I've had enough. It's time to try something new."

"In that case," said Colonel Harris, "let's begin! Out there a whole galaxy is breaking up. Soon the time will come when a strong hand is going to be needed to piece it back together and put it in running order again. You know," he continued reflectively, "the name of the old empire still has a certain magic to it. It might not be a bad idea to use it until we are ready to move on to something better."

He walked silently to the vision port and looked down on the lush greenness spreading far below. "But whatever we call ourselves," he continued slowly, half-talking to himself, "we have something to work for now." A quizzical smile played over his lips and his wise old eyes seemed to be scanning the years ahead. "You know, Kurt; there's nothing like a visit from the Inspector General once in a while to keep things in line. The galaxy is a big place, but when the time comes, we'll make our rounds!"

XVI

On the parade ground behind the low buildings of the garrison, the 427th Light Maintenance Battalion of the Imperial Space Marines stood in rigid formation, the feathers of their war bonnets moving slightly in the little breeze that blew in from the west and their war paint glowing redly in the slanting rays of the setting sun.

A quiver ran through the hard surface soil of the plateau as the great mass of the fleet flagship settled down ponderously to rest. There was a moment of expectant silence as a great port clanged open and a gangplank extended to the ground. From somewhere within the ship a fanfare of trumpets sounded. Slowly and with solemn dignity, surrounded by his staff, Conrad Krogson, Inspector General of the Imperial Space Marines, advanced to review the troops.